Loyalties

Loyalties

ALAN SCHOLEFIELD

St. Martin's Press
New York

Grateful acknowledgement is made to the Estate of Robert Frost for permission to quote from 'Stopping by Woods on a Snowy Evening' from *The Poetry of Robert Frost*, edited by Edward Connery Lathem, published by Jonathan Cape.

Library of Congress Cataloging-in-Publication Data

Scholefield, Alan.
    Loyalties / Alan Scholefield.
      p.   cm.
    ISBN 0-312-07029-2
    I. Title.
  PR9369.3.S3L65   1992
  823—dc20   91-37396
                                                CIP

First published in Great Britain by Chapmans Publishers Limited.

First U.S. Edition: April 1992
10 9 8 7 6 5 4 3 2 1

For Gordon and Vivien Warrington

Loyalties

Prologue

The Barbizon Tower was built in the 1960s when money was pouring into London. Before then that part of Bayswater had been a mass of bombed sites and pre-war shabbiness.

There are now many luxury developments in the area but the Barbizon Tower, eighteen storeys high, is the most prestigious. And the most luxurious apartment is the penthouse. Its walls are of tinted glass and on its roof are a pool and sauna and a garden of geraniums and fuchsias in large terracotta pots that give an impression of Italy.

At four thirty on a chilly morning in May, Anna Webster stood at the penthouse windows looking out over London. On a clear day the view was panoramic, from Hampstead in the north to the Surrey hills in the south. Now all she could see were millions of lights, like diamond chips set in black velvet.

She never tired of this view. But though she was staring at the lights of London, she was not really seeing them.

She had hardly slept. She had dozed between two and three, and had then had a hot shower followed by a needle-spray of cold. Then she had dressed.

That had been a problem. How do you dress for battle? She tried to visualize how her sons would be dressed.

Nico, her adopted son, favoured denims, but would he wear denims to a board meeting? Especially this one? She thought he probably would and that they would be the latest from Calvin Klein.

Peter would be wearing a double-breasted blue blazer. He

had always liked blazers. And grey trousers cut so that the shortness of his left leg would not be too obvious.

John, her third son, would wear a conventional dark grey or dark blue suit with stripes. So would the lawyers.

Their clothes would betray their characters: Peter's pink shirt, red silk tie and silk handkerchief would hint at the world of communications and entertainment.

And what of Nico? Boots? A fine gold chain round his neck? Just a touch of the playboy?

John's formality: cold and serious? And yet underneath she knew there was warmth. Sometimes, when she thought about John, she felt regret almost as deep as the regret she felt for what had happened to Peter.

If the men were dressing up, she'd dress down. It might just disconcert them, throw them momentarily off balance. She chose carefully: olive green trousers, a tan silk shirt and a yellow Hermès scarf knotted at her throat. On her left wrist she wore a man's chronometer on a bright red-leather strap and on her right wrist a chunky gold bracelet.

She spent half an hour on her face and hair and by the time she finished she felt as ready as she would ever be.

She looked at herself in the long mirror in her bedroom. It reflected a woman with dark hair greying at the temples, a trim figure, breasts still shapely under the silk. Ben had said she had the most beautiful breasts he had ever seen. She still regretted Ben.

'You're not too bad,' she said out loud to her mirror image. 'Not too bad for a grandmother.'

She went into the kitchen and made herself breakfast of freshly squeezed pink grapefruit, a couple of slices of wholemeal bread, green fig preserve, and a large French cup of black coffee.

She stood at the window drinking the coffee and watching the sky lighten behind St Paul's. She lit a cigarette. This was the time she usually liked best, the quiet overture to the day ahead. But not today. She stubbed out her half-smoked cigarette. She wanted to get going, to face it. To put matters in train so that a final decision could be made. That was the result of her many years working in newspapers, she thought, where decisions *had* to be made. Even a bad decision was better than no decision.

And God knew she had made some bad ones – as a result of which her sons seemed to want to pension her off. And then what? Take over themselves?

She smiled grimly. She wasn't ready to be pensioned off and the thought of Peter, Nico and John getting together over *anything* was hard to imagine.

There was a discreet buzzing on the door-phone. She crossed the pale grey carpet that covered the floor of the sunken living-room, picked her way round the large steel and smoked-glass coffee table, and lifted the receiver.

'Car's ready, ma'am,' a deep Caribbean voice said.

'Thank you, Shelford.'

She fetched her bag, briefcase, and an Azzedine Alaïa leather jacket which she slung over one shoulder, looked once round the apartment, and closed the door behind her. The thickly carpeted elevator took her swiftly and noiselessly down to the underground garage. Her car was idling near the security gate and Shelford, large and smiling, was giving the windscreen a final polish.

She had given the buying of a car a great deal of thought. Flashy sports coupés were too young for her, and she did not want the 'developer's' image of a Rolls or a Jaguar. But after what had happened with Peter, she wanted something strong; strong yet fast and individual. She had found it in a Bristol.

Usually, as she slipped behind the wheel and smelled the rich aroma of hide, and felt the softly throbbing engine at her feet, she would get a rush of pleasure. But not this time.

'I got a good one today, Miz Webster. Runnin' in the two thirty at Sandown. Can't lose.'

At least once a week Shelford had a hot tip.

'That's what you always say.'

'But today . . . today we goin' to make our fortunes.'

She fumbled in her bag and took out a ten-pound note.

'If you say so, Shelford,' she said, catching his infectious smile and giving him one in return.

'On the nose like always?' he said folding the note away.

'On the nose.'

She drove out on to the Bayswater Road, warming herself at the last remnants of his smile. The park was still locked so she turned left, cut down Park Lane and made for Victoria. London was deserted. She could see the occasional derelict, wrapped up in his plastic and newspapers, asleep in a shop doorway. She felt a puckering of gooseflesh, someone walking over her grave, as her grandmother used to say, and thought: There but for the grace of God go most of us.

At this time in the morning it took her ten minutes to reach the *Daily News* in the Vauxhall Bridge Road. The big grey building, with the revolving globe of the Earth on its roof on which was inscribed WEBSTER COMMUNICATIONS, would have looked strange there just a few years before, but now Fleet Street was only part of an earlier mythology to most journalists.

The national newspapers had departed for Wapping, the Isle of Dogs, Battersea – anywhere where office space was cheaper. She had remained long after the others – for Fleet Street *was* newspapers, to Anna. But finally the move had had to be made.

She was let into the underground car park by one of the security staff and took the private elevator up to her office on the top floor.

This, in its glass and steel and airiness, was like her penthouse, but more functional, more purposeful, as befitted the ruler of an empire.

She went into her PA's office and brought back the faxes from the States which had piled up overnight. This was her first task every morning and she performed it routinely. She owned a string of newspapers in Massachusetts and Connecticut and three TV stations in upper New York State and Boston.

She let her eye travel down the pages: an editor on the *Hartford Argus* was resigning because of ill health, Turner Communications was signalling it wanted to make a deal with her TV stations to take their twenty-four hour newscasts. The circulation figures for the *Boston Mercury*, flagship of her US stable, were down two percentage points in the first quarter . . .

She tossed the pages down on her desk. Her mind could not concentrate on America.

Dawn was coming to London. When in Fleet Street, she had

looked out at the spires of Wren churches; now there was only the old Battersea power station. The thought suddenly struck her: would she have done to her mother what her children were proposing to do to her? She couldn't answer; the circumstances were so different. Anyway, she wasn't sure yet what her sons *were* going to propose, although she had a damn good idea. She was surprised at Peter. The other two, she knew, had their own reasons.

Restlessly, she left her office and wandered along the echoing corridors to the elevators. She went down three floors and came out into the newsroom. It looked quite different from the old days of typewriters and copy paper and wet page proofs. Then the floors would have been knee deep in paper. Now, with its rows of dead terminals, it looked like NASA headquarters after a space shot.

The only life in this technological wasteland came from the agency screens pouring out their unending flood of news from every part of the world.

She glanced at the Associated Press menu.

There had been a plane crash in a storm off Manila . . . an Australian had won the world's beer drinking championship . . . she flicked on and finally came to the story she thought she might find and felt her stomach clench with tension. Similar ones had been appearing for several weeks.

It was datelined Vienna and read:

The Austrian State Prosecutor said tonight that unless positive identification was made in the case of 74-year-old Franz Gregor, he would be released from custody.

Six weeks ago the French Government requested that Gregor be arrested by the Austrian police pending an extradition application. Gregor is alleged to have committed war crimes in France when he was a member of a Nazi SS detachment. It is alleged that the name 'Gregor' is an alias and that his real name is Cuno Theodor Beckerman. Gregor, a former Vienna police inspector, has been living in retirement until his recent arrest.

The Documentation Centre in Vienna, set up after the war by Simon Wiesenthal and responsible for evidence leading to the

11

arrest and trial of dozens of former Nazis for war crimes, has so far not been able to identify Gregor as Beckerman.

The French Government's application concerns the deaths of forty-two villagers shot in reprisal for the dynamiting of a train carrying German soldiers near Libourne in south-west France in 1943.

Anna printed the story, tore it off the printer and slowly made her way back to her own office. The bad times never came singly, she thought.

She looked at the three clocks on the wall: one showed US Eastern Standard Time, the second the time in Hong Kong, the third local time. Was Vienna one or two hours ahead? Whatever it was, Nairn would still be asleep but that was just hard luck, she *had* to know what Nairn had discovered. She dialled the Hotel Bristol and asked to be put through to her granddaughter's room.

The receptionist queried the name.

'Braid,' Anna said. 'Miss Nairn Braid.'

There was a pause, then the heavily accented voice said, 'I am sorry, madame, but Miss Braid has checked out.'

'Are you sure?'

'Yes, I am sure, madame.'

She put down the phone and stood looking at the dead instrument as though it was in some way to blame.

Where was Nairn? Still in Vienna? On her way back to London? She gripped her lower lip between her teeth. God damn it, she needed her! She needed her *now*!

She phoned Nairn's flat in London on the off-chance that her granddaughter had come in late the night before, but all she got was the ansaphone.

Her eye fell on the AP story again and she picked up the tearsheet, crumpled it and threw it into her wastebasket. Vienna, she thought, was where this whole wretched mess had begun.

BOOK ONE

Anna

One

In the late summer of 1937 Vienna was much as it had always been, suffused by a world-weary cynicism and cloaked in an atmosphere of superficial gaiety. But beneath the façade was a deep-seated anxiety about the future. Hitler was already making speeches about the unification of the German-speaking races (which meant bringing Austria into the German nation-state), people were flocking to join the Nazi Party, and Jews were already beginning to emigrate. But to Anna, Vienna seemed to hold out a vision of hope and change, for she came to it from a double tragedy in her personal life.

She was eighteen years old and had spent her life in the cathedral city of Winchester where her father practised as a doctor. She had had a happy childhood, had done reasonably well at school, and was waiting to hear if she had got a place at Oxford.

She had no interest in what had happened – and was happening – in Germany and in other parts of Europe. Her main concern was with herself. She had gone to an all-girls school so her knowledge of men was limited and based mainly on the received wisdom of older girls who had been 'snogging' in the back seats of Austin Sevens.

It was a carefree existence which was changed for ever one sunny Saturday when her parents' small yacht was rammed by a passenger ferry in the English Channel and both were drowned.

She was an only child and her nearest surviving relative was her maternal grandmother, who lived on a small hill farm in

Wales. Mrs Monkton had spent so long in rural isolation that she was frightened of a town the size of Winchester. After the funeral she took Anna with her to Wales.

Mrs Monkton was a small, shrivelled old lady with stringy muscles and dark facial hair. The farm hardly made enough for one person to live on, and the result was that she did all the work herself.

She had a flock of sheep, a few cows, some hens and a rooster, a couple of pigs. She thought and spoke in terms of Lammas-tide and Michaelmas. She was up at dawn and went to bed at nightfall. There was no electricity or running water in the house nor was there a wireless, and the only books, except for tomes on husbandry, were a leather-bound set of the Waverley novels of Sir Walter Scott.

The nearest town was Hay-on-Wye, pretty but remote, and at the end of a winding road. Anna and her grandmother hardly ever visited it except for supplies.

Any hope of going to Oxford disappeared and so, it seemed, did Anna's future, for her father's estate had left her with almost nothing. She was in total despair.

Then, a few months later, in early August, a letter was forwarded to her. It bore a Vienna postmark and it was from a friend of her parents called Michael Meissner. Her parents had met him on a walking holiday at Bad Ischl in the Austrian Salzkammergut and they had stayed in touch with each other. Anna had met him and his wife, Ruth, when they stayed with the Websters in Winchester.

His letter suggested, in view of what had happened, that she might like to spend a few months in Vienna with them. It would help her to get over her bereavement and, if she agreed, she could pay for her board and lodging by looking after their son, a boy of six, and a baby which was due in a couple of months.

It was like a sudden reprieve from a life sentence. She told her grandmother the letter's contents and saw a look of relief spread over the wizened face. That day she took the bus into Hay and sent a cable to Vienna. Four days later, apprehensive but excited, she was boarding the Orient Express in Paris.

*

16

The Meissners lived in the leafy suburb of Neustift am Walde. She thought Vienna the most beautiful place she had ever seen. The suburban avenues were lined with linden trees; apple and pear trees were fruiting and their heavy branches often hung out over the pavements. No one seemed to take the fruit and when she remarked on this to Michael, he smiled and said, 'We Austrians are very law-abiding.'

He was in his early forties, plump and balding. He too was a medical man – an ear, nose and throat specialist.

The house was large and sprawling and stood in several acres of fruit trees and wild lawns. When Anna arrived, Ruth, heavily pregnant, was playing bridge with three other women in a small summer-house built in the shade of a great horse-chestnut tree. To Anna, newly released from her grandmother's muddy and windswept hilltop, the house and garden seemed like arcadia.

At first everything was strange – the richness of the food, the heat, the currency, the different weights and measures – but not unpleasantly so. The Meissners had two indoor servants, a cook and a housemaid, the same number as had worked for her own family.

She soon got used to the household and its ways. Michael went to his surgery each morning, returning at six or seven. Ruth played bridge. She was a pale woman in her early thirties, herself the daughter of a doctor. She was tall and dark-haired and seemed younger than her years for she had a kind of childlike, almost fey quality about her.

Being pregnant and the weather being extremely hot, she did as little as possible. She seemed, to Anna, to have two passions, French fashion magazines and bridge. She played bridge every afternoon, mostly in the summer-house. Along with the bridge markers and the packs of cards the maid would put out little cut-glass bowls of mints and packets of long black Balkan Sobranie cigarettes. Anna was later to think of these drowsy, hot afternoons as the end of an era.

War was coming. But Ruth and her friends played on.

Sometimes when Michael came back from his surgery the ladies would still be at their cards and Anna would see a look in his eyes that was part irritation part fear, as though he knew they were on the edge of a nightmare and was annoyed with

17

his wife for not understanding, yet afraid of waking her from her dream.

One of Ruth's bridge players, Frau Beckerman, was often brought to the Althofengasse by her son Cuno. He would sit on the lawn in the afternoon heat and talk to Anna about himself. He was the Austrian skiing champion and made winning the slalom again sound like a matter of life and death.

He was in his early twenties, of medium height and build, with dark good looks and dark hair smoothed back with brilliantine. He had been educated partly at the English School in Vienna and he spoke the language reasonably well. He was now thinking about his future and waiting for the skiing season to open. He was clearly interested in Anna and she was flattered.

Like the season itself she was just coming into perfect ripeness. She was a little taller than average with dark hair and blue eyes, and a slender body from which the early puppy-fat had disappeared during the weeks with her grandmother. Her breasts were upturned and she was pleased with them. She was not pleased with her shoulders which she thought a little too square, or her face which she thought a little too long.

She felt herself to be a reasonably attractive woman and was ready for her first serious love affair.

At first she found Cuno's skiing adventures fascinating. He told her in detail how he trained, the running he did, the exercising and weight-lifting, for, as he said, he was 'serious'. There were many skiers, particularly the British, who were not 'serious' and not much good anyway. In Cuno's opinion they had no future.

When Anna remarked that it must be an expensive hobby he was outraged at the word 'hobby', and said grandly, 'I do not count the costs. It is for Austria.'

There was a swimming pool in the nearby suburb of Sievering built among apple trees and grassy banks and he took her there several times. He had a smooth brown body and would do fifty and more press-ups to show her how serious he was. He was beautiful to look at, she thought.

They would lie close together on towels in the dappled shade of the apple trees, so close that their bodies touched. Sometimes he played with her hair, sometimes he took a piece of grass and stroked it down her back and thighs. His touch activated nerve endings in her skin that had never been activated before and she would lie in the afternoon heat allowing herself to slip into a kind of waking dream.

On other days he would borrow his mother's little DKW and take Anna for drives up into the northern hills past Kahlenberg and Weidlingsbach.

The Deutsche Kleine Wunder, the cheapest car in Germany at the time, seemed to represent to Cuno a kind of social disaster for he said to her several times that he would soon be buying a Mercedes-Benz.

On one occasion he turned off the road and parked on a forest track. She let him kiss her and did not try to stop him when he loosened her bra and slipped his hand underneath it to fondle her nipples.

She had played this game before; its rules demanded that she pretended what was happening was not happening, while her lover pretended that what he was doing he was not doing; and that the buttons of her blouse and the catch of her bra had come undone by some mysterious force over which neither had any control.

Only an overt act could shatter this delicately constructed edifice and, given her upbringing, Cuno's hand forcing itself towards her groin was the overt act. She put her hand down and covered his. He pushed. She gripped more firmly. Suddenly she realized that he had been using only part of his strength. All those press-ups had not gone for nothing.

His groping hand was unstoppable. She felt his fingers in her hair. 'No!' she said.

'Why not?'

'I don't want you to!'

'Don't be so silly. All English girls like it.' He forced her head back and kissed her.

She twisted away and said, 'I've got my period.'

His muscles relaxed, his hand slipped out from under her dress.

'I think you are lying to me.'

'Why do you think I didn't want to go swimming?'

19

'You are just a little girl,' he said contemptuously. 'A cock-tease. Is that how you say it?'

For the next week there was a kind of armed truce between them but she knew and he knew that there would be other times.

She wanted to fall in love. But there was something about Cuno that held her back.

It wasn't until a few weeks after her arrival that Anna discovered all was not bridge and chocolates in the garden of the house on the Althofengasse.

Ruth's brother, Felix, came to stay. The house was so large that at first Anna was not certain whether he was living there or not and it was only when she saw other men visit him in the farthest suite of rooms that she realized he was a fixture. She discovered that his presence was supposed to be a secret. His family did not mention it and she was asked not to discuss his whereabouts. He came and went at eccentric hours.

He was several years older than his sister with the same pale skin, but where Ruth was dark, he had a mass of blond curly hair. He was a journalist and had worked for several newspapers in Austria and Germany. He and Ruth were very close.

The men who came to see him were of all ages and would remain closeted with him for hours at a time, some leaving at three or four in the morning.

Anna met several. One, Herr Doktor Professor Bloch, taught constitutional law at the University of Vienna. He was in his late sixties, small and rather frail with a thin body and a huge dome-like head.

One day he brought her a small box of expensive chocolates. 'They are from Demel's,' he said. 'For our English friend. I lived for one year in England but a long time ago.' She was touched.

At the other end of the age spectrum was an American foreign correspondent called Ben Ramsey, only a few years older than Anna herself.

She met him late one afternoon sitting out in the garden with Michael and Felix. The first thing that struck her was his size. He was well over six feet tall and built like a barn door. She learnt later that he came from a farming family in Minnesota where he was considered to be on the small side.

He had no interest in farming, instead had crossed the border into Canada, told the *Toronto Globe & Mail* he was planning a journey down through Africa and talked them into agreeing to take stories from him of his travels. In 1935 he had reached Addis Ababa in Abyssinia when the country was attacked by Italy and he had a world scoop. He had filed a series of dramatic stories from the battlefront – the first to tell the western nations about the Italian use of mustard gas – which had made his name.

He was now on the *New York Tribune* and, since he was considered to have a nose for trouble, had been sent to Vienna. He had an infectious smile, a laugh which might be heard half a block away, and a casual way of dressing. He reminded Anna of a wood carving she had once seen of an American Indian.

During the hour they spent together around the table on the lawn he spoke to her only once, saying: 'They tell me you're English.'

When she said she was, he nodded and said, 'Your prime minister's got the future of Austria – I guess you could say Europe – in his hands. I hope to God he understands that.'

She had no idea what he meant but the remark had been addressed to her with a sharpness which made her uneasy.

Two

The summer was coming to an end. The early September days were still hot but the evenings and nights had a touch of autumn in them. Anna was helping Stefan make a crane with his Meccano set one day when Ben Ramsey came out on to the lawn looking for Felix. He paused beside them. 'I hear you've been going swimming with Cuno. He's just a playboy, you know.'

Irritated, she said, 'It's none of your business.'

He smiled. It was the first time she had seen him smile properly. His big face cracked open and its warmth seemed to envelop her. 'You rose to that like a trout. I like to get a rise out of the English. Has he been telling you about his skiing? He's the world's greatest, you know.'

She wouldn't be drawn further by his irony and said, 'We've talked about skiing.'

'I'll bet. Listen, there aren't going to be too many good days left – and I don't only mean the summer. Will you come swimming with me? I'll show you something you've never seen before.'

'What?'

'A different kind of swimming pool. Warm water. Health-giving. Life-giving. What more could you want?'

That Saturday they drove to Bad Voslau, a small and dusty spa town about thirty-five kilometres south of Vienna in the Burgenland. It was a lovely day, the last true day of summer.

The swimming complex was astonishing. Pools were inter-linked by channels and there were waterfalls and fountains.

The channels were shaded by trees, and clean pebbles covered the bottom. Through these channels flowed the warm spring water and they swam from one pool to the next. They lay in the sun, and swam again, until it was nearly lunchtime. She dressed and found Ben near a fountain under which a dozen people were sitting in special wheelchairs, letting the medicinal water run over them.

Then she saw that all were limbless. Some had lost feet, others legs. They were letting the water run over the naked stumps.

They had lunch at the village of Rust, sitting outside the restaurant under straw awnings. They ate plates of smoked meats, sausages and sweet pickles, and drank a flask of white wine.

Ben said, 'Were you shocked?'

She hesitated. 'No. But I've never seen anything like that before.'

'Probably wounded in the first war. My father came back from France minus a hand. I guess it's all going to happen again if the politicians don't act now to stop Hitler.'

After he had paid the bill they walked down the little main street. On each cottage chimney-stack a pair of storks were roosting.

'They'll be leaving in a week or so to winter in Africa,' he said. 'Nobody knows what they'll find when they come back in the spring.'

Anna discovered that winter was fierce in Vienna. Ruth had her baby at home in a snowstorm. With Anna's help Michael delivered his son, Nicholas, himself. He was extremely proud of the baby and his own dexterity and went round saying to everyone, 'You see, I'm not only a man for sore throats.'

During this time Anna discovered what Felix was doing. He had started a clandestine anti-Nazi newspaper and was having to keep one jump ahead of the Austrian police. He had sent his wife and children to stay in the country.

Cuno was out on the skiing trail in Switzerland and Ben was in Berlin. Anna spent much of her time looking after Nicholas. On fine days she would take him to a nearby park, wheel him

23

up and down in the winter sun and pretend that he was hers.

She got a brief note from Ben. 'Things are hotting up here,' he wrote from Berlin. 'The suffering of the Jews is awful. But it is not only they who are being arrested and taken to camps. Anyone who openly flouts Hitler and his National Socialism quickly disappears.

'I think a great deal of the day we spent in the Burgenland. I'm planning to be back in Vienna in February. If it's cold enough we can go skating. Are you any good at skating? I'm sensational. Love and kisses to Cuno. Ben.'

She read the letter three or four times. She too had thought a great deal about the day they had spent together.

The cold increased and with it tension in the house. Felix came and went by night and Ruth and Michael began to argue. Anna's German was just good enough now to make out some of the exchanges. Mostly they concerned Felix and what he was doing and the danger they were in because of him.

It was difficult for her to understand what was really happening. Most of her time was spent in the house looking after the children, and without Ben to keep her in touch with the outside world her thoughts turned to her own future.

She could not go on looking after people's children in a foreign country for the rest of her life. But she had no money, no skills. And in Britain there was only her grandmother's bleak upland farm.

February arrived. Ben did not come back but Cuno did. He had taken part in the slalom at Kitzbühel but had fallen, the point of his ski-stick had penetrated his thigh and he had to keep off skis for a month or so. He was proud of the wound and showed it to Anna. She flinched when she saw the gaping hole.

He laughed. 'It is nothing for us. For the English perhaps, but for us nothing.'

Ruth had started her bridge again. Cuno would bring his mother and then stay on. Anna could not avoid him. She would spend hours drinking coffee and listening to him talk. Several times he trapped her in empty rooms and would fondle her breasts before she managed to escape. It was with a feeling of great relief that she went to the telephone one day towards the end of February and heard Ben's voice. He was back in Vienna.

He was thinner and looked older. He had been working round the clock, he said. All the correspondents were. Hitler was threatening Austria and the Austrian Chancellor had gone to meet him to try and bargain for time.

A few nights later Ben took her to a meeting he wanted to cover just off the Döblinger Hauptstrasse. It was a small masonic hall half full of depressed-looking workers. They sat near the back where the rows of seats were empty. On the stage was a table and several chairs. A large poster on the wall said in German: 'Austria for Austrians.' A red banner next to it displayed the Hammer and Sickle.

Three men came on to the stage and made speeches which Anna did not understand, then the chairman beckoned to someone in the wings and Felix came out. She had not seen him for a week or more for he was no longer living in the Althofengasse.

His curly blond hair was carelessly untidy. He waved his hand in acknowledgement of the ragged applause. He looked confident and it was only when he spoke that she heard the tremor of nervousness in his voice.

'Friends,' he began. 'Friends and comrades . . .'

That was as far as he got, for the doors of the hall burst open and a pack of Fascist Brownshirts, each with a club in his hand, barged in. There was instant panic. Women screamed, men fell. Ben grabbed Anna and forced his way on to the street. She looked back but Felix was no longer on the platform. The Brownshirts were tearing down the poster and the banner.

In the street more Brownshirts attacked members of the audience as they fled from the hall. One raised his club to hit Ben but Ben held his arm and said in German, 'I'm an American newspaper correspondent.'

The man hesitated, then relaxed. Ben's size alone made him pause.

Anna was trembling. 'Walk slowly!' Ben said. 'They're like animals. If we run they'll attack.' As they reached his car he said, 'You need a drink.'

He took her to the Urbanikeller in the Amhof. It was full at that time in the evening but they managed to get a table underneath a brass replica of a laughing alligator. He ordered a flask of wine and said, 'Now do you understand what's happening?'

'I . . . Yes . . . I do.' She was still trembling. 'What happened to Felix?'

'There's always a back exit in these halls. He'll be all right.'

'Did you know he'd be there?'

'Someone told me he might.'

'I'm frightened,' she whispered.

'You're British. You'll be okay. For the time being anyway.'

'For the time being?'

'The Germans'll take Austria. No one can stop them. But so far their quarrel isn't with Britain.'

'Take me home,' she said. It sounded odd. Home? The Althofengasse in a Vienna that might soon be overrun by Nazis?

It had been raining and the cobbles on the square were shining in the streetlights. Their shadows were huge and distorted as they fell on the surrounding buildings. Suddenly he drew her into a shop doorway and kissed her.

All her tension and fear, bottled up for weeks and heightened by the events of the evening, caused her body to stiffen. She felt the stubble of his cheek, the coldness of his lips, the smell of cigar tobacco.

He pulled away. 'I'm sorry,' he said, reacting to her rigidity. 'I guess you – '

'Oh God, don't be!' She turned her face and kissed him, clinging to his large frame.

'I couldn't stop thinking of you,' he said.

Suddenly her tension was released in a rush of warmth and happiness and she realized that she had never experienced such a feeling before.

They kissed again and both knew that something irrevocable had happened.

After a while they turned and went back down the steps into the Urbanikeller. Their table was still vacant and they sat as they had done before, but they were not the same people.

He ordered more wine and plates of pork knuckles and salad. They ate ravenously. They held each other's hands so that each had to eat one-handed.

26

Like all lovers, they thought that this had never happened to anyone else with quite the intensity it was happening to them. In the space of a couple of hours they talked about everything that was important to them. She told him her background, he told her his. He spoke of their future – for it was taken for granted that their future would be shared – and how much he wanted to return to the States and take her with him. He told her of the places there he wanted to show her, the life there he wanted to give her. As he spoke, England, Winchester, the hill farm in Wales, all began to disappear in her memory and imagination. America seemed to offer her a new life and long exciting vistas opened before her.

He leaned over the table and kissed her. After a moment he said, 'Have you eaten any of your onion salad? You'd better.'

Then came the reaction. He told her that he would have to be travelling for the next few months as the European story developed. Her face fell.

'But I'll be back. In and out. We'll see each other. I'll keep in touch.'

'But can't you stay? Can't you work from here?'

'I have to go where the news is,' he said. 'That's my job.'

'I'll go with you.'

'That's not possible.'

A shadow fell across her happiness. For the first time she realized he had another love, another mistress – journalism.

They finished the wine. 'Where can we go?' he said.

She knew what he meant and for a moment something in her locked up. Then she thought: I don't have to answer to anyone.

'We can't go to the Althofengasse.'

'And I'm staying in a boarding-house. No women allowed. We could go to a hotel.'

She thought of arriving in a hotel foyer without luggage. The look in the receptionist's eyes.

'Not tonight,' she said. 'Let's do it in style.'

'Tomorrow then. I'll book a room at the Ambassador. It's on the Ring near – '

'I know it.'

*

The following day she caught a tram into the centre of the city. She had not been in during the day for some weeks and was surprised at the crowds drifting aimlessly about. Groups had gathered at street corners as though they were waiting for something.

The Hotel Ambassador was at the opera house end of Kärtnerstrasse near Sachers. She had packed a nightdress in a small overnight bag and was carrying this as her luggage. She knew she was not going to spend the night but was uncertain what else to take. She was nervous and filled with tension. But it was the tension of excitement and longing.

At the hotel entrance she was nearly knocked down by a large open black car. Several army officers, also dressed in black with shining leather boots, got out. She had not seen the uniform before.

One of them turned to her and with a bow, said in German, 'Please forgive us.' They strolled into the hotel lobby where an old man was on his knees drying the marble floor. One of the officers touched his shoulder with a riding crop and indicated that he should move out of the way. He rose painfully to his feet and stood against the wall.

Anna recognized him. He was Professor Bloch who had visited Felix and given her chocolates.

He looked very different now. His head had been shaved and he was wearing a grey smock with a yellow star stencilled on the back.

She went forward to greet him but he stared at her without a glint of recognition, then got down on his knees again and continued drying the floor.

Disturbed and bewildered, she went to the desk and gave Ben's name.

'Good day, Mrs Ramsey,' the receptionist said, and handed her a key.

She took the little cage-lift up to the third floor. The room was nineteenth century, with heavy wooden furniture and over-stuffed chairs. The bed was a large four-poster. There was a balcony and she opened the French windows and stood outside in the cold looking along the Ringstrasse.

She could not get the image of Professor Bloch out of her

mind. Ben had told her what was happening to the Jews but she had hardly taken it in. Now the picture of the old man on his knees drying the floor haunted her.

She unpacked her night clothes and arranged them in the bathroom.

Ben had said to meet him there at noon and they would have lunch in the room. The minutes ticked by. Twelve thirty came . . . then one . . . then half past . . .

She stood on the balcony watching for him until she became frozen. She sat in the room. She stood by the window. By two o'clock she felt wretched and angry and worried.

She repacked her bag and went downstairs to the desk. 'Tell my . . . my husband I've gone to Neustift am Walde.'

'Very good, madame.'

There was a pile of newspapers on the counter. They were editions of that morning's *Continental Daily Mail*. The heading on page one screamed out at her: HITLER INVADES AUSTRIA.

Three

Everything had disintegrated after the Anschluss. Felix had gone on the run. Ben had disappeared on the trail of political stories and Vienna had been more febrile than ever. Jews were being rounded up; there was talk of 'camps' to which they were being sent for 'rehabilitation'. One was said to be not far upstream from Vienna on the Danube at a village called Mauthausen.

It was difficult to get at the truth, and indeed better not to, Michael said. Ruth had withdrawn into her shell. They didn't *want* to know what was really happening, and neither did Anna. She wanted Ben to return. She wanted an end to Cuno's continual pestering.

It was then that the police arrived, at seven o'clock one morning. The first anyone knew about it was when a large green Opel pulled up outside the house and four men, all wearing long black leather overcoats, banged at the front door.

The house was thrown into panic. No one was properly dressed. Nico was being fed. Stefan was running about. The police didn't bother with identity documents or search warrants. The senior officer, a large malevolent figure in shiny coat and cropped hair, said, 'We have information that Herr Felix Esslin is here.' Michael and Ruth were still in dressing-gowns. 'Please remain in this room.'

One man stayed to watch them and the other three began to search. Michael, under Ruth's agonized gaze, protested formally. The man said, 'We are under instructions.'

'But he is my wife's brother. Of course he came here. It is only natural. But he's not here now.'

'I cannot comment,' the man said.

After an hour the other three came back into the room. One was holding Felix's typewriter, another a bundle of letters.

Michael repeated what he had said. The big man turned on him and said, 'All traitors have brothers and sisters, fathers and mothers.'

Then he ordered Michael and Ruth not to leave Vienna without police permission and they drove away.

Nothing like this had happened to the Meissners before. Their lives had been lived among the middle class professional set where laws hardly meant anything because they never broke them. The only time Michael had anything to do with the police was for parking violations. It was as though they had suddenly contracted the plague and they were filled with shame and fear.

They were talking about it still when Cuno brought his mother to play bridge. Later, when Michael came back from work, Cuno said, 'A lot of people are leaving. Jews of course, but some others too. Politicals.'

'One needs exit visas,' Michael said.

'Of course.'

'And they are very difficult?'

'Very. And expensive.'

'But if one could pay . . . could one obtain such things? I ask, you know, just for interest.'

Cuno thought for a moment and said, 'There are ways, but they are dangerous. Extremely so. If one were found out . . .'

'Of course.'

Cuno smoothed back his dark, shining hair. 'Austria has a long border. There are places in the Vorarlberg where it is possible to cross into Switzerland. I have skied in places where they cross all the time and nobody asks for papers.'

'And you know exactly where these places are?' Michael said.

'Of course.'

The following day Michael phoned Cuno and asked him to come to the house.

Anna was not present at the discussion but Ruth told her that Michael had decided they must leave Austria. As long as

Felix was being hunted or even if he was arrested they would be in danger. Whole families were disappearing into the camps.

Michael sold his practice and the house to an old friend. The price was lower than it should have been but he said they were lucky to sell at all in these times.

Ruth disassociated herself from any plans apparently on the grounds that if she did not think about problems they would disappear.

Anna wanted to leave, to go down to the Westbahnhof and take the Arlberg-Orient Express to the west. But she had become Ruth's right hand and felt duty-bound to remain.

It was then that Cuno made his move.

She had learned to sleep in the Austrian way, with open windows in the severest weather and a down-filled duvet to keep her warm. One night, he simply climbed through her window. She had woken to see his shadow above her and for a second she thought it was Michael come to ask her to help with Nico. It was only when she realized he was not Michael and that he was dressed for the street, that she became frightened.

'Cuno!'

'Sssssh! Not so loud!'

They were hissing at each other like snakes.

'What do you want?'

'What do you think? That I have come to discuss Nietzsche?'

She felt his hand touch her cheek. The fingers were freezing.

'If you don't get out of my room this instant I'll call Michael!'

He sat down on her bed. 'Yes. Call him.'

'What?'

His hand had slipped under the duvet and was fondling her body.

'Call him. And when he comes I tell him to find his own way across the border.' She fought his hand. 'Let me tell you something, Miss English girl. Without me they are finished. You can always go back to England. But not them. You know what is going to happen to them? I tell you. The police are going to find Felix and they are going to make him tell them

32

what happened here in this house. That he plotted against the state. And you think they are going to believe that Michael and Ruth did not *know*? And they are going to arrest Professor Bloch and the others who were plotting here. Yes, plotting. Traitors! They will take everybody: Ruth, Michael, Stefan, Nico . . . You have heard of the "rehabilitation" camps? That is where they will be taken.'

In spite of the warmth of the bed she felt icy. It was the iciness of hate and despair. She was to be the payment for his co-operation. He began to undress.

Anna's sexual fantasies had grown more vivid since she had fallen in love with Ben. She was ready for sex. But not ready for Cuno.

That first time was the worst. While she had had no experience he seemed to have had very little. He forced his penis into her and she felt something tear. She gasped and, although she fought them, tears came to her eyes.

He finished quickly in a series of convulsive jerks and then said, 'Tomorrow buy yourself some Vaseline.'

The next few weeks were a series of nightmares for her. Because of the wound in his leg Cuno was trapped in Vienna. He was at the height of his strength and sexual power and wanted her every day and sometimes twice. When his mother played bridge he would take her back to their large old-fashioned and gloomy apartment in the Gentzgasse. She hated these times. He would take her on his mother's bed in full view of her long wardrobe mirror.

He was like an animal, yet also like a child. He wanted her as a mistress and mother but with the half-formed needs of a child, unclear even to himself. He wanted her anally and orally and these times were the worst of all.

In her innocence she had thought that the sexual act was something two people did and it was called making love. What was happening to her had nothing to do with love.

Quickly she learned how to protect herself. If she stiffened and grew tense he hurt her. If she relaxed, told herself that there was a distinction between her body and her mind, between her emotions and her flesh, then it became easier.

Every day she thought of ways to escape and every day she

knew she could never make a run for it on her own and leave the family, who had taken her in and loved her, in Cuno's hands.

She had come to realize that he lived in a world of his own making where right and wrong had almost no meaning. She had no doubt he would take his revenge. It would need only one telephone call to the Staatspolizei.

In the event the telephone call came the other way, a strident ringing in the night, just as they had always feared it would.

'Hurry!' Michael said. 'For God's sake hurry!'

Ruth, his wife, was dressing Stefan. Anna was putting fresh clothing on the baby, Nico.

Ruth's thin face was drawn, her dark hair, usually so carefully done, was tousled.

Stefan, six years old and squirming in his jacket and tie, said, 'Are we going skiing?'

'Yes, darling, skiing.'

Although the exchanges were in German Anna's knowledge of the language after half a year in Austria was enough to follow everything that was being said. The telephone call had come before light that morning. Michael was already up. So was Anna because Nico had been crying. She had taken him into Ruth's room to be cuddled by his mother when Michael had burst in.

'The State Police have arrested Felix!'

The blood drained from Ruth's face. 'Oh God! When?'

'Late yesterday. That was Dieter from the Ministry of Justice on the phone. It was good of him to ring. If he was found out . . .' His voice trailed away. 'They've arrested Maria and the kids too.' Maria was Felix's wife.

Ruth began to cry. She and her brother were very close. 'We've got to hurry!' Michael said. 'I'll telephone Cuno.'

'Are we really going skiing?' Stefan said.

'Yes, darling. We're going to Bludenz.'

'Have I been there?'

'No, you've never been there.'

'Is Uncle Cuno coming?'

'Yes, we're going with Uncle Cuno.'

'He's the best skier in the world,' Stefan said. 'In the whole world.'

Ruth was pulling out clothes and hats from her cupboards and was stuffing them into two large suitcases and a hatbox, when Cuno came in.

He was dressed in a heavy white skiing sweater. He smiled at Anna, his dark, good-looking face twisting slightly. She stared back at him trying to keep the hatred from her eyes. Only a few hours before he had been lying on top of her naked body, pumping and groaning and swearing at her in a soft voice. Keep the hatred for later, she told herself. We need him now.

'Stop!' Cuno said. 'You can't take all that!' He threw one of Ruth's suitcases on to the floor. 'An overnight bag. That's all.'

'But my hats!' Ruth said. 'I have a new – '

Michael was packing medical books.

'And no books!'

'They're my life,' Michael said. 'Without my – '

'You can buy more in Switzerland. They have medical books there too. I told you before! Just what you can carry!'

'My jewels!' Ruth said. 'I *must* take them.'

'Yes,' Cuno said. 'That's the sort of thing. Small and light. And something you can sell in Zürich.' He turned to Michael. 'Have you got the money?'

Michael opened a briefcase. Anna saw it was stuffed with high denomination notes, Swiss and Austrian.

'I'll take mine now,' Cuno said.

Michael hesitated, then reached into the briefcase and brought out a large brown envelope. Cuno stuffed it into his pocket.

Ruth spread her jewels out on the bed. There was a pendant necklace of diamonds, several diamond rings, a brooch comprising a cluster of emeralds and rubies and half a dozen other brooches and necklaces of lesser stones. There was also a medallion on a ribbon.

'What's that?' Cuno said.

Ruth put it with the rest in a leather Gladstone bag. 'My grandfather's decoration from the Emperor.'

'I'll get the car out,' Cuno said.

'No!' Michael said. 'I will! It's not yours *yet*!'

They trooped out into the dark cold morning. Anna's belongings were in a small case. She held it in one hand and Nico in her other arm. Stefan had left his little Schuko racing car and ran back to fetch it.

Michael brought the big Mercedes-Benz from the garage and they packed their belongings on to the luggage rack at the back. Anna looked at the dripping garden, so different now from when she had arrived in the summer. The apple trees were beginning to come into bud but that was the only sign of spring.

She and Ruth got into the back of the car with the two children. Michael sat at the wheel, Cuno beside him.

Ruth said, 'My mink!'

'I'll get it,' Anna said. She ran into the house and picked up the heavy coat. She didn't blame Ruth. She would have wanted it too if it had been hers.

For a moment she stood in the silent house. She had loved it here. It had been the best part of her life so far. Except for Cuno . . .

She saw the telephone. Could she have one more try to contact Ben? But where? All she got from his newspaper office was the endless ringing of the unanswered phone. She felt tears come to her eyes. Would she ever see him again?

'Anna!' It was Michael's voice. 'Hurry!'

She ran out to the car and gave Ruth her coat.

'Did you lock the door?' Michael said.

Ruth laughed, a hysterical sound. 'We're not coming back, Michael! Don't be so silly!'

He turned and said angrily, 'Silly? If it wasn't for your brother we wouldn't have to leave!'

He swung the car out of the front gate and turned towards Vienna's northern hills. They'd leave that way then cut down towards the autobahn. No one would be expecting them to take that direction.

The morning light was grey as they left the outskirts of the city. Ruth had begun to cry and had infected Nico who was grizzling in Anna's arms.

'We'll come back one day,' Michael said. 'One day the Nazis will go. One day there won't be troops in the streets. We'll come back then. I promise you.'

36

But Ruth slowly shook her head. She did not reply and Anna knew she didn't believe him. Anna didn't believe him either.

But she told herself not to think about that. Think about the border. Think about getting out. Then she could begin to think about the future.

Four

Before the war Altenkirchen was a small, picture-postcard town.
Now, because of the motorway and the dam, little of it exists.
At its centre was a white-painted church with a gilded spire.
There were three inns, two in the main street and one at the
base of the ski-lift on the slopes that overlooked the town. The
houses were mainly chalets made of wood with verandahs on
the upper floors. It was the kind of place anyone would have
been delighted to visit on a skiing holiday or, in summer, a
walking tour of the Vorarlberg.

On a cold and misty afternoon in 1938, as the Meissners' big
Mercedes wound down its mountain road there was still an
air of magic about it. But when the car came closer Anna saw
the reality.

The town had been overrun with people; the roads filled with
abandoned cars.

It did not come as too much of a surprise, for all along the
autobahn she had seen cars being stopped by police checks.
They had been lucky and the only time they had been stopped
the police had had their attention diverted by a convoy of
German armoured cars moving in the opposite direction and
they had waved the Mercedes on.

Now, as they came down slowly into Altenkirchen they saw
that the small sixteenth-century bridge across one of the Rhine's
tributaries, which connected Austria with Switzerland, was
almost invisible beneath the crowds that were pressing against
the customs barrier on the Austrian side.

Michael Meissner brought the Mercedes to a stop about four

hundred metres from the bridge. The town was built on the slope above the river and they had a good view of what was happening.

Everywhere there were families with children trying to cross. And everywhere, too, there were soldiers with guns.

The afternoon was becoming colder and the mist was descending from the high mountains into the dark pine forests which spread out on three sides of the town.

'We'll never get across today,' Michael said.

Ruth was holding Nico who had been crying during the fast non-stop drive from Vienna. The heater in the car had broken down and everyone had frozen on the snowy Arlberg Pass.

Ruth said, 'We must! I must get Nico changed and warm.'

'Give him to me,' Anna said and tried to warm him underneath her coat. He clung to her but kept up a continuous low crying.

'We're not going to cross here,' Cuno said contemptuously. 'How can you think that! It's too dangerous. They've got police and border guards with orders to shoot.'

'Where then?' Michael said.

'I told you we would cross the water by boat. We must leave the car here and walk.'

'Walk!' Ruth said, looking down at her high heels. 'Where to? How far?'

'Downstream. Maybe four kilometres. To a small village. I know they have a boat.'

'I thought you'd arranged it!' Michael said angrily. 'I paid you for it!'

'How could I arrange it? They don't have a telephone in a place like that. Anyway you can't ask for such things by telephone. Not these days. But I know the village. I've skied to it. They have several boats.'

Michael said, 'It's terrible taking a chance now – with the children.'

'You could have stayed at home!' Cuno said. 'You want to go back? Or do you want to try here?' He pointed to the bridge.

Michael shook his head. 'All right. Your way.'

'Can't we drive part of the way?' Ruth asked. 'Isn't there a track?'

39

'Maybe half a kilometre.'

'It's better than nothing,' Michael said. 'Which way?'

'Left by the first inn,' Cuno said. 'You want me to drive?'

'No thanks.'

The car lurched and swayed over the potholed street and then they turned on to a muddy track. They drove slowly for about five minutes and came to great piles of logs, freshly cut, which blocked any further progress. They sat in the car, unwilling to move. They were all cold and tired and had not eaten since the morning.

The light was cut by the trees and the mist swirled in long streamers between their dark trunks.

Cuno got out and said, 'Let's move.'

'Are we going skiing now?' Stefan asked.

'Not here, darling,' Michael said. 'First we cross the river. We'll ski in Switzerland.'

Ruth was standing on the muddy road in her high-heeled pumps and her mink coat looking like a fashion model who had wandered into the wrong shot.

All this time Nico had kept up his crying.

'It's impossible!' Ruth said. 'You can't expect him to go in a boat.' She reached out and felt his hands. 'My God, he's freezing!'

Michael looked uncertain. Cuno said, 'We can't stay here, we'll look suspicious.'

They saw a man and woman, both dressed in city clothing, walk swiftly through the trees below them.

'They're also going to look for a boat,' Cuno said. 'If you don't hurry there'll be nothing left.'

Ruth turned to Anna. 'You have a British passport. Take Nico. They'll let you through. We'll meet you on the other side.'

Michael said, 'But – '

'For God's sake, Michael, the child is sick. He's cold. He'll die if we don't get him to a warm place.'

He nodded. 'Ruth's right,' he said to Anna. 'They'll let you through. All those people will be Austrian Jews. But you're English. Your passport can take you anywhere.'

'But what about Nico?' Anna said.

'If they ask, just say he's yours.'

Cuno was already walking past the woodpiles on a narrow track. 'Are you coming?' he shouted.

Michael put his hand on Anna's shoulder. 'We'll see you on the other side. Have you any money?'

'Yes.'

'Book into a hotel and get a room for us.'

Ruth leaned forward and kissed Nico on his forehead. 'Goodbye, darling. See you in a little while.' Tears streamed down her cheeks.

She turned and, holding her suitcase in one hand and Michael's arm with the other, hobbled off along the muddy track.

Anna watched them disappear into the mist and then she turned and made her way back to Altenkirchen.

As she walked she rocked Nico on her arm trying to soothe him, and herself as well. She was alone with a baby and she had not been alone in all her life except for the few days when she had travelled from England to Vienna.

The noise and confusion at the bridge made her feel more bewildered.

Many of the women in the crush were wearing fur coats. Some were carrying a second. There were babies in arms, grandparents in their eighties.

There was a single passport control, a hut on the near side of the bridge. A queue had formed along a stretch of road for about a hundred metres. Behind that was a barbed wire entanglement and behind that the crowd. Through a gap in the wire, people were being allowed one at a time to join the queue. Many were being turned away. Some came past her grim-faced, others sobbed out loud.

Nico was crying in chorus with the other babies and Anna realized she would have to do something more than simply stand at the back of a crowd if she was to get through that afternoon. It was now mid-afternoon but she did not know how long the border would remain open.

'You're English,' said a voice at her elbow.

She turned and saw a man just over medium height with square shoulders and a wide-brimmed felt hat that was shaped to go down at the back as though to shade his neck. He was

41

dressed in a heavy tweed suit and a mackintosh. Over one shoulder was slung a Rolleiflex camera and in his hand he carried a small Hermes typewriter in a metal case.

'You're English, aren't you?' he repeated. 'I heard you talking to your baby.'

'Yes.'

His face was large and flat with thick lips. 'I've just arrived,' he said. 'How long have you been here?' He had a slight accent.

'Ten minutes or so.'

'You'll never get anywhere on your own. Hang on to my arm. Excuse me! Excuse me!' He used the typewriter as a weapon, bumping people with it, moving them out of the way. 'Excuse me! We must get through!'

People glared and shouted in German. But he seemed impervious and she hung on.

'Jews,' he said to her indicating the crowd. 'All trying to get out.'

The crush near the barbed wire was more intense and their progress was slower. A man with a megaphone came out of the passport control hut and began to shout. Anna could make out only a few words but the man in the felt hat listened carefully and said, 'Bugger it! They're closing the border for the day. Too many people. It won't reopen until eight o'clock tomorrow morning.'

'But I *must* get across.'

He looked at her oddly. 'We all want to get across,' he said.

She felt desperate. 'There must be other places. Other ways. Some people are going across by boat.'

'Here? I don't think so.'

'No, not here. Further downstream. About four kilometres. Maybe we could get a boat.'

'Are you sure?' His eyes had widened with interest.

'Yes.'

'What's the name of the place?'

'I don't know.'

'I'll go and see. Wait for me.'

The crowd was beginning to disperse.

'I'll go with you.'

But he suddenly vanished. She felt more alone than ever.

She didn't know what to do or where to go. She followed the crowd and found herself at the town hall. It had been turned into a refugee centre.

Anna was placed in a part of the hall with mothers and babies. Officials from the Swiss Red Cross gave her nappies and baby food and she was able to make Nico more comfortable. Later they received soup and bread and pallets stuffed with straw to sleep on. She was so exhausted she couldn't think straight. During the night the police came round looking at passports and exit permits. Several mothers were taken away.

A lieutenant from the border patrol looked at her passport and said, 'Come to the police station at seven o'clock tomorrow morning.'

'Why?' She wondered whether the Meissners had been arrested and were asking for her.

But all he said was, 'You will have the answer then.'

She slept fitfully. Nico was restless and when she felt his brow she thought he might be running a temperature.

She couldn't get out of her mind the thought of the Meissners on the other side of the river, searching the hotels, looking for their child. Sleep was made even more difficult by women and children snuffling and coughing and crying. This must be what hell is like, she thought, a place with a lot of frightened people.

She was dozing in the grey dawn when she felt a hand on her shoulder. It was the man in the large hat.

'You all right?' he said. 'I couldn't find you.'

He told her he had walked downstream and had seen boats ferrying people across. He had waited for hours but none of the boats had come back.

'We must go down to the bridge,' he said. 'The crowd's already beginning to form.'

She looked at her watch and said, 'I have to go to the police station.'

'Why?'

'They told me to.'

'I'll come with you.'

She was grateful.

As they walked, he said, 'What's your name?'

She told him. He said, 'Mine's Wilson Braid.' At the police station he said, 'Give me the baby. I'll hold her.'

'*Him*,' she said. 'His name's Nico.'

'Hello, Nico.' He put his typewriter down and took Nico.

She went into the police station. The officer who had spoken to her in the town hall was sitting behind a desk typing two-fingered on an old Adler. He was dressed in dark green loden with black shoulder flashes. He had a wide peasant face with a high colour.

'Grüss Gott.' Then, recognizing her, said in English, 'Oh, good morning. Where is your child?'

'A friend's holding him for me.'

'Good. Your passport please?'

He looked at it as he had the previous night. 'What have you been doing in Austria?'

She had been expecting the question. 'I was with my husband. He's a newspaper correspondent. He's in Poland now.'

'He must have a lot to write about. Too much, I think.'

He took a stamp from his drawer, hit an ink pad and stamped her passport.

'When they open the border go into the left-hand queue, it is for foreigners. You will have no trouble now.' She thanked him. 'It is not right that young mothers with children should be treated like that – ' he indicated with his thumb the general chaos outside – 'specially visitors to our country.'

He put out a hand, shook hers, and then returned to his desk.

When she told Braid what had happened he smiled. 'You're lucky. Pretty girls always get special treatment. By the way, where's your husband?'

'In Poland.'

'That's not so good.'

They opened the border at eight o'clock sharp. Anna felt a sense of lightness and relief as she handed her papers to the Swiss border control on the other side of the river. After a brief inspection one of the men stamped her passport with a 72-hour transit visa and she was through and free.

She stood by the river parapet and waited for Braid. After ten minutes or so he emerged from the customs hut and walked

44

across the bridge. His coat was flapping, his hat was on the back of his head and he had neither the camera nor the typewriter. When he reached her he was red-faced and furious.

'The bastards searched me as though I was a bloody wog,' he said. '*And* they've confiscated my camera and typewriter.'

'I must find the Meissners.'

'Who?'

'My friends. They'll be in one of the hotels.'

There were only two. They went to the first and he said, 'Let me hold the baby.'

Gratefully she handed Nico over. The receptionist had never heard of the Meissners.

They went to the second hotel, the Kaiserhof, and she was met with the same reply.

'But they've got to be in one,' she said to Braid. 'If there are only two they've *got* to be in one.'

'Unless they've gone on somewhere else.'

'But they can't.'

She took Nico as he went into the hotel. When he came out a few moments later he said, 'I've taken a room.'

'But I can't stay here. I've got to find – '

'Listen, you're dead beat. So's the kid. Let's get into the room and talk there.'

It was a large pleasant room, chintzy and warm, with two double beds and a cot for Nico. She sat on one bed and felt almost dizzy with tiredness. Then, in halting phrases, she told him about the Meissners and the fact that Nico was not hers. He took out a notebook and jotted down sentences as she spoke.

'So you're not married?'

'No. It was all a lie. In case they questioned me.'

'Well, you lie bloody well. You took me in too.'

'I'm sorry.'

'I'll check with the police and the Red Cross. I'll be back in half an hour.'

Anna arranged with reception for a maid to run her a bath. She sat in the water looking down at her dark pubic hair, hoping desperately to see slight traces of blood, but the water remained

45

crystal. She was late. If she missed her period again she knew it would be certain.

No Meissners had been registered with the police or the Red Cross, Braid told her when he returned. He began to question her about herself, and why she had been in Vienna.

Finally she said, 'What are you writing?'

'Your story. I'm a journalist on the *Daily News* in London. Didn't you know?'

'How could I?'

'I thought you might have seen my photograph next to my byline.'

'I've never seen a *Daily News*. My father took *The Times*.'

He looked amazed and at the same time irritated.

'Why are you writing about me?'

'It's my job. And you're a bloody good story.'

She felt totally helpless. If she objected he might leave and she did not want that. And she had almost no money. She had told Michael she had but when she counted it she found there were only a few schillings.

And there was Nico. What was she going to do with him? She'd have to wait for Michael and Ruth. But for how long?

The thoughts went round and round in her mind as Braid continued his questioning. An hour later he had got most – not everything – from her.

It was then that she said, 'I knew a journalist in Vienna. An American called Ben Ramsey.'

He looked up sharply. 'I knew him too. Poor bugger.'

'What?'

'He got blown up. In Warsaw. I saw the story on Reuter's before I left Salzburg. Fascists attacked a political meeting, threw a couple of hand-grenades into the crowd. Half a dozen were killed. Ramsey was one.'

The horror took her by the throat. The past weeks . . . first Ben disappearing, then Cuno . . . She stopped herself thinking about Cuno but she could not stop herself thinking about Ben.

'Did he mean anything to you?'

'Yes,' she whispered. 'I'm tired.'

'Look, I've got to go to Zürich to file a couple of stories. Yours

46

too. And I've got some pictures to send. There's a train in half an hour. I'll be back tonight or tomorrow morning.'

She curled up in a ball and cried herself to sleep. When she woke it was early morning. Fears rushed back. Again the tears came but this time she gulped them down. If she broke now she was finished. And she must think of Nico. He lay in a cot in a hotel she could not afford and he belonged to someone else. In her womb there was probably another baby. Cuno's baby. She was nineteen years old and she was alone.

Five

Altenkirchen, the Meissners, Wilson Braid, the Red Cross, Nico . . . everything had to be sorted through into a coherent narrative. The problem was that the Anna Webster who owned the *Daily News* and the Anna Webster who had woken up in the chintzy room of the Kaiserhof Hotel in Switzerland that morning in 1938 were two different people.

She remembered waking up and looking at Nico who was already awake and staring intensely at his fingers. She remembered heating milk in hot water in the basin and feeding him. Above all she remembered that the morning was sunny and that the mists of the previous day had disappeared. The little town had looked so safe on this side of the river: the streets, the buildings, the few people already about. Yet just across the bridge there was chaos, danger and death.

She counted her money again. There was hardly enough to pay for a meal, let alone the room.

She wondered where Wilson Braid was, probably halfway to London. She must forget him. She must depend on herself and the first thing was to see if the Meissners had reached the town, then pay her bill. The first she could do herself; the second, if the Meissners had not arrived, would involve help from the British Embassy. She knew they had a special fund for destitute nationals stranded in foreign countries. But where *was* the nearest embassy? Zürich? Berne? Basle?

Perhaps she should telephone the embassy and tell them that the Meissners were missing and that she had their baby. The embassy officials would guide her.

While Nico was still sleeping she asked one of the maids to keep an eye on him and went downstairs.

The woman at the desk called, 'Madame. *Bitte.* A moment. Will you be staying tonight?'

'I'm not sure.'

The receptionist frowned. 'We have much pressure for the room. There are many people crossing.'

'Yes. I will be staying.'

'And your husband?'

'He's gone to Zürich. I'm expecting him back later.'

She went out into the bright morning sunshine, into the safe Swiss streets. Already the crowds were massing on the far side of the river. They seemed even bigger than the day before.

Traffic was only one way on the bridge and the Swiss border control officials looked incredulous when she said she wished to go back into Austria.

'I need to get information.'

A middle-aged passport officer said, 'Madame, they let you out once, do you not think it may be difficult a second time?'

'I have a British passport,' she said.

'Many people have foreign passports. That is no guarantee. Here you are safe.'

She saw a group of Austrian police on the bridge staring down at the water. One was the lieutenant who had stamped her passport.

He was standing midway across the bridge and she said to the Swiss official, 'Can they stop me if I only go halfway?'

'Halfway is still Switzerland.'

'Can I go and speak to one of those men? He may know something about my family.'

They let her through the barrier. She forced her way on to the bridge through the crowds crossing in the opposite direction. Some were pushing prams filled with household goods and clothing. They stared at her in disbelief.

Her steps faltered. What if the Meissners had been arrested and taken to a camp? Would they take her too? And then what would happen to Nico? She still believed that her British passport allowed her free passage without let or hindrance.

49

Anywhere. It was something she had grown up with. She was British. And British was best. But . . . did the Austrians know that?

The lieutenant saw her. He frowned and gave an almost imperceptible shake of his head. She stopped about a quarter of the way across.

'I must talk to you,' she called.

He no longer looked the fresh young man with the ruddy mountaineer's face she had seen in the police station. Now his expression was grave, almost angry.

'This is not sensible,' he said. 'You are one of the lucky ones. Can't you be satisfied with that?'

Briefly she told him about the Meissners, how they had come to Altenkirchen together, how they had been separated.

One of the policemen who had been looking down into the water said something to him. The lieutenant turned to her. 'Maybe you can help. Please follow me.' She hesitated. 'I will bring you back.'

On the Austrian bank a man in long chest waders was throwing a grappling hook over something which had caught in flotsam trapped against one of the bridge supports. It was the body of a man dressed in a dark suit with a white shirt and tie. After three throws the hooks caught in his clothing and the body was towed ashore.

The lieutenant took Anna down to the river bank as they turned the man over on his back. 'Do you know him?'

She was looking down in horror at a man in his forties or fifties; dark, with a Semitic cast to his face. There was a blue hole in the side of his head which must have been made by a bullet.

'No,' she said with relief.

'I will take you back. But please do not come on to the bridge again. I cannot help you.'

For the second time in twenty-four hours she left Austrian soil and went back into Switzerland.

A small crowd had gathered by the bridge on the Swiss side watching the recovery of the body. From it a voice cried: 'Anna! Anna!'

For one heart-leaping moment she thought it was the voice

of Michael Meissner, then she saw Wilson Braid pushing his way towards her.

'You look surprised,' he said.

'I didn't think . . . I don't know why, I just thought you wouldn't come back.'

A flash of annoyance crossed his face. 'I said I would.'

She told him she still hadn't found the Meissners.

'We'll check in Zürich,' he said.

She heard the word 'we' and felt a huge release of tension.

At the hotel he asked for the bill. They went up to the room. 'I managed to get some money in Zürich,' he said, and he counted out twenty-five pounds and gave it to her. 'For expenses.'

'But – '

'But what?'

'I don't know when I'll be able to repay you.'

'It's not my money, it's the *Daily News*'s. It's a drop in the ocean to them and anyway they liked your story so it's yours by rights.'

'I don't know how to thank you,' she said, and meant it.

She began to collect Nico's things. He was standing behind her and she felt his arms close round her. 'There is one way,' he said.

She felt a wave of revulsion, as he pressed himself against her. She could feel his hardness.

'Wilson, I – '

There was a knock on the door. His hands dropped away. The maid entered and asked if she could clean the room.

Anna saw a flush on his cheeks and anger in his eyes.

Wilson had hired a car and they reached Zürich that afternoon. The Red Cross already had lists of missing people pinned to boards.

The Meissners were not on any list. A harassed official was unable to hold out hope. Braid asked him to phone Red Cross headquarters in Geneva.

'It is impossible!' the man said. 'I have not the time.'

'Listen, I work for the *Daily News*.' He took out his Cable & Wireless authorization card. 'If you don't phone I'm going to cable a story to London saying the Red Cross doesn't care a damn for missing people.'

The official phoned. Geneva had no word of the Meissners either. Nothing about them had come through from the field-workers in Altenkirchen, Feldkirch or Bludenz.

They went to the back of the room where there was more space.

'What are you going to do with Nico?' Braid asked.

The question had been in her mind every waking minute. She had already made a decision.

'What if the Meissners are dead?'

She had not considered such a possibility until she saw the body beneath the bridge. Now it seemed all too likely: shot by border guards while illegally crossing, the boat tipping over, the bodies washed downstream, perhaps not found for weeks.

'They'd put him in an orphanage,' she said. 'He'd never really know who he was or who he is or anything about himself.'

Braid nodded. 'Things are going to get worse in Europe. And if war comes . . .' He left the sentence unfinished.

'I'm going to take him with me. I'll keep in touch with the Red Cross and when they find the Meissners . . .' The word 'if' had come into her mind but she had resisted it. 'And when they find the Meissners I'll bring him back or Michael and Ruth can come to England to fetch him. But in the meantime he'll be safe.'

'What'll you do for money?'

She had thought about that too and then decided not to think about it. If she had to go back to her grandmother's farm, so be it. At least this time she would have Nico. But what about the baby that was possibly growing inside her womb even now?

'I'll manage,' she said.

'I'm going back on the train tonight,' Braid said. 'The *Daily News* will stand you a ticket if you'd like. We could go together.'

She agreed quickly. He booked a wagon-lit and she realized for the first time how comfortably top journalists travelled the world.

He tipped the conductor to watch over Nico and gave her dinner in the dining car. This is unreal, she thought: the glitter, the expensive evening wear. It seemed on a different planet. As the train sped through the night, out of Switzerland and into France, she was cocooned by the warmth and the luxury, almost hypnotized by the rocking of the carriage, the pink-shaded lights, the gleaming cutlery, the white napery. The outside world was a dense blackness except for the occasional rush of lights as they passed a lonely village.

She relaxed and allowed Braid to make the decisions. He ordered sole Colbert, followed by a Chateaubriand and drank a bottle of Nuits-Saint-Georges. While they ate he talked about himself. It was a subject in which he was totally absorbed.

She learned that he was a first generation South African and that his father had founded a newspaper and magazine empire out there. Wilson Braid had been sent to Fleet Street some years earlier to gain journalistic experience as other parents might send a young person to university.

'Eventually I'll go back, and take over from the old man,' he said. 'That's the arrangement.'

She found that as the wine went down she could put up with Braid and his accent did not jar as much as it had to begin with. He was quite a good-looking man, decisive, energetic, with a kind of animal attraction but she sensed an animal brutality that lay beneath the surface. He was no Ben Ramsey – but Ben was dead and she had to subdue all thought of him. The true comparison was with Cuno and *anyone* would be better than Cuno. As he talked about his Fleet Street successes, how he had scooped the *Mail* on this story and the *Express* on that, she continued to study him. Slowly a path through the maze presented itself.

Nico was asleep when they returned to the compartment. Their two bunks had been made up, one above the other.

'Which do you want?' Braid said.

'If it's all right with you, the bottom one so I can be near Nico if he wakes.'

He found a whisky flask in his bag and opened it. 'A night-cap?' She took a sip. 'A single malt. The best you can get. Why don't we sit down? It's too early to go to bed yet.'

He sat next to her and put his arm round her shoulders. There was something possessive about the way he did so, as though she belonged to him. And in a way she felt she did. He began to rub his hand up and down on her breast.

'Put the light out,' she said.

'You're not shy, are you?'

'Nico might wake.'

'So what? What the hell would he know about it?'

But he switched off the light and the compartment was dimly lit by a blue night-light in the roof. He kissed her. She kept her lips closed. She felt his hand on her brassière clip then his cold fingers on her nipple.

'Wait a minute,' she said.

She went to the bathroom and took off her underwear, leaving on only her slip.

He had taken off his trousers and was ready for her. She lay on her back and spread her legs and he penetrated her.

She listened to the click of the wheels on the track. His rhythm grew faster and faster until she felt him twitching and shuddering. He lay on her for a few seconds and then withdrew clumsily and lit a cigarette.

It had been surprisingly easy, she thought. She wasn't disgusted and frightened as she had been with Cuno. Wilson Braid was just doing what men did. She had neither enjoyed it nor hated it; she had been indifferent, as though it was happening to someone else.

For the very first time in her life she felt in control of the situation in which she found herself. And for the first time she realized that control meant power. It was a strange and heady experience.

Six

Anna often wondered what would have happened to her if she had not accompanied Wilson Braid on the train to London. At the time she was certain he would try to make love to her – and thought he would probably rape her if she did not agree. To avoid that happening, she would have had to part with him in Zürich and go to find a British consular official – and her whole life would have been different.

But she *had* slept with him, that was the important thing, not once, but twice on the journey, for he had wanted her again not long before they reached Calais Maritimes.

It had been a strange homecoming; indeed, it was like coming back to a strange country in the sense that she knew no one to whom she could turn, no old chums from school whom she could phone and say, 'Can I stay? And by the way, I've got one baby and I'm expecting another.'

Coming back with Wilson Braid made all the difference. Although he was a foreigner in Britain he seemed to know more about it than she did and was more at home than she was.

'What are you going to do?' he had asked her on the train and again on the ferry and each time she had said that the first thing was to go to the Red Cross.

Now, on the train from Folkestone to London, he said, 'They'll take Nico away from you.'

She was suddenly alarmed. In the past few days Nico had, by his very helplessness and need for her, begun to play havoc with her emotions. She had always been close to him, had spent more time with him than his mother, and had walked him in the Vienna parks pretending he was hers. She realized, young though she was, that her maternal instinct was strong. She had in fact been slightly envious of Ruth.

'But why?'

'I think you'll find that under British law you would have to adopt Nico to be able to keep him and they'll never let a single woman adopt.'

'Then what'll happen to him?'

'They'll do what the Swiss would have done; put him in an orphanage until they can trace his parents. If the Home Office really wanted to get tough they'd say he wasn't British and send him back.'

'No they won't!'

'Why not? He's Austrian.'

'Because I won't let them!'

She looked down at the baby on her lap. If he wasn't Ruth's any longer – and it looked more and more likely that something terrible had happened to the Meissners – then he was hers. Her baby. She felt a flood of love and protectiveness.

'I'll take him to my grandmother's farm.' She told him about the windswept house in Wales.

'Sounds a bit bloody primitive but maybe it would be best. But you can't go today. You wouldn't get there before night. I'm going down to stay with my father in Hampshire for a few days, why don't you come with me and then I'll drive you to Wales.'

They left London in the afternoon in Braid's dark blue Riley and were on the high ground to the east of Winchester before dusk.

That was the first time she saw Usbourne, a house which would become important to her. It was built of grey stone and stood on rising ground. It was surrounded by a park dotted with great beech and elm trees, and overlooked a small stream.

It was square and plain and grey, a description which, she realized once she had met him, precisely fitted Wilson's father, Jock Braid.

In the late afternoon sunlight they drove up a well-kept drive bordered by daffodils. On the way from London Wilson had said to her, 'My father's a Presbyterian of the old school. Fire and brimstone. So we'd better just keep your story as you first told it to me. He'd start interfering if we told him the truth.'

After one of the maids had shown Anna to her room and taken Nico from her, she and Wilson went into Jock Braid's study where she was introduced as the wife of an American colleague who had been killed in Poland.

As it turned out Jock Braid at that moment could not have cared if she had been the widow of a Martian. Some hours before he had been struck down with severe pain in his head.

He lay with his dressing-gown on over his day clothes on a sofa in his study in front of a blazing fire. The pain was so severe he could not move his head to greet them. He simply lay with his eyes closed and his lips moving slowly in prayer.

Wilson questioned the butler, and discovered that Jock had been coughing and sneezing the night before.

'How long has he been like this?'

'Since luncheon, sir.'

'And the doctor? Where's the bloody quack?'

'Sir, he has his own doctor, a homeopathic gentleman in Winchester. He won't have anyone else.'

'And?'

'Well, sir, he is away at a conference.'

'Get someone else then, for Christ's sake!'

'Who, sir?'

'Jesus, I don't know! There must be someone. Get a man down from London if you have to.'

Anna broke in. 'I think I know what's wrong. My mother used to have attacks like these. It's sinus.'

'That's just a runny nose, isn't it?'

'Not if you've ever had it,' she said. 'I've seen my mother crying in pain.'

'What'd she do for it?'

'There's nothing you can do except use steam.'

'If you know what to do, then do it.'

The staff found oil of eucalyptus, a basin, boiling water and a towel, and Wilson was sent off to buy aspirin.

'He'll never take them,' he said, but went anyway.

The pain was so severe that Jock went against his religious and homeopathic convictions and took them gladly. She gave

57

him four and when Wilson expressed surprise she said, 'My father was a doctor and he gave four to my mother.'

Between them they got Jock into his chair behind the desk with the steaming basin in front of him. She covered his head with a towel and made him breathe the eucalyptus-smelling steam.

She sat with him most of the night. Every three or four hours she gave him more aspirin and kept filling the basin with boiling water. In the early hours of the morning he began to feel better. His sinuses became unclogged and the pain diminished.

Wilson had gone to bed, so Anna helped Jock on to the sofa and fetched blankets and pillow. She could see where Wilson got his burly frame. Jock must have been in his late middle age and was heavy-set. His hair was grey but his skin had a pink well-scrubbed look and his eyes, which had been dull with pain when she had first arrived, had regained some of the sharpness which was part of his character.

'You're a good girl,' he said and she could hear the deeply resonant tones of the Scottish Highlands.

He lay back and she asked if he wanted some warm milk with a little whisky in it.

'I'll be grateful for the milk,' he said, 'but I havna touched spirits since I took the pledge as a young man.'

Later, in her room, feeling secure for the first time in weeks, she suddenly saw the ludicrous side of what was happening to her. Upstairs she was caring for a baby that wasn't hers, downstairs for an old man she'd met only a few hours before. 'You're a regular little Florence Nightingale,' she told herself.

After another twenty-four hours of Anna's treatment Jock was almost clear of discomfort and was up and about conducting his affairs.

She spent several days at Usbourne and during that time she came to know Jock quite well. The doctoring had formed a bond between them.

Wilson had told her of his father's newspaper and magazine empire in Africa. Now she discovered he also had a string of provincial papers in the south of England, in towns like Farnham, Chichester, Winchester, Guildford, Southampton and Portsmouth. Some were dailies and some weeklies. When he was in England, Usbourne was the nerve centre. He could reach any of his papers in his chauffeur-driven motor in less than an hour, and he was able by daily fixed-time calls to Africa to keep in touch with events there.

He moved constantly between Africa and England and he had a stateroom permanently booked on one of the Union Castle liners.

She began to see Wilson in a different light. In Altenkirchen and in Switzerland he had been a man of impatience and aggression – virtues then. Now she saw someone who was afraid of his father. Jock treated him as though he was still a boy; and Wilson acted as though he was. He never smoked or drank in front of his father. She saw him smoking out of doors. At night, when he came to her room, he smuggled in a flask of whisky.

The day at Usbourne started with prayers. All the servants would assemble in the drawing-room and Jock would read from the Bible and lead them in a hymn. Then he would get down to business. Usually a manager or an editor would arrive during the morning and be shown straight into his study. An hour later the man would emerge looking white and shaken. Often she would hear Jock's voice on the phone, his harsh tones echoing through the downstairs rooms, as he spoke to his general manager in Johannesburg.

In spite of his great wealth he lived a simple life. The food they ate was plain and washed down with water and the conversation was usually about the cost of newsprint or the fall in advertising revenue. He seemed to have little interest in the content of his newspapers. When Wilson tried to tell him what was happening in Europe, Jock said, 'I never trusted papists and never will.'

His brusqueness did not extend to Anna. The contrast was so marked that Wilson said to her, 'I've never seen him like this with anyone except my mother just before she died.'

Once Anna was playing with Nico in the sunshine on the terrace. She was aware of Jock looking out of his study windows at them. He did so for some minutes then opened the French windows and joined them.

He sat in a basket chair and watched Nico lying on his

59

stomach kicking his legs and moving his arms as though trying to swim on the rug.

After a moment's silence he reached into his pocket and brought out a wallet from which he took a browning snapshot. It showed a woman in a long Edwardian dress leaning over a play-pen in which there was a baby trying to stand.

'My wife Agnes,' he said. 'And Wilson when he was a wee boy. That was taken in Cape Town. I always wanted six sons and six girls. I came from a large family myself. Eight of us. But all dead now.'

She thought she could see him at the head of a table with his twelve children down the sides and his wife at the other end: the religious patriarch.

'Aye, a large family. And a flock of grandchildren. That's what a man like me needs. When you've founded something, built it up, you need sons and grandsons. Now I dinna ken what'll happen when I go.'

She saw that he was in a somewhat lugubrious mood and said, 'There's always Wilson. I'm sure he'll run things the way you want. Anyway, that's a long time ahead.'

But the pain had given Jock intimations of mortality and he wasn't to be cheered up so easily.

'Aye, he's done well right enough. The *Daily News* is a good paper. But writing's the easy part, it's running the show that's hard – even with the Lord to help you. I hope you say your prayers.'

'Yes.' She did but more out of superstition than belief.

'You're a good girl.' He bent down and let Nico grip his finger. 'That's what I want. A grandson. I've met some of Wilson's lady-friends. Didn't take to them. All eyelashes and red lips. Tell me about your husband.'

She told him about Ben and found that she could talk about him without tears coming to her eyes.

'He sounds a good man. I'm sorry for you.'

Abruptly, as though he suddenly remembered that it was a working day, he rose and went into the study. She realized she had witnessed one of his rare moods of softness and sentimentality.

The following morning Wilson took a call from the *Daily*

News. When he found her he was filled with suppressed excitement and said, 'They want me in London. My guess is they're going to give me the diplomatic correspondent's job! They hinted at it a couple of months ago.'

She felt a sudden chill. She knew what she had to do but the time wasn't right yet. 'Congratulations,' she said.

'Thanks. I know they've been bloody pleased with my stuff from Europe. Especially my copy from Austria. I beat the hell out of the competition. I had half a dozen exclusives.' He was too caught up in his own euphoria to see her change of mood. 'You won't mind getting the train to Wales?'

'No.'

'And I'll drop in some time. See how you and Nico are settling down.' He had been half expecting gratitude but she looked at him blankly. He took her chin in his hand and kissed her on the forehead. 'You know, I'm rather taken with you. So is the Old Man.'

She took a train to Hereford, a bus from there to Hay-on-Wye and a taxi from Hay to the end of the rutted track that led to Cold Hill Farm.

'I'd take you right up to the house, love,' the taxi driver said, 'but the springs would never stand it.' He patted the side of the Morris Twelve with affection.

She paid him out of the money she had left from the twenty-five pounds Wilson Braid had given her and, settling Nico on her left hip, she walked up the track to the farmhouse.

The day was bleak and the wind bent the yellow grass. Here, high up on the hills above the Wye, winter lingered. There was still snow on the top of the Black Mountains.

The house lay back against the grey sky. It too was grey, with a black slate roof, shiny now after rain.

She had steeled herself on the journey, had told herself that her sojourn would not be long, but even so her spirits were at their lowest when she reached the door of the house.

She had forgotten how uncared for it was. Broken window panes had been boarded up. The paint on the door was peeling and the wood had split. Underfoot everything was mud.

'Grannie!' she called. But there was no answer.

She went in. The black cooking range, which she remembered as being permanently lit, had gone out and the kitchen/living-room was ice cold and in a state of chaos. Two old chairs faced the empty fireplace, one of which had blankets on it and a pillow. At one end of the room stood a smelly oil heater.

She went upstairs. The room in which she had slept was precisely as she remembered it and, she thought, precisely as she had left it. Some of her hairclips were still on the bedside table, and so was a novel she had been reading. She thought that her grandmother could not have come into the room at all.

There were twin beds and she put Nico on one. She went out to the shed and came back with a bucket of coal, cleaned out the range, got it alight, then took the oil heater upstairs and lit it. When she came down her grandmother was standing in the doorway. 'Oh,' she said. 'You're back. Did you bring the post?'

She was the same wizened, dirty, shrivelled thing that Anna had remembered with such dread. But now she had a limp and Anna discovered she had had a fall soon after she had left for Vienna.

The fall had made it difficult for the old woman to get upstairs so she lived on the ground floor. She slept in one of the armchairs. What food she ate – all of it was tinned – she warmed on the top of the oil heater. The range had not been lit for months. This was her world: the armchair, the heater, a basin of cold water to wash in, the muddy farmyard, and the sheep on the hill.

That first night, as Anna lay in her bed listening to the wind raging across the tops, she knew that if she had had any doubts about what she was going to do, she had none now.

The fall had aged Mrs Monkton and affected her mind. She was descending quickly into senile dementia. She thought, for instance, that Nico was Anna's baby brother, and Anna allowed her to continue to think that. She had never talked much; now she hardly spoke at all.

Anna went to see the district nurse to get some things for Nico and told her about her grandmother.

'I used to go and see her,' the nurse said, 'but she threatened to shoot me.'

The evenings were the worst times. There were only oil lamps and candles and Mrs Monkton would spend the time adding up the money in her bank savings book while Anna read *Ivanhoe* and *Rob Roy*. Sometimes her grandmother did not recognize Anna and thought she was the daughter of a long-dead neighbour who had lived over at Bredwardine.

Anna took over the housework. She scrubbed and cleaned the rooms, blacked the range, and cooked proper meals. Mrs Monkton seemed to have forgotten how to use a knife and fork, for she sometimes used the blunt back of the knife to saw at her meat.

Anna centred every waking thought on Nico; it was her way of disassociating herself from what was going on around her. She was waiting – just to make certain.

Then, about two weeks after she had come to the farm, on a day of racing black clouds and rain, she laid the table for the midday meal and got everything ready. She put on an old mackintosh and walked down the muddy track to the road and fetched the post. Usually, by the time she got back, Mrs Monkton had come in for her meal for now that her granddaughter was cooking she looked forward to them.

She wasn't in the living-room. Anna banged an old ploughshare that hung on the cottage wall and went to get Nico out of his cot to start feeding him. It was empty. For a moment she couldn't believe her eyes. She was frozen with shock. Then she rushed upstairs thinking she might have left him in the other bed. But the bedroom was empty too.

She ran to the barn. In her mind was the old thought: gypsies. They could have come to the house while she was away getting the post. It was a childhood fear built on fairy stories. Gypsies and wolves.

'Nico!' she yelled.

But there was nothing in the barn except a few chickens.

'Grannie!'

Only the wind shrieking round the corners answered her.

She ran down the hill at the back of the house to the small stream where her grandmother fetched the house water.

She saw her almost immediately, a black shape half on the bank, half in the stream.

'Oh God!' she screamed. She couldn't see Nico.

The old woman had slipped or been pulled forward by the heavy bucket and had fallen face down in the water.

Ten yards away, behind a tuft of grass and huddled in a blanket, was Nico. The old woman, for some mad reason of her own, had brought him down to the water's edge.

Anna saw that he was unharmed, then she caught Mrs Monkton by the shoulders and pulled her out. Water poured from her nose and mouth and it was obvious she was dead.

She took Nico first, then struggled to get the old woman's body up to the house. The slope was steep and it took her a long while. She thought of going for help but the nearest neighbour was more than a mile away up another hill and by the time she had heaved and pulled the body into the house she knew she would never be able to walk there carrying Nico as well – and she couldn't leave him.

That night she and Nico kept to the upstairs bedroom but all the while, until she fell into a troubled sleep, she thought of the body lying on the kitchen floor. The wind was still blowing and the house was restless. Timbers expanded and contracted. She heard noises she had never heard before and her dreams were of drowned children.

The following morning, carrying Nico, she walked two miles along the road to a public telephone and called the undertakers and the police and soon others were making decisions on her behalf.

She knew no one in Hay but everyone seemed to know Mrs Monkton. The police knew her lawyer and her lawyer knew her bank. If Anna had had any thoughts of inheriting and selling the farm they were soon dashed, for she discovered that her grandmother had been renting for many years. Cold Hill Farm would never be hers, the bank owned it. And the money her grandmother had spent so many evenings counting amounted to less than thirty pounds.

All this she learned in the space of a few hours while the undertakers went to the farm to fetch the body. One thing the old lady *had* owned before she died was a cemetery plot, and she was buried in it the following day.

Anna knew she could never spend another night on the farm.

She and Nico stayed in a bed-and-breakfast place just off the main street and after the funeral she sat on the bed with him and counted her money. The bank had paid for the funeral but had then frozen the account until probate of the will. After she had paid for their lodgings she would have less than five pounds left.

The time had come.

Even though she was not positive that she was pregnant she had to take a chance. There was no other way.

She went to the post office, asked for a handful of change, closed herself in the red telephone kiosk near the marketplace and put a call through to the *Daily News*.

'Mr Wilson Braid, please.'

'He's not here.'

'Is he out on a story?'

'No. Not here. Gone.' There was a half-smothered laugh and then faintly she heard the voice saying to someone else, 'One of Braid's floozies.'

'Has he gone to Europe?'

'No, gone. As in left. Finished. He's left the paper.'

There was a click as the receiver at the other end of the line was replaced.

She called Usbourne House. 'Is Mr Braid there?'

She had meant Wilson but it was Jock's voice. 'I'm sorry to trouble you,' she said. 'I wanted to speak to Wilson.'

'It's no trouble at all. But Wilson's not here. He's up in London.'

'Oh.'

There must have been a slight quaver in her voice for he said suddenly, 'Are you all right, Anna?'

'Yes.'

'And Nico? There's nothing wrong with the wee boy, is there?'

It was the concern in his tone that did it. No one else had been remotely concerned about either of them since she had come to Wales. Her throat seemed to constrict.

'Are you there?'

'Yes,' she said.

'What's the matter? You're upset. I can hear it in your voice.'

'No. I – '

'What's happened then? *Tell* me!' The tone was imperious.

She told him everything except that she was almost certain she was pregnant.

It came out haltingly at first, then the words spilled over each other leaving sentences half formed. But the gist of what had happened began to reach him.

When she'd finished she felt drained and wretched. Then Jock said, 'Right. You're coming here. Is there a hotel in the town?'

'Yes.'

'Go there. Get a room. Have a meal. I'm sending the car immediately.'

After she put down the phone she stood for a few moments before emerging into the street. That's what you could do when you were kind and had money, she thought. You could be the magician, the fairy godfather who could change people's lives.

She arrived at Usbourne for a late dinner. Just the two of them. Jock and herself. She felt a sense of belonging she had not felt since Vienna. He told her that Wilson had had a row with the *Daily News* and walked out.

'Something about not getting promotion,' he said. 'I think he's been stupid. Got into a pet. Anyway he's left and gone to the *Examiner*. It's a bit of a rag but I suppose it's all good experience for when he comes out to Africa.'

The following day Wilson arrived. She was walking Nico just below the terrace when he pulled up in his blue Riley. He came up to her, his face dark with displeasure.

'What are you doing here?'

It was easier because he was ungracious. 'I'm carrying your child,' she said.

'What!'

'It's true.'

'Oh, my God!' Then fear entered his eyes. 'Have you told the old man?'

At that moment Jock came out of the house and walked towards them.

'*Have* you?'

'No.'

66

'Oh, it's you,' Jock said, by way of greeting to his son. 'You haven't left the *Examiner* yet, have you?'

Wilson smiled gamely. 'No, Father.'

'Well, that's something.' Then, nodding towards Anna, 'Look who's arrived.'

Later in the day Wilson came up to her room. He'd been drinking.

'What's the game?' he said.

'There's no game.'

'Come on, you know bloody well what I mean.'

'I know I'm pregnant.'

'Yes, but by whom?'

'That's a silly thing to say.'

His face darkened again, this time with more than displeasure. He had come up to try to frighten her, she thought. To throw her off balance. She told herself to stay calm.

'If you're pregnant, we'll have to do something about it.'

'Like what?'

'I know some people in London. They'll know what to do.'

'You mean an abortion?'

'What else?'

Once, when she was thirteen, a woman in her early twenties and pale as death had come to the house door in Winchester and asked for her father. Dr Webster had taken the woman in and Anna had seen blood on her legs. Soon an ambulance had come and the woman had been taken away on a stretcher. Her father had not commented but her mother had. She had learned then about back-street abortionists.

'You're not thinking of keeping it, are you? A single woman with a baby has a pretty rough sort of life.'

She could see how his mind was working: frighten her, soften her up, then pay her off.

'I don't think your father would like to hear you talk like this.'

The effect was profound. His eyes widened and he half turned as though to see whether Jock had suddenly materialized behind him.

'You wouldn't.'

'Why not?'

'Well . . . you'd have to tell him about Nico, that he wasn't your child.'

'I'm going to tell him anyway. I don't think it was very bright not to tell him in the first place. I'll simply say the story was your idea.'

'And if I deny it, who do you think he'll believe? I'm his son.'

'That's true,' she said. 'Then it doesn't matter if I tell him since he'll believe you and not me.'

They stared at each other for a moment and that was when she knew she had won.

They were married at Usbourne parish church three weeks later. It was done in a rush because Jock was sailing for the Cape of Good Hope. The speed suited Anna. She had missed her second period.

Seven

Few places in London have changed as much as Chelsea. When Anna went to live there with Wilson Braid just before the war, it meant the area between Sloane Square and the Town Hall and it meant having a Flaxman telephone number.

It was a village and the King's Road was its high street. There were butchers and greengrocers, small cheap restaurants, fish shops and corner grocers and gents' outfitters; there was a snooker hall and a dozen tobacconists with boards in their windows offering rooms and flats for rent. In winter the streets were filled with the smell of coal fires.

There were no hamburger joints, no pizza parlours, no boutiques, no record shops, no rock music.

What it did have was a great number of writers and painters, sculptors, musicians, and their hangers-on who did nothing very much except booze in the pubs at lunchtime. Most people did not have much money. It was raffish, bohemian, and sexually emancipated.

Wilson Braid had an apartment in the heart of Chelsea.

Anna had lied to achieve the marriage and when the ceremony was taking place she had made a resolution that she would try as hard as she could to make it work. That much she owed Wilson.

This decision was put to the test almost immediately for she discovered that the man she had married was not one she had known before. The Wilson she had met in Austria had been a professional newspaperman doing his job with aggressive enthusiasm. The Wilson she had known at Usbourne was young Master Wilson on his best behaviour in front of daddy. But her husband in his London surroundings was quite different.

He was a strange mixture of naïvety and decadence. London impressed and fascinated him. He devoured it all and seemed to be saying: 'Look, this is me!'

She got a view of the darker side of his nature the day after the wedding. They had spent the first night at Usbourne and then gone straight up to London with Nico because Wilson had so recently started on the *Examiner* that he couldn't ask for leave.

They pulled up in Walpole Street and the first thing she noticed was that the curtains were drawn over the downstairs windows of his apartment. When she went in she realized why. The sitting-room might have come out of *The Arabian Nights*. The walls were painted dark red and the curtains were black. There were two divans piled with cushions and more cushions on the floor. Dim shaded lamps gave the only light.

The bedroom contained a large double bed. It was unmade and the black sheets were rumpled and smelled frowsy.

These were the two main rooms. There was a second bedroom which was bare of furniture, a bathroom with rusting pipes and decaying wallpaper, and a kitchen which looked out over a barren yard and which was piled high with dirty dishes.

He saw her expression as they returned to the sitting-room. 'Don't you like it?'

'It's just . . . I haven't seen a room like it.'

'Marvellous, isn't it? Denys thought up the colour scheme.'

'Who's Denys?'

'Denys Keane. You'll meet him. Want a drink?' He held up a bottle of Nicholson's gin. 'I'm afraid there isn't anything to go with it.'

She shook her head and he poured half a glass of neat gin and threw it into the back of his throat. 'You'll meet them all. Denys and Pamela and Ralph. You'll meet the whole gang.'

He had been resentful right up to the moment of the wedding. Now he was more human and she wondered if he was beginning to accept a fait accompli.

Nico would sleep in the spare room and she looked round

for something to use as a bed for him until they could buy proper furniture. She chose one of the divan mattresses, but Wilson didn't want the sitting-room disturbed.

'He'd got to sleep somewhere,' she said.

'Not on one of these. He'll make it dirty.'

'Wilson, he's a baby.'

'He's not *my* baby.'

'Of course he is. Until we can find Michael and Ruth.'

'Don't talk bullshit. You know they'll never be found. Face it. You're saddled with their kid. You. Not me.'

He gave himself another shot of gin and then put the bottle down. 'I'm going out,' he said.

Tired and angry, she began to throw the cushions off one of the divans.

'What the hell are you doing?'

'You don't listen. Nico's got to sleep somewhere.'

'Not on these!' He grabbed a cushion and tried to pull it from her hands. She hung on grimly. He was a powerful man and she slid to the floor in a heap.

He looked down at her. 'Don't do that again. When I say something I mean it.' He paused and then said softly, 'You got what you wanted. Now you'll have to live with it.'

He turned and left the room. She heard the door slam and then the engine of the Riley turn over and fire. It had an open exhaust and made a terrific din as it pulled away. She wondered if he was going to see Denys and the rest of the gang. It was not a good way to start married life, but perhaps no more than she deserved.

Europe was moving towards war. The Anschluss between Germany and Austria was followed by the German takeover of the Sudetenland. The British prime minister, Neville Chamberlain, flew backwards and forwards to talk to Hitler in Munich in an effort to keep the peace. There was a feeling of suppressed hysteria and in the London pubs people were drinking up and having another . . . and another . . . It was a time to gather ye rosebuds.

The early part of Anna's pregnancy was marked by severe spells of sickness and it took her all her strength to look after

Nico. Mostly she was on her own. After a few weeks in London the *Examiner* sent Wilson back into Europe to cover the growing crisis.

She was relieved. It gave her time to become acquainted with her role as wife and mother, a role into which she had forced herself in a matter of months. It seemed barely credible that less than a year before she had left England for Vienna. From that moment everything had started to spin out of control.

Wilson's absence gave her time to catch her breath, to get her world back on to its axis even though it was such a different one. It was still too early to think of the future. The present was all she could cope with.

Slowly she began to know Chelsea and her neighbours. The first member of the 'gang' to whom Wilson had introduced her was Pamela Kincaid who lived in the basement of the house next door. She was large and red-faced with short hair and wore a tweed hacking-jacket. She smoked Abdullah No. 7 in a short black holder, wore a monocle, and swore a great deal. She called Wilson, Willie.

Before Wilson left for Europe he took Anna to several of her parties. All the guests seemed to be women or effeminate-looking men. Later she discovered that some of the women were men and some of the men were women.

Once he had gone Pamela was in and out of Anna's flat, wanting to borrow an envelope or sticking plaster or a couple of bob for fags.

She liked to come when Anna was bathing Nico. She had a bluff hearty manner and would sit on the lavatory and put a towel on her lap and say, 'Can I dry him?'

Her hands were big and clumsy. Once she screwed her monocle into her eye and stared down at the baby who was lying on his back, and said, 'The wolves used to call Mowgli "little frog". They do look like little frogs. Except for that.' She pointed to the tiny penis. 'It doesn't look menacing now, but my God, just you wait.'

Some weeks after Wilson had left, Pamela invited Anna to a party. She was the first to arrive. Pamela moved behind her chair to get her a drink – she always offered a cider punch laced with gin – and stroked her head in passing.

'I love your hair,' she said.

Anna said, 'When are the others coming?'

'It's only a small party. Just you and me, darling.' Then she tried to kiss her.

It was a clumsy pass, and Anna easily avoided it.

'No?' Pamela said.

'Definitely not!'

Pamela smiled. 'Pity. It would've been so convenient. But, fair enough. I'll be good. Scout's honour.'

Denys Keane was older than the others and was an actor when he could get the work.

At first he was suspicious of Anna, as though her arrival would spoil their little group. But his own good nature got the better of him and soon they were on terms of genuine friendship.

'He's as queer as a coot,' Pamela said to Anna, as though her own desires were perfectly natural.

As far as she knew, Anna had never met a male homosexual. She had heard about them and if she had thought of them at all she would have considered them as remote from her life as the Ethiopians. However, there was nothing remote about Denys. He gave her what she so desperately needed at that time, friendship.

She was almost housebound and often in the evenings he would bring round a bottle of cheap wine and they would talk. She felt she could relax with him. She wasn't threatened. There was no sexual tension. He was cosy. He liked to gossip and knew a great of what was going on in Chelsea, mostly in bedrooms.

His hobby was fine needle-point and many evenings they would sit together in front of a coal fire while she knitted and he made a cushion cover.

He was funny about Wilson, which amused her. He always called him Bwana. She discovered that most of his gang treated him with the same irony. They took his money and his drinks and his hospitality and then made fun of him.

All except Ralph. Ralph made her uneasy. He was in his early twenties, had broken away from his family in the West Country, to their relief, and had become a remittance man in reverse.

They gave him a large allowance as long as he remained in London.

He was very beautiful and was often photographed by the gossip columns dining at Quaglino's or the Trocadero.

He was slender and pale with fine dark hair. There were smudges under his eyes. Anna never saw him without thinking there was something unwholesome, almost evil, about him and she came to view him as a Dorian Gray figure. It was no surprise to her later to discover that he was a morphine addict.

Denys had been desperately in love with him for more than a year and they had lived together briefly, but then Ralph had started an affair with someone else and Denys had tried to kill himself. He showed Anna the scars on his wrists.

'Can't *you* find someone else?' Anna had said.

'You can't just give someone up, love,' he said. 'Even though your head tells you to.'

Peter was born in the early part of 1939 in St Giles's Hospital in Kensington. She had a private room. Wilson was away but Denys came with her and when she went into labour sat by her side and read her articles from *Punch*.

By the middle of the year Anna was dividing her time between London and Hampshire. When Jock was in South Africa she stayed in Chelsea, when he arrived at Southampton she would have the house ready for him. She was pregnant again and Jock was in his element.

Wilson had always called him the 'old man' and now it was coming true. He was beginning to look old.

'This climate's no good for me.' He tapped his wheezy chest. 'I've a mind to sell everything I own here but I wouldn't get a penny now with all this talk of war.'

'Do you think it's coming?' she said.

'The Lord knows. I want you to come out to Africa with me, then you'll all be safe.'

But it was more than that. He had become dependent on her and she realized what a lonely old man he was.

She had no wish to go to Africa, but the thought of three small children in a Chelsea flat was daunting. Even now if it hadn't been for Denys coming to baby-sit she would not have been able to get out by herself.

All this time she continued trying to find out what had happened to the Meissners. Wilson also made further enquiries in Europe. He consulted lists of prisoners in concentration camps and persuaded the Red Cross Tracing Section to redouble their efforts, but nothing was found of Michael or Ruth or Stefan or Cuno. It was as though the ground had opened up near Altenkirchen that day and swallowed them. As far as Anna could make out from reading the papers, it was not a rare occurrence; hundreds of thousands of people had disappeared as Europe disintegrated.

People were now saying that war would not come before the New Year and Jock had arranged all their passages for early October. But things suddenly accelerated and the declaration of war overtook them. Chamberlain made his speech on Sunday, 3 September, and Britain found herself at war with Germany at eleven o'clock that morning. One day later a German U-boat sank the liner *Athenia* and two weeks later another sank the aircraft-carrier *Courageous*.

Suddenly the voyage to Africa began to look suicidal and the passages were cancelled.

John Braid was born in 1940, during the period they called the phoney war when nothing much was happening between the Allied and Axis forces. But later that year the blitz on London began.

Wilson was hardly ever at home. The *Examiner* sent him round the country to write stories about the Home Front and there was talk of him becoming a war correspondent.

Anna had not seen him for some weeks but was expecting him and had returned to London. One evening Denys took her to a party. They walked along the King's Road in the blackout towards Oakley Street. He seemed more than usually tense. They stopped at the Six Bells for a quick drink and she gave him some money to buy a bottle of gin. This was now a normal part of her life – handing money to Wilson's friends. They all seemed to be broke much of the time.

The party was being given by Georgina somebody whom Anna had not met. The night was pitch dark and smog was

75

lying over the river. They groped their way down Oakley Street, found the right house and let themselves in. The blackout curtains were drawn but inside the house was brightly lit.

'Hello, darlings,' Georgina said, coming from a room on the ground floor. 'Coats upstairs.'

The house seemed to be throbbing. The air was thick with cigarette smoke and a wind-up gramophone was playing an Ink Spots number. They picked their way through couples sitting on the stairs.

'Which way?' Anna asked as they looked for the room in which to drop their coats.

'I've never been here before,' Denys said.

He turned right and went along a landing, opened a door, switched on the light, and gave a choking cry. She was just behind him. Looking past him, she saw Wilson lying on a bed against the far wall. He was naked and there was another figure on the bed with him, their bodies entwined. The other figure turned and looked at them and she saw it was Ralph.

'Fuck off!' he said.

'Bastard! Bastard! Bastard!' Denys yelled, and then he burst into tears.

Wilson smiled as though challenging her to comment.

'Come,' Anna said. 'Come away.'

They went down the stairs and out into the street again. She felt numb. Denys was sobbing. They walked towards the river and she guided him along the Embankment. Finally they reached her flat. She gave him a drink and settled him by the fire. She did not dare leave him in case he tried to kill himself again.

It was an hour or two before he regained control. It didn't even seem strange for her to comfort a man whose lover had been in bed with her husband.

The sight of Wilson in that room jogged her out of the cocoon in which she had been living. It was three days before he came home and during those three days she made up her mind that she had to find a way of life in which she could become independent. She knew now she would never go out to Africa with Wilson. She knew that their marriage, as far as it had ever been a marriage, was finished.

When he did come home he pretended that nothing out of the ordinary had occurred and she took her lead from him. If she had used him, he had used her. In that sense they were quits.

'I'm going down to Usbourne,' she said. 'I won't be coming back to the flat.'

He smiled at her. It was the same patronizing, knowing smile he had used in the past. 'You'll go down when I say so.'

That was in the late afternoon. She heard the Riley thunder off down the street and knew that if she stayed she would be sacrificing a position in the kind of game they were now going to play. Yet she had almost no money.

That night the sirens started up soon after dark. She gathered the children and took them to a nearby air-raid shelter. There she listened to the crump of bombs falling on the City and the Docks and two or three much closer.

The all-clear sounded about midnight and she wheeled the children back to Walpole Street. A bomb had fallen near Sloane Square about three hundred yards away and the King's Road was blocked by fire-engines. Another had exploded even closer, in the gardens of the Royal Hospital. They had never come as close as this before. It underlined her determination to leave London whatever Wilson said.

She managed to get the children to bed and was pouring herself a drink when Pamela Kincaid arrived.

'You'd better come down,' she said. 'It's Willie.'

They went to Pam's basement. He wasn't dead or injured. She found him standing, his feet against the bottom of the doorframe and his hands near the top, in an open doorway in the middle of Pam's flat. He looked almost like Christ on the Cross. His eyes were fixed and his skin had gone a kind of greyish colour.

'He's been like that for an hour or more,' Pam said. 'Ever since the bombs fell. I'm damned if I can do a thing with him.'

Anna said his name but it was like talking to a statue. She touched him. His arms were like iron bars.

'I saw a chappie like that once,' Pam said. 'He had a near miss on a motorbike. Rigid with fear. We had to lift him from the saddle.'

Between the two of them they forced his arms away from the door. He began to whimper. They managed to get him home, up the stairs and into his own flat.

'He'll be all right now,' Anna said, dismissing Pamela.

Wilson moved slowly. He reached for the gin bottle and put it to his mouth.

After a moment he said, 'Joke. It was a joke.'

They looked at each other and he saw the mix of pity and contempt in her eyes. There was nothing more to say but both knew he would not stop her now from doing whatever she wanted to do.

Eight

One day during the Second World War, Anna said to Jock Braid, 'I need something to do.'

'You've got something.'

'I mean something more than the children.'

A south-westerly gale was lashing Usbourne House. Jock was sitting near his study fire, a rug round his knees. Anna was standing at the window, staring at the sodden countryside. The room smelled of eucalyptus oil and resonated to the sound of Jock's chesty breathing.

'There's no something *more* than the bairns.'

She knew he doted on his grandsons but she had made up her mind. As the war had continued month after month, year after year, with food and fuel rationing, icy winters, and a general air of depression and dowdiness, she had felt increasingly that her own life was slipping away.

For the first time she saw a chance of freedom, for Wilson had gone off to North Africa as a war correspondent.

At the time she had said, 'I don't think you're going to like it out there.'

'Think what you like.'

His behaviour on the night of the bombing had not been repeated and the old arrogance and aggressiveness had slowly seeped back into him. But she knew and he knew that she knew . . .

Jock Braid had been appalled that Wilson had agreed to report the war. He was terrified that his only son would elect to put himself in danger.

The two of them had closeted themselves away and talked for hours. Anna knew that they were bargaining, or at least that Wilson was bargaining. At last he came out of the study looking smug and satisfied. She had waited for him to tell her what had been discussed but he did not and her pride kept her from asking.

She was to discover it for herself over the following months. Jock took the *Examiner* with all the other national papers and she read Wilson's dispatches from Egypt. Most had an 'exclusive' tag on them. He often started his stories with sentences like, 'As I write these words German shells are falling all around me . . .'

Then the stories ceased and a few weeks later she heard that he had left the *Examiner*, joined a hospital ship bringing casualties back to Britain round the Cape of Good Hope, left the ship in South Africa and joined Braid Communications.

Jock was ecstatic. 'It's what we planned,' he said. 'But I couldna tell you for fear something might have gone wrong.'

'But doesn't it look as though, you know . . .'

Jock chose not to understand her.

'He's entitled to do what he wants,' he said. 'He's got a South African passport. He doesn't have to report the war or fight in it. It's not South Africa's affair anyway.'

But she felt he was making excuses for his son and when she went up to London Denys said, 'I understand the Bwana's had enough of bang-bangs and gone home.' Others seemed to think the same.

Wilson had clearly bargained well with his father for in a matter of months he became the chief executive of Braid Communications in South Africa, a position he was due to hold until Jock was able to return.

Jock's hair was white now and grew in a fluffy tonsure. His skin had lost its ruddy look and his eyes – except for moments when he spoke of returning and taking up the reins again – lacked their usual fanatical sparkle.

She did not know how she would tell Jock that she would never go out to Africa. She left it to the future to solve. What she did know was that she must be prepared to look after herself, to go it alone with her children. She was still young enough to learn, and learn she must. The obvious place was on one of Jock's provincial newspapers.

She returned to the subject the following day. He said, 'The war will be over soon. You'll be in Africa. Ladies don't work there.'

'You've told me often enough about all the servants and nannies, but I can't just . . .' She had a sudden glimpse of Ruth Meissner playing cards as the world changed . . . 'I can't just sit around playing bridge.'

Another time she said to him, 'When you were a young man in Africa, would you have wanted to spend your time telling servants what to do?'

'Of course not.'

'Well, I don't want to either.'

Knowing that this was her only real chance, she wore him down until finally he said, 'Let me think about it.'

A week later he grudgingly told her she could work on his newspaper in Winchester. 'But only a couple of hours a day, mind. I've spoken to the editor and he'll take you under his wing.' Then he said, 'There's no need, you know.'

But there was every need. She started at the beginning of the next calendar month, by which time she had hired a nanny to take care of the children while she was away.

The *Winchester Mercury* was a daily broadsheet which had not changed much in two hundred and fifteen years. Its main function was carrying advertisements for stock and property sales. Its biggest scoop was in 1805 when it beat the London papers with the news of Nelson's victory at Trafalgar and this story had been framed and placed in the waiting-room.

She had agreed to Jock's stipulation that she worked only in the mornings and arrived in his chauffeur-driven Daimler. The staff were mostly retired journalists brought back to run a paper denuded by the conscription of its younger members into the army. Some had worked in Fleet Street and took a jaundiced view of the newest cub reporter arriving in such state.

Anna knew how offensive it must be to 'real' journalists to have to put up with the boss's daughter-in-law but by now her

81

resolve to give herself a profession had become so powerful she was able to withstand the cynical looks.

For the first few weeks she was very lonely. She was given the simplest of jobs to do: the weather, the time of high and low water at Portsmouth and Southampton, the time of sunrise and sunset. She knew that a child of five could have managed them, but she stuck to her self-imposed brief and did exactly what she was asked to do. She was left severely alone by other reporters and was never drawn into the endless discussions on the newsroom floor.

She would start at nine and the car would arrive before lunch to pick her up. Sometimes, if she was given an additional task like finding out when the next Women's Institute meeting was to be held, and was not ready to leave, she made Jock's chauffeur wait. This upset the editor who would hover over her desk and say, 'Don't worry, Mrs Braid, I'll get someone to finish for you.'

But mostly she had so little to do that she would spin it out to fill the hours. In the afternoons she would be back at Usbourne with Jock and the children. Journalism seemed to her the dullest and most overrated job she had ever come across. It was also unpleasant to be resented quite so openly.

She began to realize that she was gaining no real experience and not making the kind of impact that would stand her in good stead for the future.

She went to the bank in Winchester, borrowed a hundred pounds, and bought a small Hillman car.

'What for?' Jock said, impatient with her.

'Because I need one. I can't always be dependent on you. Anyway, I want to learn shorthand and typing. I'll never get anywhere doing the weather.'

'You've no need to "get anywhere". Can you not see that? In South Africa you'll be the daughter-in-law of the owner and the wife of the managing editor of the entire group.'

'I'm not there yet,' she said, and left the question open as she always did.

Her change of direction paid off. Now, on Jock's petrol coupons, she was able to drive herself to work. The little car had a canvas top and on summer days she would put it down and let the wind blow through her hair as she drove to and from the *Mercury*. Just this simple physical act gave her more pleasure than she could ever remember experiencing before. It meant freedom.

She took shorthand and typing in her spare time. She learned on an ancient Underwood upright and took down page after page of company reports and parliamentary speeches. At night she would practise her outlines while she and Jock listened to the war news on the wireless.

At first he scowled at her but slowly her interest in newspapers began to revive his own. They talked about stories that had come up during the day, for she was now beginning to cover more important subjects than the weather. And grudgingly he began to accept her for what she was: a female eccentric who wished to work in newspapers.

After a while she found herself being accepted by her colleagues. Now that she was putting in a full day and working as hard as anyone else, they responded by taking her along when they went to the pub for a drink at lunchtime.

They began to help her; to show her how to go out and get a story, write it and put a heading on it. After six months she led the paper for the first time with a story about a rapist preying on Land Army girls who were working on surrounding farms. For the first time she felt the excitement of the job.

But she was doing a balancing act. On the one hand was her work, on the other was Jock. She knew that if he thought she was neglecting the children, he would terminate her job.

And there was further pressure. Now that the Royal Navy had won the U-boat war, ships were sailing more frequently between South Africa and England. Mail was getting through, so were food parcels. Letters began to arrive for her from Wilson demanding that she bring the children out to Africa. Jock unwittingly became her ally. He would not hear of them being put at risk.

The D-Day landings took place and the war moved into its final European phase. At the beginning of 1945 a taxi drew up at Usbourne and a small man in a long black overcoat and black Homburg hat clutching an armful of newspapers was taken in to see Jock. It was a Saturday and Anna was at home doing what she loved most – entertaining her three children.

The man spent most of the day with Jock before leaving in the late afternoon. She waited for her father-in-law to join her but he remained in his study. She dined alone in the big dining-room while he refused a tray. By mid-evening she was worried about him and went into the study.

The floor was covered in newspapers; so were the desk and the big table near the windows. He was bent over one, studying its pages, and when he looked up she thought he had aged five years.

'What is it?' she asked. 'What's happened?'

He did not reply but she followed his eyes to the front pages. They were all newspapers from his African company, each from a different city, but most carrying similar lead stories of sex killings, rapes, robberies – with the political and war news relegated to inside pages.

'Do you know who that was?' Jock said, meaning the man in the black Homburg hat. 'My general manager out there. The man who sat at my desk and in my office. A month ago I was told he was resigning because of ill health. Ill health! Wilson got rid of him. And look. Have you ever seen anything dirtier than these? I started all these papers, they're my bairns if you like. But . . . I never thought to see the day when they'd look like that. How am I to face my church?'

He began to pace slowly up and down the room. 'I wondered why I wasn't getting proper reports. I put it down to the war, to conditions. Now I know. He's hired a new staff. Combed the gutters for specialists in dirt. That's all this is!'

His head was twitching and his hands were shaking and she feared he might have a stroke.

'Maybe it isn't Wilson,' she said. 'Maybe it's someone else.'

'Na, na. There's no one else. He's got his hands on the reins . . . He's always wanted that. Wanted me out of the way . . . Look at that!' He flicked his finger at a long account of a sleazy divorce action. 'I don't want stories like that in my papers. I've never had them before and I don't want them now.'

She began to gather up the newspages.

'Ever since he was a boy he's had a nose for dirt. Things

happened at school . . . Well, better forgotten . . . I've tried to stamp it out. But . . .' He had forgotten who he was talking to, he was communing with himself. 'Well, there's only one thing to be done.'

'What's that?'

But he did not reply. Instead he walked out of the study and up the stairs to his bedroom.

The following day he left early for London. She went into work that day feeling worried and tense but this was soon wiped out by the story she was pitched into.

A woman's body had been found in bushes by the roadside five miles out of Winchester. Normally Anna would never have been put on to a major murder, but the crime reporter was ill.

She drove up to the scene of the crime, told the police inspector in charge who she was and began to question him. He was as inexperienced in major crime as she was and instead of refusing to be interviewed he took her over to a mound covered by a blanket and pulled a corner away.

The young woman's face was swollen and purple, the eyes bloodshot, and a piece of yellow material was knotted so tightly around her neck that parts of it had disappeared into the folds of her skin.

This was not the first dead body Anna had seen. She had had to identify her dead parents, had seen the body brought out of the river in Austria and had had to deal with her grandmother. But looking down at the dead girl she felt sick at the waste and the brutality.

But she had a job to do. The inspector told her he thought the woman had been raped then killed. She looked more closely at the strangling material and saw that it was a yellow silk scarf.

The *Mercury* suddenly had a scoop in which everyone was interested. She was the only journalist to have seen the body. The *News Chronicle* in Fleet Street asked her for an exclusive and ran it with her byline. It became known as the Scarf Murder.

She worked on it for seventeen hours without a break and, late that night, when she lay in bed, the events of the day unreeled in her head like a movie and she was so excited at being sucked into the vortex of a major story that she could not sleep.

She stayed on the story for two more days before an RAF officer at a nearby camp was arrested and held in Winchester Prison. By that time Jock had returned to Usbourne.

Nine

Jock brought with him a man called Montague Axe. Anna had heard his name before but had never met him. He was a large man rapidly going bald which made it difficult to judge his age, but she would have guessed he was in his late twenties, although he dressed and acted older.

He was tall and wide and plump but carried his weight lightly. He wore a dark blue suit with a loud white chalk stripe, a black and white polka-dot bow tie, and over his distended waistcoat, a gold watch and chain. He was Jock's London lawyer.

He spent the night at Usbourne and set out to charm Anna. His interests were wide. He spoke about books and paintings, the theatre. He kept up a flow of conversation – which was just as well, for Jock sat at the other end of the table picking at his food and fiddling with the salt-cellar until finally he said to Anna, 'I've booked a passage. I'm leaving in a fortnight.'

She had been waiting for something like this and cold fingers seemed to close over her heart.

'If you need anything for the boys or the house – or yourself, Mr Axe here will see to it. And as soon as it's safe he'll book passages for you all.'

He was agitated and inward-looking and went to bed early, leaving Anna and Montague Axe to take coffee in the drawing-room.

Axe pulled a flask from his pocket and said, 'It is writ: Take a little wine for thy stomach's sake. Would it matter if it was brandy? I can vouch for its quality.'

'I'm sorry we couldn't offer you wine but my father-in-law . . .'

'That's why I came prepared,' he said.

She found two small glasses and he poured them each a measure.

'My husband always carried a flask here too,' she said. 'Can you tell me what's going on?'

'Some of it. You probably know a lot anyway. Jock's been on the telephone to Johannesburg. I managed to get him a diplomatic line. I know he's talked to your husband.'

'And?'

He placed the tips of his chubby fingers together on his stomach in a gesture she was to become familiar with.

'Family battles are always destructive. What we're trying to do now is limit the damage. You've seen copies of his new-style papers?'

'Jock showed them to me.'

'This is where I have to be delicate. Wilson is, after all, your husband as well as Jock's son.'

'I think I know enough about journalism to see that he's taken the papers down-market. And I don't have to agree with his aims.'

'His aims are impeccable. He wants to expand. Jock wants the status quo and to remain good friends with the Lord.'

Her eyes widened with laughter. 'Sometimes I wonder if he's not in direct contact. Is there no middle path?'

'Have you ever been to South Africa?' She shook her head. 'I know it well. There's a saying out there: "You don't sell newspapers, people just buy them." That's all right in a static situation such as we have now. But once the war ends everything will become fluid and there will be a free-for-all.'

'So you think my husband is doing the right thing?'

'I didn't say that.' The fingers met over his belly.

'I'm worried about Jock. He's nothing like the man I first met. And this has hit him hard. Is there anything I can do?'

'I'm afraid there's nothing anyone can do. As I say, it's a question of damage limitation.'

She pressed him further but he avoided her questions with elegance until finally she gave up and asked him about himself.

He seemed more ready to talk about that. He was a Lithuanian. His family had emigrated to South Africa after the First World War. He had been educated there and at Cambridge and had then remained in England. Now he had a flourishing London practice.

When she went to bed she felt herself stiff with tension. At first she did not know what had caused it, then she realized that the time was fast approaching when she must tell Jock or Wilson or both that she would not be going out to Africa. She didn't give a damn about Wilson, but she did about Jock. But how could she talk to Jock without first telling Wilson that their marriage was over? Of course she needn't tell Jock at all, but the thought of the ship sailing away from Southampton Water with this old man – whom she had grown to love in spite of himself – perhaps never to see his grandchildren again, was hard to contemplate.

Was she wrong in her decision not to go to Africa? But if she went she would ruin her life – a life she had only recently discovered. And would that be good for the children?

The following morning after Axe had gone, Jock said, 'He's a good man. Clever. A Jew of course. I'd rather have a Jew than a papist. But my father wouldn't have allowed either to cross the threshold of his house.'

During the next few days as her father-in-law made his plans to leave England, almost certainly for the last time, she tried to bury herself in her work. But at the back of her mind was always the thought of what she had to do.

As she arrived home one evening, having made up her mind to approach the subject obliquely, she saw a strange car parked in the drive and felt a moment of relief. A visitor would mean postponement. But when she went into the house she found that the visitor was a doctor; not a homeopath or a naturopath but the local GP with a stethoscope around his neck and a grave expression on his face.

She froze. 'The children!'

'No, Mrs Braid. It's your father-in-law. I asked the staff to try to contact you.' He was an elderly man and his tone was accusatory.

'I was out on a story. I work for the *Mercury*.'

'So I believe.'

'Well, tell me!'

'Mr Braid's had a heart attack. I've sent for an ambulance.'

'Where is he? When did it happen?' The questions encompassed the butler and one of the maids who were standing nearby looking worried.

'In his bedroom. That's where he was found. The butler heard a noise. Mr Braid had fallen. We managed to get him into bed.'

'I must go to him.' She ran upstairs and went into Jock's room. It was like himself, plain and severe. He was fully dressed still but all his clothes had been loosened, and he lay on his back breathing stertorously. His eyes were closed and his skin was grey. She sat down and held his hand and felt tears at the back of her eyes.

There were times she did not like Jock, but there was a side to him, a kind of innocence, that really appealed to her. And there was his love for her children.

She went along the passage and found them all with their nanny in the playroom. 'Grandfather's ill,' she said.

She picked up John and sat down on the sofa. Peter and Nico climbed up beside her and she managed to get her arms around them all.

'We know,' Nico said, solemnly.

'He's going away for a little while.'

Nico clamoured to ask her questions but before she could answer the ambulance arrived. 'Where are you taking him?' she asked the doctor.

'I've reserved a room at the Royal Hampshire in Winchester. He'll be better off there than in London. At least there are no V2s exploding all over the place. Don't worry, Mrs Braid, they've looked after coronaries there before.'

Anna was following him but he held up his hand. 'No visiting until . . . well, until he rallies.'

She watched the ambulance and the doctor go down the drive then phoned Montague Axe.

'The doctor's probably right,' he said. 'He's better off in the country. But I'll get one of the top heart specialists in London to go down and see him just in case.'

'What now?'

'I'll cancel the passage.'

'And I'll cable Wilson.'

'Will you be all right? Would you like me to come down?'

She heard a different note in his voice. He wasn't just a lawyer asking about a client's daughter-in-law. There was warmth and she felt grateful.

'I'll be all right.'

The hospital was not more than a mile from her office. She was allowed to see Jock briefly the following day. He looked older and smaller and she had difficulty in hiding her distress.

It was bitter winter weather and snow blanketed the country. Usbourne was almost cut off, but each day she managed to drive in to work and also to visit the hospital. Jock was fighting a lonely battle in his private room. At times he seemed to be sinking, at others rallying.

When she arrived back in the office one icy afternoon a messenger came into the editorial department and said, 'There's a gentleman to see you in the waiting-room, madam.'

She went into the room expecting to see Montague's plump figure. A man was standing with his back to the room looking out at the drifting snow. When he turned, the light fell on his face and she saw that the left side was badly scarred.

'Hi,' he said. 'Remember me?'

She recognized the voice and reached out to brace herself on a chair. 'Ben?' It came out as a whisper.

'Yes,' he said. 'It's me.'

'But I thought – '

'What?'

'I was told you were dead.'

'Dead?' He sounded surprised. 'It's a well-known fact that the Ramseys are indestructible.'

'But – '

'Take it easy,' he said. 'We've got time. At least I have if you have. We could go out and find a drink.' The strong Minnesota accent was music to her.

'Oh, Ben, I can't. I have to see someone in hospital and then get home to my children.'

He raised his eyebrows and the scar tissue around his left

91

temple and down his cheek seemed to become whiter. 'Jesus. Children? Is that plural?'

'Three. But only two are mine.'

'Wow, I guess I've got a lot of catching up to do.'

'How on earth did you know where I was?'

'I saw your name in the *News Chronicle* over some murder down here. I thought the chances of *two* Anna Websters were pretty remote.'

She felt shaken and confused. He was like a ghost from the past. Then impulsively she said, 'Why don't you come with me? Have some supper and we can catch up. I've got a car.'

'So have I.'

She gave him directions then went to visit Jock.

She was nervous and regretting her impulse as she drove back to Usbourne. She had enough on her plate just now without adding more. She saw in her mind's eye the scar on his face. If it hadn't been for that she would have recognized him instantly; the same big frame, the same broad face with the widely spaced eyes. She felt her heart thudding as she remembered their brief interlude in Vienna. Nothing remotely like it had happened to her since. In her memory she saw them holding hands in the restaurant and heard them talking of what they would do and where they would go. It was like looking down the wrong end of a telescope. The two people she saw were like children. Now they were grown up.

He was at Usbourne when she arrived.

'My God, this is some place you've got.'

'It isn't mine, it's my father-in-law's.' She told him briefly about Jock. 'Come up and meet the children.'

Ben looked reluctant.

John was being bathed but Peter and Nico were in the play-room. It was a large room with a rocking-horse and climbing-frame, well-worn furniture, and a mass of drawings and paintings pinned to the walls.

The two boys ran at her and she gathered them in her arms. This was their time for uproarious games with her. She laughed as they tugged at her.

'Can we play blindman's-buff?' Peter said. 'Please!' He leapt on to the sofa and began jumping up and down.

'Peter, the springs!'

'No! No!' Nico shouted. 'Sardines! Let's play sardines!'

Anna turned to Ben. 'You go down and fix yourself a drink. I'll join you shortly.' Ben's expression told her she had said the right thing.

Peter at five and Nico a year older were more than a handful and she was flushed and short of breath when at last she went down to the drawing-room.

'Have a good game?' he asked.

She laughed. 'I'm away all day. This is the time I love best.'

'I'm sorry if I – '

'No, no. We had our romp.'

She kept her own supply of liquor in the house now and gave herself a gin and tonic.

'They're lovely children,' Ben said and she smiled at the effort he made.

They had supper in front of the fire and Ben, unthinking, ate the entire month's ration of bacon and cheese.

She told him about Nico and the race for the border and what happened there and how she had never heard from the Meissners.

'A lot of people went missing then,' he said. 'I guess half of Europe was on the move.'

She told him about meeting Wilson and going to the Red Cross. 'You mean Wilson Braid?' he said. 'I didn't make the connection. He's your husband? I knew him.'

Something in his eyes told her that the acquaintanceship had not been a good one.

'He got me out,' she said. 'He was the one who told me you were dead.'

'Almost. Not quite.'

'I waited for you,' she said, remembering the overstuffed bedroom in the hotel on the Ringstrasse. 'What a strange day to try and start an affair.'

He lit a cigar. 'You wonder if it really happened . . .'

Then he began to speak in a soft voice, telling her about himself as though he might have been telling a story about someone else.

'I heard the news of the German advance after I left you that

93

night. I checked the agency tapes as I usually do and there it was. I wish I could say I remembered to leave a message for you but I didn't. Europe was on the road to war just as I'd always thought it would be. There wasn't anything else in my head, I guess. Only the thought of heavy artillery crossing the border and Hitler expected in Linz.'

'And there was I with my frilly nightie and my overnight bag with nothing else in it, pretending to be someone I wasn't to the hotel receptionist. You never wrote.'

He shook his head. 'I hadn't been in Linz twenty-four hours when I was tossed out of the country along with half a dozen correspondents. It seemed the government thought we'd been writing anti-Austrian propaganda. We were taken to Salzburg. That was the last time I saw Wilson.

'After I'd been thrown out I was ordered by my paper to go to Warsaw. There had been border incidents and they thought Germany might invade Poland too.

'When I got to Warsaw it was in chaos. I was on my way to the Foreign Office to get a permit to work in Poland. Someone was haranguing a large crowd. I stopped to find out what was happening. And that's the last I remember for a long time. I was told later that someone had thrown a home-made bomb into the crowd. Several people were killed.'

He touched the scar on his forehead. 'I was in hospital in Warsaw for seven weeks. At one time they thought I was going to die and they put me in a cot and closed the screens.

'I was on morphine. That's when I began to dream about Vienna. I couldn't believe it had ever happened. But I could see the Meissners' house and you and the time we went to Bad Voslau and swam and saw the wounded men with their stumps. It was all mixed up with the tanks and the armoured cars. Nothing seemed real.

'And then this English doctor came. I couldn't speak Polish and they couldn't speak English and maybe they thought I had some last request to make. I don't remember much about him but he saved me. He phoned my paper in New York and said they had to get me out and they did. They took me to Germany by ambulance and then I was flown to the States.'

'How long were you there?'

'Nearly a year. Most of that time I was on sick leave. It was a strange time. I went to my folks and they looked after me and there was this girl there, the daughter of a neighbour I'd known since I was a kid. She'd become a nurse and she used to come over and change the dressings and bathe me and help me to learn to walk all over again.

'The stronger I grew, the more I wanted to get back to journalism. I guess it's a kind of fever.'

'So you came back to Europe?'

'First I went to New York. They wanted to keep me there. Wanted me to cover City Hall, for Christ's sake. Can you imagine me on a beat like that? London was in flames, Germany was attacking Russia, and they wanted me to write about the municipal budget deficit. I said the hell with it and if they didn't send me back to Europe I would resign. So they flew me back via Lisbon and I've been in Europe ever since.'

'And the girl?'

'She was well out of it. She wanted a home and kids. She's a nest builder. I guess you could say I'm a nest flier.'

'So what now?'

'Now I go back to France in a couple of days. But I just *had* to try to find out whether you were *the* Anna Webster.'

'Now you know.'

'Not quite. You're Mrs Wilson Braid, mother of three.'

'And you?'

'You know the song, "It's not the same old me"? Well, I'm not the Ben Ramsey of Vienna 1937 either.' There was a kind of bleakness about the way he said it.

He looked at his watch and looked at her. She knew what he was thinking because she had been thinking it too.

'I'd better go,' he said.

'I'd ask you to – '

'No, no, I must get back to London.'

It was an uneasy, artificial parting. Both said they must see each other again. She watched the war-dimmed headlights bobbing off down the driveway and went back into the house. She poured herself a small drink and sat looking into the dying fire. All she could see were ghosts.

She went upstairs and looked in on the children, lingering

by Peter's bed. A night-light burned low and his face beneath the dark thatch of hair was totally innocent. From the moment he was born she had kept a special watch over Peter. Always in her memory was his father. Always in her mind was the thought of those dark and savage genes emerging once again. She had read several books about heredity versus environment but how could anyone be *sure*? So far there had been no hint of Cuno in Peter's make-up and she prayed there never would be. She touched him now on his head, stroking his hair, as though to stroke away the demons.

Ten

Winter was drawing to an end and so was the war. Jock struggled on. From the person Anna had first known, authoritative and in control, he had become a little old man with white fluffy hair in a large hospital bed. He had grown a beard and this made him seem even older. Mentally he had changed too. There was a kind of pathos in the way he greeted her. He complained constantly about the food, about lack of attention, about the nurses not answering the bell when he rang it. He also wanted to be moved somewhere else.

When Anna enquired into these complaints she found that in many cases he was wrong and that he was suffering from a well-known syndrome that overtakes old people in institutions, a kind of paranoia.

But the most common subject for discussion was Wilson and what he was doing to Jock's papers. Anna had been in touch with her husband both by letter and telex. His letters were curiously flat and badly written for a journalist. He seemed to have little interest in his father's health and wanted him to remain in England.

'He will get much better medical treatment there than in South Africa. I think he must be perfectly recovered before he even attempts the long voyage.'

Anna agreed even though she knew Wilson's reasons had nothing to do with Jock's health.

Most of her husband's communications concerned the boys, especially John for whom Wilson's fatherly feeling was much stronger than for the others. Again Anna wondered if human beings could detect their own genes in some primitive and unexplainable way.

He wanted her to send the boys out to him. 'The war's over bar the shouting,' he wrote. 'I can get them passages easily. And it's safe now. All you have to do is find a professional companion to accompany them.'

She hedged. Who would look after them? She was their mother. She certainly was not going to let anyone else take them out. His letters became more angry, sometimes even threatening. But she was adamant, and she used Jock as an excuse. She delayed replying to Wilson's letters so that sometimes two or three would arrive before she wrote.

She played the game skilfully, waiting and watching Jock. If he survived she would have to tell him what she had postponed telling him. If he didn't . . .

He clung to Anna's visits and also to those of Montague Axe, who came down from London in his big grey Bentley.

He also clung on to a belief that Africa would cure him. Once he got out to the sun and the clear air, everything would return to normal. And Anna was to take him back.

This plan had arrived fully grown in Jock's mind – and it added another potential nightmare to her life. Axe, he said, would book them several staterooms. They would take with them an additional nurse. The sea air would do him a power of good – and they would be together as a family.

'I'm in bed here,' he said. 'There's no difference between being in bed here and being in bed on a ship.'

Anna nodded and made sympathetic noises and repeated that Wilson was definitely against him travelling until he was fully fit again. That would send him off on another diatribe against his son and often he would give her glimpses into her husband's youth and early manhood that she had never known before.

'He was spoiled, you know. His mother spoiled him, being an only child. I couldna give him all the time I wanted to, I'll admit that, but there was something in the boy that wasna quite right. There was a' that carry-on at school.'

He had been involved in some way in the theft of money from another boy but how she wasn't clear, for although the police were called in nothing was ever proved. The impression was of a childhood torn between an overprotective mother and a dominant father.

Jock seemed not to understand that he was disparaging his son to his son's wife. With time on his hands he brooded, and most of his thoughts centred on what Wilson was doing to him and to his empire. It added to his paranoia.

Early one Sunday morning the telephone rang at Usbourne and Montague Axe asked Anna whether she was going in to see Jock.

'I'm just about to leave.'

'Right, I'll give you luncheon.'

'That would be lovely, but I keep Sundays for the children.'

'No, I mean lunch at Usbourne. You and the children. Everyone.'

'How do you mean?'

'I mean, don't do anything. Don't let anyone start cooking. Leave everything to me.'

She went to see Jock and when she returned she found the Bentley parked outside the house.

Axe was wearing what she thought of as his 'country clothes' – a three-piece suit of snuff-coloured tweed and his regulation bow tie. The suit made him look immense.

He lifted a wicker hamper from the car, carried it into the kitchen and began to unpack it. He took out a leg of lamb, the size of which she had not seen since before the war, a tin of pâté de foie gras, a dozen eggs, a bag of new forced potatoes, a tin of haricots verts, a tin of raspberries, a jar of raspberry jam, a bottle of sherry, a pound of yellow butter, a pint of thick Jersey cream, a small Stilton, and a box of crème de menthe chocolates.

As one delicacy followed another, first the butler, then the maids, then the children, crowded round the big kitchen table to watch.

Anna said, 'Where on earth did you get all this?'

He turned to her, smiling a smile that was full of smugness and pride. 'Just say a grateful client.'

'And the cream and eggs and butter?'

'I know a farmer not a dozen miles from here.'

She felt a moment of exasperation – he was enjoying his triumph just a little *too* much. But that was almost instantly forgotten, for he abruptly tore off his bow tie and jacket and covered his large belly with a blue and white striped apron.

'Now,' he said, turning to Nico and Peter. 'Which of you two young gentlemen is going to help me?'

'Me!'

'Me!'

'All right, you can both be my special chefs. Now, first of all, we're going to make a trifle.' He turned to Anna. 'A bowl, please.'

She brought him a small cut-glass bowl which he held up to the two boys. 'We're not going to get much trifle in that, are we?'

From the wicker basket he lifted a sponge-cake that would have filled three such bowls. The onlookers gave a united sigh.

'Monty, this is absurd. *Where* did you get a cake like that?'

'I made it, of course.'

She could see that he was revelling in the effect it was having on everyone in the room.

'Right,' he said. 'Now we cut it up and lay it in the bowl. Nico, you lay the pieces down flat when I've cut them – and Peter, you slosh on the sherry. A good slosh, mind.'

None of the adults had seen a trifle for at least five years, the children never.

'Now,' he said, 'the gigot. We're going to have it the French way . . .'

Anna never forgot that lunch. And even the two boys marked it as one of their earliest memories.

After lunch they put on coats and walked through daffodils down to a small lake.

Peter and Nico were full of energy and wanted her to race them to the water.

'But I've just had lunch,' she said.

The boys would not accept this as an excuse and she ran through the grass with them, finally flinging herself down by the water's edge, a bad third.

'Oh Lord,' she said to Axe as he arrived with John on his

shoulders. 'I shouldn't have done that, not after being such a glutton.'

She found him a strange mixture of the pompous and the childlike. He walked with his belly thrust out and his arms almost still at his sides. She thought he looked like a Roman emperor and needed only a toga. But with the children he changed. He had the ability to talk to them as though he was one of them and she had not seen them take to an adult the way they took to him.

As he was leaving, she said, 'I can't remember when last we had such a lovely Sunday.'

He held her hand, lingering over it. 'There'll be plenty more,' he said.

Anna was succumbing to the drug of daily journalism where each day is wiped clean with the printing of the paper, and each new day is completely blank. Every morning she drove in to work full of pleasurable anticipation.

Her handling of the Scarf Murder had done her good on the *Mercury* and she became a utility reporter, covering for colleagues who were sick or on leave. She wrote for the women's pages, sometimes the daily column; she covered the courts, helped on crime stories and political stories; she even did some sports reporting. She was also taught sub-editing.

The *News Chronicle* in London had liked her murder coverage and was asking for any local stories or features with a possible national interest. They paid her well for what they printed but, more importantly, they used her name.

One day Ben phoned. 'I've got to go to Southampton to do a piece on the reconstruction of the docks after the bombing. I'll be passing Winchester. Why don't we have lunch? You must know a good pub around there.'

She was pleased to hear his voice. She asked around the newsroom for advice about a pub and the consensus was the Troutbeck Inn, which stood alone in a field overlooking the River Test. They met there on a warm early April day with a light breeze from the south-west. They sat on the terrace drinking gin, and watching trout rising to a hatch of early flies.

The light was brighter than when she had last seen the scars on Ben's face. They seemed more pronounced. She noticed that he always sat with his good side to her.

'Look,' he said, 'I've been thinking about last time. I don't know about you but I guess it was uncomfortable. And it shouldn't have been.'

'It was for me too.'

'It was my fault. I was resenting your marriage and your kids and I imagine you were resenting the fact that I hadn't been in touch.'

'Something like that.'

'Listen, what d'you say we wipe the slate clean? Everything starts as of now. Okay?'

'Okay.'

He called the publican and asked what there was to eat: rabbit stew, spring greens, boiled potatoes.

'Sounds great,' Ben said. 'Got any wine?'

He had some Spanish Rioja from before the war.

Anna had begun to feel tense and she was able only to pick at her food. Ben was not eating much either. But they enjoyed the wine.

'How's the job?' he said.

'Fine.'

'You'll be in Fleet Street soon.'

'Not with Jock ill.'

'And the kids?'

'Fine.'

There was a pause, then she said, 'When did you get back?'

'Yesterday. The war will be over in a few weeks.'

'You'll be going to Germany?'

'Sure . . . Let me see if I can get another bottle.'

He went into the bar leaving her in the warm spring sunshine. She was beginning to feel more relaxed.

He filled her glass. 'Here's to the loss of innocence,' he said.

She knew he meant their own lost innocence from the time in Vienna.

'Don't say that.' She felt a sudden sadness. 'I don't like thinking that anything is lost for ever.'

'Well, what shall we drink to?'

'Something more cheerful.'

'Us? You know, there's one difference between now and then.'

'What's that?'

'Don't you remember? We were eating with only one hand.' He leaned across the table and took her hand. 'Like this.' His felt cool and dry, hers was hot.

'Yes, I do remember,' she said, and made a slight move to regain her hand.

He held it more firmly. 'We've had a date for a long time,' he said. 'Do you think we'll ever keep it?'

'Some dates are not meant to be kept.'

'Ours was. Listen, they have rooms here. Don't let's pass up this chance too. There might never be another.'

She shivered in the sun. 'Don't say that. Please don't say "never".'

'Well then?'

She drew a deep breath. 'Why don't you ask if they have one free.'

'I have and he has.'

She rose and picked up the wine and the glasses. 'I know the way,' he said.

They made love in a small attic room with a sloping ceiling, cottage-garden wallpaper, and a window looking out at the river. The warmth of the day had heated the air under the roof and they lay naked on the bed in the rays of a slanting sun.

'I knew it would be like this one day,' she said.

He lay on his back, one arm flung over his face to shield his eyes from the sun and she could see the scars on his chest and stomach. She touched them with the tips of her fingers and felt his skin twitch.

He turned to her and said, 'I guess I've never been able to understand . . . well, let's just say Wilson doesn't seem an obvious choice for you.'

Faint white hairs glinted on her breasts in the sunshine and he began to stroke the firm flesh.

'What was her name?'

'Who?'

'The girl back home. The one who nursed you.'

'Valerie. Val. Why?'

'I just wondered. How long have we got the room?'

'As long as we like.'

'I want you to make love to me again. Slowly this time. Last time it was too fast. No, no, I don't mean in that way.' She laughed at his look of relief. 'It was just so good I wanted it to go on and on.' She slid on top of him and sat astride, easing him into her. She began to move very slowly, rhythmically.

They parted in late afternoon, he continuing down to Southampton, she driving slowly to Usbourne. She felt content, happy in a way she had never felt before. She kept thinking of his body and the scars and seeing the cosy, chintzy room, and feeling the sun on her naked breasts. 'I knew it,' she repeated to herself. 'I knew that one day it would be like this.'

Eleven

The Troutbeck Inn became their place. They would meet there as often as they could. Ben would ring her from London and tell her he could be down at such-and-such a time and could she make it? She always did. She switched jobs with other reporters, worked late, changed her duty rosters, even lied. But she got there.

She began to live in a dream world. The war, her job, her children, visits to Jock – all these had their place in her life but moved out of sharp focus. Her relationship with Ben was at the centre of everything.

She had been waiting to fall in love ever since Vienna, seven years before; it had been a long time coming but at last it had come. That it should have been Ben was simple irony, for she had struggled hard to eradicate him from her memories and had almost succeeded.

But that was all demolished by the power of her love. Each day she waited for his call and each day it did not come was a day wasted. Each time she saw him her life was renewed, each time they parted she felt bereft. She hardly ate, and she slept badly.

It was no problem getting 'their' room at the Troutbeck for there were no other takers. Occasionally a middle-aged man in a tweed cap came into the bar, talked fishing and took snaps of the place, but otherwise they had it to themselves. The publican, a taciturn man, supplied them with food and drink, then ignored them. It was like being in a foreign country.

'Tell me about Wilson,' Ben said one day. 'Why the hell did you marry him?'

She had been expecting it and had edited her life in the way she would have if her own obituary had landed on her desk in the office.

'Why does anyone do anything? It seemed right at the time. I had to look after Nico. My grandmother died. There wasn't much else I could do.' That seemed to satisfy him.

She loved his body, loved to touch and smell his skin. Often as they lay naked in the warmth of the room, listening to the river splash over a weir, she would lie with her head on his stomach and let her fingertips touch the scars on his chest and stomach.

'I hate them,' he said once. 'I'm going to get them fixed.'

'Fixed?'

'If the war's contributed nothing else to humanity it's brought advances in plastic surgery. They can take the skin from the inside of your leg and graft it anywhere.'

'But the scars are *you*,' she said. 'I can't remember you without them.'

'I can,' he said.

'Don't change.'

'Beneath that cool exterior you're a romantic at heart.' He held her close.

On other occasions, he talked about the Meissners. She did not like thinking or talking about them now. They raised the spectre of the past and the question of Nico's and Peter's parentage. She wanted to bury all that for ever.

When she asked why he was constantly returning to it, he said, 'They were friends. I'll do what I can to find out what happened. I owe them that.' Then, almost as an afterthought, he added, 'It'll make a good story.'

'Yes, it will.' She said it without thinking and realized she had passed a milestone; anything now was grist to the journalist's mill.

Jock came home and Anna took a week's leave. He was able to spend most of the day sitting up. The spring weather turned warm. His nurse would dress him and Anna would walk with him slowly on the terrace. His steps were weak and shaky.

He talked almost solely about Africa. He wanted to stay in his house by the sea. The sea air had mysterious properties; it would bring him back to strength.

Axe came down whenever he could. He was working on booking sea passages but the war in the Far East was still raging and troops were being sent there so shipping was at a premium.

One early evening when Jock was already in bed and they were having a whisky from her private stock, he suddenly said, 'I know things are not well with you and Wilson.'

'Oh?' she said sharply. 'How? You didn't get that from me or Jock.'

'No, but it's my job to read between the lines.' He held up his hand. 'Please don't say anything. I just want you to know that I'm here if you need me.'

She was touched but tried to keep the conversation unemotional and said, 'That sounds final. What haven't you told me?'

'I think I've got a passage for you in one of the Ellerman ships.'

'When?'

'Next week.'

It was like a knife turning in her stomach. The moment he'd gone she phoned Ben in London. There was no reply from his office or from his apartment. She phoned at intervals until midnight then went to bed but couldn't sleep.

She had not heard from him for days. It sometimes happened like that when he was on a story. Now, suddenly, she felt cut off from him and was terrified that something unexpected had happened, like his being suddenly recalled to the States.

She was having breakfast the following morning when she was summoned to the phone. It was Ben.

'Hello, darling.' She tried to keep her voice calm. 'I tried to phone you last night.'

'Sorry, I was out.'

'Yes, I know. How are you?'

'I'm okay.' He sounded slightly distracted. And then he said, 'Listen, the reason I'm phoning is I'm going back to Germany.

The war's just about over. They want me to cover the race for Berlin.'

'When?' She felt as though the ground was opening up beneath her.

'Tonight. Half a dozen of us have seats on a VIP flight.'

'What time do you leave?'

'Northolt at nine.'

'I've *got* to see you.'

'It's going to be difficult.'

'Jock's back from hospital. We're supposed to leave for Africa next week.'

'I thought you weren't going. I thought that was the whole idea.'

'That's what I want to see you about.'

He didn't reply. She felt tears of desperation come to her eyes, then he said, 'Okay, I'll be there by three.'

She was supposed to take Jock for his first drive in the spring countryside but told him she'd forgotten she had to take Peter to the dentist.

'I'll come with you,' he said. 'I'll just sit in the car.'

'No, no. What if it suddenly turns cold?'

'I'll take a rug.'

'What if something happened? What if we had an accident, even a minor one. You'd never get out to Africa.'

'Well . . . Aye, I suppose so.'

'I'll take you out tomorrow.'

'Being ill is like being a child again,' he said. 'You have to do what others tell you to.'

She phoned the Troutbeck and reserved the room. During the morning she read the papers to Jock and after lunch went to fetch Peter. 'But you didn't tell me,' he said. 'You said you were going out with Grandpa.'

'I know, darling, I forgot.'

She bundled him up and drove to a colleague's house on the outskirts of Winchester. Anna had met Margaret Fowles on several occasions but did not really know her. 'I have to go to the dentist,' Anna said. 'Could you possibly look after Peter for an hour or so?'

Margaret was somewhat taken aback but agreed. Anna went

back to the car and said, 'Mummy's made a stupid mistake, darling. It's not you, it's me who's got to go to the dentist. You'll stay here with this nice lady until I get back.'

She drove to the Troutbeck. The man in the tweed cap was the only one in the bar. She went up to their room and sat at the window, remembering another time she had waited for Ben. She began to feel afraid that he might not come, that something might have occurred to stop him. But after a quarter of an hour he walked into the room and locked the door behind him.

They took each other in their arms and she clung to him. 'God, I'm glad to see you!'

'Tell me what it's all about.'

'Afterwards.'

They made love, but she was tense. Afterwards there wasn't the usual feeling of warmth and love.

'Why the sudden change of plan?' he said.

'It's not sudden. I've been thinking about it for ages. If I told Jock now that I wasn't going to Africa and that the children weren't going either, God knows what would happen. It might bring on another heart attack and kill him. I thought I'd take him out and that'll give me a chance to talk to Wilson. There's nothing left between us and he knows that too.'

'You mean a divorce?'

'Yes.'

'And then?'

'Come back here, of course.'

'And the children?'

'Bring them with me, naturally.'

There was just the faintest trace of something puzzling in his tone, but she brushed it aside.

'What did you think I'd do?'

'I just wondered.'

'It doesn't have to be here,' she said. 'Wherever we can be together.'

'I might have to go back to the States.'

'Well, then it'll be the States.' She frowned. 'Don't you understand, I want to marry you. I want to be your wife.'

He got off the bed and brought a cigar back from his jacket.

He took some time to light it. During those moments a series of thoughts raced through her mind, but the central one was of the children. She wanted to reassure him that she would not expect him to sacrifice himself for children who were not his. She wanted to tell him that he would get used to them, that no one was expecting him to be an instant father. Then she realized that if she said those things it would sound as though she was begging and something inside her turned to steel. She would not beg, ever. But that did not stop her from asking the straight question.

'Darling, I'm asking you to marry me,' she said.

He took her hand and held it tightly. 'I know,' he said, 'and I'm – But – '

'But what?'

'Look, you're going to Africa, to your husband whom you haven't seen for a long time. I'm going to Germany. I don't know what will happen there. I know the war's coming to an end in Europe but my paper could send me to the Pacific and God knows how long the war out there will last. I could be there for months, even years.'

'War correspondents get married.'

'I know they do. Of course I know that. But it takes time to get a divorce. Darling, why don't we see what happens in the next few months.'

She felt her emotional energy drain away leaving a kind of void. They talked and talked but the more they talked the more they seemed to her to become like two acquaintances rather than two people deeply in love.

It wasn't until he said, 'I'd better get going,' that she felt the desperation return.

She suddenly saw her life stretch out before her like a bleak winter landscape. How would she get through the days without him? But there was nothing she could do. She put her arms around him and held him for a long moment and then said, 'You go first.'

He dressed and they said goodbye at the door. Even that was spoiled by the man in the tweed cap coming along the corridor. She heard Ben's car start up and drive away and then she finished dressing.

She looked at her watch and realized with dismay that they had been at the inn for two and a half hours.

The clouds were dark and it had started to rain. She drove fast into Winchester. Peter was in tears and had apparently been difficult. Margaret Fowles was controlling her anger with both of them as Anna apologized profusely.

'You're a big boy,' she said to Peter as he got into the front seat beside her. 'Please stop being such a cry-baby.'

The rain was coming down more heavily now, beating on the canvas roof of the car. She drove out of town and began to wind up towards the top of the Downs. It was Jock's supper-time and she knew he would be anxious about her for she always sat with him.

Peter had begun to snivel and she said, 'Peter, *do* shut up!'

On the top of the Downs in the half-light she saw the lorry too late. It was stationary just round a blind bend. She swerved. The tyres lost their grip on the wet road and the car spun. She had a sickening sensation of flying and then the car was rolling and she hit her head on something hard.

Peter! He was lying half on top of her. There was broken glass everywhere. She heard voices and felt the car being pushed upright. The canvas hood was ripped and hands lifted Peter and her on to the grass. It was the lorry driver and his mate.

'You all right, miss?'

'Yes. Yes. But Peter . . . Where's my son?'

'He's here,' the lorry driver said. And she saw his face and knew that something terrible had happened.

Anna sat in the hospital waiting-room. It was the same room in which she had waited so often to see Jock. Except for herself it was empty. How long she had sat there she had no idea. It was dark now. Her hair was matted with mud and there were streaks of mud and blood on her clothing. Her dress was torn and her shoes broken. There was a painful throbbing in her head. None of that mattered.

A nurse came to her with a blanket and a cup of tea but she shook her head.

'Are you sure you're all right, Mrs Braid?'

'Yes.'

Why should she be all right? Why couldn't it have been *her* in casualty? Peter. Oh, Peter.

She had relived every second of the accident a dozen times since she had been sitting there.

Again she saw the lorry, the rain lashing down. And then she saw Peter's crumpled body as the two men brought him out: the blood on his face, the short grey trousers, the bare legs, and then, at the bottom of one leg . . .

Her stomach clenched and her mind veered away. She managed to blot out the picture but she couldn't stop the words of the lorry driver to his mate.

'Jesus! The bone's sticking out!'

Then the journey in the lorry. The bumping. The lurching round corners. She had held Peter in her arms trying to absorb all the bumps and shocks, and also his pain.

'Anna?'

The name penetrated from a great distance. She saw Montague Axe, huge and dark in the dim lights.

'Anna! What on earth are – ?'

'What is it?' She cut across him.

'I've got very sad news. He's gone.'

'Gone?'

'He's dead.'

She gave a cry of despair. 'Oh no. No. He can't be!'

'I'm sorry that I was the one to have to tell you,' Axe said. 'They say the second attack is usually the finish.'

'What?'

He seemed to see the mud and blood for the first time. 'What's happened to you? Are you all right?'

'Tell me!'

'It was after you left. He had a stroke.'

'Jock?' she whispered.

'Of course.'

She closed her eyes.

Just then the double doors at the end of the room opened and the surgeon came towards her. 'I'm sorry you've had such a long wait, Mrs Braid. But I wanted to be sure.'

She held her breath. They were the longest seconds she would ever endure.

He said, 'It might have been worse. The head injury is not as bad as we thought. Mild concussion I should think. And he'll be over that soon. He won't remember a thing about the accident which is just as well. But the leg . . .' He paused. 'I'm not sure we'll be able to save his foot.'

She stared at him without speaking. Her jaws felt locked. Then she said, 'But there must be *something* you can do. He's such a little boy.'

'We know that, Mrs Braid. We'll do everything in our power.'

Twelve

For Anna the next thirty-six hours were the worst she had experienced, worse than the death of her parents, worse than her meetings with Cuno, worse than her time on her grandmother's farm. Apart from the overwhelming misery she felt about Peter, there was the guilt. It was like having a separate self, who stood just outside the periphery of her consciousness, always there, always accusing. She was filled with self-loathing.

Axe had taken her back to Usbourne from the hospital. Nico and John were asleep and she had sat by their bedsides for hours, simply looking down at them.

The telephone rang constantly. All the London papers wanted stories about Jock. Axe handled the calls but, as one followed another, Anna cried in anguish, 'How will the hospital get through if there's any news?'

For the first time in many years she prayed. Not just the usual hurried and superstitious mumblings before she went to sleep, but anguished personal prayers.

Then there was Wilson. He bombarded her with telexes and cables. It was pointless, they agreed, him coming over for the funeral since the sea voyage took a fortnight. Instead they planned a memorial service in Usbourne parish church at some later date, when the war was over and life became normal once again.

She passed the hours between the house and the hospital and each time she made the journey she heard her own last irritable words to Peter and cried.

She hated herself, too, for the lies that surrounded what had

114

happened. She wanted to confess. She wanted absolution, but she couldn't bring herself to tell even Axe.

The burst of calls ceased and now each time the telephone rang she heard it with dread. Once it was Ben.

'Darling, I've managed to get a later flight. I want to see you. I can't just leave yesterday as it was. How soon can you get to the Troutbeck?'

'Ben, I don't think –'

But he interrupted her. He spoke for a long time, his voice urgent and filled with love for her. He told her how much he regretted the day before, how much he needed her, how they would work things out, how he would finish reporting the war and then they would all settle in America, he and Anna and the children, and they would have kids of their own . . .

A torrent of words flowed over her.

They were words she would have longed for at any other time, but now they were just words, words, words . . .

Finally he stopped and waited for her comment, for her support. But she could not give him any.

'I must go,' she said. 'Goodbye, Ben.'

Soon after this conversation came the call she had been waiting for. Axe took her in to the hospital in the evening. She followed a consultant to the children's ward. Peter's bed was surrounded by screens and he lay white-faced against the pillows. The walls of the ward were enlivened by children's crayon drawings, and the floor was covered in toys. She put his teddy bear at the foot of his bed.

'He's stable,' the doctor said. 'And I think we can save the foot.' She felt a flood of relief. 'But it's going to mean a lot of hard work for him. He'll have to get used to wearing a surgical boot to give the leg support as he grows. And then, with luck, and if he's careful, it should improve.'

'Will he be able to walk?'

'Oh yes. But he'll have to be careful. No rough games, but swimming would be good.'

'Will he limp?'

'He will at first. But later . . . possibly not. We'll know more as he grows. I don't want to raise your hopes too high, Mrs Braid, but remembering what he was like when he was brought in I think his chances of living a normal life have improved considerably.'

She had to be content with that.

Axe took her to the best hotel in town. 'This calls for champagne. And there's something else to celebrate.'

He made a little ceremony of ordering and pouring the wine. It was ice cold on her tongue and she found herself with a raging thirst. She drained her glass and he gave her a second.

'What else?' she said.

'I didn't tell you earlier because you probably wouldn't have listened.'

'I'm listening now, Monty.'

'Jock's left you his British estate.'

'What?' She was shaken. 'Usbourne? But –'

'I'm using the word "estate" in the legal sense.' He touched his fingertips together over his stomach, enjoying the moment. 'Not just the house. The newspapers, the printing works, everything.'

She placed her glass carefully on the table in case the trembling in her hands caused the wine to spill.

'I don't believe it!'

'I wouldn't joke about something like that. Do you remember when he came up to London and I brought him back?'

'That's when we met.'

'I had drafted a new will for him. You're not the sole beneficiary but you are the main one. He's left the house to you outright, but Braid Provincial Newspapers Ltd is left to you and the children and Wilson. Each of the boys has twelve per cent, you have thirty-nine per cent and Wilson twenty-five. Jock wanted it that way because twenty-six per cent would have given Wilson a blocking minority . . .' He saw the look on her face. 'Sorry. I'll explain everything later. But in simple terms it means that if you have the support of one son you have a fifty-one per cent share – and you're in charge.

'Jock was very disappointed in Wilson as you know but he wanted to leave him something because he was the old man's only child and Jock always set great store by blood relations. However, he wanted you to have the power, but only if you had the support of at least one son. If you didn't, then he reasoned you didn't deserve the business. And if Wilson could get the support of all three boys, then he did. In the meantime, until the boys are twenty-one I hold their proxy votes. Congratulations, my dear.'

But all she could think of was that she would give up everything to make Peter whole again.

It took some time to sink in. When she walked around Usbourne she told herself that it belonged to her, but nothing had ever belonged to her before and she found it difficult to understand that the bricks and mortar, the grass and the trees, were hers. Her new responsibilities were a blessing. Had she been left with nothing to do but hospital visiting, she felt that she would have sunk into a bottomless pit of depression. But a company does not stand still, decisions have to be made, orders have to be given.

At first she was on the edge of panic. 'I don't know anything about running a company!' she said to Axe. 'I'm not even sure I want to try.'

He had been managing the company since Jock had become ill and he soothed her now. 'I told you before – I'm here when you need me.'

'I wish you'd take it over, Monty.'

'Then what would you do? You could hardly go on being a reporter on a newspaper you owned. Anyway you need something like this. You'd just rot down here otherwise.'

They talked about the company for hours. He would arrive from London with briefcases filled with papers, some of which she could understand, but some, the legal documents, might have been written in Sumerian or Old Slavonic for all she could make of them.

But Axe had the ability to reduce a complicated picture to a simple one with a few deft strokes. In reality he was giving her lessons in fiscal and commercial theory. She learned quickly but realized that to do justice to Jock's creation she needed Axe at her right hand. She wanted him to join the company but he was cautious.

'Let's see how things go,' he said. 'We're only at the start. But decisions have to be made. You need to be in London. You can't run the company from Usbourne.'

'Jock did.'

'He hated London. But it's not really practicable. You need an office there and you need a place to live.'

'That's impossible at the moment. I have to be near Peter.'

In May 1945 the war in Europe ended and Anna spent VE day sitting beside Peter's bed in hospital, reading to him from *The House at Pooh Corner*. A few days later she and Axe went to the cinema in Winchester to see the latest newsreels of the German surrender and the scenes outside Buckingham Palace.

Axe pressed her about London and she began to realize he was right. When she went up he would meet her train at Waterloo and they would drive around the shattered city looking at offices to rent. She liked none of them.

'Aren't there any in Fleet Street?' she said one day.

They drove down from the Strand and for the first time in weeks she felt a quickening of interest. Every great newspaper name was there. Later she would recall that drive, for she knew that it was then that the seed of Webster Communications was sown. It was a grey day and Fleet Street was dingy and thick with traffic fumes. Most of the buildings were still standing but further on, past Ludgate Circus, a large area had been flattened by bombs.

They parked the car and walked. 'This is where I want to be,' she said.

On these day trips Axe would take her out to lunch at expensive restaurants which seemed not to have heard of rationing. Once he took her on a tour of properties he had bought at the height of the bombing, when owners were selling cheaply to get out of London.

'Didn't you ever think we might lose the war?' she said.

'Of course. But then there wouldn't have been any point in living. Not for a Jew, anyway.'

There was a particular house near Victoria Station that he wanted to show her. It was one of a terrace in an elegant square. 'I'm going to do it up,' he said. 'You could have the two top floors or the whole house as a London base if you liked.'

She laughed. 'Where would I get the money for a place like this?' she said, unthinkingly.

He looked at her with raised eyebrows. 'My dear, you could buy the square.'

The place was damp and rat-infested and hadn't been lived in for years, but there was something about it that appealed to her. When she looked from the windows she saw that the square was large. There were trees and grass and an old tennis court. It would be a place where the boys could run about. The word 'run' made her cringe and blink back tears.

'I'll think about it,' she said.

Axe took her to his own house. It was in one of the most beautiful streets she had ever seen, Church Row in Hampstead, one of a terrace of tall Georgian houses with old brickwork that glowed. It had a long garden, large for London, which was overgrown and neglected. The house itself was dark and gloomy, except for the kitchen which was modern.

Some of the rooms still had gas lighting and the walls were crowded with paintings. Axe, she discovered, was a compulsive collector, not only of paintings but also of porcelain. There were oils and etchings, pen-and-ink drawings, charcoal sketches, water-colours. There was hardly a space between the pictures. She recognized a Renoir and a Matisse, an early Picasso, Dufy, Klimt, a Gwen John, a Schiele. They hung in no particular order but wherever a space could be found.

The furniture was heavy, with leather chesterfields and chairs which gave the drawing-room the look of a London club. He lived alone except for a daily woman – he had told her once he could not abide permanent servants – and the house had a chilly, unloved look. She longed to fill it with flowers and throw open the dark velvet curtains.

He gave her a drink and said, 'I have two tickets for a show tomorrow night. Why don't you give yourself a break? We'll dine afterwards and you can stay here. I've got more spare rooms than I know what to do with.'

'Thanks, Monty, but I must get back.' She said it automatically then softened the refusal by saying, 'Peter's home.'

'Yes, you told me. Look, I'll drive you back afterwards if you like and you can give me a spare room.'

'I like to be there to say good night to him.'

'You have your own life, Anna. You can't go on lacerating yourself. Of course you feel guilty but don't destroy yourself. If you do you'll hurt Peter worse than he is now. He must learn to live his own life. He can't be dependent on you for ever.'

She was aware that since the accident she had channelled her caring and her love to Peter. Monty might be right but she could not help herself. She spent every free moment with him. He was in pain most of the time but hardly ever complained. This touched her deeply.

Peter had his crutches now. She hated the word. It seemed to come out of a Dickensian world of crippled children. They would spend hours playing word-games and from these the crutches became his 'legs' as in 'Where are my legs?' and when the pain became bad he called it 'My you know what,' which later evolved to Unowot. Peter drew Unowot as an Eskimo on crutches.

She said to Axe, 'I must get my train.'

'I'll drive you down.'

'There's no need . . .'

'I'd like to. It would give me pleasure.'

She put up her hand and patted his cheek. 'You're very good to me, Monty.'

He caught her wrist and said, 'I think I'm in love with you.'

'Monty, please don't!'

'It started that very first evening.'

'Please . . .'

'I wanted you to know.'

'I'm very touched.'

Suddenly he was no longer the somewhat pompous lawyer, but a young man, embarrassed and fumbling for words.

At last he said, 'I won't say anything more but I think you should know that I'm a patient man. The law teaches you that.'

They left London in late afternoon sunshine. Traffic was light because petrol rationing, like food rationing, had become even tighter.

Anna remarked on this to keep the conversation on neutral ground. Axe replied, 'The great British public thought that when they'd won the war the spoils would be to the victor.

Now they're angry. I think they'll ditch Churchill for a socialist government at the next election and then we'll have trouble.'

'Who's we?'

'The industrial and commercial worlds. Taxes will go up and we'll be under pressure from the unions. The print unions are the most militant in the country.'

'I don't know anything about industrial unions.'

'I'm afraid the learning process isn't going to be pleasant.'

She listened to him talking about the industrial landscape with only half an ear, thankful that they were on unemotional ground.

There was a strange car in the drive when they reached Usbourne.

'Are you expecting visitors?' Axe said.

'No,' she said, frowning.

He followed her into the house. A figure rose from a chair in the drawing-room and came towards them. Anna's heart almost stopped.

'Hello, darling,' he said, taking her in his arms. 'Surprised?'

Thirteen

Of all the people Anna might have expected to cross the floor of her drawing-room that evening, Wilson Braid was the last. She had not seen him for more than a year. He had become part of her past; one of her ghosts. She had thought about him less and less, had answered his letters perfunctorily, and if it had not been for Jock she would already have asked for a divorce.

Now, as he came towards her with his arms outstretched and a stage smile on his face, she was so stunned she could hardly move. He clasped her to his square, powerful body, and she swiftly jerked her head to one side in case he found her lips.

'Well, well, well . . .' he said.

The following few minutes were filled with embarrassing and brittle pleasantries until Axe excused himself and drove back to London.

'I must see to Peter,' she said, using him as an excuse to break the silence which had fallen.

'I'll come with you.'

He had already seen the children. Nico and Peter were in the playroom. As usual she made a great fuss of Peter. He was still pale and thin, unlike Nico, who was robust, but of the two, Peter was the better looking.

'Why does he call his crutches his "legs"?' Wilson asked.

'Crutches is such a horrible word,' she said.

'That's avoiding reality.'

'Why not, if that is the reality?'

He seemed ill at ease with Peter. He spoke to him with a bluff joviality that sounded out of place, and again she wondered whether he suspected that Peter was not his child, for he was a different person with John. He picked him up and played with him. He was altogether softer and more loving.

After they had said good night to the children he walked out on to the terrace and looked across the lawns to the parkland and the lake beyond, then he took an exaggerated breath of air and said, 'My God, it's good to be home.'

It was the word 'home' that set off alarm bells in her head.

He put his arm out to encircle her shoulders but she slid away, saying, 'I'll have a room made ready for you.'

He opened his mouth and she prepared herself for a row but his face relaxed and he said, 'It'll take a little time for us to get used to each other again.'

This was a new Wilson, one she did not understand. For the first time since she had lived in Usbourne she locked her bedroom door. She lay awake for hours staring into the darkness, trying to work out what he was planning – but failed.

The following morning at breakfast she came closer to finding out. She was finishing her coffee when he came down.

'Good morning, darling,' he said and pressed her shoulder. He ordered kidneys and bacon from the maid who stood at the sideboard. 'There's nothing like an English breakfast.'

He sat down opposite her at the long oak refectory table and tapped it with his knuckles. 'And look at this table. It was probably made three hundred years ago. History. That's what Africa lacks.' Then, through a mouthful of food, he said, 'We must have a talk.'

'I've an appointment in London,' she said hastily.

'There's no hurry. All the time in the world. The South African papers are doing well. Now we've got to make something of this end. Father never really put his mind to it. The company here was a kind of hobby. A foot in British publishing. But I think I can turn it into something pretty good.'

She choked slightly on her coffee but decided not to begin an argument before she had all the facts – just in case there was anything she had not been told.

She phoned Axe from Winchester station and he met her in London. 'I've found the very place,' he said.

'Where?'

'You wanted Fleet Street. You've got it.'

Suddenly there was an urgency in her life which had been lacking.

'No. 85. The Reuter Building. There's a suite of offices for rent on the second floor. I've taken an option.'

'That's excellent, Monty.'

'You sounded strained on the phone.'

'Let's see the offices and then we'll talk.'

The Reuter Building, dressed in grey granite, was at the bottom of Fleet Street, near Ludgate Circus. It faced, on the opposite side of the street, the *Daily Express*, the *Daily Telegraph* and the *Daily News*. It housed the Reuter's News Agency on the top floors, the others being rented by foreign newspapers and agencies.

'Perfect,' she said, as she wandered round the empty rooms. 'I want to change the name of the company – can I do that?'

'To what?'

'Webster Communications.'

'It sounds more American than English. But why not?'

They went to Ning's Coffee House and sat in one of the high-backed booths and she told him briefly what had occurred.

'I think I can see his ploy,' Axe said. 'He wants control of the English company. The only way he can get that is through you. As things stand, his twenty-five per cent of the equity gives him no power at all. But as the head of the family he's in a much stronger position.'

'But he's not the head of the family. I don't even want him as my husband.'

'Then you'll have to do something about that.'

'Would you – ?'

'I'd rather it wasn't me. I don't handle divorces and anyway I have a personal interest. But I'll find you the best man in London.' He sipped at his coffee and then said, 'He's using you as a stalking-horse.'

'Yes, I know. And I think his ultimate object is to get a foot into Fleet Street. If the papers were his I'm sure he'd sell them and buy a national newspaper.'

'As things stand, he wouldn't get much for them.'

She looked up in alarm. 'Are things bad? You didn't tell me! Aren't we making profits?'

'Not very handsome profits. But first things first. My dear, you mustn't . . .' He paused, selecting the precise words. 'You must not take up your marital life again in *any* sense, no matter what Wilson says or demands.'

'I've not the slightest intention of letting him into my bed, if that's what you're getting at.'

'That's precisely what I'm getting at. No conjugal rights. And you've got to shift him out of the house or get out yourself. Don't share the same roof.'

'I'm damned if I'm getting out,' she said. 'It's my house and it's the children's home. The strange thing is he's being sweet and charming – or at least trying to be. I can hardly recognize the man I married.'

'You're not supposed to.'

'What does that mean?'

'It's an act. Are the servants in hearing distance when he's being this new charming self?'

She recalled breakfast. 'Yes.'

'That's why he's doing it, in case he needs them for evidence. His defence, if you brought an action for divorce, would be: here's this loving husband who is consistently charming to his wife and now she wants to end the marriage. And the servants are trotted into the box to say how loving and charming he is and how unresponsive she is.

'You've got to be careful, Anna. The courts don't like "hard" women. But having said that, you must find some way of getting him out. I know it's not going to be pleasant but it must be done because if you share the house with him a judge will say, well, if you can live amicably under the same roof even without the exercise of conjugal rights – and that'll be a very messy cross-examination with servants talking about who was in what bedroom and when – then why ask for a decree nisi?'

She arrived back in Winchester in mid-afternoon. The day had turned hot and the car was not there to meet her. She waited for twenty minutes, then found a taxi and arrived back at Usbourne feeling sticky and irritable.

Jock's Daimler, which she had inherited along with his driver, was standing at the bottom of the steps. When she enquired why it had not been at the station she was told that Wilson had countermanded the orders. She felt a sudden flare of anger and went to look for him.

She found him in the billiard room. He was leaning over the table, a cigarette between his lips, looking for all the world as though he owned the place.

'You're looking very beautiful,' he said.

She closed the heavy door behind her. 'No one can hear you, Wilson. What happened about the car? It was supposed to meet me at the station.'

'You found a taxi, didn't you?'

'That's not the point. What happened?'

'I had to go to Chichester.'

'What do you mean by countermanding my orders?'

'What do I *mean*? *Your* orders? You're sounding like a head prefect.'

She ignored that. 'Yes, my orders.'

He slowly chalked the tip of the cue. 'I had to see the editor of the *Chichester Argus*. I'm sure you're familiar with the paper. My father owned it. I'm on a fact-finding mission.'

'What facts? And anyway, what have they to do with you?'

'You must be joking. These were my father's newspapers we're talking about. My family's.'

'If he wanted you to have them he'd have left them to you. But it's the other way round. He left them to me!'

'You don't seriously believe that's the end of it, do you? That I'm going to lie down and be trampled on by some bloody gold-digger?'

He leaned over the table and potted a long red.

'I want you out,' she said.

'Look – ' his voice was like butter – 'why get into a fuss about this? We've got an excellent company. With a little rejigging we can turn it into – '

'It's not "we",' she said. 'That's what you don't understand.'

He said, 'I realize you don't want to take up the marriage again. But there's no reason why we shouldn't rub along together. You see, I find Africa too restricting, too provincial. I want to come back and live here. I've got a good man in Johannesburg. He can run things out there and I can do what my father did, except in reverse. Instead of making my base in Africa I'll make it here. I'll live in Usbourne, and the flat in Chelsea, and go out to Africa three or four times a year. We could have what's called an "open" marriage. I don't think that's unreason—'

'Save your breath! You're not going to live in Usbourne, you're not going to have a say in the company, we're not going to pretend to be man and wife and we're not going to have an "open" marriage. You're going to leave Usbourne and we're getting divorced.'

'I suppose Axe has put you up to this.'

'Monty has nothing to do with it.'

'I suppose he's been bedding you. He's a bloody yid, you know.'

'You disgust me.'

'And vice versa. But what if I contest the will? Listen to this and try to imagine how it would sound in court. Here's a woman who was pregnant before her marriage – that's a black mark for a start – and this woman insinuates herself into the emotions of a sickly old man while his only son goes bravely off to report the war and then to take over his father's company and save it from ruination. The wife talks the old man into changing his will . . .'

'That's a lie!'

'The court may take a different view.'

'I want you out of this house! I'm going to tell the servants not to take orders from you, not to feed you, not to make your bed . . . on pain of being sacked. As far as this household is concerned you'll be invisible. I'll fight you with everything I've got, Wilson. I'm not going to allow you to ruin the family and Jock's memory.'

As she went out of the room she slammed the door behind her.

*

The following day she was supposed to be in London but stayed close to the children. A taxi came at half past nine and Wilson left without seeing her.

She phoned Axe and told him what had happened. He listened in silence then said, 'Did you really tell the servants not to feed him?'

'No. I didn't in the end.'

'Thank God for that.'

'Monty, I'm afraid. I can't seem to judge him. I don't know what his next move will be. I just think it'll be something in keeping with his ideas of revenge.'

'You've no idea where he's gone?'

'To the flat in Chelsea probably.'

'I'd have you all here but that would complicate things tremendously in any divorce action. I might be cited as co-respondent. Not that I'd mind but it would make things difficult for you – and they're going to be difficult enough as it is. Look, I've got a weekend place on the Dorset coast near Lulworth. There's no reason why I shouldn't lend you that. Why don't you take the children there, there's room for the nanny as well. They'll be safe and out of the way. The weather's good and you can have a few days' holiday yourself without the need to be looking over your shoulder.'

'That sounds wonderful. Especially for Peter. When could we go?'

'I haven't been down for months. It needs a good airing and a good cleaning. I've got a woman in the village who looks after it but she's not on the phone. I'll send a telegram to her and have it made ready for you. Why don't we say three days from now unless you hear from me? And, Anna . . . don't let the staff know why or where you're going. And you don't have to tell the nanny either.'

'I'm taking the kids off on a touring holiday,' she said. 'We won't know where we're staying until we get there. Right?'

'Perfect.'

For those three days she stayed close to the children, hardly leaving the house. She would stand at the upstairs windows

128

looking out at the parkland, scanning it. Every time the phone rang her heart gave a jerk. But she neither saw nor heard from Wilson. The silence was ominous.

Axe's cottage was in its own little cove and about half a mile from the nearest neighbour. It was as remote as she desired. The weather was warm and the sea was a dazzling blue. She played with the children on the sand as she had never had a chance to do before.

The beach was still covered in barbed wire and concrete tank obstacles and part of it was closed off because of mines, but they managed to find enough space to build sand-castles.

She took off Peter's surgical boot and massaged his withered leg with its livid scars. He loved the water. She began to teach him to swim. Nico begged to be taught too and she promised she would after Peter had learned.

She soon realized her mistake, for Nico reacted badly. He flung sand at Peter and John and generally made a nuisance of himself. She quickly invented a game in the shallow water, holding their hands as the small waves broke on them and the boys shrieked and jumped and laughed and pretended to be afraid.

It was bucket-and-spade weather, long sunny days and only a light breeze. She should have been happy and to a large extent she was but the spectre of Wilson was like a shadow in the back of her mind. But gradually, as one lovely day followed another, she found herself sleeping better, eating better and beginning to relax.

She spent a week in Dorset with the children and then drove back to Usbourne. She was going through her post when the phone rang. It was a former colleague on the *Mercury*, a middle-aged man called Harold Chester who had been one of the first to extend friendship to her when she had joined.

He said, 'I thought you should know there's been someone round the office asking questions about you.'

'About me?' She was puzzled. 'What sort of questions?'

'General questions at first, but then they became more particular: how long you'd been working, what sort of jobs you'd done, had you been successful . . .'

'Who was he?'

'A chap with a London accent. Ordinary-looking but sharp, if you know what I mean.'

'Go on.'

'And then he started talking about the car crash. Said he was from the insurance company.'

'Do they usually ask all those questions?'

'I don't know. Never had a claim.'

When she put down the receiver she found that her hand was shaking. Why would they want to know all about her? Were they investigating her character? Were they thinking of challenging the claim? And if they were it would mean they might find the dentist and then *everything* would come out. She'd rather drop the claim!

She had a sudden thought and dialled the number of Margaret Fowles who had looked after Peter on that terrible day.

'How's the little boy?' Mrs Fowles asked, without warmth.

'Getting on.'

'I was sorry to hear about it. I remember you were in a bit of a rush that day.'

'Was I?' Anna said, grimly. Then, 'I was wondering whether anyone had come to you asking questions about the accident?'

'You mean the police?'

'No. Not the police.'

'There was someone a day or two ago.'

She felt chilled.

'What sort of questions did he ask?'

'He seemed to know more than me. Anyway I don't stand on my doorstep answering strangers. I didn't like the look of him.'

'Did he tell you who he was?'

'He said he was a reporter working for one of the London rags.'

'He wasn't a big man, was he? Square and powerful-looking?'

'Just the opposite. Sharp-faced. Like a rodent.'

Anna stood by the phone after she had replaced the receiver. Could it be the same man? But why call himself an insurance investigator one moment and a London reporter the next?

Unless . . .

Unless he was neither.

130

Suddenly the thought was fully fashioned in her mind and she ran to the car.

She drove furiously across Hampshire and into Dorset, flinging the sedate Daimler round corners and pushing it to the limit on straights. Even so it took her more than three hours to reach the cottage.

She saw smoke coming from the kitchen range as she ran down the path. The sun-umbrella was up on the little beach and she could see a figure beneath it.

The nanny was lying on a towel reading a book.

'Where are the children?' Anna shouted from twenty yards away.

The young woman got to her feet. 'I thought they were with you,' she said. 'Mr Braid said he was taking them to meet you.'

Fourteen

Anna drove as fast as she could into Weymouth and parked on the pavement in front of the police station. She blurted out the facts as she knew them to the duty sergeant in the charge room.

He said, 'Just take it calmly now. First of all give me your name.' They went through her particulars but she was so breathless she could hardly form the words.

At the end of her account, which he forced her to tell in coherent sentences, he laid down his pen and said, 'Kidnapped? But you say this gentleman is their father.'

'Yes, but – '

'May I ask if you are divorced?'

'No.'

'Are your children the subject of any court action?'

'No.'

'Are they wards of court?'

'No.'

'Then, madam, the word "kidnapped" is not applicable.'

'But don't you see – ?'

'No, madam, I do not see. If what you have told me is the truth then what I see is a father coming to fetch his children and removing them to his place of residence which he has a perfect right to do.'

It was useless, she thought. How could she explain? She hurried down the steps and drove back to Usbourne. All the way there the thought of the three children being with Wilson battered at her.

He had known all the while that they had gone to Dorset!

The secrecy was a joke! He'd been having her followed. The man asking questions at the *Mercury*, the man on the doorstep at Mrs Fowles's house hadn't been an insurance investigator at all but a private enquiry agent.

Sometimes rage gripped her so fiercely that the road blurred in front of her, but more often fear for the children turned her stomach to ice.

She must get in touch with Axe. He had been like a rock at the time of her accident. She needed him now as she had never needed him before. She knew that this was a seminal moment in her life. She would have to tell him everything: that she lied about the dentist, that she'd been having an affair with Ben. She would inevitably forfeit his respect and love but there was no help for that. The children were paramount. They were all she had.

But when she phoned his office he was out.

She felt drained, almost cheated. She wanted to release everything into Axe's emotional keeping, to let him tell her what to do. And he wasn't there!

She gathered up her post and went into Jock's study and closed the door behind her. Anything to take her mind off what had happened . . . anything to pass the time until Axe returned.

She flicked through the bills until she came to a large buff-coloured envelope and opened it. There were half a dozen typed pages with a covering letter which came from V. Hardiman and Co., Solicitors, of Bedford Row, London.

The letter was addressed to her and read simply, 'Dear Madam, My client, Mr Wilson Braid, has asked me to send you these copies of affidavits, the originals of which are in our possession.'

She felt suddenly sick with apprehension but glanced at the first typed page.

It read:

I Reginald Sibthorpe, Garage Proprietor, of 42 Cowley Road, Southampton swear upon oath that the following account is true.

For the past few months I have been in negotiations with the owner of the Troutbeck Inn in the County of Hampshire, with the object of leasing fishing rights owned by him. For this purpose I

*made several visits to the Inn. During these visits I observed the
woman later shown to me in photographs and whose name I believe
to be Mrs Wilson Braid, in the company of a gentleman I know
of as Mr Ben Ramsey, a journalist.*

*On several occasions I observed them conducting themselves in
a very loving manner such as holding hands and kissing. On a
separate occasion I saw Mr Ramsey leave one of the upstairs
bedrooms and kiss Mrs Braid who was standing inside the doorway
in a state of semi-nudity . . .*

At the bottom of the page was the seal of a Notary Public and
the signature of Mr Sibthorpe who must, she thought, be the
little man in the tweed cap they had seen occasionally in the
bar.

She remembered him passing the door of their room as Ben
was leaving on their last visit.

She turned to the following page. This was a longer statement
by the owner of the Troutbeck Inn swearing that he had let a
bedroom to a Mr and Mrs Ben Ramsey on twelve separate
occasions. Although Mr Ramsey had paid for a night's stay
each time, they had never in fact spent more than two or three
hours in the room at a time. He too swore that the photograph
he had been shown was that of a woman known to him as Mrs
Ramsey whom he now understood to be Mrs Braid.

Then there was a list of dates on which the room had been
used and a separate list of wine and food consumed, even of
cigars bought.

There was a third deposition from a chambermaid employed
by the Troutbeck Inn. She described the room after the couple
had left it, glasses, bottles, food trays, the untidy bed, even the
discovery of a used contraceptive.

To Anna this was like reading a horror story. She was filled
with feelings of guilt and shame. She knew that if Wilson
brought these witnesses to a divorce hearing not only would
she not obtain a decree nisi, but she might even lose the
children.

What did Wilson mean by these affidavits? A warning? A
basis for negotiation? She had to find him, to talk to him, to
bargain. She thought of phoning the Chelsea flat, but if she

did she would give him the opportunity of spiriting them somewhere else. It would be best to go and surprise him.

She had not been up to the flat since well before Jock's illness. In memory she hated it, she had been unhappy there. In her mind it was Wilson's flat and nothing to do with her. Now, as she parked the car and walked towards the house, she felt her nerves begin to twitch.

Everything looked the same. The street was dowdy and the paint was peeling from the terraces of houses. Chelsea was still recovering from the war. She went up the steps and rang the bell. She waited but there was no answer. She banged on the door.

'There's no one there,' a voice said.

She looked round and saw the large masculine figure of Pamela Kincaid on the pavement. She was wearing a duffel coat and a brown trilby hat, carrying a walking-stick and had her shopping basket in her hand.

'Anna? Is that you? Shit, I thought I'd seen a ghost.'

She put down her stick and bag and opened her arms to enfold Anna but only got her hand.

They exchanged greetings and Anna said, 'I was looking for Wilson.'

'I thought the Bwana was in Africa.'

'Then you haven't seen him?' She was tempted to add, 'And the children?' but Pamela would instantly grasp what had happened and it would be all round Chelsea in an hour and in the gossip columns tomorrow morning.

'As far as I know there hasn't been a soul in the flat since you left. Feel like a transfusion? I've got a drop of gin. Nothing to go with it but to hell with that.'

Anna refused. She was uncertain of what to do next. Again she had screwed herself up to do something and again she had been thwarted.

'You sure you won't change your mind?'

Anna shook her head and said, 'How's everybody?'

'God knows. They all seem to have disappeared. It isn't like war-time. There was a spirit then. But it's gone, vanished.'

Pamela looked older and Anna saw her as a lonely middle-

aged woman for whom the war had been a period of comrade-
ship and 'transfusions' and living for the moment before the
next air-raid threatened to blot everyone out.

'I see Denys occasionally. But that's about all.'

Anna had not thought of Denys for a long time. Now a frisson
fell like a shadow on her skin. 'Is he still in the same room?'
she asked.

'No. He moved in with Ralph for a time but then Ralph was
picked up by an American and whisked off to San Francisco.
Denys pines. Keeps telling himself that Ralph will come back
but it's wishful thinking. San Francisco's just the place for
Ralph. Denys's got another room somewhere down the cheap
end of the King's Road but if you'd like to see him he's working
at that new self-service grocer round the corner.'

'I'd like to very much.'

'Come on then.'

They walked down the King's Road. Pamela had linked her
arm in Anna's. It was like walking with some large, retired
major-general, she thought.

Near Royal Avenue there was a new shop which called itself
a supermarket, a name which Anna had not seen before. She
said goodbye to Pamela and walked into the shop looking for
Denys. Eventually she found him at the far end. He was
standing behind a little counter with a frilly sign on its front
which said, 'Belton's Little Bangers'. He was dressed in a chef's
apron with a tall cap and was frying small sausages on a
hot-plate and offering them to shoppers on cocktail sticks.

He greeted Anna with an embarrassed smile. 'I'm only doing
it between parts,' he said, then he took off his tall hat and
kissed her on the cheek. She saw that he had lost some hair.

'Would you like one, darling?' he said holding up a sausage.
'They're a promotion.'

'No thanks. I'm not hungry.'

'I don't blame you. There's only about ten per cent meat.
God knows what the rest is, I've not had the courage to ask.
Wood pulp probably.'

'Is there anywhere we can talk?'

He looked at his watch. 'What about a drink? I could do with
one after smelling this all day.'

136

'When do you get off?'

'Oh, to hell with it. I'll pack up now.'

They went to the White Hart and sat at a corner table and she caught up on his life. Things had not gone well with him. He had not worked on the stage for more than a year. He showed her his hands. The fingers were beginning to twist and buckle with arthritis.

'And my knees are going. I'll lock solid soon. Still, not to worry. Down the hatch.'

After a couple of large gins Anna felt herself beginning to unwind. She always felt better in Denys's company.

'What about you?' he said. 'Still married to the Bwana? Last I heard he was out in Africa bossing the blacks.'

She began to tell him what had happened to her since they had last met, first hesitantly then more fluently. As she spoke about Jock's legacy to her his eyes widened with pleasure.

'That's fabulous, darling!'

She thought it was like talking to a close cousin or an aunt. Someone who wouldn't make judgements. Then she told him about Ben and Peter and what was happening now.

'Poor Anna,' he said. 'And poor Peter. What a ghastly creature the Bwana is to be sure. And you came up to beard him in his den.'

'Only he wasn't there. And then I saw Pamela and we talked about you and I had an idea.'

'No one's had an idea about me for a long time,' Denys said, and gave her his old roguish grin. 'Tell me. The filthier the better.'

'I need your help.'

His eyes were suddenly wary. 'Go on.'

'Do you remember that night we went to the party in Oakley Street. The night we found Wilson and Ralph in – '

'Of course I remember!'

'I want you to swear an affidavit that you saw them in bed together.'

'Why?'

'Wilson's got people to swear affidavits about Ben and me. The only way I can see to hold him off is to give him some of his own medicine. It's the only thing he understands.'

'But that would involve Ralph.'

'Pamela tells me Ralph's gone to San Francisco with an American.'

'She could never keep her bloody mouth shut!'

'Well, it's true, isn't it?'

'What if it is? It's only temporary. He said so when he left. He said he'd be back. He said he was like a bad penny. That I'd never get rid of him.'

'Denys, you don't really believe that.'

'Why the hell shouldn't I? It's the only thing that keeps me going.'

'Darling, you *know* what San Francisco's like. If he falls out with his American friend it doesn't mean he'll come back to you.'

Denys's face had drawn in. His eyes were angry. 'What would you know about it? You know nothing about us. Oh, you think you do but – '

'I know exactly how you felt and how you feel. I sat with you all those evenings and listened to you. I've seen the scars on your wrists. Darling, of course I know!'

'I'm sorry.'

'Please help me. Think about the children. For God's sake, unless I do something fast I may never see them again.'

The anguish in her voice roused him.

'The point is, if Ralph ever found out it would be the end. I mean the finish!'

'But why should he find out?'

'Because it could go to court. Think what the tabloids would do with it. Newspaper proprietor found in bed with young gigolo. That's what they'd say.'

'It'll never get to court. I promise you. Never.'

He shook his head. 'I'd do anything to help but you're asking me – '

'I'll give you money,' she said. 'I'll give you a thousand pounds. No one will ever know.'

'A thousand pounds . . .' he said. 'It's usually thirty pieces of silver.'

'I'll make it two, three thousand. Whatever you want. For God's sake, Denys, I can't put a price on my children!'

He was silent for some moments and then he said slowly, 'When do you want it?'

'Now. We'll go to a notary. Have it sworn properly.'

He shrugged. 'Why fool myself? He probably wouldn't come back anyway.'

It was late when she arrived at Bedford Row but the lights were still on in Victor Hardiman's office. His secretary had gone but Anna kept her finger on the street bell until someone came.

'I want to see Mr Hardiman,' she said.

'I'm Victor Hardiman.'

She was surprised. He was younger than she had thought, not much more than thirty. Tall and slender, with light hair smoothed back. He was elegantly dressed in a dark blue suit and foulard silk tie with suede ankle boots.

'I'm afraid the office is closed for the day. If you ring my sec—'

'I'm Mrs Wilson Braid.'

'Oh, I see.' His voice had an exaggerated drawl but his eyes were sharp as razors.

'I don't want to come in. All I want is to deliver this to you.' She handed him a copy of the affidavit Denys had sworn. 'I would like you to read it and let my husband have it, preferably tonight. You can tell him that unless I hear from him by tomorrow evening I shall release it to the William Hickey gossip column of the *Daily Express*.'

He stared at her for a moment then said, 'Very well, Mrs Braid. It shall be as you say.'

All the following day Anna waited by the telephone. At noon Axe phoned but she kept the conversation short.

At two o'clock it rang again. It was Victor Hardiman. He said, 'Your children will be at my office this afternoon at five o'clock, Mrs Braid. Would you like to come and fetch them?'

She felt a sudden release of tension, as though a knot in her heart had come undone. 'I'll be there,' she said.

'Your husband asked me to make his excuses. He felt sure you would not mind if he missed the meeting.'

She was driven up in the Daimler and reached Bedford Row on the dot of five. She had stopped at Harrods on the way and bought a train set for Nico, a speedboat for Peter and a paint-box for John.

'I'm Mrs Braid,' Anna said to Hardiman's secretary as she entered the office. 'Are my children here?'

'Yes, Mrs Braid.'

Anna felt the last vestiges of apprehension disappear.

She followed the secretary along a corridor and into an office.

'My darlings!' Anna said, throwing her arms wide. Peter came clumping across the floor to her as fast as he could, but Nico stayed back. She held Peter tightly then said to Nico, 'Aren't you going to give me a hug?'

But Nico's eyes were troubled.

'What is it, darling?' she said, gathering him to her.

He struggled and she released him.

'I hate him,' Nico said.

'Who?'

'The man.'

'Well, you don't have to worry about him any longer. Where's John?'

The two boys stood like statues in front of her and her happiness disappeared in a single moment.

'Tell me! Is Johnny hurt?'

'He took him,' Peter said.

'Who?'

'The man. Father.'

'Oh my God!'

She ran into the secretary's office. 'Where's Mr Hardiman?'

The secretary's eyes wore the same look she had seen in Nico's. 'Through there. He's expecting you, Mrs Braid.'

Victor Hardiman was seated at his desk and rose elegantly.

'Where's John? Where's my son?'

Hardiman picked up an envelope and handed it to her.

'You knew, didn't you?' she cried.

'Open it please, Mrs Braid.'

She ripped open the envelope. It was from Wilson:

By the time you read this, John and I will be well on our way to Africa.

Did you really think you would get everything?

140

When your anger has cooled, reflect on this: if you try to get him back you will have to fight in the South African courts, a different legal system from the British. Everything will be revealed. Certainly you will tarnish me but you will not escape.

However, if that means nothing to you then remember this, Peter will find out about you and Ramsey and the lies you told. What that will do to him no one knows.

My advice to you is settle for what you've got and I will settle for what I've got. And I shall not contest a divorce . . .

Fifteen

There would come a time in the months and years that followed when Anna would be free – for days at a stretch – of that moment in Victor Hardiman's office. It wasn't a case of forgetting, but rather one of not thinking about it.

But for a long time she was raw with the memory. It jumped out at her when she saw in print the name 'John', or when she saw someone else's little boy. At first she was unable to see his clothes, his toys or his empty cot without feeling a combination of rage and loss.

If she had not had an affair with Ben she would not have taken Peter into Winchester, there would have been no crash; if there had been no crash, there would have been no lever for Wilson to use against her and she would not have lost John.

If . . . It was a word that came to haunt her.

She wanted someone to whom she could unburden herself and thereby gain some relief from guilt. Monty was the obvious person but she couldn't tell him without explaining everything, or at least without him suspecting that there was a great deal more to tell. This might weaken his love and respect for her, which she needed just as much. In a strange way, although their ages were much the same, he had assumed a paternal role in her life.

She knew that she was not fooling him when she said that she and Wilson had come to an agreement over the children. He had looked at her closely. But as the months passed and the divorce proceedings got under way and as they became embroiled in the company's business, the awkwardness faded.

The children recovered quickly from their experience and were soon themselves again. But Anna found she could not refuse them anything. She knew she was spoiling them yet she could not help herself.

The orthopaedic specialist had suggested more than once that Peter would benefit from swimming, so she built a heated indoor pool at Usbourne and gave it to him on his next birthday. She and the staff stood at the edge of the pool on which floated a specially made birthday cake decorated with ribbons.

But her gesture did not turn out as she had anticipated.

Peter was delighted but Nico hung back and said, 'Will I be able to swim in it?' His face wore a worried frown.

'Of course you will, darling.'

'But it is my pool, isn't it?' Peter said.

She saw the trap she had prepared for herself. She could not say it was only a bit of birthday fun. He had taken the gift seriously. Instead she answered his question with a question. 'But you won't mind if Nico swims in it?'

Peter thought for a moment and said gravely, 'No, I don't mind. He's my brother.'

But Nico would not go near the pool. He sulked and finally Anna had to ask Peter to agree that half the pool was Nico's and half his. Peter seemed to realize this was a compromise he would have to accept. Even so, Nico made life difficult for all of them for a while.

One day soon after this Peter lost his surgical boot. As he grew stronger he was leaving off the boot for an hour or two at a time because, he said, it eased the Unowot. Nico was instantly suspected of hiding it as he had done several times before.

'But I didn't,' he protested. 'I didn't touch it.'

A search soon revealed it in his toy cupboard and Anna was so angry that she said, 'You little liar!' and smacked his face. It was the first time she had ever struck one of her children and she was instantly appalled and horrified.

'I'm sorry, darling. I didn't mean to do that.' She tried to gather him in her arms but Nico fought and screamed and fled to his bedroom. What made things worse was the discovery that one of the maids had tidied the boot away by mistake.

When she told Axe he said, 'He'll get over it and so will you. Most children get smacked sometimes. I know I did. It's not the end of the world.'

She did get over it and so did Nico but it lingered in her mind for a long time like a bad dream.

The time came for the boys to go to school. She thought of employing a tutor for Peter so he would not have to endure the rough-and-tumble of a boarding school, but Axe talked her out of it.

'Let him find his place in life,' he said. 'It's going to be difficult at first, but if you mollycoddle him now you'll turn him into a semi-invalid who'll always have an excuse for failure.'

She saw the logic of his argument so she sent the two boys to a prep school near Usbourne. Because Nico was the elder and more robust she begged him to take care of Peter. 'He's your brother and he isn't as strong as you and he won't be as strong as other boys of his age so you must look after him. Don't let the other boys take advantage of him and don't let them bully him. You'll have to stand up for him.'

Nico looked uneasy at the responsibility being placed on his shoulders but said he would try. 'I'm sure you will, darling.'

But he ran headlong into a problem no one had foreseen: his name and the fact that he was an adopted child. From the time he had been old enough to understand anything, Anna had told him about his parents. She had told him everything except the fact that they had vanished. Instead, she had told him that they had died.

She reasoned that to have them inexplicably lost might produce traumas for him later. Death was a fact and one could get used to it. She had not been able to take the route of many adoptive parents by telling Nico she had chosen him, but she was able honestly to say she had attended his birth and that she had brought him up and loved him and been just as much a mother as his own mother. Whether he understood this she was not certain, but sooner or later he would.

And so they had kept the name Meissner.

None of this had bothered Nico or anyone else in the family, but now the name Meissner, so soon after the war, had become

144

a dangerous label. He was bullied and humiliated and it was Peter who came to *his* defence.

The headmaster told Anna that on several occasions he had to break up fights in which Peter and Nico were taking on four or five other boys.

Anna was horrified and she talked it over with Axe.

'This is the kind of thing that happened during the First World War,' he said. 'People changed their Germanic names to English, even little dachshunds were stoned because their origins were German. But I had no idea it had come back.'

'I'm worried about Peter.'

'I should have thought that Nico was the one who – '

'Don't you see? Peter's so loyal. He could be seriously injured.'

When she spoke again to the headmaster he said, 'I'd suggest putting Nicholas in another school, but I don't think it would be any better. The young of the human animal can be extremely cruel and my colleagues tell me that the same anti-German feeling is rife in all our prep schools.'

After one incident in which Peter was sent to the sanitorium with a possible fracture of his collar-bone, Anna knew she had to act.

Axe had heard of a school in Switzerland. It was called the Helvetian Academy and had been started in the twenties as a school for the sons of League of Nations' employees. Now it had become a place for the offspring of the very rich.

'I don't like the idea of a kind of Drones' Club,' she said.

'Look at it this way, the education is first class and the name Meissner won't matter a damn. If you let him remain at school in this country he could suffer permanent psychological damage.'

They talked it over several times before she said, 'All right, I'll write to the Academy.'

The following term Nico went off to school in Switzerland while Peter remained in England. His own status had been greatly improved by defending his adoptive brother.

The problems that had arisen over Nico, and the number of times she had discussed them with Axe, had caused Anna to take a close look at all their lives. Peter and Nico needed a father. And who better than Monty whom she was already drawing into the family circle? She did not feel sexually drawn towards him. But she did feel a warmth and gratitude, a kind of love. And she knew that his own feelings had not changed. But was warmth and gratitude enough to sustain a marriage?

For the first time in years Anna had no children at home. She took Axe up on his offer of the house in Eccleston Square, near Victoria Station. She said to him, 'There doesn't seem much point in buying just part of it, specially if the children come up to London in the holidays.'

They agreed on a price and he drew up the papers. The house was to be bought by the company and leased to Anna. This again brought up the problem of the company's profitability. Now that she had graduated from Axe's private school of economics and knew how to read a balance sheet, she reminded him that he had once told her of an idea he had for the company.

'It wouldn't have done much for you then, but I was thinking about it again the other day,' he said. 'The country's shaking off the post-war blues. The economy will start to grow soon. Perhaps the time has come.'

'Don't be mysterious.'

'There's nothing mysterious about it, it couldn't be simpler. But hang on till tomorrow, then I can show you.'

The following day he picked her up in his Bentley and they set off through the south of England.

'Have you ever seen the whole of your kingdom? We'll have what royalty used to call a "progress".'

They drove first through Hampshire then Sussex and back into Surrey, visiting Winchester, Southampton, Portsmouth and Chichester, and back through Haslemere, Guildford and Farnham. In each place Axe stopped the car outside the local newspaper office with its adjoining printing works. The buildings were neglected and needed refurbishing. Some of these print works covered half a block. Axe marked the position of each of the buildings on a street-map of the relevant town.

When they returned to Usbourne he spread the street-maps out on Jock's desk and said to her, 'Do you notice any similarities?'

She wasn't sure what he meant and did not want to make a fool of herself, for an air of smug mystery had surrounded him all day. She looked closely at the pencil outlines of the buildings she owned.

'Only that they all seem to be in the centre of the towns.'

'Precisely. They're all on prime sites. If my guess is right and the country is on the brink of a boom, the first need will be for building sites in city centres.'

'I don't follow, Monty. What's that got to do with selling newspapers?'

'I'm suggesting that you sell most of these properties.'

She was stunned. 'But that'll mean closing down the papers. The end of the company.'

'No, not – '

'And all those people losing their jobs! Why? Just so that the company can make a profit? I'm surprised at you, Monty.'

He was giving himself a drink and his face flushed with annoyance. 'You don't seem to understand, Anna, that it simply isn't viable to have a printing works in each of these towns. Most of the plant dates from the turn of the century. It's old-fashioned machinery in old-fashioned buildings. Everything is labour intensive, with large staffs needed to keep it going, and every bloody printer is a member of the most militant union in the country.'

'But, Monty – '

He held up his hand. 'Hear me out. My idea isn't to close down newspapers. Quite the contrary. But to print them in a specially designed, centralized, modern printing works.'

'All the papers?'

'All of them. The journalists will remain in their local towns but in different premises and send their copy through to the print works. And everything will be distributed from there. That's the key to it; distribution. You can then sell the buildings occupied by the individual print works and invest that money in more newspapers or magazines or whatever you like.'

He reached into his pocket for a small notebook and said, 'I've done some rough estimates on what the properties might fetch.'

147

She saw a final figure with a series of noughts at the bottom of a column, and blinked.

'That's a conservative estimate. It'll take time and the unions won't like it because of the job losses but if we can show them that if we don't the company will go under – '

'Will it?'

'We can't stand still, Anna. Times are changing and we have to change with them.'

'I wonder what Jock would have said.'

'You can't look over your shoulder at Jock's ghost. These papers were a hobby. You don't try to make a profit from a hobby. I think Jock liked the old machinery and the smell of hot metal. He once said it reminded him of his youth.'

Axe was difficult to argue with when he was in full flow, she thought. He knew his subject and she didn't. All she could think of was people losing their jobs, of families and wives without a breadwinner. But if Axe was right they would have to prune to save the whole tree. If they didn't it would come crashing down and *everyone* would suffer.

They talked about the idea several times and slowly she found herself being convinced. She could see the logic, she could see the need, she could see the elegance of his grand design, and yet . . .

Finally she said to him, 'I think you're right, Monty, but I want you to put your faith where your mouth is.'

'What's that supposed to mean?'

'I want you to join the company. Become its chief executive. I asked you once before but you weren't ready then. Are you ready now?'

He shook his head slowly. 'I'll work with you. I'll be your non-executive chairman if you want me to. But I won't be an employee, I won't work *for* you.' He smiled to take the sting out of his words.

'Why? Because I'm a woman?'

'I thought you'd ask me that. And I'm not certain of the answer. If I said yes, I wouldn't be telling the truth, and if I said no, the same would apply. Let's just say I value my freedom too much.'

And that's where she had to leave matters. It was unsatisfactory but there was nothing she could do about it. So, with Monty's help, she began the long process of heaving Webster Communications into the latter half of the twentieth century.

Sixteen

If Anna had considered in advance what running a small news-paper group would involve she might have said that it would be a bit like her job on the *Mercury* but on an enlarged scale. She would have been wrong. She did little or no editorial work. Everything was managerial.

She was running a company, as Axe had warned her, which was old and in need of cash injections. Much of her time was spent trying to stem the haemorrhaging of more money. Her worn machines were constantly breaking down and she was forced to spend time finding extra printing capacity; newsprint was in short supply, which meant journeys to Finland and Norway to negotiate contracts for paper; senior managers and editors became ill, died, left and had to be replaced; news agency contracts came up for renewal; the fleet of delivery vans was ancient and distribution managers were on the phone several times a month asking for replacements.

But her main task was dealing with the print unions which had grown stronger and stronger over the years until they were run like fiefdoms, with jobs for life for the favoured few.

Feather-bedding, overmanning, official strikes, wildcat strikes, meetings during working hours . . . she found that she was paying top wages to men who had no actual jobs, some of whom did not even bother to come in to work except on Fridays to draw their pay. The faintest criticism from management led to a threat of strike action.

Her managers were not much better. Weak, status conscious,

work-shy, weekend orientated and afraid of militant shop stewards, they were little help.

She began to realize what running a group like this in the late 1950s and early 1960s really meant. It meant money, money, money . . . and worry.

And time.

She worked from early morning until late at night. She never had enough *time*. She ran Webster Communications from her offices in the Reuter Building. At first she did little without referring to Axe but gradually she got the feel of the business and was able to make her own decisions and stand by them – and, of course, suffer from them when they went wrong.

Slowly, too, she began to judge the staff she had inherited. Some she found wanting, others had been kept back by the seniority system. She shifted some sideways, offered others early retirement, and leap-frogged others into senior positions. The company groaned and heaved with apprehension and resentment, but eventually she surrounded herself with a young team of bright managers who did not simply tell her what they thought she wanted to know, but were prepared to fight for money and changes and structural reorganization.

As she became more successful she realized two things. First, that Axe was right about the economic climate. At the end of the 1950s corporate Britain accelerated; property prices rose sharply, especially in city centres. She began to sell her prime sites. A new print works was built at a central point and all her weekly and some of her daily newspapers were printed there and sent out by fleets of vans. Soon she began to see a change for the better in the balance sheets.

Secondly, she realized that this kind of newspaper publishing held little appeal for her. It was both too small and too large. The papers were parochial but spread over a huge area. There was little excitement for her in provincial journalism.

She said to Axe, 'If I'm going to run a newspaper I want it to be an important one and an exciting one and I want it to be at the centre of things. I want the best, Monty. I don't want to be running things "from" Fleet Street, I want to be running things "in" Fleet Street. I want my own newspaper.'

'Have you thought of the costs involved in starting one?

Anyway, the other owners would kill the idea before you put together a dummy.'

'I don't want to start one, I want to buy one.'

'That presupposes someone wants to sell, and there isn't anyone that I know of.'

'I don't mean now. I'm content to go on as things are, to make this company as good as I can – but then one day, if the chance comes along . . .'

In spite of the long hours she worked, she missed the children terribly. She looked forward all week to seeing Peter each weekend either at Usbourne or in London. He was in his teens now and growing fast. He was dark-haired and good-looking. People saw in him his mother's eyes. But Anna looked more closely. Was his mouth Cuno's? His forehead? His chin? Her memory of Cuno's face was imprinted on her but she could not – or *would* not? – see a likeness.

She wrote once or twice each week to Nico in Switzerland telling him what she planned for their next vacation – she always took hers to coincide with the boys' – or what she had been doing with Peter. But it was John's absence which nagged at her. She received little news of him. Her divorce went through and it seemed as though there was never going to be an opportunity to see him.

Axe went out to Africa to visit his parents. She made him promise to see John and take photographs of him. The snapshots showed a solemn boy dressed in a school blazer and short trousers. She realized, with anguish, that she would not have recognized her own son if she had passed him in the street.

Axe told her that he had been put down for one of the best private schools in the country. But that wasn't the kind of news she wanted. She questioned him about details – how he spoke and how he smiled and what he thought and had he liked his presents, and had he asked about her? Above all, was he happy?

Axe did his best to answer them. Yes, he lied, Johnny had asked specifically about her, wanted to know all about her – his lie was rewarded when he saw the look in her eyes – and as far as he could tell he was an ordinary, happy little boy. This made

152

her glad for John but sad for herself: his happiness owed nothing to her, nor would she witness it.

She asked about Wilson. Axe told her that he had not remarried but over the years had had a succession of mistresses.

'Isn't that what all grown boys want?' she said.

He looked suddenly uncomfortable and saw a flash of an embarrassment she had not seen before.

The photographs of John made her realize how quickly he was growing up; how quickly all the children were growing up, and the corollary – how quickly the years were passing for her as well.

Running a newspaper company was exciting and exacting and to a certain extent fulfilled her, but sometimes, at night when she could not sleep, she would feel a deep sense of loneliness. She had never had a successful domestic relationship with a man and she began to feel that perhaps she should. She told herself she wanted a successful marriage, wanted the feeling of sharing her life with someone who was sharing his with her.

Sometimes, during these wakeful nights, she would decide to put her relationship with Axe to the test. But then, when morning came and the worry and loneliness faded, she baulked. It just seemed too clinical. If she loved him there would be no need for a test.

Then news came from Switzerland which forced her hand. She received a letter from the school saying that Nico had been accused of stealing, that he had been expelled, and would she come and fetch him.

She caught the first plane and was in Zürich by midafternoon. She took a taxi from the airport and drove up the winding mountain road to a castle whose turrets and towers might have come from the overheated mind of Ludwig, the mad King of Bavaria.

As she crossed the courtyard her eye was drawn to the array of expensive cars parked below the walls. There were Alfa Romeos, Lancias, Spanish Pegasos, gull-winged Mercedes and a dozen Porsches. She knew these belonged not to the staff but the senior boys.

The academy had changed since the days when it took in the

sons of diplomats and League of Nations' officials. She saw young Arab men in flowing robes, black Africans, and she knew there were Indians and Americans, some English, a few Germans and French: but wherever they came from their parents had to be very, very rich.

There were few rules in the ordinary sense. Senior boys could smoke, drink in moderation, keep sports cars or horses, spend weekends skiing – or in bed with their girl-friends so long as they did not get them pregnant, and even then there were doctors who, for a fee, would attend to that. Surprisingly, the education was of the best and many old boys had done well for themselves in business, medicine and the law. Others had no need to do anything after leaving school except count their money or be weighed in diamonds.

Theft in such a place was more serious than in ordinary schools where petty larceny was endemic. Here it was an onslaught against the natural order of things and therefore anarchic, which frightened the school authorities. Nico had 'stolen' a radio.

'But I gave you a radio,' Anna said. 'You didn't need to take one.'

They were in Nico's room. Each boy had his own room and his was up at the top of the castle under the leads with a view over a darkly forested valley. A river ran like a silver thread below and skeins of mist encircled the mountain peaks. It suddenly reminded Anna of the slope down to Altenkirchen when she and the Meissners had arrived at the Austrian border that terrible day.

His room was filled with expensive playthings, a Tandberg stereo with Leak speakers, a Grundig reel-to-reel tape recorder, the latest ski boots, racing skis, an M3 Leica, a silk dressing-gown from Sulka. She had given him all this or at least given him the money to buy it.

Once Axe had looked surprised when she had bought Nico a gold Parker pen for his birthday. She had seen the look and instantly flared up. 'He didn't ask to be born,' she said. 'He didn't ask for his parents to vanish, he didn't ask to be brought up by me. Anyway it's not your business, you're not his father.'

Axe was taken aback by her aggression and instantly she

regretted it. 'I'm sorry, Monty. It's just that . . . I've never had enough time with Nico. There's always been . . . Well, you know all about it.'

Now, in his room, she tried to look dispassionately at him. He was dressed in strawberry corduroys and a white American sweat-shirt three or four sizes too big for him. He was in his late teens and going through an unattractive phase physically and emotionally. His face was dotted with spots and his manner was resentful and challenging.

'But you've got a radio,' she repeated. 'A good one. You didn't need to take anyone else's.'

'It's broken.'

'Couldn't you have had it mended?'

'I wanted to listen to the football commentary.'

'Couldn't you have asked someone to lend you a radio?'

'They don't lend things here.'

'Couldn't you have listened in someone else's room?'

'I wanted to listen in my room.'

'So you simply decided to take someone else's?'

'Yes. Anyway I only borrowed it.'

'The headmaster says the boy you took it from is an Arab.'

'Yeah. A desert prince. He's pathetic. I hate him.'

'Why do you hate him?'

'Everybody hates him.'

It took some time to unravel this. The Arab was the son of one of the Saudi princes and the wealthiest boy in the school. He and Nico had had a feud for a long time, the origins of which were lost in the complexities of juvenile hatreds and humiliations. Reading between the lines she realized that the taking of this particular radio had been a calculated provocation.

The school authorities, she discovered, had begun by adopting the view that Nico had just borrowed the radio and that the whole thing was unimportant. But there were half a dozen Arabs at the school and they forced the headmaster's hand. Either he did something about Nico or they would speak to their parents. All kinds of things reared up: racism, the possibility of the boys being withdrawn, negative publicity. It was simply easier to get rid of Nico.

She helped him pack and took him to a hotel in Zürich. After a silent, morose dinner, she went to his room to say good night and sat on his bed.

'Don't worry, darling. We'll work things out.' She tried to take his hand but he moved it. 'We'll find another school.'

He was reading and did not look up. He put his finger on his place on the page.

She rose and went to the door. 'Maybe I've spoiled you,' she said.

'Why not?' he said. 'You spoil Peter.'

Some weeks after Anna had found a place for Nico in a 'progressive' co-educational school in Dorset known for its handling of 'difficult' cases, she said to Axe, 'All work and no play makes Jill a dull girl.'

He looked at her carefully, his antennae quivering, and said, 'Why not let me take you to a show and then we'll have supper.'

'Exactly what I had in mind, Monty,' she said. 'But please, no Brecht. I'd fall asleep.'

'I promise. What about *Orpheus in the Underworld*? It's on at Sadler's Wells.'

It was light and frothy. She should have enjoyed herself but she was very aware of Monty's physical presence in the seat beside her. Since his declaration of love a long time before, he had been careful never to touch her, even accidentally. Now, as though testing her reactions, he rested his hand on her shoulder to attract her attention, and when he leaned close to speak to her in the darkness, his hair touched hers. He had brought a box of Harrods' chocolates and had ordered champagne for the intervals. He was almost too attentive.

He looked what he was, a successful lawyer. He was impeccably dressed in a dark grey worsted suit and a white silk shirt. His hair was brushed back so that his head was one smooth dome.

Why did she feel tense and uncomfortable? Was it his size and shape? Was it the feeling that he was a father-figure and that what she was contemplating was incest? He reminded her of Orson Welles and like Welles he was not an unattractive man, there was just something . . .

The opera ended and they made their way out to the car.

Instead of driving back to the West End he turned north. 'I thought we'd have supper in Hampstead.'

He pulled up outside his house in Church Row. It was the first time she had been there late at night and she realized that by candle-light the club-like drawing-room lost its sombreness. On a side table there was a smoked salmon mousse, duck in aspic, and a mound of profiteroles. He opened a bottle of Krug.

'This looks magnificent, Monty. I take it you did it all?'

'The salmon's a new recipe. I hope it's all right.'

He excused himself and returned some moments later. He had removed his jacket and tie and put on a long dark-green paisley silk dressing-gown and had knotted a white scarf at his throat. He went to the radiogram and put on a record. As he did so she smiled to herself. The gown and the scarf were straight out of a movie. Melvin Douglas might have been wearing them. But while most men's music for seduction might have been Nat King Cole or Ella Fitzgerald, only Monty would have put on Bruckner's Seventh Symphony.

Her tension returned. She picked at her food and noticed that he was not eating much either. When they had finished he gave her another glass of wine and sat beside her on the big leather chesterfield.

'It was an experiment,' he said, waving at the food.

But she knew he did not only mean the food. It was a symbol for the evening. *That* was the experiment. He put his arm along the back of the chesterfield and she felt his fingers touch her neck.

He began to talk in a slightly high voice about smoked salmon mousse and the difference between London and Scottish smokings. She was shaken by a gust of laughter, almost spilling her drink.

Monty flushed and said, 'You find salmon amusing?'

She put her glass down and caught his face between both hands and kissed him firmly on the lips. 'I'm fascinated by salmon mousse but are we going to play cat-and-mouse here or are we going to the comfort of your bed?'

She saw the same quick flash of angry embarrassment cross his face. 'If that is what you want,' he said.

'Yes, Monty, that's what I want.'

The next half hour would linger in her memory for a long time. Anna's sexual experience did not equip her to deal with someone like Monty. The moment they went into the bedroom his anxiety was obvious. She could see his hands trembling as he folded down the counterpane as neatly as the best chambermaid. The room had been specially prepared. There was a second box of chocolates, a bottle of cognac, cigarettes. He filled two snifters with brandy and said, 'To us.'

'To us, Monty.'

She sipped at hers and felt it go down her throat like fire. He threw most of his into his mouth and then excused himself. While he was gone she undressed quickly and slipped into bed. A few moments later he returned. He had removed his clothes but was still wearing his silk gown. Now he switched out the light and the room was plunged into complete darkness, for the velvet curtains did not let in the streetlights.

She heard the clink of the bottle on the glass and said, 'Where are you, Monty?'

'Right here.'

She put out both hands and touched his body. He was sitting on the edge of the bed. His skin felt cold and clammy. She heard him swallow the brandy then he came into bed beside her.

He lay inert but breathing heavily. She waited for him. He remained still. She sensed that she would have to take over. She put her arms around him and it was like putting them round a tailor's dummy. He felt stiff, rigid. She began to regret what she had started but knew there was no opting out now.

Somehow she had to get him to relax. She rose on her elbows and kissed him. He kept his lips together primly like a schoolboy and she began to wonder if he had been in bed with a woman before.

She stroked his body, gradually moving her hand further down. She felt a spasm run through his muscles. Her fingers reached his scrotum. The penis was small and flaccid.

She began to realize that something was seriously wrong. She tried in vain to stimulate him. She kissed him again. 'What can I do for you?' she whispered. He did not reply.

He turned to her and she heard a choked sob. 'I'm sorry, Anna. So sorry.'

She held his face against her breasts as she might have held a child. 'It's all right, Monty. Don't worry. It doesn't matter.'

But she knew it *did* matter. And as she held him, she was wondering how this would affect their future relationship. She knew she would have to be more sensitive and more careful. She had laughed at him for talking about salmon mousse. Would he remember it? Would he forgive her?

After a while he turned away and she heard the bottle and glass again. Then there was a flare of a lighter as he lit a cigarette.

'You can give me one,' she said. She smoked rarely.

'I love you,' Monty said.

'I know you do.'

'I want you to know it isn't you.'

'I don't think that.'

'I thought that because I loved you . . . I thought it would be different . . . I've been to psychiatrists . . .'

'Monty, you don't have to tell me. It doesn't matter.'

'One of them said, go to brothels. I did. They didn't help. One said was it boys or children that I wanted? I was appalled . . . No one seems to know why . . . The experts say that some people are like this and that we must learn to live with it . . . But I find it hard . . .'

'You've got everything else, Monty. You're a marvellous lawyer, a marvellous businessman, a marvellous friend . . .'

'Friend! It's like a dirty word to me!'

He took her back to her house in Victoria in the early hours. In the bathroom she looked at herself in the long mirror. 'Some femme fatale!' she said to her image and, smiling ruefully, went off to bed. But she couldn't sleep. She lay thinking about him, wondering how she would retain that friendship he thought he so despised.

But when they met again two days later he gave no hint of what had happened and she, taking her cue from him, tried to blank it out of their shared experience. Once or twice she caught him looking at her with a longing that turned her heart.

She worried about him. But not for long, for when she went down to Usbourne that weekend there was a letter waiting for her from Ben. The address was a private hospital in Surrey. The letter simply read: 'I'm about to go under the surgeon's knife. I'm scared. Would you come and hold my hand? Love, Ben.'

Seventeen

'It's called the Beauty Parlour,' Ben said, indicating the hospital. 'That's what the flyers used to call it during the war. It was an RAF hospital and they sent the bad burn cases here.'

He and Anna were walking in the wooded grounds. It was dusk and in the half-light he looked thinner, even gaunt. He was wearing his hair modishly long, allowing it to cover the scarring on his left ear. But the remainder of the damage to his face seemed more obvious to her now than when they had been having their affair.

His letter had come as a sudden gut-twisting shock, bringing back into sharp focus that last meeting: the rain, the crash, even the smell of the hospital in Winchester when she had waited for the verdict on Peter.

A voice inside her head had told her not to go to see Ben, but the letter was like a cry in the dark. Those brief words hinted at loneliness and anguish and she could not help responding.

She still felt conflicting emotions. In one sense he was a stranger, in another more close to her than any other person.

He was still talking to her about the hospital and the operation on his face. It was due the following morning and he was apprehensive.

'But at least I know it's the best place there is for what I want, and I guess I can thank the war for that.'

She had expressed surprise that he had waited this long and had learned that, while she had been building up Webster Communications, he had been going from one war to the next: Korea, the Congo and Algeria. He had the leathery look of someone who has been out in all weathers and slept rough; of someone who has been drinking too much and eating too little.

He was talking about the plastic surgeon. 'He'll rebuild the eyebrow. He's going to take skin from the inside of my arm. And he'll do the same here.' He touched the pitted scarring along his jawline. 'There's nothing much they can do about my ear. But at least when they've finished and if it works, I won't look quite so much like the Phantom of the Opera.'

She might have said several things: that he'd never looked like that to her, that she had stopped noticing the scars after the first few hours – but she had said all that before. There wasn't much point now since he had decided to go ahead.

The wind was chilly and they went in. His room was small. He offered her the single chair then propped up the pillows on the bed and leaned against them. He brought out a bottle of whisky and gave himself twice the amount he gave her.

All he could talk about was war. There had been no time for marriage. He'd written two books. She had seen neither. He was now writing a third.

He asked her about herself and she told him briefly. It didn't seem to sink in. He kept returning to his own life, asking if she knew so-and-so of the *Mail* or so-and-so of the *Express*. Some of them were famous correspondents whose bylines were in the national papers.

These were men and women who seemed to move in a group from one war-torn hotel to another, who followed their wars in helicopters and in taxis. He spoke of Algerian cafés blown to pieces by *plastique* and of photographers and reporters blown to pieces with them.

As he spoke she thought of the man who had said he would give up this kind of journalism to settle down with her and the children. She realized how impossible that dream had been. He would always have had to cover just one more war, one last battle, one final attack.

But there was still something special between them. She felt it and she knew he felt it too. He was the one man she had ever truly loved and she wondered if she fulfilled a similar role in his life.

When she left him he kissed her on the lips and held her. 'Come and see me again,' he said.

She felt an uncharacteristic constriction of the throat. 'Of course I will.' Then she wished him luck.

On the way back to London she carried in her mind the picture of him sitting on the hospital bed, a drink in one hand and a cigar in the other, and his face half turned away from the light in that self-conscious way which delineated him more clearly in her mind than anything else.

She went to see him later the following day. The nurse said, 'You'll get a bit of a shock, but please don't make it obvious.'

He was still drowsy from the anaesthetic and his face was in bandages. He had a tube in his mouth and holes had been cut for his eyes. He put out his hand and she took it and sat by the bed. She wasn't shocked by his appearance. She had been expecting the bandages. He looked like something in a movie, perhaps from *The Invisible Man*.

She did not stay long for he could not talk but when she was leaving she searched out the sister in charge and discovered that it would be weeks before the bandages were removed and that there was no reason for him to stay in hospital.

The next time she visited him she said, 'I don't want you going to a nursing home. The staff at Usbourne have nothing to do when I'm not there. You'll be far more comfortable.'

'What about the proprieties?' he said, mumbling from behind the bandages.

'To hell with the proprieties. I won't be there most of the time anyway.'

After a few days she moved him into a room above her. If the staff – now only a cook and a housekeeper – were surprised they didn't show it.

She spent the week in London and usually phoned in the evenings to find out how he was. She came down to the country late on Friday.

She had been expecting Peter but he had developed into an expert swimmer and was representing his school at a gala in the north of England. The staff usually had the weekends off.

Some of the bandages had been removed from Ben's face.

His eyes and mouth and the whole of the right side were uncovered.

She had brought smoked salmon and a cold game pie from Harrods and they had their supper in front of the study fire. They talked about the Meissners. He asked if there had been any trace at all and when she said no he said, 'I'd sure like to do a book one day about some of the people who disappeared. The Red Cross has a tracing section with hundreds of thousands of names on their lists. They reckon people will be searching for relatives and friends for thirty or forty years. Writing about Michael and Ruth would personalize the story.'

She found it difficult to sleep that night. She dozed, her mind twisting and turning in dreams, the past and the present intermingling; the Meissners, Altenkirchen, Cuno's leg with its gaping wound, the body in the river – and like some photographic image, Ben's bandaged face swam in and out of each scene.

She woke with a start and lay listening to the house, hearing the long-case clock in the drawing-room chime two o'clock. Outside there were the night sounds. She could hear an owl in the distance, and then closer, a short jerky scream, perhaps a rabbit caught by a fox.

Then she heard the sound of footsteps above her. She followed them with her eyes. Ben was walking backwards and forwards across his room. She turned over and tried to sleep but couldn't. Sometimes the footsteps stopped for minutes on end, then they would start again.

She put on a dressing-gown and went into the corridor. She could see the light under his door above her. 'Ben!' she called.

The door opened. 'I'm sorry,' he said, 'did I wake you?'

'I couldn't sleep. I'm going to make some tea. Would you like a cup?'

'I'll come down.'

They sat in the big kitchen, warmed by the Aga.

He offered her a cigarette but she shook her head. 'Sometimes it gets to you,' he said.

'I'm sure it'll be fine. The sister said it was routine.'

'I don't mean this,' he said touching his face. 'No, no, I mean my . . . the way I live. The wars . . . I guess you can't continue

164

. . . I mean, you can't keep on going from one to another . . . Six of my friends have been killed. You realize it's only a matter of time . . . Will it be the next one? Or the one after that? And how will it happen? Will you step on a mine or get blown out of the sky . . . ?'

He began to pace up and down. She rose to give herself another cup of tea and he caught her arm and pulled her towards him. Gently and gingerly, so as not to disturb the grafts, he kissed her on the lips. It was enough. The charge was there still.

He began to unbutton her dressing-gown and covered one of her naked breasts with his hand. She stood outside herself, watching. She had known this was going to happen – why else had she invited him to Usbourne? She felt the edge of the table. 'Not here,' she said.

They went to her bedroom and made love in the dark. But it wasn't the dark of Axe's room, nor were there chocolates and brandy. She was in her own territory; she was safe, relaxed. As he entered her, she knew she had been wanting this moment for a long, long time. Her flesh responded to his, her need to his, and when it was over they lay together in silence, drowsy, their muscles as soft as dough.

Throughout she had kept one thought in her mind: be in control. That was what she had lacked the first time round, control.

It was a strange time. In a way it was like being married. He went up to London with her and lived in her house. She would leave Fleet Street as early as she could to have the evening with him. Normally the London house was a place where all she did was sleep. Often, because of cocktail parties and dinners which she felt obliged to attend, she would crawl between the sheets in the early hours utterly exhausted.

Now that Ben was there she cancelled all her evening appointments and put her social life on hold. At first he seemed content to spend the day regrouping his forces; reading all the papers, watching the newscasts on TV, going to the Tate Gallery or a movie. Sometimes they would eat out, sometimes he would bring in take-aways.

She felt a growing sense of the rightness of what she was

doing. This was what she had missed all her life; someone to come home to.

'Darby and Joan,' he said to her one evening as, after dinner, they lay naked in her bed, watching an old B-movie.

'You make us sound in our dotage.'

'We're not getting any younger.'

There was a tone in his voice she had not heard for a long time; a chilly, bleak note, that sent a shiver down her spine.

Another time he said, 'I can't remember a better period in my life than now. I mean it. I love you. I always have . . . it's the reason I've never married. I've thought about you in bars in Brazzaville, in cafés in Algiers, in hotel bedrooms from Seoul to Budapest . . . longing for you and wishing you were there.' She put her arms round him and held him. 'I'm sick of it all . . . sick of the travelling, sick of sleeping on floors and in aircraft . . . sick of being cold and wet and above all sick of the panic you feel if you've missed a story. I guess there's a time in life when you need the old adrenaline but then . . . you grow out of it.'

She knew that each statement contained a sub-text. It would have been easy to pick up that sub-text and develop it. Could she? Could she still have Ben? She decided to give it a little more time.

And during that period he began to change. He grew bored and restless and the tensions returned to him. Sometimes he was not in when she arrived home. She found out that he would often go to the Press Club where he would meet other war correspondents and they would drink the afternoon away.

They went down to Usbourne for the weekend and Peter came from school. Ben did his best but he tried too hard to be friendly and Peter was at an age where he held people at arm's length. That meeting gave Anna a new perspective. She had never told him the truth about the accident and now she knew she never would.

Peter was much stronger and it was only when he grew tired that he limped. The boot was gone, so was the crutch. But not the Unowot. It was hard enough to forget for a time how it had all happened – and now Ben's presence was a constant

166

reminder. The thought of marriage disappeared into the great void of things past.

The day arrived for Ben to go back to the hospital to have the bandages removed. She had arranged to pick him up there in the afternoon but when she arrived he had gone. There was a letter for her at reception.

My darling,

I think we both knew that this is how it would have to end. The grafts have taken. They look a bit white but that's only natural.

War's like a drug, and Indo-China seems to be the place now to find it. I'll miss you of course. I'll lie in empty bedrooms remembering you and cursing myself for ever having left you. One day, if I don't have my feet blown off, I may even walk back into your life. All my love, Ben.

She drove for a long way without any sense of direction and found herself in the wilds of Hampshire. She stopped the car at the highest point of the road and looked out over the rolling countryside.

Her feelings were mixed. This was the second time that Ben had disappeared from her life. At least this time he had written her a note. She was sad that nothing permanent would ever come from the relationship, but glad that she had not had to make a decision because she knew what it would have been and had no wish to hurt Ben.

She went home. For a long time she missed him badly, especially when she woke in the morning and saw the empty space in her bed. But she recovered more quickly than before. She was not as vulnerable. She was her own woman. And she knew he would come back. That was enough.

And over the years things had not changed all that much. Ben *had* walked back into her life – and out of it again – many times. There would be a phone call from London Airport and an hour later he would be with her, for a day, a week, a month. Indo-China became Vietnam, and when that was over there was Cambodia and Angola and Ethiopia and the Falklands and Nicaragua . . . so many wars.

167

Sometimes she flew to a Greek island or an African lake, to join him for a holiday. This way of life suited them both; it became their raison d'être.

And as one war followed another, Anna's children grew up and married and had children of their own . . .

'I'm a grandmother,' she said to Ben one day. 'Imagine that.'

'I'm trying to. But grannies don't have breasts like yours. Or at least they shouldn't. It's too much of a temptation.'

By this time she had sold the house in Victoria and bought the penthouse overlooking the park. And by this time she was the owner of the *Daily News* and had an empire stretching to America.

'I've always liked older women,' Ben said. 'Mature. Like strong cheddar cheese.'

Now, standing in her office in the *Daily News* and looking at the morning traffic building up as it came over Vauxhall Bridge, she thought of him, wondering where he was. He no longer worked for a newspaper; instead he followed only the best wars and wrote books about them. She knew he had been in Eastern Europe when the Berlin Wall came down but had not seen him since.

She heard the cleaners move into the building. Like the *Daily News* itself, it was renewed every day. This was what had kept her going over the years, the need to focus all her attention on this taxing master of hers so that there was no time to brood on the might-have-beens.

And now her family wanted to take it away from her! It was true she was no longer young, it was true that she tired more easily; it was just possibly true that if someone of probity had come along and offered her a good price for the *Daily News* she might have been tempted to sell it – for she had had a good run for her money. But take it from her? Force her to sell? Never! Not without a fight to the bitter end.

Wars, as Ben had often told her, were won in stages, single battle by single battle. The first of those battles would be today in her boardroom. But it wouldn't be the last. There was always Cuno waiting in the wings. That's if he was Cuno and not this other man, Gregor. And only she could tell. And if he was and she did . . . ? She hardly dared to imagine the effect it would have on her family.

This was what Nairn was supposed to be finding out!

Nairn – John's daughter – had been like a gift from heaven to Anna which partly made up for John's loss. In her she had found not so much a granddaughter but a second self: the young woman she might have been if things had been different . . .

She dialled her London flat again but all she got was the answering machine.

The sun had come up, the day was upon her. She dialled Monty's house in Hampstead. He was usually up early but just in case . . .

'Hello, Monty,' she said when she heard his voice. 'You know what day it is?'

'As well as you. I'll be with you in an hour.'

169

BOOK TWO
Nairn

One

Wilson Braid leaned back against the pillows in his hotel room and sipped a cup of tea. It wasn't the same strong, brick-red liquid he was used to in Africa; this was weak London tea, but still it was better than nothing.

Grey dawn was seeping into his room. He always woke early these days; he seemed to need less sleep than when he was young and in Africa he was usually awake by five. That was when he often phoned John in Cape Town. He knew John hated it, which was why he did it. Kept him on his toes. Mary too.

He also found it the best time of day to plan and to ponder. He was not a philosophical man so the pondering had little to do with life, much more to do with the people who worked in Braid International, and was usually on the lines of who he was going to fire and who he would hire or move up as a replacement. It was also a time when he planned his strategy for the future – what newspaper he wished to add to his stable, which he had lost faith in as a money-maker and wanted to sell.

On this particular morning, he was doing his pondering in a hotel suite not far from the London *Daily News* building. Anna did not know he was in London; few did. He had flown in the day before and instead of going to the Savoy as he usually did, had booked into the Imperial. This hotel was also on the Embankment with a view of the Thames, but less conspicuous and, more importantly, he was not known there.

He had flown first from Johannesburg to Zürich and Frankfurt to see his merchant bankers. Instead of catching the shuttle to Heathrow he had flown to Munich and picked up a late morning flight to Gatwick, travelling economy class – something he had not done for more years than he cared to count.

'So this is how the other half lives,' he had said jokingly to the air hostess and received a cold stare in return. He had seen no one he recognized and was as certain as he could be that no one had recognized him.

The past few days had been hectic and when he had woken in his suite in the Imperial a few minutes ago, with a waiter hovering above him with his tea tray, he had, for a few seconds, not known where he was.

Now he felt life come back to his stringy muscles. He was no longer the square, heavy-set man Anna had married. Age had thinned him down to gristle and bone. He was bald and nut-brown from the African sun. He picked up the phone and asked for room service. His South African accent was still marked and the timbre of his voice was gravelly.

'I want some breakfast,' he said. 'I want bacon and eggs and fried – '

'I'm afraid the kitchens are not open yet, sir, but if you'd like to give me your order I'll – '

'Don't talk crap to me. This is supposed to be a first class hotel. I want bacon and eggs and fried bread and toast and decent Seville marmalade. And I want it in fifteen minutes.'

The adrenaline produced by this exchange fed his ageing sinews with energy. He got out of bed, poured himself a second cup of tea and stood at the window. His bedroom was at a corner of the building and he could look across the roofs of London to the dome of St Paul's. In between was Fleet Street where everything had started for him.

Strange to think it wasn't the world's newspaper mecca any longer. But times changed and you changed with them or you went under. He mightn't be coming back to Fleet Street, but he was certainly coming back to London and this time it was to stay. He just wished more of his former colleagues were still alive so he could say, 'Fuck you!' to them, especially the ones on the *Daily News*.

He got out his address book, looked up the number of Braid International's house in Chester Square and dialled. The phone rang for almost a minute before a sleepy voice said, 'Ja?'

''Morning, John.'

'Dad?' Braid could hear his son rearrange his mental furniture. 'Hello. How are you?'

'Fine, fine . . .'

'When did you get in?'

'Late yesterday.'

'And you're at the Imperial?'

'Ja. Haven't set eyes on anyone who knows me and I came in on a completely different route. Munich to Gatwick. Have you seen Hardiman?'

'Yes, everything's set.'

'What about Nicholas?'

'What about him, Dad?'

'For Christ's sake, you know what I mean.'

'Nico's okay. Still the same.'

'I want you to go to his place this morning. Be with him. Drive him to the office. Don't let him out of your sight. Okay?'

'Sure, if that's what you want. But he's short of funds. He won't change his mind.'

'He's always short of funds, and his mother's bailed him out before. I want him safely delivered.'

'I don't think there's going to be any problem.'

'Don't think, John. I'll do the thinking. Okay?'

'Sure.'

'We're going to make them eat shit today, son.'

'Absolutely, Dad.'

'I'll see you later.'

Wilson replaced the receiver and nodded to himself. That would get John up and keep him on his toes, he thought. And that was half the battle with people. Keep them rattled and on their toes.

There was a knock at the door. 'Breakfast, sir.'

When he had finished his breakfast he smoked one of the five cigarettes he allowed himself each day. He thought of phoning Victor Hardiman, his lawyer, but it was too early. The trouble with the British, he thought, was that they slept too long.

The early morning was bright but cold. He dressed, put on

175

a heavy coat, pulled his hat well down over his eyes, and went for a walk along the Embankment. The pale early sun glinted on the Thames, burnishing the water like copper, but he did not see it. He was looking inward, planning for the day.

It was a day he had been waiting for. He'd promised himself that one day he'd come back and now he had. It had taken a long time for there were always other things that had occupied the immediate future, but he had known that it would come in the end.

He walked through the Inns of Court, drawn like a magnet to Fleet Street, and came out at the Cock Tavern. In the old days the Silver Grill had been the only place to eat in the vicinity. He went on towards Ludgate Circus, past El Vino where he had drunk so much claret, past the building where Ning's Coffee House had stood, then crossed at the Reuter Building and walked back along the other side.

Where had they all gone, those great newspapers? The place was just like any other city canyon now. That's where the *Express* had been. That had once been the *Daily Telegraph* building. He stopped before the new façade of the building that had once been the *Daily News* and which now housed an insurance company.

Standing in the chilly morning air he remembered his last day as though it had been yesterday. He felt his heart begin to race. He mustn't let memory ambush him like this! It was long ago. But he had a long memory and anyway there were things you carried until you dropped.

When Anna owned the building it had had a circling globe on the roof with the lettering WEBSTER COMMUNICATIONS on it. Webster! Christ! What a bloody piece of crap. Anna Webster! Why the hell he'd ever got mixed up with her he'd never know, nor ever forgive himself. He'd seen her as a good screw on the train out of Switzerland and that was all – and look what it had cost him. A whole newspaper group. The most expensive fuck in world history.

He wondered if she had put the circling globe on her new building in Victoria. If not, he would. Once the place became his, that is. Just the name BRAID. That was all. Everyone would know – at least, everyone who needed to know.

He turned and walked back along Fleet Street to the hotel and the telephone. If people weren't awake by now they bloody well should be.

Two

'He can't even let you get your rest in London!' Mary Braid said, angrily. 'It's bad enough at home, but we've just had this long flight and *still* he rings you up at daybreak!'

'It's only his way,' John said.

'That's what you always say! Only his way. What about your way? My way? Everyone else's way?'

'He's too old to change now,' John said. 'Anyway, it shows he cares. I mean, I'd be more worried if he didn't phone.'

They were in the big kitchen in the basement of the house in Chester Square. In the distance they could hear the rumble of traffic beginning to pick up in the King's Road and every now and then the house gave a faint tremor as an underground train left Sloane Square and made its way towards Victoria.

They were both still in their nightclothes. John was wearing a dark blue silk dressing-gown and Mary a cream satin gown cut on masculine lines. He was unshaved, while she had put on a quick face and brushed her short grey hair.

'Coffee's ready,' she said. 'Do you want something with it? Toast? An egg?'

He shook his head. 'Let's take it into the study.'

The study was on the first floor: black leather, dark green velvet curtains, a grey carpet. It was a sombre room furnished to Wilson's specifications. Mary had made tentative suggestions about brightening it but John had been unwilling to put them to his father in case he felt insulted. The only personal addition John had made was a series of eighteenth-century water-colours of African animals.

She watched him drink his coffee. He was tall and dark and once had not been unattractive, but now he was losing his hair and had become slightly stooped. This was her husband. He was a good man and a decent citizen and she had not wanted anyone else. She still didn't, but had recently begun to consider life without him. It had been unthinkable until the children were off their hands; now she could think the unthinkable.

Wilson couldn't last for ever, she had told herself, and her life would change once he was out of the way. That too had been enough to keep her from thinking the unthinkable. But now there was something else.

She no longer wanted to live in southern Africa. She no longer wanted to live in a white ghetto protected by black guards against black robbers. And she wasn't alone. Most of their friends out there dreaded the future. It was all very well for Nelson Mandela to talk about sharing, but what would happen when he was put to the test? Why would southern Africa be any different from the rest of Africa? It wasn't so much the politics she feared – she did not think much about politics – but simple domestic crime. With a black population explosion already out of control, not enough work and few welfare benefits, the answer, as far as some blacks were concerned, seemed to be to take what they wanted and kill anyone who stood in their path.

A Cape Town family she had known for years had been wiped out in a blood-bath when their house had been robbed. Few of their friends had escaped burglary or mugging.

She and John were lucky. She had been born in Britain and still had her British passport. John too had been born in Britain and she had gone with him to the British consulate in Cape Town to apply for a British passport. That had been depressing. The queue for passports was made up entirely of young white South Africans. She had been on the point of delivering an ultimatum to John about leaving South Africa and living in Britain when Nico had written to him asking for a loan. And that's when John had come up with his idea for the *Daily News*. If he could take over Webster Communications they would be able to live out their lives in peace in England. But because of the way the shares were divided he'd had to go to Wilson, who had taken charge, of course. But the plan still stood. John would head the British operation and they'd move – lock, stock and barrel.

If only John had defied his father early on, just once, it would have given her hope. It had been one of her ambitions, to persuade him to fight, to struggle out from under his father. She had to admit that so far she had failed.

Had she managed it his life would have been different, and so would his relationship with their daughter, Nairn. But she hadn't so they both had to make the best of it.

And the best of it would be for John to take over the *Daily News*. It would get him out from under Wilson and it would mean they could leave Africa. She still, after all these years, thought of England as 'home'.

She had met John at a Christmas party in London in the swinging sixties. He had been sent by Wilson to gain experience in Fleet Street. He had a bleak room in Chalk Farm, knew few people, and was homesick for the warmth and colour he had left behind.

At first she was sorry for this lonely and displaced figure. Even then she tried, by innuendo, to make him see himself as a separate person from his family and specifically his father.

Slowly their romance had blossomed. She never pretended it was a devouring passion but she was a sensible woman, knew she was no beauty, and doubted if she would ever do better for herself. When he asked her to marry him and return with him to Africa, she agreed. Had she met Wilson Braid before the register office ceremony she might have decided differently.

Now John was in late middle age and beginning to run out of steam and she had no desire to spend the rest of her life with a man who did not believe in himself.

She said, 'Your father's always behaved like this to you and you've always taken it.'

He glanced up at her sharply. She had tried to keep the contempt from her tone.

'It's easy for you to make judgements, you don't have to keep the family peace.'

'You're making excuses, darling. Don't do that.'

'That's what you always say. I know you've never liked him and I can understand that. But you've become obsessed by him. Ever since the Nairn business.'

'I'm not the one who's obsessed.'

'You know you blame him for – '

'Look, John, your father was interfering in every aspect of her life as though she was *his* daughter. And to get her away from him I had to send her to school in England. Six thousand miles from me, her mother. I missed all those years of her growing up. That seems to me a good enough reason to be obsessed by him. For God's sake, she's seen more of Anna than she has of me.'

The 'Nairn business' did not specifically apply to one single incident but to the years of Nairn's childhood in the large house overlooking the sea in Cape Town which had originally been built by Jock Braid. It was a phrase that, in their shorthand, allowed them to talk of Jock Braid and Wilson Braid and the whole set-up without mentioning anyone by name – for names sometimes acted as triggers for resentments and arguments.

She had been carrying Nairn when they first moved into that house. She had wanted a place of their own, somewhere they could decorate and personalize. But no, they had to move into the big house. That's where things had started to go wrong for Mary. She wasn't a traditionalist – and you had to be one in this family, especially in Africa where Jock had founded his newspaper empire at the turn of the century in a small printing shop in Cape Town.

They'd even had to name Nairn – this was Wilson's pressure – for the small town in the north-east of Scotland from which Jock had emigrated.

She had been told often enough that the old man had had a direct line to God; that he'd get down on his knees every day and ask God to give him health and wealth and to smite his competitors – and God did just that. By the time he was forty-five he was a millionaire in the days when money meant real money.

The house was evidence of that. It had fourteen bedrooms and a billiard room and a full staff of servants to run it. It was furnished in the heavy mahogany that the old man had loved. The paintings of his severe Scottish parents still hung in the front hall and were dusted every day. In the big dining-room there was a painting of Jock himself in his late middle age, a bald man with a tonsure of white hair, a not unfriendly mouth, but piercing, fanatical eyes.

Mary tried many times to have the paintings removed to storage and the house modernized, but John was adamant.

'What would Father say?' was his stock reply.

Wilson Braid ran his company from the Braid Building in Johannesburg, to which John would have to go every few months to give an account of how he was managing the Cape Town end. Each Christmas Wilson would descend on them for a month's holiday in the 'family' home. He still did. These were trying times for everyone and when the children were little – Nairn had an older brother Frank and an older sister Barbara – they would be spring-cleaned like the house itself.

There was a five-year gap between the older children and Nairn, and Mary sensed that this was part of the 'Nairn business'. It was the gap that was important. Frank and Barbara had formed a bond which Nairn could not share. They did things together, they had a secret language, they trusted and depended upon each other.

Nairn, of course, had no defence against this other than to try to capture for herself as much of her family's love and attention as she could.

Mary saw what was happening and tried to give Nairn as much affection as she was able, but John was irritated. When he failed to respond Nairn pushed herself further into the limelight, always wanting to be on his knee, always wanting to be with him, drowning him in her love.

Below their house was a sea pool, built out into the Indian Ocean breakers. Sometimes John would come back early from the city and go down for a swim. He liked to be alone at these times but Mary, who knew that Nairn was waiting anxiously for her father through the long hot afternoons, would beg him to take her. Often he did so with reluctance.

When Wilson arrived on the Blue Train for his summer holiday their lives no longer seemed their own. He ran – or tried to run – the house. He would order the servants around and countermand Mary's instructions. He would make new times for meals or change menus or invite people for dinner without telling anyone. He had to have special soap – grandfather's soap – and he liked a special brand of breakfast cereal – grandfather's corn flakes – and there were other special commodities which were brought in specially for him and from which the other members of the household were barred.

John put up with these irritations without comment, but Mary did not, and an antagonism grew up between her and her father-in-law.

Mary was especially protective about Nairn. The child was frightened of her grandfather. He criticized her way of dressing, her manners, her accent, the way she played unselfconsciously with the little coloured children of the household servants. As she grew older she kicked violently against such criticism.

Mary tried to take her side but John was fearful of upsetting his father. It didn't take more than a few days from the time of Wilson's arrival before the house was seething with tension.

When Nairn was ten, things came to a head. In Cape Town the second of January is known as Second New Year and there is a traditional Mardi Gras type of carnival. For the Cape Coloureds – a race of mixed blood – it is their special time. Bands are formed from the different suburbs, costumes are created and they play and dance through the streets.

One of the Braids' servants, a young Cape Coloured woman called Sarah, wanted Nairn to join her group. Secretly they made a costume and secretly – because her parents would never have given her permission – Nairn joined a suburban troupe.

Within an hour she was missed. The house was turned upside down. The police were called. Rescue boats searched the bay because Mary thought she might have gone down to the pool and fallen off the wall into the sea.

Late that evening Nairn and Sarah returned. Sarah was sacked on the spot and Nairn was put to bed without any supper.

Mary made a decision. She wanted Nairn to be removed from

the atmosphere of the big house and educated in England. John and Wilson fought her but Mary found new depths of courage and determination and finally she got her way.

When Nairn was twelve years old Mary flew with her to England and saw her settled into a conventional girls' boarding school in Sussex. Even as it was happening she knew it wasn't the best plan for her daughter but anything else – or at least anything else that she could think of – would be worse. As she left Nairn at the school, a little girl standing in a deserted driveway, it was like leaving part of her own body.

Now, in his study in the house in Chester Square, John tried to take his wife's mind off Nairn. Whenever Mary spoke about her these days he heard the mixture of anguish and jealousy in her tone and felt a stab of anger himself. It was true. Nairn *was* Anna's child more than his or Mary's. And Nairn probably loved her more.

'This bloody family!' he said. 'Sometimes I wish I wasn't a Braid. I'd have been much happier as someone else.'

'You're doing it again, John. You *are* a Braid. You can't change that. And you shouldn't be thinking like that today. You've put too much time and energy into this deal. Anyway, the *Daily News* is a good paper.'

'But it's losing money.'

'I suppose that means you'll take it down-market.'

'Why do you say that?'

'Your father's done it with all his papers. Tits and bums and scandal.' She heard her voice rise but could not control it. 'And all the time a holier-than-thou attitude. "The people know best. Give them what they want!"'

'But why not? The people do know what they want. And if it's tits and bums, let them have it.'

'That's Wilson speaking, not you.'

They paused. They knew if they went further they could damage each other emotionally.

After a few moments John changed the subject. 'I suppose it's too early to phone Nico.'

'Why?'

'Dad wants me to keep an eye on him just in case. Stiffen his resolve. We don't want him collapsing on us.'

'Wilson's like a bull-terrier. Once he starts he never lets go of anything.'

John took this to be a compliment and after finishing his coffee said, 'You know what he made me do once?'

'Who? Nico?'

'Dad. I must have been about eight. He'd given me a tape recorder, an expensive one. When I came back from school for the summer holidays he asked me where it was. I told him I'd left it in my locker at school. Christ, you'd have thought I'd left the Crown Jewels. I'd never seen him really angry before. His face went all knotted and red and his eyes became bloodshot. I thought he was going to hit me, really belt me. But he didn't. He made me go and fetch it.'

'He made you go back to school to fetch it?'

'I was at Napier then. Nearly a thousand miles away. Two days and two nights on the train. Second class. In the heat of summer too. He said it would teach me to appreciate possessions. And it has. You've got to hand it to him.'

She looked at him in amazement, opened her mouth to comment, changed her mind and kept silent.

'How do you think Nairn will react to what's going to happen?' he said.

'She'll be upset about Anna, I suppose, but you're her father. Perhaps you should call her.'

'I did. From Johannesburg. She wasn't at home. So I wrote to her.'

It was the way he said it that caused her to look at him sharply. 'Oh? About the takeover?'

'No, just a note saying we were coming over and that we'd be in touch.'

As he spoke his voice grew thicker and she waited for him to continue but he remained silent.

Then he said, 'I've always been sad about Nairn.'

Not now, she thought. Not today of all days. She could tolerate no lapse in concentration. 'We'll talk about Nairn later.'

'That's what I always said to myself: I'll play with Nairn later. Then suddenly it was too late.'

'Not now, John!'

With a convulsive movement, he reached out and placed his

hands on her breasts. It was like a little boy reaching for his mother. She took his hands in hers and moved them away. 'Perhaps later,' she said. 'When it's all over.'

He nodded and turned to leave the room.

'John.' He stopped, hearing the change of tone once again. 'No going back. And I mean that. I'm not going back to Africa with you.'

Three

Nico knew that this was going to be one of his bad mornings. His mouth was dry, his throat raw, and a throbbing pain had worked its way from the back of his neck across the top of his skull, and settled behind his eyes. He reached out, felt for a glass of water and drank thirstily. Then he opened his eyes.

The room was in semi-darkness, the light of early morning making it shadowy. He sensed that he was alone and when he turned he saw that the other bed had not been used.

Slowly the events of the night before began to form in his mind. Some friends of Jacqui's had come round to the apartment in the late afternoon and they'd had a few drinks. He could just about remember their names. There was Myles someone-or-other and his girl-friend, a Swedish bit with a name like Birgit. And another man, Raoul. Egyptian. Someone had said he was a currency dealer.

He didn't know where his wife had met them. They seemed like old friends, dating from before he and Jacqui had married. Anyway they'd had three or four bottles of Moët and then gone on to Deal's. He hadn't been there for more than six months. He'd sworn he wasn't going back. But Jacqui had pressed and so had the others and when it looked as though they might go without him, he'd said all right.

They had driven there in Raoul's stretch Mercedes with a cocktail cabinet in the back and black glass windows. Nico remembered Raoul saying it was bullet-proof, though why anyone should want a bullet-proof car he didn't know unless he was into drugs or Middle Eastern politics or both. He had used coke – they all had – but you didn't need a bullet-proof car for that.

He lay there in the grey morning light with his head throbbing and a sick feeling in his stomach, trying to remember what had happened at Deal's.

He'd shot craps for an hour and Jacqui had come for more money. She'd won a bit on roulette and then that streak had fizzled out and she'd lost her bundle. He'd tried to sign an IOU but the manager had refused and become unpleasant because of problems in the past with IOUs. Myles and Raoul, neither of whom looked more than twenty-five, had stood around, smiling. Finally Raoul had staked Jacqui.

They had gone on to Flicker's and had more drinks and the others had danced, and then on to Michael's Place, which he'd never been to before, but which the others knew. It was a rotten little club in Earl's Court packed with yuppies. Raoul had put his arm round Jacqui and Nico had told him to cut it out.

Not that he could have done much, he supposed; the age difference would have told in the end. But he was bigger than Raoul who was just a fat little fart with one of those Zapata moustaches.

That's when the arguments had started with Jacqui. She had been sulky ever since the money thing at Deal's. By two o'clock he was tired and wanted to go home but she wanted to go on and on. She'd kept on saying, 'I want a bacon sarni . . . I want a bacon sarni . . .'

The others said they knew some caff at the market in Nine Elms on the other side of the river where you got the best bacon sandwiches in London. But by that time he'd had it. He'd tried to get her into a cab in the Earl's Court Road but she'd fought him.

'Piss off!' she'd shouted. 'If you can't take it, piss off!' She was drunk of course. She never would have said such a thing otherwise.

Gingerly he got out of bed. The throbbing instantly became worse. He made it to the bathroom, tried to be sick but couldn't. He put four Alka-Seltzer tablets into a glass of water, waited for the hissing to stop, then drained it. His hands were shaking. He examined himself in a mirror. A wide-shouldered figure with a big, open face and a balding scalp stared back at him from bloodshot eyes.

'I'm fifty-three years old,' he said to his mirror image. 'I can't go on like this.'

But then he smiled. It hurt, but he smiled. 'You always say that in the morning, old sport. And after the second bloody Mary you're rarin' to go.'

He went through his range of pills, chose several and began throwing them into his mouth: B Complex, iron, liver, vitamin C, garlic, ginseng. Then he shaved and combed his hair over the bald patch. Well . . . not bald, thinning.

He put on a gown and padded along to the kitchen. It was a large apartment but the kitchen was small and every surface was covered with dirty plates and overflowing ashtrays.

At this time in the morning the street outside was quiet, but he could hear the traffic from Park Lane. It never stopped, day or night. That was one of the things about living in Mayfair; the rest of London closed down at two or three in the morning but in Mayfair there was always something doing.

He carried his coffee into the drawing-room and opened the long yellow velvet curtains. The room was orange-and-gold and when the sun came in it glowed. Now in the early light it looked tatty. He lit a cigarette but it tasted so foul he instantly put it out.

He wondered if they had ever got to Nine Elms – or had that simply been an excuse to get rid of him? He felt anger and jealousy and his head hurt worse than ever. Where the hell *was* Jacqui?

On the coffee table he saw a small pile of envelopes: yesterday's post which he hadn't bothered to look at. Most were bills and he could see from the red printing they were final demands. He tossed them aside. There was an airmail envelope postmarked Australia. It would be from his daughter Natalie by his first marriage. He tore it open.

Dear Daddy,
    You haven't heard from me for a long time and I must apologize, but Herman and I [who the hell was Herman?] *have been living*

*up in Queensland – 'gone bush' they call it here. We went so far
north there were hardly any other surfies.*

*I learned to live rough, cooking on the beach, things like that,
that I would never have learned in England. Herman says I'm
the best barbie cook there is!*

*Anyway, we have at last come back to Sydney and Herman
and I want to open a surfers' boutique in Palm Beach selling
underwater gear and boards and all that.*

*Now here comes the 'crunch', Daddy. We're going to need some
money to start because the area is up-market and the shops are
expensive.*

*But we've got our eye on a shop that's coming up for sale. The
only thing we need is money.*

*We've been to see the agents and they reckon that we'll get it
for between two and three hundred thousand dollars.*

*We don't want the money as a gift. Perish the thought! Herman
would 'kill' me if I asked you for money. No, Daddy, it would
only be a loan. We'd pay you back.*

*I'm really keen on this and I know Mum thinks it's a good idea
too.*

Lots of love, Natalie.

Twenty-five years old, he thought, but stuck with a mental
age of about seventeen. That's what happened when you were
a surf groupie from the age of twelve.

In the envelope was another sheet. He knew with a sinking
feeling that this would be from her mother.

Doreen had got lost in the shuffle of his life somehow. She'd
been his first wife, an Australian model he'd met in London.
Beautiful body but not much upstairs. And after Doreen there
had been Geraldine and she'd got lost in the shuffle too except
for the alimony cheque that disappeared every month in the
direction of the Algarve where she was living with an ageing
pop singer. Sorry. Artiste.

Doreen, thank God, was married again, but that had never
stopped her from bombarding him with demands for money
for Natalie.

He opened her note now, knowing what it was going to say.

Dear Nicholas,

I'm enclosing this with Natalie's note. Please read hers carefully. I don't want you to say no to her. She's twenty-five years old and this is the first time she's ever given any indication of settling down.

Herman's all right. I don't think they'll ever marry, he's not the marrying kind, but she's happy with him.

You've got to think of her future. She's spent most of her life on the beach and that doesn't seem to me to fit her for much else.

I mean, how is she going to develop a feeling of responsibility? How will she bring up a child?

You can easily afford what she's asking so please don't say no, I don't want her to turn out like you.

Yours, Doreen.

How about that for a begging letter!

What they were asking for was more than a hundred thousand pounds sterling. Jeee-sus! He'd paid for her schooling, her music lessons, her ballet lessons, her teeth. He'd paid for her to go round the world. He'd paid for courses in ceramics and furniture restoring, enamelling and oil painting. She'd dropped out of every one of them. He'd paid for three cars – two of which she'd written off. He'd bought her clothes and jewellery. And now she wanted a shop. Sorry. Boutique. Not to sell clothes in but bloody surfboards.

No wonder Herman wasn't the marrying kind. Why would he be when she had old moneybags in London?

'You can easily afford it,' Doreen had written. Christ, if only she knew.

He heard the door open and close and stuffed the letters into his dressing-gown pocket. Jacqui came into the room. Even in this light, even without much make-up left, even with her hair uncombed and her mascara smudged, even with all that, she still looked terrific. Someone had once said, before they were married, that she was a production-line Barbie doll. That was bullshit. She was terrific and she had a terrific body.

'Oh, you're up,' she said.

She was wearing a short tight skirt, a gold top under which her breasts jigged up and down, and a black jacket.

'I'm up.'

'After what we went through with you last night I thought I'd find you out cold.'

She had lost all of her lipstick and her lips had a puffy, used look. He turned away. He didn't want to see, didn't want to think. She was back. That was the main thing.

'I wasn't as bad as that.'

'You were awful. I've told you before you shouldn't drink so much. You can't handle it.'

'Look who's talking.'

'Don't be silly, I wasn't drunk.'

'Of course you were. At Deal's.'

'I was having a good time. There's no law against that, is there? That's not being drunk. Anyway you look awful.'

'I'll be all right.'

'I'm going for a bath.'

'Where have you been?'

She looked at him with raised eyebrows as though to say, 'What business is it of yours?'

He said quickly, 'I mean, did you go and have your bacon sarnis or whatever?'

'You can remember that, can you?'

'Of course. I told you I wasn't drunk.'

'No. We didn't in the end. Raoul knew of a party in Kensington. We went there instead.'

'Whose?'

'You wouldn't know him.'

'I might.'

'I didn't get his name. He's a . . . a financier. I mean a property developer. A friend of Myles's.'

'I thought you said Raoul knew about the party.'

'Did I? I meant Myles.'

'Whereabouts in Kensington?'

'What's this, the Inquisition?'

'I wondered, that's all.'

'I don't know. Raoul drove us.'

'Good party?'

'Very good.'

'See anyone we know?'

She moved towards the door. 'No.' Then, 'By the way, they want us to go to Deauville at the weekend.'

'Who does?'

'Myles and Raoul.'

'No chance. I hope you told them.'

'I said of course we'd go.'

'Jesus, don't you understand anything? Didn't you see what happened at Deal's last night? The guy who talked about the IOUs. Didn't it register with you?'

She stared at him, her eyes indifferent. 'So?'

'So we can't afford to go to Deauville. I can't afford to stake your famous winning streaks at the Casino. You know, the ones that always end up with you losing your bundle. We just haven't got the bread.'

'Listen, Nico, I'm up to here with that kind of talk. When I married you, you made out you were this big wheel, this director of a communications company. And ever since then you've been like Scrooge. Don't buy this. Don't buy that. We can't go here and we can't go there.'

'Look . . .' He felt an overwhelming sense of rage. She waited for him to finish the sentence but he didn't. Instead he said, 'The company's going through a bad time.'

'So am I.'

'Things should start improving after today.'

'Why today?'

'The meeting's today.'

'Oh Christ, the bloody meeting. That's all you can talk about. You and John are always on the phone. The meeting. The meeting. You think you're going to run Webster?'

'Of course not. But there are certain things I can do.'

'Like what?'

'Like design.'

'Design! It isn't a fashion house, it's a newspaper.'

'Newspapers have to be designed. The pages. The type. It's going to be completely revamped.'

'What do you know about newspaper design?'

'You forget I went to art school.'

'That was thirty years ago. People who design newspapers are Nairn's age these days.'

193

It was like a slap in the face.

She began to unbutton her jacket.

'Did you really go to a party?' he said, angrily.

'Believe what you want to believe. I'm tired.'

She made to go through the doorway, stopped, turned and said, 'And I'm going to Deauville whether you come or not. Raoul says he'll stake me.'

She went off down the passage.

He gave himself a drink. His hands were shaking so much he could hardly pour. Lots of vodka, not too much tomato juice, tabasco. It was like fire going down his gullet. On an empty stomach the charge was tremendous and it brought sweat out on his forehead. He began to feel better. He lit a cigarette. It tasted just fine. He took a couple of draws, stubbed it out and drained the bloody Mary.

He heard the bathwater running and imagined her undressing. Had she undressed for Raoul?

He walked along the passage and into the bedroom. She was naked, just about to put on a dressing-gown.

'Can't you knock?' she said.

'I want you.'

'Not now.'

'Yes, now.'

There was something in the way he said it that made her look up. He saw her eyes widen slightly.

'Nico, I'm tired and I'm dirty. I want a bath.'

'Whose dirt? Raoul's?'

'What that supposed to m—?'

He grabbed the dressing-gown and pulled it out of her hand. Christ, he thought, what a body.

'I don't want to, Nico.'

'To hell with you!'

He forced her down on the bed. He forced his way into her.

'For God's sake, you bastard, you're hurting!'

But he was past caring. He went at her like a bull. He shouted, 'I'm coming . . . ! I'm coming . . . !' Then he came and it was like being hit between the eyes. He lay on top of her feeling as though all the energy and adrenaline and all his lymph and

194

bone marrow, every atom and neutron, all of him, had exploded and drained away leaving a black void.

She pushed him off her. He lay on his back, inert, boneless.

'Enjoy yourself?' she said.

Four

'Suzy! Suzy! Heel, killer!'

Suzy, the killer dachshund, paused briefly at Peter Braid's command and then went on about her business of investigating an overflowing refuse bin.

They were taking their regular constitutional on Hampstead Heath. They did a circular walk most mornings around dawn, long before the joggers arrived. Sometimes Suzy would investigate the occasional tramp sleeping rough who would wake from an alcoholic daze to a cold wet nose on his face.

On this spring morning, at this hour, the Heath was almost deserted.

Peter limped after Suzy, hardening the tone of his voice, until he realized, as he always did, that he was not going to win, put his hand in his pocket and came out with a biscuit.

'Come here or I'll make a waistcoat out of you!'

Suzy instantly ran back to him, accepted the biscuit, and for a little while pretended to be a well-trained dog.

These daily walks were as much to dominate the pain in his leg as to exercise Suzy. Years ago he had identified the pain as a personality. Sometimes it was strong, sometimes weak, but always there. He had decided to fight it on a person-to-person basis and taking it for walks was one way of carrying the fight into its territory.

The day ahead loomed ominously in his mind. It was the day of the meeting. Today was the day he would have to make up his mind whether or not to go against his mother.

This was something that a fortnight ago would never have

entered his mind. Now he would have to decide. And there was something else: Laura was flying to New York to open in a new play – just when he needed her.

He turned left below Kenwood, walked through the Vale of Health and came into Christchurch Place. The small tree-lined street was quiet. His house was tall and elegant.

He gave Suzy her breakfast and then went into his study on the first floor. His leg was aching now. He said out loud to it, 'That'll teach you, you bastard!'

He was dressed in chinos, a faded blue shirt and a white crew-necked sweater. His hair was still dark. At the studios most of the make-up girls would have gone to bed with him like a shot even though he was old enough to be their father.

He turned away from the window and looked round the room. It had been part of his life for many years. The books he had written were on the shelves, the typewriter and word processor on which he had written them and several dozen TV scripts, were on the desk, and the videos of his heavyweight question-and-answer show, *Talking Heads*, were in a special cabinet. Almost his whole working life was here and he wanted to keep it unchanged.

But he knew, with a sense of sudden panic, that things would change today and that the changes would be irrevocable.

'Bad night?' Laura was in the doorway. Nights were often bad for Peter.

'No, I woke early,' he lied. 'Coffee?'

He gave her a mug. She was wearing a pale green see-through nightdress which highlighted her dark red hair. She was full-breasted and, though nearing forty, had kept her figure. Of course, he thought, it was easier if you didn't have children. Soon it would be too late for that.

'What time is your plane?' he said, knowing to the minute.

'Noon.'

'I wish you weren't going.'

She turned away and stood looking down at the street. The light fell on her rich hair picking up the highlights.

'I postponed it as long as I could,' she said. 'The rehearsals start tomorrow.'

'If we were married you wouldn't be going.'

'Don't, Peter.'

'Well, probably wouldn't.'

'I don't want to play the game this morning.'

'Why call it a game?'

'Because it is. You're being Peter Braid and this is *Talking Heads* and I'm one of your panel and the subject is marriage. A good thing or a bad thing? And I put the woman's point of view and you start to ask questions like what would become of society if more and more couples just lived together and didn't have children.'

'And?'

'And what?'

'What's your answer? What *would* happen to society? No, never mind society. What would happen to *us*?'

'Why should anything happen? We've been living together, mostly happily, for nine years – why start changing things now?'

'Because life *is* change. That's the one damn certainty: nothing stays the same.'

'*You* want change, so *I* must change! That's it, isn't it? Look, we've been over this a dozen times. The next subject for discussion is usually kids. And I just don't feel like going over the same ground for the umpteenth time. You didn't want them either, you said. We both had our careers, you said. And you were right. *And* they're important to us. I know how much yours means to you and I know that without mine, without the money I'm able to earn which gives me independence, I probably wouldn't be living with you.'

'For God's sake, you know I wouldn't begrudge you money.'

'You've never understood my need to have my own income. Never understood that most women hate having to take money from their men.'

'Don't talk rubbish! Of course I have. It's just that at the moment – '

'Listen, we love each other, we're happy, we're okay for money, our careers are going well – *don't rock the boat*.'

'Is that one of the important lines?' His tone was suddenly soft, dangerous.

'What d'you mean?'

'I mean from the new play. You know, deep and transcendental. *Don't rock the boat!* Christ! It sounds like shit to me. A real dog.' She turned and made for the door. 'That's right. Just disappear like you always do when things get rough. Go to America and act in your play. It's not even on bloody Broadway!'

She stopped. 'Are you in pain?' she said flatly.

'No, I'm not in pain! And I've told you a million times to save your compassion for the stage.'

'Okay, what is it then? If it's not your leg, why have you started on me? Is it because I'm going away? I've gone away before and I've come back. And what about you? How many times have you been away? Last year you were in America for nearly two months! I didn't complain. That's what we agreed. That's how we've survived.'

Suddenly the pain struck him and he sat down. The anger vanished as his energy was marshalled to cope with it. She knew what was happening for she had seen it many times. She ached to go to him but knew it would be a mistake and she stood at the door, hurting in a different way and sad for him at the same time.

He said, 'I'm sorry.'

'You want me to rub it?'

'I feel so bloody helpless!'

'I don't mind. I like to rub it.'

He eased his leg on to a footstool and she sat on the stool and began to rub the part where screws were holding the bone together.

For some minutes they didn't speak and then he took her hand and kissed it. 'I hate hurting you. It wasn't really me, it was Unowot.'

'You want your pills?'

'No. They make me feel muzzy and I can't afford that today.'

'When I get back let's do it.'

'What?'

'Get married.'

He stroked her face.

'I mean it.'

'Balls. You're just feeling sorry for me.'

'You must stop that, Peter.'

'Stop what?'

'Stop turning my love into your version of pity. I mean it about getting married. If we don't like it we can always divorce and go back to living together.'

'The tabloids would make a real meal out of that!'

'I'm not going to let you wriggle off. You started it. You brought it up. You said we should be married. Okay, I say we should be married. Now your shot.'

'Maybe you won't want to when you get back.'

'Maybe I won't. Maybe you won't. But right now . . .' He dropped her hand and turned away. 'What is it, Peter? I know there's something. I've known for a week or more. Is it someone else?'

'Christ, no!'

'Can you tell me?'

He was silent for a moment, then said, 'I had lunch with Baxter a couple of weeks ago.'

'Kevin Baxter?'

'The very same. Kev.'

'What'd he want?'

'The *Daily News*.'

'What?' There was shock and disbelief in her tone.

'Nice, isn't it? Mother's paper. My income – except there hasn't been any lately.'

'How do you mean?'

'I mean no income. Zero. There are no dividends because there is no money to pay dividends. And when the half-yearly figures come out there's going to be a hefty loss. That's what today's meeting is all about.'

'Why didn't you tell me?'

'You've got your own life. Remember?'

'That's a really bitchy thing to say.'

'I'm sorry. Put it down to a mixture of Unowot and worry.'

'Tell me about Baxter.'

'Well, friend Kev rang me a couple of weeks ago and said would I have lunch with him at the Ritz? I've never liked the sod, he's the worst kind of Australian. Chip on the shoulder. A Pommie basher. Old mates and cobbers. Just one of the boys.

With a carefully cultivated okker accent when we all know his daddy was one of the richest men in Sydney, that he comes from old money, went to posh schools, and Cambridge. He's like one of those dreary socialist millionaires who pretend they're still a son of Barnsley or wherever and live in St John's Wood and, as a sop to their consciences, don't have their Rolls-Royces washed. The French have a phrase for them: vote to the left, live to the right. Oh yes, I almost forgot: a man of the people. That's how Kev looks on himself.'

'But you went.'

'Surely. When the chief executive of the TV channel that owns your contract asks you to lunch you do not offer a prior engagement.'

'Does he look like his pictures?'

'Younger, if anything. Big and suntanned and only about mid-forties. Eyes too close together. And he never quite looks at you. Always just over your shoulder as though he's expecting someone more interesting to come into the room.'

'He's got a pretty nasty reputation with women.'

'You know from experience?'

She gave a thin smile. 'Go on.'

'So we went to the Ritz and after we'd talked about the famous ceiling and the views of the park he said how were things with the *Daily News*. I said fine and he said that's not what he'd heard. He'd heard that things were bloody awful. And he's right, of course. But in the middle of all this, just to show me who and what he was, he calls the head waiter over and complains that the plate isn't hot enough. Tears him off a strip. And when the head waiter apologizes profusely Baxter says, "Oh for Christ's sake, get up off your knees. That's what's wrong with all you Brits."'

'Charming.'

'I thought so. He said it loud enough for the whole room to hear. Then as calmly as anything he goes on about wanting the paper.'

'But why you, why didn't he go to Anna?'

'That's not the way these people do business. I have a contract with Channel 14. I'm available to do his work for him, in other words talk Mother into it.'

'Which you're not going to do.'

'Which I'm not going to do.' He tried to make his voice sound totally convincing but there was just a moment when her eyebrows arched slightly.

'Go on.'

'To string him along I asked him what he thought it might be worth to him. He'd been waiting for this because he took out a little leather-bound notebook and read out a figure. It was all just theatre. He didn't have to look it up at all. Anyway it had been calculated more or less on the buildings and plant alone. There was nothing there for good-will or the name. It was just dotty.'

'So what did you say?'

'I said he'd better talk to my mother or Monty but I was pretty sure what her answer would be.'

'Anna loves that paper. It's her whole life.'

'Yes, it is.' His voice was uneasy.

'How did he take it?'

'Not a flicker. These people never show emotion except about things that don't matter. Just thanked me for my time and courteously asked his chauffeur to take me home. He said he preferred a walk.'

He paused then said, 'The movies get it absolutely wrong, you know. There's never any hysteria about people like Baxter. They're always calm at times like that. It's only sometimes when I get them on my programme I can raise the temperature. They hate journalists. Really hate them.'

'Has he gone to Anna?'

'Not as far as I know.'

'So the whole thing's over?' She looked at him closely. 'Or isn't it?'

'Not really. The Kevin Baxters of this world never start something and then just forget about it. He wants the *Daily News* and he proposes to get it. He's like a kid: I want therefore I will have. He wants to be up there with the other Australian and Canadian media tycoons and owning a national newspaper is one way.'

'Is Anna vulnerable?'

'No. It's a family business. The family own all the shares. If

202

it was a company floated on the stock exchange all Baxter would need to do would be to buy up enough shares on the open market and he'd have control. But the only way he can get control now is if he can buy our shares.'

'Anna would never sell.'

'It wouldn't matter. The way the articles of association are written we, the sons, could sell out if we all agreed.'

'But you've never agreed about anything.'

'That's true.'

'Anyway, you're out of it. Baxter hasn't come back to you.'

'Yes,' he said, lying. 'I'm out of it.'

She looked at him for a long moment, lines of worry forming on her brow, then she said, 'Darling, Anna can't go on for ever. Have you thought about taking it on yourself? I mean you've had the training; you worked on the *Financial Times* and the *Telegraph*.'

'That was years ago. And thanks but no thanks. I wouldn't go back to the grind of daily journalism for anything. I've got my books and – '

'And your programme,' she prompted.

'And *Talking Heads*. And you.'

'You make it sound as though you've got a collection and I'm part of it.' She looked around the room. 'Maybe it would be better if I was stuffed and you could put me in a corner.' She smiled to take the edge off the remark, then said, 'You know, darling, it doesn't *matter* what you have or don't have. Love doesn't depend on that.'

'Are you quite sure?'

'All your life you've been trying to prove things. You don't have to prove anything to me. I love you anyway.'

'Thanks.' The acid was back in his voice. 'You mean these things I've collected, including you, are just symbols. "Look at me! I may be a cripple but I've got a beautiful woman and a high-profile TV job. So I'm just as good as you."'

'Something like that. I'm going to get dressed.'

He gave himself another cup of coffee. Well, he'd told her. Now, if something went in a way it wasn't supposed to go, she would know the background and would be in sympathy with him. Or would she? You could never tell with Laura.

Anyway, he wasn't going to be Kev's commercial pimp. Absolutely not.

But there was something that Laura had touched on which came back to him. What if he could get the editorship of the *Daily News*? Daily journalism had seemed dowdy in comparison with TV but now that people like Baxter were coming into the industry he wasn't so sure. It would mean . . . well, what would it mean? It would mean giving up a high profile. But would that be so very undesirable?

On the other hand he would be out from under Baxter. He could tell him to shove his television station. That would be a pleasure.

But he needed to test the water and there was only one person to contact – Nairn. She knew more about his mother than even Monty did. He picked up the phone and dialled.

'I'm sorry I'm not in to take your call . . .' Nairn's voice said from the machine. 'But if you'd like to leave your name and . . .'

He waited for the tone. 'Nairn, it's Peter. Something urgent's come up. Can you ring me as soon as you wake up?'

Five

Nairn Braid, the object of these telephone calls and discussions, was sitting at that moment in a British Airways airbus as it took off from Schwechat Airport, Vienna, en route to London.

And she was afraid . . .

She was afraid of what she had found out, but even more of things she thought were there, like rocks under water, which she could not see. She was afraid for Anna, and for John Braid her father. And, for entirely different reasons, she felt a growing anxiety for herself.

'Would you like coffee or tea?' the stewardess said, bending towards her.

'Coffee, please.'

She had a bank of seats to herself. She was grateful for the coffee for she had been up all night. She took it in thirsty mouthfuls and finished it quickly. Then she leaned back and closed her eyes and tried to relax by making her mind a blank.

But pictures kept flashing on to the backs of her eyes. The most frightening was the picture of Gregor sitting in the visitors' room of the prison at Stein. Even in so heavily guarded a place she had felt afraid of him. But that might easily have been caused by the atmosphere of the place; prisons create fear.

Then there was Paul's face and the faces of the people at Altenkirchen, photographs Paul had shown her of the Meissners, even one including Anna in the garden of the Vienna house taken before the war.

She took it from her wallet and looked at it. It was black and white with scalloped edges and showed a group round a table near a large horse-chestnut tree. There was a flask of wine on the table and glasses.

Paul had told her who the people were: there was Michael Meissner looking plump and amused, Ruth, his wife, her expression inscrutable as she stared at the camera, and Anna looking young and beautiful. Behind Anna stood two men. One was Felix Esslin, Ruth's brother, but who was the other? He was tall and powerful but his face was half hidden by the shade of the tree. Was he Beckerman?

That was just one of the many questions she had asked – there were many more questions than answers. The whole investigation had become like a jig-saw; some pieces fitted, others seemed not to belong to the puzzle at all.

She put her small case on to the seat next to her and opened it. The camera lay on top of her clothes. Its leather case was badly scarred by fifty years of usage. That was something else she would need to investigate.

She pulled out a small laptop word processor, set it up on the pull-down table and raised the screen. It was one of the characteristics of journalists that they thought better when their fingers were on a keyboard and she was no exception.

She did not know exactly what Anna wanted, a leaderpage piece or a straight feature or just the information on a personal basis, but getting things straight to Nairn meant writing them down.

She wrote the heading GREGOR-BECKERMAN then she searched her mind for a first sentence. Usually she had no trouble with intros but this one stubbornly refused to come, and after a few moments she realized why. Gregor might be Beckerman or he might not, but that was only one issue. The other was what she had found out, or half found out, which was important to Paul and herself and possibly her family.

That was what scared her. The lid had been kept on this particular Pandora's box for a long time. She had prised open a corner and now no one knew what was in the box or what had already escaped.

'Get it straight,' she said to herself.

She tapped out:

WHO'S WHO?

THE MEISSNERS *Michael, medical specialist, his wife Ruth, son Stefan disappear Austria 1938 presumed killed by border guards.*

FELIX ESSLIN, *journalist, brother of Ruth Meissner, executed by Austrian Gestapo 1940. Lily Esslin, his wife, died Mauthausen concentration camp 1942. Johann Esslin, their son, survived the war, married, died 1976. One son, Paul.*

PAUL ESSLIN. *29, First meeting,* Daily News, *April.*

'Sorry to interrupt you,' Anna said, as Nairn entered her office, 'but I want you to sit in on this. This is Mr Paul Esslin.'

A man uncoiled from one of Anna's chairs and bowed slightly to Nairn. He was tall and slender and his aquiline face with its fierce eyes resembled a bird of prey.

They were in Anna's big airy glass office high above the Thames with the tall chimneys of the old Battersea power station sticking up like fingers on the skyline. A pale April sun streamed through the windows as clouds moved up over London on a south-west wind.

Usually when Nairn walked into a room she was conscious of the look in men's eyes. She was tall, in her mid-twenties, with dark hair cut short and pale blue eyes. She moved with the grace of an athlete and her walk was long-striding and purposeful. Monty had always said she reminded him of Anna at the same age.

Nairn had grown accustomed to these looks. She knew that half the men were undressing her with their eyes, and when she was in her teens it had caused her embarrassment. Now she told herself that it was better than indifference; the look she was getting from Paul Esslin was of a total lack of interest. His nod to her had been so brief as to be barely discernible and he turned back immediately to Anna.

'What are you doing?' he said.

'I wanted you to meet Nairn because she'll be going to Vienna.'

'Perhaps I have not made myself clear!'

'You've made yourself perfectly clear, Herr Esslin.' She turned to Nairn and said, 'Have you read the stories coming

207

out of Vienna and Paris about an alleged war criminal – ?'

'Alleged!' Esslin said scornfully.

Anna said, 'Yes. Alleged. You're a lawyer, it's a lawyer's word.' Then to Nairn, 'A man called Gregor.'

Nairn felt her own irritation increase. She turned away from Esslin, ignoring him, and addressed herself entirely to her grandmother. 'We had something on an inside page this morning. Isn't he alleged' – she pronounced the word slowly and with emphasis – 'to have executed a group of French Resistance – '

'Not Resistance,' Esslin cut in. 'Ordinary people.'

'Hostages,' Anna said.

'Please . . . we are wasting time,' Esslin said. 'I have a plane to catch.'

Esslin, who had sat down, now uncoiled his long limbs once again and hovered over Anna's desk.

'I beg you, madame,' he said. 'If you do not come they will release him and once that happens he will never be rearrested. There will be no extradition. He will go free.'

Anna turned to Nairn, 'Mr Esslin thinks I might know this man Gregor.'

'I tell you he *is* Beckerman!'

'And that I might be able to identify him as a man called Cuno Beckerman I knew in Vienna a long time ago. I think it's highly doubtful.'

'Madame, I – '

'I knew Mr Esslin's grandfather before the war and – '

'What has this to do with her?' Esslin said, pointing to Nairn. 'It is you I have come to ask.'

'Mr Esslin, I liked your grandfather and I would like to do something to help because of that. I can perfectly well understand your feelings, but I simply cannot get out of this chair and fly to Vienna to identify in court a man who might or might not be Beckerman. I have a newspaper to run, a business to look after – '

'And you think that running a business is more important than identifying a murderer?'

'I didn't say that. I agree. It *is* important. But even if we were talking about Eichmann I simply couldn't leave everything

208

and go to Vienna with you. It's not realistic. I would need a great deal more information.'

'But you have all the information.'

'All I know is what you've told me.'

They stared at each other.

'Do you mean by that you don't believe me?'

'I mean that you are not unbiased. Your family was almost obliterated. I can well understand that you want revenge on *all* war criminals but – '

'Beckerman knew where my grandfather was hiding. He knew it through Ruth and Michael Meissner. He also knew that Felix had been working at the Meissners' house.'

'You can't be sure of that.'

'Of course I am sure. He telephoned the Staatspolitzei.'

'How do you know that?'

'My father had a friend in the Ministry of Justice. He found out that Beckerman was paid ten thousand schillings for the information. Not only that, but Ruth Meissner and her whole family disappeared when Beckerman – '

'I know that better than you do. But I still can't get up from this desk and rush to Vienna. There are ways of doing these things and my way is to ask Nairn to go and find out as much as she can.'

'Why her?'

'Because I can trust her.'

Nairn saw him flinch.

She stayed on in Anna's office after Esslin had gone. 'Do you think it could be Beckerman?'

Anna said, 'I doubt it. He disappeared at the same time as the Meissners.'

'But Herr Esslin seems so sure of his facts.'

'Obsessed people usually do. First you have a theory and then the facts are made to fit it. What Herr Esslin is really about is revenge. The need for revenge and the growing obsession blot out everything else.'

'He seems to think it's just a matter of identification. Isn't there anyone else who might know Beckerman?'

'If Herr Esslin knew of anyone else he wouldn't be in London.'

'So it's only you.'

'It looks like it. And you can see how fragile even my testimony would be in court; how easy it would be to break down. I mean it's more than fifty years since I knew Beckerman.' Anna's voice was rising as though in defence of herself and Nairn looked at her oddly.

'Almost every war crimes trial held now comes down to the identification of old men. In recent trials the prosecution has put dozens of camp victims on the witness stand and even *they* can't agree. What would one person's testimony be worth?'

'It could be worth a lot if the person was sure. Don't forget Herr Esslin says he has circumstantial evidence.'

'Yes, well . . . That's what I want you to find out. I don't believe in taking people's word for things – journalism teaches you that – and you shouldn't either. Go to Vienna. Go and check his facts if he has any. And then maybe we'll run a campaign in the paper to have Gregor or Beckerman extradited. And perhaps I'll go to Vienna. But first let's see what you find out. And Nairn . . . I don't want you talking about this to anyone.'

She smiled to take the ring of authority from her words. 'Okay?'

Nairn frowned slightly, then she shrugged. 'Okay.'

She left the *Daily News* early that day and drove to her flat in Swiss Cottage through heavy traffic. Mentally she was preparing herself. Neil was usually irritable when she had to go away, even for a day. It was flattering, but made telling him difficult. 'A day is a lifetime,' he had once said. It was true for her too. She didn't like leaving him either. And God knew how long this trip was going to be. A week? A fortnight?

She wondered if he was at the flat. Often he worked at his other studio. At least that's where he said he was. He usually worked on two canvases at the same time, one at her flat and one in a room in Camden Town.

As she opened her door she heard the soft notes of his guitar. 'Hi,' she said as she went into his workroom. It was the best room in the flat and should have been the living-room, but it was the only room with the light he needed for painting.

He was sitting on the floor near the big French doors that opened on to the wild and weedy garden, strumming on his guitar and singing an old Bob Dylan. She bent to kiss him on the head then opened the window. The smell of hashish was heavy on the air.

He had a seraphic look on his face and began to sing 'The times they are a-changing'. It was a ballad that always affected her deeply. He had sung it when they had first gone out together. He sang softly in a clear, low voice, and she was taken off guard by his beauty, as she often was. He had long black hair caught behind his head in a pony-tail, and wore a single earring. She thought, as she had done many times before, that his thin, chiselled face could have come out of a pre-Raphaelite painting.

She leaned against the wall and watched him and then remembered what she had to say and decided to take him out to dinner. It might be easier after a few glasses of wine.

He finished the song. She clapped and he rose and bowed slightly. She kissed him on the lips and felt how cold they were.

'Had a good day?' she said.

'So-so.'

'How's the canvas coming on?'

'I was working on one of the hands today.'

She stared at the half-finished oil on the easel. It was of a voluptuous nude and it seemed to her that it was in much the same state of completion as it had been for a week or more. It was Harriet, of course. Most of the nudes were. He denied it, naturally, but it was Harriet all right with her big breasts and red hair and what he had once called 'deep-thewed thighs'. She was a kind of Earth Mother.

She wondered if he was using Harriet as his model again, or if this was from memory. She daren't ask. What if he simply said, yes? It was just the sort of thing he might say if he thought she was checking on him. When he had first come to live in her flat she had phoned at odd times of the day just to say hello and hear his voice.

Finally he'd said angrily, 'We're not married. This is how we agreed to live, right? So for Christ's sake stop checking up.'

Now she said, 'I don't feel like cooking. I thought we'd eat out.'

They went to an Italian restaurant in the Finchley Road. They walked and she hoped that the exercise would clear his brain. As usual he drew all eyes. He was tall and wore a long cloak and a wide-brimmed black hat.

'God, I'm starving,' he said when they were seated. 'And thirsty.'

A waiter hovered. 'You order,' she said.

'I'm going to have *penne* and then spare-ribs.'

'I'll just have the spare-ribs.'

'And a bottle of Barolo.'

He ate and drank voraciously and then rolled a cigarette.

'I've got to go to Vienna,' she said quickly.

'When?'

'Tomorrow.'

He leaned back and stared at her through the smoke. 'I thought we were going to Brittany.'

'I'm sorry, Neil.'

'Whose idea was it that we take the car and roam the little coast roads – and you can paint, darling, and I'll catch up on my reading and we'll have lovely seafood meals and – ?'

'Don't! It's my job. On a newspaper you don't have choices.'

He shrugged. 'Well, as they say, if you gotta go you gotta go. How long?'

'A week, maybe a bit longer. I'll keep it as short as I can.'

'Don't worry about it. I'll be okay.'

'And we'll go to Brittany when I get back. The weather will be warmer anyway.'

She paid the bill and they went back to the flat. 'Want to smoke?' he said.

She shook her head. 'Why don't you come to bed?'

'In a little while.'

She packed quickly and got into bed, waiting for him. She heard the soft notes of a Bach chaconne.

She had been with Neil a long time now. She had met him at university and left before taking her degree to wander with him through Europe. That had almost caused a break with her parents. Finally they had met him and it was obvious they disliked him. Was that why she'd stuck to him? Sometimes she wondered. Or was it the fear of loneliness?

Anyway, Anna had simply absorbed this new phase in her life and had taken her on to the *Daily News*. As she had said at the time, 'With your background you probably have ink in your veins, not blood.'

It could have been a disaster; in fact Nairn had been a brilliant success.

'Neil!' she called.

The guitar stopped. She waited. Then she heard it start up again. She put out the light and stared at the ceiling. Why didn't he seem concerned about her going away? Would he wait for the front door to close then pick up the phone and call Harriet? Did he *want* her to go?

Six

Nairn landed in Vienna on an early spring day and took a taxi into the city. Paul Esslin's office was in the First District and he was on his way out of the door when his secretary called him back.

'Grüss Gott,' he said, shaking her hand formally.

He wasn't dressed like an international lawyer, she thought. He was wearing black corduroy trousers, a half-length brown suede car coat and a white scarf wrapped round his throat. His hair was longer than was fashionable and Neil suddenly flashed into her mind. But he didn't look like Neil at all. His face was not really handsome, but strong, and the nose was slightly hooked, like a raptor's. His eyes were dark brown and she had forgotten that there was something fierce about them.

'I have to go out.' His voice was deep, his tone cool.

She looked at her watch. 'We had an appointment at two. It's just on two now.'

'Something has come up. Can you wait?'

'Look, I've flown all the way from London to – '

'Maybe it would be better for you to go to your hotel and we'll meet later.'

'And maybe it wouldn't. I think – '

'All right, then. Come with me. We have to hurry!'

'But where are you – ?'

He shoved her case behind a desk, caught her by the elbow and before she knew what was happening she was back in the street and being hurried along the pavement.

Even with her long stride she was hard pressed to keep up with him. His coat and scarf billowed out behind.

They cut down two or three streets and she lost her bearings. Then abruptly they were in front of a large building and he swept her into the entrance hall.

'Silver room,' he said waving at a doorway. 'Oriental carpets.' He waved at another. 'Stamps. Coins.' He waved at a third.

He began to bound up a large flight of stairs and she followed him. 'This is the State Auction House, the Dorotheum,' he said over his shoulder. 'Like your Sotheby's or Christie's but not so grand.'

He plunged into a large hall. She could hear a voice intoning German numbers. The hall was full of people and there was a crowd around the door.

'Just in time!' he said. He stood her against the wall. She realized that his long body was brittle with tension.

The auctioneer was selling something but Nairn could not see what it was. Paul's hand shot up. A fat man on the far side of the room was bidding and the two men looked at each other with what seemed to her like anger.

The bidding rose furiously with Paul's hand jerking up and down, and his passion was so great, she even thought he might be bidding against himself.

It became a duel, the fat man and Paul. The other bidders dropped out and turned to watch them. At each bid Paul's expression became fiercer, more taut, until finally the fat man slowly shook his head.

She saw a look of triumph cross Paul's face as the object was knocked down to him. But when he brought it back after paying for it, she was surprised and disappointed – it was only a coffee-grinder.

He pushed his way through the crowd towards the exit, and for a moment she thought he had forgotten her. She tugged at his sleeve. 'Remember me?'

He frowned then smiled suddenly. It was the first time she had seen his face soften. 'Forgive me. That was bad manners. Come. Let's have a drink to celebrate.'

'Celebrate what?'

'This.' He held up the grinder.

215

They went to Sachers and sat on the narrow terrace. She was frozen. He seemed impervious to the wind.

'Have you had something to eat?' he said. 'Yes? On the plane? Are you hungry still? All tourists want a Sachertorte.'

'I'm not a tourist. Or had you forgotten why I came?'

'No. I have not forgotten.' A waiter stood at his elbow. 'Coffee and a cognac,' Paul said. Then to Nairn: 'And for you?'

'Just coffee.'

'Black? White? Turkish? Dark? Medium? We are a coffee culture.'

'Black.'

He examined the antique coffee-grinder and she felt he had lost interest in her. Irritated, she said, 'What if you had lost it?'

'But I didn't.'

'But if you had? To the fat man.' She remembered Anna describing him as obsessive. 'You *had* to have it. Just like you *have* to get Beckerman.'

He stared at her for a moment without speaking, then said, 'Here in Vienna we invented psychiatry. Parlour psychologists are a cliché.'

'Look, I know it's my grandmother you're interested in but you're stuck with me for the time being, okay?'

He did not seem to be listening. His eyes had shifted to the street. It was as though he was looking for Beckerman among the afternoon crowd. She began to feel that she had strayed into *The Third Man* and any minute Harry Lime would come rolling down the street. Perhaps it was the atmosphere of Vienna, she thought. Under the veneer of Gemütlichkeit and Sachertorten, there had always lain something deeper and darker. She recalled Anna's description of Vienna after the Anschluss with the Jews wearing their yellow stars and the Nazi officers swaggering along the Graben to the admiring glances of the Viennese.

'I'm sorry,' he said. 'You were saying?'

'I said it was delicious coffee.'

'Ja. Delicious.' He was restless, shifting in his seat. He lit a cigarette, stubbed it out. Then he said, as though she were keeping him, 'I have work to do.'

'So have I.'

'Yes. Of course. I apologize.' His moods changed with bewildering rapidity. She noticed that he never stayed in one position for long but shifted his lanky legs, or fiddled with the ashtray, touched and stroked the coffee-grinder. He did not sit so much as perch.

They went back to his office and he showed her into a room at the far end of a corridor. It was sparsely furnished with a large table, a chair and three grey metal filing cabinets. He carried her suitcase into the room and then said, 'Everything I have on Beckerman is in these cabinets. They are all open, you may look at anything.' He closed the door and Nairn was alone.

She was wearing a long tweed coat and the room was so cold she decided to leave it on. This wasn't what she had expected. She had thought he might have a couple of box files full of clippings and documents. She was used to photocopying machines and microfilm and reading machines, word processors and discs. Here there was nothing of that kind. She hardly knew where to begin.

She opened the top drawer of the cabinet nearest her. It bulged with files. She pulled one out at random and opened it. On the cover was written in German *1941 (August–December)*. Under the date was the one word FRANCE. She opened it and discovered that all the papers were in German. Her knowledge of German was good enough to order a meal and book a room but nothing like good enough for this. Most of the papers seemed to be letters or official documents.

Usually in such a situation she would have gone to the commercial section of the British Embassy and asked for a list of interpreters. But an interpreter would need months to sift through this amount of material. She pushed back the file, pulled out another – the same mass of indigestible, incomprehensible official jargon greeted her.

The door opened and Paul's secretary came in with coffee.

'Do you speak English?' Nairn said.

'A little.'

'Is there anyone . . . I mean . . . The problem is I don't read German very well.'

'I am sorry,' the secretary said. 'Here is not my work.'

Nairn drank her coffee then marched along the corridor. 'Is Herr Esslin free?' she said and did not wait for an answer.

Paul was sitting at his desk. The room was beautifully furnished in dark wood, the walls lined with books. He was dictating into a small hand-held machine.

He switched it off and looked fiercely at her for interrupting, but she ignored him.

'There's so much material,' she said. 'I – '

'Don't you read German?'

'No.'

'Then you have a problem.'

The expression on his face seemed to indicate that he had known this was going to happen; that he had known she was going to be humiliated.

'You're not being very helpful,' she said. 'I should have thought you'd have wanted me to – '

'Listen. I *know* he's Beckerman. But I'm a lawyer. I must prove it.'

'So I'm just an irrelevance.'

'Yes.'

'Thank you very much!'

'Please don't be angry. We have a deal, don't we?'

'What sort of deal?'

'You work for a newspaper. You will get a story.'

'Is that how you see it? You get Beckerman, I get a story? You think that's how it works?'

It was as though she had touched a nerve. 'Let me tell you how it works,' he said. 'First your grandparents must be put into a concentration camp. Then one of them must be murdered and the other must die of disease.'

'For God's sake, I didn't mean that.'

'Then try to understand. I need someone to prove he's Beckerman. There is only your grandmother who *might* be able to identify him.'

'Might?'

'Not even I think that after all these years she could go up to him and place a hand on his shoulder and say this is Cuno Beckerman. However, she is all I've got. But she is too busy.'

'But she has a huge organization to run. Of course she's busy.'

'I only need her for one day, two days at the most . . .

well, maybe three. We go out to Stein-in-Wachau. We talk to Beckerman. She says yes or no. Easy, yes? But instead she sends you. What can you do?'

'I can do my job. I'm a journalist. I can ask questions.'

'That is why I left you in that room. I wanted you to see for yourself how many questions have been asked, how many answers have been given. Do you think you can come here for a few days and match that?'

Despite her anger she began to see his point.

'Of course you can't. But I'm not just playing games with you. I thought your German would be poor. The British expect everyone to speak English. It can make life difficult, especially in a situation like this. Am I right?'

'Okay. You're right. If you wanted to embarrass me then you've achieved that. But does it help you?'

'It cuts away a lot of the dead wood. In those filing cabinets are years of work, hundreds of documents, affidavits, statements, invoices, bills, army lists, sales slips, certificates of birth and of marriage, death lists from Mauthausen, sick lists, doctors' lists, recruitment lists, promotion lists . . .'

She heard his voice begin to take on a rising note, as he became more passionate.

He went on: 'And that's not even scratching the surface. In those three metal cabinets there is everything a court needs to find that Cuno Beckerman killed innocent civilians during the war. Not only in France but we think in Italy as well. I know he caused my grandparents to be sent to Mauthausen but I have no proof of that. There were no tape recorders bugging telephone calls in those days. All he had to do was make one telephone call.'

'So you're trying to use France as your weapon?'

'It's the best documented case. There's a mountain of evidence to prove that he had a group of civilians killed near Libourne. But where is he? Is he in Stein prison or did he die a long time ago? It's not much use having cast-iron evidence if you've got the wrong man.'

'I assume he has papers to prove he's Gregor.'

'After the war such papers were offered to many Nazi criminals on the run. Even faces were changed by plastic surgery.

So we can prove over and over that Beckerman was this and Beckerman was that. But no court will send this man to France for trial unless it is sure he *is* Beckerman. And your grandmother is the only person who might be able to tell us.' He rose and opened the door. 'Now please . . . I must work. I am trying to arrange an interview for you.'

'With whom?'

'Beckerman, of course.'

'In gaol?'

'In Stein. It's your Wormwood Scrubs or America's Sing-Sing. The one that everyone wants to escape from. You should get a good story for your paper.'

She went out of his room feeling more than embarrassed. His passion was such that she was almost convinced that the man *was* Beckerman without reading a line or seeing him. But she cautioned herself to remember that passion by another name was obsession.

She went to the Bristol, unpacked and had a bath. Then she wrote everything she could recall about the day on her laptop word processor.

It was only seven o'clock and the evening yawned ahead of her. She sent down for food and a bottle of wine. The television was showing a football match so she turned the radio to the classical music channel, and used it as a kind of wallpaper while she made notes.

She found it difficult to concentrate. The events of the day kept on spinning past her eyes like a fast forward video. She needed someone to talk to. She picked up the phone and dialled her own apartment in London. As she did so she kept telling herself that there were millions of things that might take Neil out of the flat and that she must not be disappointed if he wasn't in. The phone rang four times and there was a click and then her own voice told her there was no one home and to leave a message after the tone.

She replaced the phone and sat on the bed feeling schizoid, one personality in London and one in Vienna. She went to bed and dozed, waking suddenly and fearfully at midnight.

Abruptly she knew what had woken her and, feeling a crawling sensation in her stomach, she grabbed the telephone book and looked up Esslin. There was a Paul Esslin in Gustav Tchermakgasse. She had no idea where that was but dialled anyway.

'Ja?' a man's voice said, warily. She could hear soft music in the background.

'Is that Paul Esslin, the lawyer?'

'Nairn?'

'Sorry about the hour. But one question. In all those pieces of paper in the filing cabinets have you any details about Ben Ramsey?'

'Who? Oh yes, the American journalist. Of course. Why?'

She felt deflated. 'I just wondered. Good night.'

She was having breakfast downstairs when Paul arrived. She watched him. He stood near the door letting his eyes move slowly round the room. She had rarely seen a man with so much natural confidence. He saw her and crossed. 'Grüss Gott. May I join you?'

'I'm not at my best at breakfast. As long as you don't mind that . . .'

'It's not my best time either, not after a late night.'

'Work?'

He ordered hot rolls and coffee then he said, 'That was a terrible thing to do to me. To ring me up in the middle of the night and throw a name at me. I went into the office to look at his file.'

'But why? You recognized the name immediately.'

'Ja, but you wonder if you've remembered everything. I checked. It's all there. He's not important. He was working for a New York paper. We have some of his cuttings. He covered one or two of my grandfather's meetings and he did a couple of interviews with him. What made you think of him?'

'Anna. He's been her lover for years.'

He began to look bored. 'But what has this to do with Beckerman?'

'He may have known him, that's all.'

'Hundreds of people *might* have known Beckerman. If I had to – wait, wait! Your grandmother's lover?'

'They met in Vienna.'

221

'Where? At the – ?'

'Yes. At the Meissners'!'

He sat back staring at her. Then he pushed his food away and lit a cigarette.

'Go on.'

'He often went to the Meissners' when your grandfather was there.'

'That's where he must have interviewed him.'

'Anna told me that he once took her to a meeting where your grandfather was going to speak. And then the Brownshirts moved in and beat up the audience.'

'And he was your grandmother's lover?'

'She's never kept it a secret. The whole family knows about Ben. When I was a little girl she used to tell me about their first meeting. All about Vienna in fact. I've often told her she should write it but she won't. I'm pretty sure that at one time she thought they would marry, but they never have.'

'But where is he? He may be dead!'

'No, he's around. He blows into London every now and then. They're still very close.'

'My God, I must see him! Talk to him! I never knew. Never guessed. But *of course* that's where he would have interviewed Felix, at the Meissners'.'

'And Beckerman was there constantly. Anna says he was a pest. He was always hanging around her.'

'Phone her now. Ask her.'

She was caught by his excitement and went out to the lobby and dialled the *Daily News* in London. She told Anna what they had discussed.

'He's in Europe but I don't know exactly where,' Anna said. 'I know he was doing some research for a book on the collapse of Communism in the Eastern bloc.'

'If he phones please get his address.'

'He tends not to call, except from London Airport. But if he does I will.'

She went back to the table and told Paul. He seemed to take it badly, as though there was a conspiracy not to give him all the facts, that it was somehow Nairn's fault.

'It's so important!' he said.

'Of course it is but it may not be the only important thing you've missed. You've asked hundreds of questions, you've got drawers full of information but you still haven't asked all the questions. Journalists don't think like lawyers.'

'Bravo.'

'I'm not saying that to score Brownie points. It's just that for you this is personal. You're trying to gain rev—'

'Not revenge,' he said, sharply.

'All right. Justice. On behalf of your grandparents. Because of that it seems to me you built a wall around yourself. The wall is the Esslin family. You say you know everything there is to know about them. Okay, I believe you. But I'd like to know what happened in Altenkirchen, because that's where Anna last heard of Beckerman. And it's where she met my grandfather – '

'And without them there wouldn't have been Nairn.' He made a slight face. 'You're a romantic.'

He lit another cigarette.

'You smoke too much,' she said. 'And you should eat a good breakfast.'

He ignored her. Suddenly he reached into his pocket, brought out his wallet and took from it an ageing photograph. 'This was taken at the Meissners' house before the war.' She leaned closer. It showed a group of people sitting round a table in a garden. 'That's Michael Meissner,' Paul said. 'And Ruth his wife and Felix – '

'And that's . . . that's Anna!' Nairn said. She was looking at an attractive young woman seated between the Meissners. 'Who is the man standing behind the table? Beckerman?'

'I don't know. Unfortunately the shadow from the tree is over his face. It could be your Ben Ramsey.' He looked up. 'When do you leave for Altenkirchen?'

'I thought of going after lunch. I want to see the Meissners' house first. That's where the trail starts.'

'The trail that ends in a newspaper feature article, ja?'

'As you said, that's the deal. I haven't come all this way to look at three filing cabinets.'

He glanced at his watch. 'I have a conference at eleven. I can drive you there first.'

He drove her up to Neustift am Walde in a thirty-year-old

Lancia that had been beautifully restored. The house took her by surprise. It was bigger than she had anticipated. Anna had always talked about the apple orchard. Now it was a square of tarmac in front of the house where half a dozen cars were parked.

'It has been subdivided into flats,' he said.

They walked round to the back. She took the photograph from her handbag. 'Look, the horse-chestnut tree is still there. This is where the table was. It gives me an odd feeling to think of Anna being here on this grass so many years ago.'

As they were leaving, she said, 'If you'll drop me at a Hertz or an Avis I'll rent a car.'

He shook his head. 'I'm coming with you. I'll drive you.'

Seven

Nairn had expected Paul to drive as he walked, impatiently, but even though the autobahn was not busy, he rarely pushed the car to its limit. He drove well, she thought, nursing the highly strung Lancia engine.

She had told him what she knew of Anna's flight from Vienna in 1938 and as they passed the interchange with St Pölten he said, 'This is where they would have joined the autobahn.'

The tyre hum and the wind noise made talking difficult and she leaned back and closed her eyes, trying to visualize that grey dawn so many years ago when the big Mercedes had sped along this same route.

It was a cold spring afternoon with broken cloud and they swept past Linz and Salzburg in pale sunshine.

'We could make Altenkirchen late tonight,' he said. 'But I've never been there. I know a good hotel near Innsbruck.'

She was glad. The evening had turned grey and oncoming cars were covered in snow from the Arlberg Pass. He turned up the Wipp Tal and stopped at the Europahof in Steinach-am-Brenner. The hotel, with all its flags and lights, was welcoming.

'Herr Esslin!' the manager said, coming out of his office and shaking Paul's hand. He was smiling and talking rapidly. Nairn stood in the background and the manager looked at her over Paul's shoulder with questioning eyes.

Then Paul turned and introduced her in English. 'Miss Braid and I are on a case,' he said.

The manager shook her hand and said, 'Herr Esslin is an old friend. I give you my best rooms.'

They had dinner on the glassed-in balcony with a view of snow-covered peaks which turned dark and menacing as night moved up the valley.

They ate local trout with almonds, a fluffy sweet omelette called a Kaiserschmarrn, and drank a bottle of Riesling.

'Do you often stay here?' she said.

'I used to. Mainly in the summer. My wife and I loved walking.'

'I didn't know you were married.'

'She died last year. She was researching into leukaemia and died of the disease. Ironic, isn't it?'

'I'm sorry,' she said.

'We came here six or seven times. We would plan a walk to one of the villages, have lunch, then return by another route. She loved this region.'

He ordered coffee and brandies.

She said, 'What will happen if no one can identify Beckerman and they let him go?'

'It's not a question I ask myself,' he said. 'I'll face it when it comes.'

'My grandmother thinks you're obsessed.'

He opened his mouth to answer her sharply, then shrugged and said, 'It's possible. Ever since I left university I've been working on this. Not full time, not every day; sometimes weeks and months would pass without any progress, but it was always at the back of my mind. I worked for the Documentation Centre in Vienna after I graduated. You've heard of Simon Wiesenthal?'

'The Nazi hunter? Of course.'

'He founded the Centre. That's where I first saw references to my family and Beckerman. Of course we had always known about him but it was a shock to see his name in official files. I began to investigate. Most of the leads went nowhere. That's typical. Someone writes to the Centre from Paraguay or Bolivia saying they have seen so-and-so but by the time you check it you find it was only a rumour, that they didn't actually *see* the person themselves but heard of someone who had. Or else it's a case of mistaken identity. I knew if I wanted to go on I'd need money and the ability to travel, so I studied International Law at Harvard and then set up my practice. Now the problem is to find the time. As my workload increases I have less time for Beckerman. That's another irony.'

He sat back and stretched. 'We'll be in Altenkirchen before lunch.'

'Lieber Gott!' Paul said. 'Where's the town?'

They were in the Lancia looking down the mountain road at Altenkirchen – or where once it had been. Now there was a dam, the surface of which glittered in the morning sunlight. What was left of the town spread along one bank. The houses were modern and had clearly been built in the past twenty or thirty years. There were two churches and, surprisingly, they looked old. Nairn tried to recall the postcards Anna had shown her. In her mind's eye the town had lain at the bottom of the slope on the bank of the river.

'Are you sure this is the right place?' she said.

'The dam's changed everything. What now? It's your expedition.'

'If this was New York or London I'd interview a taxi driver. They're always good for a few quotes.'

'Let's do it. Let's ask a taxi driver.'

They drove down to the great concrete wall of the dam and then along the Austrian bank to the cluster of churches and houses. They came to a little square, on one side of which was a rank with two taxis both of which were empty. A piece of cardboard in the front window of the first had the word BUDA-PEST on it and an arrow.

The Café Budapest was across the road and the proprietor indicated a table where two men were playing cards. These were the drivers, he said, this was where they waited. One was a young man in his twenties, the other twice his age. Paul stood back and waited for Nairn.

She approached the table and, embarrassed in front of Paul, said, 'Bitte, sprechen sie Englisch?'

The young man shook his head, the older man held up his thumb and forefinger indicating a small amount. She knew Paul was watching her, waiting for her to ask him to help. He turned to the proprietor and ordered coffees for the drivers. The older man smiled, the younger continued to look at his cards.

Paul pulled up chairs and he and Nairn sat down. Then he turned to her and said, 'What would you like me to ask them?'

'Ask him if there are any old people in the town who remember the events just before the war when Altenkirchen was a border post.'

The young man's face seemed to close up. He said something to Paul. 'He wants to know why you need this information.'

'Tell him I'm trying to trace the movements of my grandparents. They came through in 1938.'

The young man threw down his cards and pushed past them, leaving the café.

Paul spoke to the older man and said to Nairn, 'He says his young friend is touchy about the past.'

'Why?'

'Austria is going through a bad period. It thinks the world is against it for what happened in the war. It all re-emerged after the presidential elections a couple of years ago when an ex-Nazi was elected president.'

Paul and the second taxi driver spoke for a short while and then the man turned and pointed through the window. Paul shook his hand and rose. He and Nairn went out into the square again. Only one taxi stood on the rank.

'What did he say?' she asked.

'He said there were few old folk left. When the dam was built most moved elsewhere. They hated the new houses. But there is one old man who lives on the outskirts. He might be able to help.'

They drove through the village and took a lane that led up the mountainside to the edge of the pine woods. Paul stopped in front of a small wooden house with a great woodpile at the back and a few apple trees. She saw an old man sitting in a wheelchair in the morning sun. He was wrapped in blankets and wore on his head what Nairn took to be an old Austrian army cap.

A small gate led into the garden and she pushed through it

and walked towards the old man. His face was painfully thin and his eyes were closed.

A middle-aged woman, short and stout with a ruddy face, came out of the rear of the house as though she had been expecting them. She looked angry and upset. She took Nairn by surprise, saying in English, 'What do you wish with my father?'

'Just to ask him a few questions.'

'He was never a Nazi! Why can't you people leave him alone?'

The old man's eyes snapped open. He said something to his daughter then turned to Nairn. His voice was thin. 'Who are you?' he said.

'My name is Nairn Braid. I wanted to ask you some questions about the time of the Anschluss, when the refugees were coming through Altenkirchen.'

His fingers began to pluck at the blanket on his lap. 'Why must you disturb him?' his daughter said. 'Why must you make his last days a misery?'

'All I want to know is about my grandmother. She was one of the refugees. An English woman about twenty years old. She had a baby with her.'

The old man began to cough and shake.

'You have no right!' His daughter turned the wheelchair and pushed it into the house.

As she did so, a voice behind them said, 'It is better you go now, otherwise there will be trouble.' They turned and saw the young taxi driver standing at the fence.

'Why is everyone frightened?' Nairn said to him.

'It is better you go.'

They drove down the lane, re-entered the village and parked in the square. 'Touchy?' Nairn said. 'I'd say they were paranoid. Let's go to the local newspaper. That's always a good place to start.'

The offices of the *Altenkirchner Zeitung* were above a chemist's shop. The entire paper was produced by the editor and his wife. But when Nairn asked if she could see the files for the Anschluss period, he smiled and said they had been destroyed many years ago, just before the great move.

'What great move?'

'When the town moved up the hill,' he said. 'Before the dam was built we all lived down by the river.'

Something clicked into place in her mind. 'The churches,' she said.

'Ja. They were taken down piece by piece and built up here. If you wish to see what it was like you must go to the museum. That is all we have now of the old days.'

The museum was in an old farmhouse about half a kilometre from the village. They were the only visitors. Each room had been set aside for a different aspect of the town's history. There was an 1860s living-room with furniture of the period. Another room was decorated with paintings and photographs of Altenkirchen as it had been before the war. One of the photographs showed lines of refugees struggling to cross the bridge.

'Anna could have been there when this was taken,' Nairn said.

In a shed outside was an old horse-drawn hearse and an old fire-engine. Alongside, in a new extension, they found a room dedicated to the Great Move.

Photographs showed various aspects of the dam being built; the concrete foundations, the coffer dams, the taking down of the churches, the rebuilding of the churches on higher ground.

By the time they finished at the museum they knew much more about the history and geography of Altenkirchen but that was about all.

They checked into the local hotel and after dinner Paul said he was going for a walk.

'May I come with you?'

'Of course.'

It was dry and cold.

'Wherever we were, Maria and I always walked a little after dinner, then we would look for a bar and have a coffee and cognac. Would you like a nightcap?' Across the square were the lights of the Café Budapest.

Except for the owner, the place was empty, and he looked pleased to have company. They sat at the bar. He said, 'Did you meet old Novotny?' He spoke English well with a Viennese accent.

Paul told him briefly what had happened.

'The old man is our George Washington. Never told a lie in his life, they say.'

He was short and bald with a pitted skin and was in constant motion while he talked, either wiping the top of the bar or polishing glasses. He seemed to do these things without thinking.

'He didn't have much of a chance to say anything,' Nairn said. 'His daughter took him away.'

'She looks after him. She has done for years. There was some trouble long ago. He was in the Staatspolizei and there was a bribery scandal. He gave evidence against his comrades. They made his life hell so he left the force and became a forest ranger. Trees don't take bribes.'

'Little places like this often have scandals under the surface,' Paul said. 'People get hurt.'

'Sure. If it was me I would have kept my mouth shut. I've been in this business long enough to know what can happen.'

He poured them each another brandy. 'Prost,' he said, and threw his into the back of his throat. 'Ja. Ja, I would have said, "Otto, keep your nose from their business." But that wasn't old Novotny's way. He only knew one way. There were some threats against him.'

'They seemed to know we were coming,' Nairn said.

'That would have been Franz, the young taxi driver. A grandson. He would have warned them.'

'Why "warned"?' Nairn said. 'It sounds as though there's some sort of conspiracy, as though we – and others – were trying to extort information. I mean his daughter said he wasn't a Nazi and we should leave him alone. All I want to know is about my grandmother and a family she was with.'

Otto stopped polishing the glass in his hand. 'But that is what the other man wanted to know. About a family.'

She felt her skin crawl. 'What other man?'

'He was here two or three months ago. He spoke to Novotny.'

'Was the family called Meissner?' Paul said.

'I don't know. He had breakfast here. He mentioned the name but I can't remember.'

'What was he like?' Nairn said. 'What did he look like?'

'Once he'd been quite a big man. Now he was thin and dry. Like a stick.'

'Did you hear his name?' Paul said. 'Was it Gregor?'

'I meet so many people. Hear so many names. They go in one ear and out the other. But he upset old Novotny, I think, with his questions. Or upset his daughter which is the same thing. People don't like questions about the past.' He turned to Paul. 'You're right, sir, about one thing. In a place like this you only have to scratch a little below the surface to find the worms.'

'What worms?' Nairn said.

Otto pretended to inspect his glass carefully and then shrugged. 'All communities have their worms. Another?'

They said no and left. In the square Paul gripped her arm and said, 'He knows a lot more than he's saying.'

'You think it was Beckerman?'

'Of course. Otto said two or three months ago. That was just about the time Beckerman was arrested. He knew we were working on the case. He probably came here to find out what people remembered or *if* anyone remembered him personally.'

'Paul . . .' She paused and then said, 'What do you think happened here?'

'God knows. But in the morning I'm going back to Novotny.'

When they reached the hotel he went over to his car to fetch a pack of cigarettes. She waited by the front door and then heard him swear.

'What's wrong?' she said, going across the pavement.

He was bending at the front of his car looking at one of the tyres. It was flat. As she bent down with him he put his finger into a slash. 'Someone doesn't want us here,' he said. 'Too damn bad!'

It was barely ten thirty. Nairn had made her notes, had a bath, and was lying in bed. She suddenly reached for the phone and dialled her London flat. The phone rang four times, then again . . . and again . . . Then the receiver was lifted and a woman's voice said, 'Hello?'

'Who's that?' Nairn said.

There was a click as the receiver was replaced. Had she dialled the wrong number? She must have. She called again. The phone rang four times and then her own voice answered, telling her to leave her message after the tone.

Eight

The following morning Paul was edgy and withdrawn. He had had a new tyre put on the car and was nearly finished his breakfast when she came down. He'd eaten only half a roll and was lighting a cigarette. She looked at his plate and he caught her look.

'Stop mothering me!' he said. It wasn't a light-hearted statement, it was scratchy. Then he held up his hand. 'I'm sorry, but I didn't sleep much last night.'

'Nor did I.'

'Beckerman?'

'Yes,' she lied.

'Me too. I feel him all around me. His ghost if you like. No wonder Novotny didn't want to talk to us. Maybe Beckerman threatened him. Anyway, we'll find out.'

He waited impatiently for her to finish her coffee then they drove through the town square. The place no longer looked like the graveyard of the previous night, for it was full of shoppers.

Suddenly Paul swung the car over to the far side of the street and pulled up next to an old diesel Mercedes. Nairn saw that Franz, the young taxi driver, was sitting in the front seat. Paul stopped level with his window and spoke rapidly in German. The young man looked uneasy.

'What did you say?' Nairn asked, as they drove off.

'I told him we were going to see his grandfather again and if he wanted to warn him he could. I also told him that if I found my tyres slashed again I'd go to the police.'

The morning was chilly and grey, the garden empty. Paul banged on the door and Nairn saw a curtain in one of the windows drawn aside and the daughter's square red face stare out at them. She shook her head violently and waved them away. Paul went to the window and shouted through the glass, turned to Nairn and said, 'I told her we would stay here the whole day if necessary.'

There was a rattling of door chains and locks and the woman let them in. The interior of the house was dark and full of knick-knacks made of horn. A fire was burning in a small porcelain stove, and the old man, dressed as he had been the day before, was sitting close to it.

'Can't you see he is sick?' the daughter shouted at them. 'Can't you see he has only a small time left?'

The old man cut her short and said in English, 'Come. Sit please.' His face had a kind of translucent quality.

'We are sorry to bother you again,' Nairn said.

The old hands rose slightly from the blanket and dropped again. 'We will take a slivovitz,' he said.

It was barely nine thirty in the morning but she accepted the small glass of plum brandy which burned like fire in her stomach.

'A man came to ask you questions a few months ago,' Paul said.

'Ja.'

'What about?'

'The time after the Anschluss. The time of the refugees.'

'What did he want to know?'

'About a family, and about a young woman with a baby.'

'Can you remember what the family's name was? Was it Meissner?'

The fingers began to pluck nervously at the blanket. 'Ja. That was the name.'

'And the young woman?' Nairn said.

'That I cannot remember. I saw her passport only for a few moments, and it is more than fifty years ago. An English name. She had a baby. She tried to cross the bridge but they closed it early that day. I managed to get her across the next day. I was in the Border Guards then, a lieutenant.' He touched his cap. 'It was a bad time. I was ashamed. Not only for Altenkirchen but for Austria. That is all I can tell you. I never knew what happened to her.'

'She's my grandmother,' Nairn said. 'Her name is Anna. She came from Vienna with a family called Meissner.'

'And a young man called Beckerman,' Paul said. 'They had no exit visas and this Beckerman said he would take them across the river by boat. That's the last that was heard of them.'

The daughter made angry noises in the background and said, 'What is the use of this?'

The old man cut her off then said, 'It was not a good time. People were robbed. Jews, you know. They were robbed of everything they had. Clothes, money. They left their autos in the streets and they too were stolen. We did it. We Austrians. Don't ask me why but we did. We even found bodies in the river, some with bullets in the head. This family Meissner; were they Jews?'

'No. He was a medical specialist from Vienna, but his brother-in-law was a Communist and he had helped him.'

They talked for nearly half an hour. Mostly the discussion was between Nairn and Novotny. The daughter listened without interrupting again. The old man did most of the talking. He had a clear memory of Anna. He kept on saying, 'She was so young, so beautiful.'

The translucent pallor seemed to leave his face and blood began to flow in his cheeks. His daughter watched him, her face softening.

But it was when Nairn mentioned the meeting between Anna and Wilson Braid that true animation entered Novotny's eyes.

'A newspaperman? Ja! Ja! The English *Daily News*. I remember that! Not him, of course, it is too long ago. But I remember we had a telegram from Salzburg about him. And he was the only British reporter to come to Altenkirchen. He had been writing bad things about Austria. That's what they said. And they had been looking for him. Maybe that is why he came to such a small border post and not to Feldkirch. We could not do much except deport him so our orders were to make it a little . . . well, not so pleasant for him.

236

'If I had known he was helping your grandmother I would have done nothing. But I followed my orders. I told customs to make it difficult for him.

'They made him strip and they searched him and took away his typewriter and his papers – '

'And his camera,' his daughter said.

There was a pause. 'Ja, and his camera. Fetch it, *liebchen*.'

It was as though his daughter had been waiting for this moment for she returned a short while later with a Rolleiflex camera in a scarred brown leather case.

Novotny took it in his old hands and began to stroke it. 'I am ashamed to tell you that I have kept this all these years. I should have handed it in, but I had never seen such a camera except in shop windows. For us, on our wages, to own such a camera was not possible.'

Nairn watched the expression on his face change to one of sadness and she felt her heart go out to him.

'I took it from customs. It and his typewriter. I sent the typewriter to headquarters. I said to myself: the camera will be taken by someone higher up than me – then why not me? This is how one lies to oneself. I wanted it badly. But when I took it I could never use it. Sometimes I would look at it. Such cameras are nice to feel, you know.'

'It's true,' his daughter said, breaking in. 'Sometimes he would sit with it on his lap and touch it.'

'When something is well made it is pleasant to touch,' the old man said. 'Now you must give it back to your grandfather.'

Nairn thought of Wilson Braid with his money and houses and boats: he could buy himself all the cameras he needed.

'I want you to have it,' she said. 'For what you did for my grandmother.'

Old Novotny slowly shook his head. 'It is too late for taking pictures now.'

As they were leaving his daughter came down the path with them. 'Please . . .' she said. 'A moment.' They stopped and waited. 'You were kind to him,' she said to Nairn. 'For the first time in weeks he looks a little better. Maybe it is giving up the camera. He was always an honest man. Just this one little thing. It has worried him all the years.'

'I wish he'd taken it,' Nairn said. 'It's such a little thing and it would be repayment.'

She shook her head vigorously. 'No, it is better this way. Now he feels free. This is the first time he has talked about the old days. He is a good man and he does not like to think of the bad things that happened then. That is why he did not tell you of the bodies.'

'What bodies?' Paul said, sharply.

'When they dug the foundations for one of the churches in its new home they uncovered three bodies. They had been buried in the woods. All this was woods in those days. Two adults and a child.'

'Was there any identification?' Nairn said.

'Only a medal. It was from the last century. A medal from the Emperor for public service. The police took it with the bones of the people. You will find an article in the newspaper.'

Paul said, translating: 'The headline reads "Three bodies found in grave. One a child. Evidence of bullet holes."'

They were in the offices of the *Altenkirchner Zeitung* in a small storeroom where the bound copies of the papers were kept. The one Paul was reading from had been published in September 1968.

He went on translating '"Three bodies, one of a young boy, have been found by workmen digging the foundations of the St Margaretan Church which is due to be re-erected above the dam next year.

'"All three are thought to have been shot. They were found on Tuesday when a mechanical digger turned up bones.

'"The digging stopped immediately and Professor Kleist of the University of Innsbruck made a special examination in the presence of members of the police force then took several bones to his laboratory.

'"According to a police spokesman Professor Kleist has dated the burial approximately thirty years ago just before the start of World War II.

'"This would place it at an unhappy time in our town's history when it was besieged by refugees and when some were murdered for their belongings by criminal elements from Vienna and other large cities.

'"Police are now working on the identities of the group but the spokesman said that after this time there was almost no hope of this being established."'

Nairn said, incredulously, 'That's all?'

'That's all.'

'And buried away on an inside page. I love that phrase "criminal elements". My God, this town really is ashamed of its past.'

They spent another half hour going through successive copies of the paper but without finding any further references.

'Now we check with the police,' Paul said.

The police station was modern, with the busy green and grey screens of terminals and the high-pitched whine of printers. Paul told the duty sergeant that he was a member of the Vienna Bar and was in Altenkirchen on official business.

They were shown into the office of a plain-clothes lieutenant. Nairn estimated his age to be in the late forties and his fleshy face wore a sullen expression.

Paul established that he could speak English and told him briefly why they were there.

The lieutenant lit a half-smoked cigar. 'What is it with you people? What's suddenly brought this story out of its grave?'

'You mean the other man?' Paul said, taking a chance. 'The one who was here two or three months ago?'

The lieutenant remained silent, staring at them through the smoke.

'Did you see him?' Paul said.

'No. He was seen by a colleague.'

'Can we talk to him?'

'He's on vacation. What is this all about anyway?'

Nairn told him about her grandmother.

'You're going to all this trouble just to find out about the early days of your grandmother? But you say she's alive in London. Can't she tell you herself?'

'There's more to it than that,' Paul said. 'We think that the man who came with them, their guide who had promised to take them across the river, was Cuno Beckerman.'

'So? Who's Cuno Beckerman?'

'Haven't you read the newspapers? The French want him for war crimes.'

'I don't read stories about war crimes. It's a long time ago and anyway I don't believe in them. War is war.'

'Okay,' Paul said. 'I'm not going to get into an argument with you about that. We understand that three bodies were dug up in the 1960s. We think this may be the family. The Meissners. We've seen the local newspaper report. It says almost nothing. We'd like to know what the police found out. Especially about the medal.'

'This wasn't in the newspaper.'

'No, it wasn't. The Novotnys mentioned it.'

A shadow crossed the lieutenant's face. 'Oh, that old – '

Paul said: 'About the medal . . .'

'You people think you can come from Vienna and – '

'I could get a court order. Why make things difficult? It's possible we might be able to help you with this case. Wouldn't you like to solve it after all these years? Think of your name in the papers.'

The lieutenant crunched out his cigar and said in a different tone, 'We always like to solve crimes, no matter how old.'

'Have you got the report here?'

He rose and left the room, returning a short while later with a plastic bag and a typewritten report. 'Please take these into the waiting-room,' he said.

The waiting-room was empty and Nairn and Paul sat side by side at a low table. Someone had tried to cheer the place up with floral curtains and a vase of plastic flowers.

Paul flicked his eyes down the typewritten pages. 'It's all forensic. The angles of the bullets. That kind of thing. The man was shot in the side of the head. The woman too. The child in the back of the head.'

He opened the plastic bag and emptied the contents on to the table: some buttons, moulds of teeth, separate plastic sachets with hair, and a rusted medallion, so corroded that it was almost impossible to tell what it had originally been.

He rubbed it with his finger. They could see the faint outline of a double-headed eagle but that was all.

'Not much for three lives, is it?' Nairn said. 'What do you think happened?'

'I think Beckerman killed them here,' he said. 'I think he shot them and robbed them and buried them. That's what I think.'

Nine

'But why?' Nairn said. 'Why did he need to kill them?'

She and Paul were in the Café Budapest, sitting at a table in one of the windows, sharing a bottle of white wine. It was mid-morning and they had gone there from the police station.

'So as not to leave any evidence,' Paul said. 'The same thing happened in France. The bodies were buried in woods.'

'But Anna told me Michael Meissner paid Beckerman well. He was also to get the car.'

'Maybe he didn't think that was enough. Maybe he wanted everything.'

'You're saying he shot them in the forest and then buried them?'

'That's my guess.'

'But you need something to dig holes with.' She was unwilling to accept the horrendous scenario Paul had sketched.

'Many drivers carry a shovel in the boot of their car, especially if they're going over the Arlberg in early spring.'

'Paul, it's too terrible to contemplate.'

'Hundreds of people were trying to get into Switzerland from this little town alone. Most of them were Jews. They could take only what they could carry. Money, share certificates, insurance policies, bonds – and jewellery. There was no wedding ring in the envelope, no engagement ring, no brooches, no necklaces. No jewels of any kind were found in the grave. And the Meissners were wealthy. Doesn't that strike you as odd?'

He reached out, took both her hands, placed them palms down on the table and counted her rings. There were four.

'Rings are fashionable these days.'

'Even so, Ruth would have had at least two rings on her fingers, maybe more. In her position would you leave your jewellery behind?'

'Gladly. You should see mine.'

He brushed this aside. 'Do you have any other explanation?'

'No. Everything just goes round and round and comes back to that same scene. But it's hard to imagine even a man like Beckerman doing that.'

His fingers lingered on her hands and then he moved them away and poured them each another glass of wine.

He said, 'Reading between the lines of the police report, my guess would be that Beckerman shot Michael first, suddenly and without warning. Then a second or two later, before she could react, he shot Ruth. Both were shot in the side of the head. The boy, Stefan, must have turned to run. He probably didn't get more than a step or two then Beckerman shot him in the back of the head.'

'I don't want to talk about it any more. Anyway you're only assuming that these are the Meissners and that Beckerman shot them. They could be another group altogether.'

'Do you believe that?'

'For God's sake, Paul, I don't know what I believe, but I know I don't want to talk about it!'

'Now you can understand the kind of facts I've been dealing with. I'm hungry. What about you?'

She shook her head. He went to the bar and came back with another bottle of wine and a large bowl of *frites*. She looked at him in amazement.

'*Zweitesfrühstück*,' he said. 'Second breakfasts are an old custom in Austria.'

She began to nibble at the French fries. 'I don't want to talk about the murder any more, not at the moment anyway, but there's one thing that bothered me earlier: old Novotny and the camera.'

'What about him?'

'He says he didn't use it. Does that sound logical?'

'There's a well-known case in the States of a man who bought every new model Leica but never took a picture in his life. He just liked to look at the cameras and feel the precision with which they were made. They're like worry beads for some people.'

'My uncle Peter says stroking a dachshund is better than worry beads.' She began to talk about her family, using them to distance herself from Paul's grisly reconstruction of what he thought had happened in the woods half a century before. She talked about Anna and Wilson Braid and their three sons; about her years at school in England when she and Anna had grown more like sisters than grandmother and grand-daughter.

Suddenly he broke in: 'Except for Anna, you don't sound as though you like your family very much.'

She frowned. 'That's not true.' Then after a moment, 'Maybe it's because of what they're trying to do to Anna.'

'What's that?'

'They're going to try to take her newspaper away from her. Or at least that's what she thinks.' She told him of the forthcoming boardroom battle.

He ran his fingers through his hair. 'Jesus!' She could tell he was not thinking of what might happen to Anna but only that it would delay her arrival.

She watched him as he ate the last of the French fries. He was an attractive man, she thought. Not in an obvious way, but he had an inner vitality and an unpredictability that made him exciting to be with.

'What do you do for relaxation?' she asked.

'Play tennis. In the winter I ski.'

'Is that all?'

'I have a season ticket for the Musikverein. For the Sunday morning Philharmoniker concerts.'

'You go by yourself?'

'No, not by myself.'

He was making it difficult for her. 'Who with?'

He grinned at her. 'I have three mistresses, I take each in turn.'

They walked back to the hotel. When they crossed the first road he took her arm as though to guide her through the traffic. She realized that in all her time with Neil he had never done that once. He kept his hand on her arm and she enjoyed his touch.

They were crossing the foyer of the hotel when the receptionist called: 'Herr Esslin. Telefon, bitte.'

'Excuse me,' Paul said.

She continued up to her room and stood by the window looking out on to the waters of the dam. There was a knock at the door and Paul came in. 'That was my office in Vienna,' he said. 'The interview with Beckerman has been arranged. We must leave immediately.'

The day deteriorated as they drove east. First there was snow on the Arlberg and the signs were on for snow-chains. But Paul still had winter tyres on the car. As they left the snowline on the far side he let the Lancia have its head and it responded like a racehorse.

Innsbruck . . . Salzburg . . . Linz . . .

They left the autobahn at Melk and crossed the grey Danube in the late afternoon with mist on the water and a thin, driving rain puckering the surface. The signs began to point to Stein. They passed apricot orchards, their blossoms drooping in the dismal weather. The prison was gaunt and forbidding in the half-light. Rain beat against its walls and much of it was obscured by mist.

As a journalist, Nairn had once had to visit a London prison. It had been built in the middle of the last century. This grim Austrian fortress reminded her of that building. There were the same thick walls and painted brickwork, the same clanking of steel doors and jangling of keys, the same faint smell of disinfectant and cooking – and the same dry warmth from central heating. Prisoners and prison officers were wearing shirts and trousers and she felt stifled in her heavy coat.

They were met by the Deputy Governor, a hard-faced man in his early forties, who said stiffly that she must be searched.

'Only me?' she said, with a sudden frisson of apprehension.

'I thought we were both seeing him,' Paul said.

'Only the lady. It is Herr Gregor's decision.' His tone was curt and dismissive. It was clear he disapproved of the visit.

She was taken into a separate room. A female prison officer

searched her handbag and her coat pockets and then ran her hands up and down her body. The Deputy Governor waited outside the room and when the search was over and she was allowed her notebook, pencil and miniaturized recorder, he said, 'Follow, please.'

They went down a short corridor and into an ante-room which, like the interrogation rooms she had seen in British police stations, contained a table and two chairs, a barred window, a steel door, and a bright light in the ceiling.

Hurriedly she arranged her recorder and notebook on the table and hung her coat on the chair. When she looked up a man was standing just inside the door. She had not heard a sound. Her apprehension turned to alarm. No one else was visible though she knew that someone must be in the passage outside.

The man was standing perfectly still, watching her. The words used by Otto at the Café Budapest – 'thin, dry, like a stick' – leapt into her mind. It exactly described him.

He moved forward slowly in a kind of shuffle. He was dressed in his ordinary clothes, a white open-necked shirt, grey trousers and sandals.

'Grüss Gott,' he said.

'Good evening.'

He closed the door behind him. She felt her skin crawl. His eyes were purplish-blue and seemed to dilate as he looked at her. He made a sudden movement and she had to force herself not to step backwards. But he was only putting out his hand in greeting. She shook it. It felt dry and cool. He was a head taller than she, with deeply incised lines on his face. He still had a full head of white hair and it was combed backwards over his domed skull.

'Please,' he said, indicating one of the chairs.

She sat and he sat opposite her. He had a presence, she thought, which filled the room. It was overpowering. His face was expressionless and he waited for her to speak.

'I . . . It was good of you to see me, Herr Beckerman.' It slipped out without thought. Paul was so convinced this man was Beckerman he had planted his certainties in her subconscious. 'I'm sorry – '

He smiled. The lips drew back and she saw stained teeth. But there was no mirth in it. 'I was a police officer. I attended many interrogations. I understand psychology.'

'I can assure you it wasn't meant. I wasn't trying to trap you. It's just that this whole business – '

'Please . . .' He held up his hand as though her apologies only made things worse.

She wanted to avoid looking into his eyes. She tried to focus instead on his mouth or his jaw but his eyes seemed to become enlarged, drawing her own eyes upwards until they locked on to the two purple beams.

She had to take a grip on herself. 'First of all, Herr Gregor, may I ask why you granted me this interview?'

He paused, as though thinking out the exact words in English, and then said, 'Here in Austria we have a president the world does not like and this has made things difficult for us. Because of this the Austrian press and television no longer have a position in the world. My story needs to be known. It is better for me to have the facts put down in a newspaper in England or America.'

'But what if you get an unsympathetic press in England? It's an emotional subject.'

'This is why we must stay with the facts.'

She forced herself to relax. 'Okay, let's start with the facts. Tell me about yourself. When and where you were born. Marriage. Children. Early life. That kind of detail.'

He spoke slowly and deliberately. His English was rusty after long disuse. He told her he had been born in Villach in Styria where he'd gone to school. On the outbreak of the war he had joined the army and become a sergeant in the Mountain Corps. He had married during the war and had fought in Italy and France. After the war he was part of a construction unit rebuilding Vienna.

'When the Russians attacked they knocked down everything in their way. First with big guns then with tanks. All was broken buildings. There was a lot of work to do.'

He had become a clerk, he said, in the British Administration when the Allies governed the First District of the city. Later he had joined the police service, had risen to the rank of lieutenant and retired fourteen years before. He was now living north of Vienna on a smallholding where he bred trout for the table.

'Why do you think you've been arrested, Herr Gregor?'

'Mistakes are often made. It is a long time ago.'

'Are you bitter?'

'I am not happy. I have few years left. This is not a place to spend even one day.'

'Have you ever been to Altenkirchen?'

'Never.'

'Are you quite certain?'

His eyes were suddenly angry. 'I said no!'

'Altenkirchen was where my grandmother escaped from Austria. You never knew her?'

'How could I know her? Who is she?'

'Her name was Anna Webster and she worked for a family called Meissner. You never knew them either?'

'Never.'

'Perhaps you will meet her. She owns the newspaper I work for. The *Daily News*.'

'How can I meet her?'

Nairn suddenly threw caution to the winds. 'Because she will probably come here, to this prison, to see you. She knew Cuno Beckerman in Vienna. They were friends.'

If she had expected a reaction she was disappointed.

'I will look forward to it. Then the story of my injustice will go round the world.'

'Why do you say that?'

'Because if she knew Beckerman then she will be able to say I am not this man.'

'But what if she says you are?'

For the first time she saw a slight reaction. He drew his lips together and swung his head away from her, so that his eyes no longer bored into hers.

'Young lady, I agreed to see you because it could do my position good. But I think I have spoken enough. I think you came here with your decision already made that I am someone you want me to be.'

'Why you are here has nothing to do with me. It is because the French Government believes that you are Beckerman. My

248

own interest is simply this: my grandmother took a baby out of Austria in 1938. It belonged to the Meissner family. Beckerman was to guide the Meissners across the border because they did not have papers. No one saw them again.'

He took a pack of cigarettes from his shirt pocket and lit one. His hands were rock steady. 'Please continue,' he said. 'As a policeman these stories interest me.'

She caught the sarcasm and smiled to herself. It was the first time she had pricked him.

'We think we know what happened.'

'We? Who is we?'

'Paul Esslin and myself. You must remember Felix Esslin. No, no, of course you wouldn't. I'm sorry. I'm getting confused again.'

Nairn was surprised at herself for answering sarcasm with sarcasm.

She went on, 'He was a left-wing journalist and Paul's grand-father. He was also Ruth Meissner's brother. He was arrested by the Austrian police after a tip-off. It has been suggested that Beckerman made that phone call to the police. You see how it all ties in?'

'Ties in? How is that?'

'With what happened in Altenkirchen. Did you know that three bodies have been found there? They were dug up when the dam was built and the village moved. Or didn't you know that they had put a dam there?'

'I told you I do not know Altenkirchen.'

'A man, a woman, and a child. They had been shot. The man and woman in the side of the head, the young boy – his name was Stefan – in the back of the head. We think he was just starting to run away when he was killed. We think Cuno Beckerman killed them and robbed them and then buried them.'

Herr Gregor smiled. 'Thinking something because you wish it is one of the problems in the police service. But thinking is not evidence.'

'We know that. We don't think there is anything at this late stage that can be done in Austria. But the French case is different. There is documentation. All that remains is identification. That's where my grandmother comes in.'

249

He rose suddenly. 'I am an old man. I become tired easily. I hope you make good propaganda for me. I say to you goodbye.' He turned and shuffled from the room.

Ten

'We are making our approach to Heathrow Airport, London,' the voice of the air hostess said. 'Would you please extinguish all cigarettes and fasten your seatbelts.'

Nairn zipped up her case, fastened her seatbelt, and sat back. Usually, after being away on a job, she looked forward to getting home – but not this morning. Too much had happened and was about to happen to allow her that comfortable feeling of anticipation.

There was Neil and herself.

There was Beckerman and Gregor and Paul and Anna – and herself.

There was Anna and Peter and Nico and her father and the *Daily News*.

And herself.

It seemed ages – but was only a matter of days – since she and Anna had talked at length of what she would do in Austria. Now she was on her way back. And what was she to recommend? Would she tell Anna she must go to Austria?

That was the question that Paul had asked her. They had been having a late dinner at Tulln after she had seen Gregor in Stein gaol. The restaurant was glassed in and the Danube spooled blackly past, only a few yards away.

Through the first part of dinner he had questioned her in detail about her interview. She had told him everything she could remember, had read to him everything in her notes, and had played over her tape recording twice. Still he was not satisfied and seemed to want to drag from her facts that she did not have.

'All I can say is what I feel,' she said.

'Not women's intuition! Spare me that.'

'I can't explain. His eyes had a quality of . . . well, of evil in them. And he just seemed right as Beckerman.'

'What do you mean by "seemed right"?'

'The way he looked, his manner, the way he answered questions. I mean, wouldn't someone who was trying hard to pretend he was innocent . . . wouldn't he say he wanted the world to know his story?'

'So would an innocent man.'

'And if you were a murderer on the run where better to hide than in the police force? Who would look for you there?'

'Conjectures. Supposition. There must have been *some*thing that gave him away. He can't be that perfect!'

'Why not?' He's a different person from the one who went to war in 1940. That's fifty years ago. People can change in a matter of weeks.'

'Not completely. Anyway, what are you going to say to your grandmother? You realize there are only a few days left. I spoke to the French legal team a week ago. They're optimistic that their files contain enough circumstantial evidence for the extradition to go ahead. I don't believe it. Austria is in a funny mood. Since the Waldheim election when all our sins were dragged out again, many Austrians in high positions have reacted badly. They say if the world thinks we're barbarians then to hell with the world.'

'But if the French case is watertight then the law is the law.'

He smiled grimly. 'That's what I thought when I first began to practise. Now I know that the law is one man's interpretation of it. And extradition is one of the most difficult parts of the law to interpret. What we need is a definite identification. This journalist, Ben Ramsey, may take months to find. No, it has to be your grandmother. What are you going to say?'

Now, on the plane coming in to London, the question was still in her mind and she still did not have an answer. How could she place this added burden of responsibility on Anna's shoulders when her professional world was about to be turned upside down?

After dinner Paul had driven into Vienna over the northern hills. She had wanted to go to a hotel but he had said, 'There's a spare room in my apartment.'

She was dead tired and the thought of phoning hotels at midnight and being told there was no room held little appeal. She was grateful for the offer and accepted it.

His apartment was in a post-war block near the Türkenschanz Park. The streets were dark, the trees buffeted by the wind, the streetlights swaying on their overhead wires. In the distance she could hear a late tram.

His apartment was warm and welcoming. The main theme was dark wood against light walls, with curtains and fabrics in hot tropical colours. Nairn felt sure the design was his wife's.

After showing her the bathroom and the spare room, he said good night and she heard him close his bedroom door.

Even though she was tired she transcribed her notes on to the word processor and added some sentences of atmosphere while she still recalled it.

She got into bed and for the first time in many months felt lonely. She told herself not to be stupid and soon she was asleep.

It seemed she had only just closed her eyes when a noise in the room wakened her. She switched on the light and saw Paul standing near her bed. He was in his dressing-gown and was holding a mug of coffee. 'It's nearly time to get up,' he said.

'I'm absolutely zonked. I thought I'd just got to sleep.'

'This'll help.' He handed her the mug of coffee and she drank gratefully.

He went to the window and opened the curtains. Grey dawn seeped into the room.

'I couldn't sleep,' he said.

She sipped the coffee, feeling it begin to work on her nervous system. 'Beckerman?'

'I asked you the same question in Altenkirchen. See how he haunts us?'

There was a moment's silence and then he said, 'You are the first person, male or female, who has slept in this apartment since my wife died. I used to bring her coffee in bed like this in the mornings. You forget the little things.' He looked at his watch. 'I'll take you to the airport. We'll leave in about an hour.'

At that time in the morning the traffic was light. Instead of taking the Gürtel ring-road, they drove straight through the centre of the city.

She said, 'Everywhere I look I see the ghosts of Anna and Michael and Ruth – and Ben Ramsey.'

'And Beckerman,' he said.

'Of course. And Beckerman. It's odd though, I seem to see everything in black and white, not in colour.'

'That's because you've seen the Vienna of that period in old newsreels.' He was silent for a moment, then said, 'Do you think she told you everything?'

'Who?'

'Your grandmother.'

God, she thought, he simply *never* leaves the subject.

'Does anyone tell everything?'

'Do you think she'll fight this takeover business?'

'You've met her. Don't you? I think she'll fight like hell.'

They reached the Rennweg, that seemingly endless road that runs past the cemeteries.

She wanted him to go on talking, to keep in contact, but he turned away, retreating into his own thoughts. There had been moments at Altenkirchen when she had almost got through to him. And again that morning, when she had woken to find him in her room. She had the impression that he had been there some time, minutes perhaps, watching her as she slept. But the moments had passed. Instead of Paul, he had become Herr Esslin again: a man obsessed with the past. The whole Austrian experience had baffled her. She knew she was an attractive woman and it was somewhat humiliating to have made so little impression on him.

She touched his arm and said, 'You'll get him.'

Then she thought: But if you don't, how will you get over it?

The airport was busy. Most of the passengers were grey-suited businessmen carrying black attaché cases bound for Frankfurt and Bonn, Milan and London.

Nairn and Paul waited together in an uneasy silence punctuated by little flurries of inconsequential conversation.

Suddenly she needed to say a great many things, to make some kind of mark on the iron of his psyche, a kind of NAIRN WAS HERE sign, so that she would not be just another blank face in his memory. But she couldn't find the words. His defences were in place – or she thought they were, so she was taken by surprise when he said, as though reading her own mind, 'I wish things were different.'

The flight was called. He bent quickly and kissed her on the cheek. He held her at arm's length and said: 'When I was in the States I used to read Robert Frost. "The woods are lovely, dark, and deep, But I have promises to keep, And miles to go before I sleep." – Well, I have promises to keep . . .'

He seemed about to say something else. She waited but the moment passed and he gave a slight smile, a slight shrug. 'Have a good trip.'

Heathrow Airport was busy but Nairn had only hand luggage. She took a tube into London and was soon in Swiss Cottage crossing the Finchley Road in the direction of her flat.

She was tired, depressed at leaving Vienna for a reason she only partly understood, disorientated from the flight, and apprehensive. She had phoned the flat from the airport but all she had got was the answering machine. She was sick of that machine and sick of hearing her own voice!

When she opened the door and was hit by a blast of hot air she knew that something was wrong. The central heating was on and Neil had also left a fan heater running in the hall. She switched it off and flung open several windows. Then she looked around. In her bedroom the bed was unmade and there was an empty red wine bottle on the floor. A wine glass stood on each side of the bed.

With mounting anger she went into Neil's 'studio'. His paintings had gone, so had the easel and brushes. So had a stereo recorder with amplifier and speakers. So had some of her books.

There was no note. No 'Dear Joan' letter. But then, she thought, the place hadn't been left this way by chance. This was his note; his goodbye; his thanks for the memory.

If it hadn't been for her books she would have sat down then and cried. That was the unkindest cut, the one that made the statement loud and clear.

'Okay,' she thought. 'To hell with you.'

She was about to start tidying up when the phone rang. She switched off the machine and answered. It was her uncle Peter.

'I've been trying to reach you for days!' he said.

'I've been away.'

'I realize that. Listen, I must see you urgently.'

'I've just walked in the door from Vienna. What about tomorrow?'

'No, it has to be this morning. Now.'

'Look, I want to bath and change and talk to Anna. And then you've got the meeting.'

'That's why I've got to see you. Before you talk to Anna. I'll be there in an hour.'

She replaced the receiver, slumped down in a chair and kicked off her shoes.

'Welcome home, Nairn darling,' she said to herself. 'Welcome home.'

BOOK THREE

The Meeting

One

The boardroom of the *Daily News* was on the same floor as Anna's suite of offices. It was a plain room with a long beechwood table. There were eight chairs on either side of the table but none at the ends, a gesture of Anna's towards equality. This was the room where she usually held editorial conferences and where the editor, the foreign editor, the news editor, the picture editor, a leader writer or two, the features editor, the women's editor and three or four senior journalists would meet. Those who could not find chairs would stand and lean against the light oak panelling on which hung framed political cartoons.

The windows of the boardroom looked out over the roofs of Pimlico to the Thames and to the Surrey hills which, on this morning of breeze and cloud, were darkly defined against the sky.

In the boardroom were Anna and Monty – now Sir Montague Axe. He had arrived some minutes earlier preceded by his chauffeur who was carrying a small wicker hamper.

'A little sustenance,' Monty said. 'I don't suppose you've had any breakfast.'

She shook her head.

He looked disapproving. 'Coffee and cigarettes, though.'

'Don't fuss, Monty.'

'Well, at least you won't have them on an empty stomach.'

He opened the hamper and brought out a bottle of Bollinger and another of orange juice and proceeded to make Buck's Fizz. 'Alcohol and vitamin C, the perfect combination for this time in the morning.' He held up his glass. 'To the smiting of our

. . . I was going to say enemies but perhaps that's going too far. I've brought some *pâté de campagne*.'

'I don't want anything.'

'Worried? A couple more glasses will change that. I'm a great believer in Dutch courage.'

He made them both another drink and then sat down facing her at the long table. 'Anything I should know?' he asked. 'I always like to have all the facts.'

'Nothing that you don't know already.'

'Then let's work on the assumption that you're right.'

He opened a scarred briefcase and spread his papers on the table-top. She lit another cigarette and watched him.

She had known him for so long she had taken him for granted. Now she tried to see him with fresh eyes. The large plump man who had once wanted to marry her had given way to an elderly plump man, with a great bald dome of a head and two tufts of grey hair above his ears.

She wondered what might have happened if she had married him. Would he have been one of the top company lawyers in London as he was now, or would he have been head of Webster Communications and not just its non-executive chairman? She couldn't imagine anyone but herself in that position yet how would she have stopped him? He was much cleverer than she.

Over the years he had become more and more distinguished. He was now a member of the Jewish Board of Deputies, had served a term as President of the Law Society and had been knighted. She might have been Lady Axe. In any case she would have been 'a wife'. And that was the point. She couldn't imagine herself as being 'the wife' of anyone. She'd been too long on her own. Sometimes she regretted Ben, but if they had married she would have missed the excitement of their irregular and unexpected encounters.

'I want to play devil's advocate,' Monty said.

'Fire away.'

'We're working on the assumption that pressure is going to be put on you to resign.'

'Yes.'

'What if you did?'

'Did what? Resign?' Her voice had risen slightly.

'Have you considered it?'

'Absolutely not.'

'Do you think you're indispensable?'

'Monty, I – '

'Save your anger. I said I was going to play devil's advocate. Just consider it for a moment. You're not young. Why not pass the crown to someone else? Why not use the remainder of your time to . . .'

'What you're really saying is, why don't I put myself out to grass?'

'All family firms, large or small, whether it's a grocer or the *Daily News*, face this eventually. The head of the family usually stays too long. Sometimes only death can release new energy.'

She felt as though he had opened a door on her future and had forced her to look on to a cold, bleak landscape. She didn't want questions like this, not today.

'Is that what you think?'

'No, it isn't. But let's say that for reasons we don't know you might want to hand over the reins.'

'Monty!'

'Bear with me. None of us is immune from being run over by the dreaded omnibus and it'll help narrow our focus. The shares are held by you and Wilson and Nico and Peter and John. So the field is small. Leaving Wilson out of it, what about Nico? He's the eldest.'

'All right, we'll play your game for a moment. Can you see Nico facing up to even the simplest problems? Can you see him even getting in to work every day? I can't. You remember when he asked me for a loan to pay off his gambling debts?'

'I advised against.'

'I said I wouldn't lend him the money but I'd give him a job. I said I'd pay him well and he could use that to pay off the debt. He was doubtful but he finally agreed.'

'I remember that.'

'What you don't know is the trouble I had. I had to find him a job which justified paying him a salary. That was hard enough. But it also had to appear to be a real job, so as not to wound his pride. I told him we were thinking of producing a Sunday edition and asked him to design a new front page banner.

'It took him four months. He went to New York and Paris and Rome to look into typefaces and the latest in newspaper design. His expenses alone were double his salary, and at the end he produced nothing. Nothing usable anyway. Then the dividends on his shares came through and he decided to take his annual leave and went to Las Vegas where he lost again.'

'But you did lend him money in the end.'

'I had to. If I'd just given it to him in the first place, it would have been cheaper. So, since you ask me, no, I don't think Nico would make a good chief executive. Apart from anything else his private life is a mess and I don't think he could change. Nico just isn't a businessman.'

'I've always liked him,' Monty said. 'There's something about him . . .'

'Yes. There is.'

'If only he'd found himself a niche.'

If . . . she thought. If she'd had more time for him. If she'd tried harder. If . . .

'What about Peter?'

'Peter.' She paused. 'I don't know.'

She suddenly saw him as a small child. The tiny face in the big hospital bed, the surgeon leaning over him, and the agony while she waited to hear the prognosis. It was a long time ago yet she could even smell, in her memory, the faint odour of ether that lingered in the hospital.

'I don't know, Monty. Sometimes I think he's quite brilliant and at others I feel that his looks have been his passport to success.'

'They've certainly helped.'

'It's just that . . . no, I can't put my finger on it. There seems to be a piece missing – for this kind of job anyway. He never did very well in journalism. I got him those jobs. He doesn't know that, and I'm only telling you because I'm playing your game.'

'Truth or consequences,' he said, and she felt a sudden chill.

'I think he was glad to get out of newspapers. Television suits him. It's the adrenaline. He told me once that when he's interviewing on camera the pain in his leg simply disappears.'

'He writes good books. Not deep but fresh, an interesting view.'

'It's the television show that's made him. I don't think you can give up that kind of life, unless you're forced to. And he's too damned good at it. No, I don't think Peter. He wouldn't want to do it, and I'm not sure he could. I think it might bore him and that would show and the staff would resent it. Sometimes his manner is patronizing and that spells trouble in this business.'

'I've often wondered about the changes pain causes in people.'

'I'm so close to Peter I can't judge.'

'Anyway, he's the one we don't have to worry about today. I assume he's only coming to block the others.'

'Peter's totally loyal. He always has been.'

'Right. What about John?'

'I'm not sure about John either. I don't really know him. From what I hear he's done well in Braid International.'

'From what *I* hear he's his father's messenger.'

'Wilson was the same when Jock was alive. He was always looking over his shoulder. It was one of the characteristics I liked least about him.'

'Jock was typical of the self-made man. They're always a problem to live with.'

'Like the self-made woman?'

'I didn't say that.'

'I suppose John could run things if Mary were behind him. I've a great deal of respect for her and I'm sorry things haven't worked out between us. We could have been friends.' She paused and then said, 'When I first lost John it was like having an arm or a leg ripped off. I always thought I'd be able to put things right eventually. But by the time he'd grown up it was too late. I was the villain.'

'And the fact that Nairn became so close to you. That would have been enough to sour any family relationship.'

'I was here, they were six thousand miles away. She was my granddaughter, was I supposed to ignore her?'

'You did the only thing you could, my dear.'

'We're so alike. No one could have foreseen that.'

'All right. If you had to choose, which would it be?'

'John. Because he's had experience of managing a newspaper. But I'm sure that if he got his hands on the *Daily News* it would only be as a stalking-horse for his father. And that will never, never happen. Not while I'm alive!'

She got up, walked to the windows and stared out unseeingly. 'Monty, do you really think I'm past it? Is that what you're leading up to in your devious lawyer's way?'

'I didn't say that at all.'

'No, but maybe you're thinking it.'

'I'm not. But . . .'

'I was waiting for that. But me no buts as the man said. What that *but* means is that you think I've made a mess of things recently.'

'All enterprises, big or small, have their downturns.'

'Don't prevaricate, Monty. I don't need mollycoddling now. Save that for later.'

'If fingers are going to be pointed – and I suppose they are – then let *them* do the pointing, not me.'

'We know that I made some bad decisions.'

'No single human being makes the right decisions all the time.' He stood up and leaned over the table to emphasize his words. 'What I need to know is how much you want to hang on to what you've created. I don't want to discover doubts, uncertainties, hidden areas.'

'Like what?'

'I don't like surprises, as you know. Especially at times like these. There's no doubt that if they all want you out they have enough voting clout to achieve it. Divide and rule. That must be our game plan until our balance sheets start to improve. We've talked about selling the American assets, so at least we have something to offer. No, the real point is that I don't want to find a side of you that you may not know yourself.'

'Which is?'

'A side that has had enough and is ready to cave in. Family rows are the worst rows.'

'Take it from me, Monty, I haven't had enough and we fight with everything we've got.'

'That's all I needed to know.'

He took out a yellow legal pad from his briefcase, drew four columns on the top page and wrote down the names of each shareholder and his holdings. Then he said, 'Let's do a preliminary vote. John?'

'We must suppose he'll vote against me.'

'Nico?'

'I imagine he'll vote with John.'

'Peter?'

'He'll vote with me.'

'In that case why are the three of them so keen to attend?'

'That's what we have to find out,' she said.

Two

Nairn tidied up the flat, showered, changed, made herself a cup of coffee and then rewound the tape on her ansaphone. It seemed as though her whole family had been trying to contact her, even her grandfather from Johannesburg. The one voice that was missing was Neil's.

Just as she was coming to terms with the thought that he really had left for good, the doorbell rang stridently. For a moment she held her breath, but when she answered the door-phone it was her uncle Peter.

She had never thought of him as 'uncle', just as she had never thought of Anna as 'grandmother'. This part of the family seemed so much younger than the African section. Even her own parents seemed older than Anna. And of course to apply the word 'uncle' to Nico would have been unthinkable.

Peter entered the room and she thought, as she always did, how good-looking he was. As a teenager she had enjoyed being taken out by him, hoping that people might think he was her boy-friend.

'Hi,' he said, taking her face in his hands and kissing her. 'Where have you been? Somewhere exciting?'

'Vienna. For the paper.'

'Big story?'

'It might be. Coffee?'

He settled down in one of her large armchairs. The room where Neil had painted was still looking as though something strange had happened to it but Nairn decided not to apologize or explain.

'Is Neil . . . ?' He left the sentence hanging.

'He's working in his other studio.'

He sipped at the coffee and she waited. At last he said, 'The meeting's today.'

'Yes, I know.'

'I've never been to an Annual General Meeting of Webster Communications. Not in all these years. I don't really like meetings, do you?'

'No.'

'You ring anyone now and their secretary inevitably says they're in a meeting. It's a knee-jerk reaction. Gives them time to decide whether they want to talk.'

He's waffling, she thought. Something's up. She wanted to say, 'Peter, I've got a hell of a lot to do,' but instead she waited.

After a moment he said, 'What's it like on the *News* these days?'

'How do you mean?'

'Well . . . still enjoying yourself? Still zipping round the world?'

'Sometimes.' She was wary now. She knew that the last half-yearly figures had been bad and that the next lot were said to be horrendous.

'I suppose you're on a pretty tight regime, aren't you?'

'In what way?'

'Isn't there some sort of economy drive?'

'You mean like not using the office phones for private calls?'

It was the way she said it that made him realize she was well ahead of him.

'No, of course not.'

But it was precisely the kind of thing he meant. Channel 14 had gone on an economy drive after their *Breakfast Special* had bombed and there'd been jokes about not using more than three pieces of loo paper. Even people of Peter's stature had received memos about telephone calls and office stationery and paper-clips. Someone had put up a cartoon on the notice-board showing an emaciated kangaroo with Baxter's features, holding out a begging bowl. But someone else had taken it down. Jobs were scarce. People were scared. It wasn't a good idea to stick it to Kev.

267

'What I meant was, you know, a general tightening.'

'Like what?' Nairn was determined to make him spell it out.

'You know as well as I do how a newspaper soaks up money. Do you still have correspondents all over the world as you used to?'

'Of course we do.'

'Quite a few papers work only with stringers these days. It's murderously expensive to keep a man and his family in a foreign post.'

'I'm not sure I understand your point, Peter.' She tried to sound as gracious as she could.

'I should have thought you'd be the first one to figure that out. We've been losing money.'

He sounded uncharacteristically pompous. Was this the Peter she had known since she was twelve? The Peter who had been fun to be with and who had taken her to the movies and the theatre and sailing at Cowes? He sounded more like her father. Or her grandfather. They were the ones who always talked about corporate affairs and money and used words like equity. Like most journalists she did not understand business and was bored by the commercial world until its venalities became page one stories.

'Anna hasn't said anything about an economy drive. We're just getting on with our work. This'll blow over. We're still the best-informed and most brightly written daily in England. We're not worried.'

'But I am. And so are the other shareholders.'

'Is that why you wanted to see me? To tell me you're worried?'

'Well, yes, in a way. But there is something else. I wanted to sound you out. I want your advice.'

She waited once more then said, 'More coffee?'

He shook his head. 'I don't know how much you know, but things are bloody serious. I mean really grim. The *News* has got itself into a downward spiral. You think it will turn around, but I'm not so optimistic. It seems to me that fresh blood is needed, a fresh initiative.'

'Sackings? That sort of fresh blood?'

'Only partly. They've happened in every other business. Why not in newspapers?'

'Because newspapers aren't like other businesses. Who are you going to sack? You know that our editorial staff can't be cut any further.'

He wasn't looking at her, didn't seem to hear. 'It needs changes at the top.'

'Right at the top? I thought you were on Anna's side.'

'Of course I am.'

There had been the slightest hesitation before he responded and she looked at him searchingly.

'What changes then?'

'I mean, well, the editor, for instance.'

'Jackson? You must be joking, Peter. He's the best editor in London. You know that, everyone knows that.'

'I didn't mean get rid of him,' he said hastily. 'I meant the introduction of some kind of super-editor. Someone above the editor. A guiding hand, so to speak.'

'But we have one. Anna. She's above the editor, she's the guiding hand.'

'No, I meant someone specifically charged with the *Daily News*. Anna's got the whole group to run. She can't concentrate only on the paper.'

'You sound as though you're thinking of a managing editor.'

'That's it. An editor who manages as well.'

'We had one. Anna let him go. Managing editors are the kind of people who know where the crosswords come from. And the comic strips. Not much else.'

'That's only when they're no good.'

'You?'

'I'm only giving a kind of example. Do you think the staff would wear it?'

'Wear you?'

'Not necessarily me.'

'You couldn't, anyway. Not doing *Talking Heads* as well.'

'There'll come a time when I'll get bored with *Talking Heads*. Nothing goes on for ever. Just say, for argument's sake, that we decided it might be a good thing for someone . . . all right, me, to take over a senior position. How do you think . . . you know, being family, the staff would take to it?'

She leaned back. He *was* thinking about it! 'Peter, I can't speak for anyone but myself.'

'Fine. Fine.'

'I don't think it's a good idea.'

'Oh?'

'You don't really know anything about newspapers.'

'That's not true. I worked – '

'That was in the old days when everything was hot metal printing and correspondents were using cables and telex. Everything's changed.'

'Not the ethos.'

'Maybe not but don't you see, you're part of the past. If what you say is true, we need someone who is part of the future.'

He tried to smile his winning, camera smile, but it slipped down his face and disappeared.

'I see.'

'Sorry, but you did ask.'

'Sure.' He rose. 'It was only hypothetical, you know.'

She saw him out into the street. As he was getting into his car she said, 'Peter, I think you should know something before you go to the meeting. If anyone tries to mess with the present structure there's likely to be a walkout.'

'You too?'

'The first to go.'

'If that's the attitude of all the staff it might just close the paper for good. 'Bye.'

She watched him drive away and went back into the flat. She was mystified as well as irritated. He was involving her in something she didn't need right then. There was Neil. There was Paul. There was Beckerman. Her own life seemed to be chaotic. This was something the older members of her family would have to sort out – it wasn't her affair.

When Peter reached his house in Hampstead there was a hire car at the door and Laura was on the front steps. He looked at his watch. 'So soon?'

'I have to be at the terminal two hours ahead of takeoff,' she said. 'They've tightened up on security.'

She was looking marvellous, he thought. She was wearing a

dark green suit with a white blouse and a thin gold chain round her neck. Green was her colour. The dark green set off the rich red of her hair. Again he wished she wasn't going. Especially now when he felt tense and uneasy.

They kissed and he held her tight. 'Don't forget what we agreed,' she said.

'Do you want me to ask you formally for your hand? On my knees?'

'Let's just say you've asked me already and I've said yes. That'll solve it.'

'What happens if one of us reconsiders?'

'Let's wait and see.' She kissed him hurriedly again. 'Anyway, you've always wanted to make an honest woman of me.'

The house seemed very quiet and empty without her. Even Suzy had taken to her basket as though she knew Laura was going away, and regarded Peter with dark suspicious eyes, rimmed with white.

He wandered into his study. The morning papers were in a pile on his desk and he began to skim them. A heading in the *Chronicle*'s media column caught his eye.

BAXTER TO GO DOWN-MARKET

Aussie would-be tycoon Kevin ('call-me-Kev') Baxter looks slated to zoom downwards in search of ratings. Baxter-watchers say he's looking for ways to expand into newspapers and/or magazines and wants a viable TV base as starters.

So far Channel 14, which, to retain its original licence, promised to break up its junk-TV schedules with morsels of culture, has been losing money.

Baxter, famously tight with an Aussie dollar, says he knows what the public wants and is preparing to give it to them.

But to do that he has to start wielding the axe.

First on the block is said to be Talking Heads, *which means baby-faced heavy, Peter Braid, will be looking for new pastures.*

It was like reading your own obituary. Baby-faced heavy . . . new pastures . . . the phrases seemed to come sniping out of the text to attack him.

He fetched his address book and looked up the name of Roddick, Norman. Roddick was Programme Controller at Channel 14. Peter knew he wouldn't be in his office yet and phoned his home. A woman's voice said, 'Hang on a minute!' In the background were the noises children make at breakfast.

Roddick's voice was soft and wet, like his lips.

'Have you seen the *Chronicle*?' Peter said.

'Just this minute, old lad.'

'Well?'

'Well what?'

'I'm waiting for you to deny it!'

There was a pause then he said, 'I wish I could.'

'Are you telling me . . . ? Christ! Are you saying that you're dropping *TH*?'

'That's about the size of it. Look, Peter, I'm just as pissed off about it as you are. But it's orders from the Abo. There's not a damn thing I could do.'

'I'll bet.'

'I fought like a dog. We all did. *TH* is the best thing we do – by miles. You know that. I know that. But – '

'When did you know?'

'Late last night. Too late to call you. I was going to do it when I got to the office.'

'So you just let me read it in the bloody *Chron*. I suppose you placed it there.'

'Now that's not fair. I wouldn't do a thing like that.'

'I'll just bet you wouldn't!'

He put the phone down. He was shaking. He went into the sitting-room and poured himself a brandy and threw it into his throat. He wanted Laura. She'd know what to do, how to calm him, to reassure him.

'But she isn't here,' he said out loud. 'She's not bloody here.' He sat down and began to rub his leg. 'Think!' he said to himself. 'Think it out.'

He sat for nearly half an hour, thoughts tumbling over each other, then he picked up the phone again and rang Kevin Baxter's private line at Channel 14.

'Is that you, Mags?' he said to Baxter's PA.

'Hi, Peter.'

'Is His Grace in?'

'Not yet.'

Was there some hesitation?

'Would you ask him to ring me the moment he arrives?'

'He's got a full diary, Peter.'

'Tell him he'll hear something to his advantage.'

'Okay, I'll do that.'

He gave himself another brandy and sat down to wait.

Three

'Damage limitation,' Monty said, 'that's what we have to think of.'

He and Anna were sitting side by side at the boardroom table, a mass of papers spread out before them.

He went on, 'Let's assume the vote goes according to our calculations. We can't simply say, "Well, that's that and thank you for coming." If we don't do something, Peter might change his mind. How is he off financially, by the way?'

'He depends on his income from Webster. Channel 14 is notorious for low pay and Laura is out of work more than in. They've got a large house in Hampstead and do a lot of entertaining.'

'The point is we've got a liquidity crisis and disgruntled shareholders. We've got to satisfy them somehow.'

'I've got salaries to pay. Those come first.'

'First the shareholders or you won't have to worry about paying salaries. You won't be here to pay them. Have you ever read Clausewitz?'

'You're exaggerating. This isn't war. We're talking about my family.'

'The psychology is the same. The defending side always has the advantage in battle provided the territory to be defended is not too large. We're the defending side and I don't think we can defend everything; not the *Daily News* and the American papers and the TV stations.'

'Are you suggesting I get rid of them?'

'It's time to sell the family silver – that's if you want to hold on to the *News*.'

She considered the proposition for a moment. It had not come out of the blue.

'You know, Monty, I've never been a collector. I'd hate to lose Usbourne but I could survive without it. The same applies to the American division. If I have to, then I have to. But the *News* is different. I'd sacrifice any – ' A telephone rang. It was loud in the quiet building. 'Excuse me, that's my private line.'

She hurried from the room and went into her office. She heard Nairn's voice and said, 'I've been trying to ring you for hours.'

'I only got back a short time ago. It seems like everyone's been trying to get hold of me. I have a lot to tell you.'

'You know the meeting's this morning? Can it wait?'

'Don't you *want* to know?'

'Of course. But not the detail.'

'I think he's Beckerman.'

It was like a blow.

'And Paul Esslin is absolutely certain.'

'He was when he came to London. That doesn't mean a thing.'

'I've seen his files.'

'Any other witnesses?'

'No.'

'Then no one's certain. We're back to square one.'

'I met Beckerman.'

Anna felt another jolt and it caused her to lash out. 'For God's sake, call him Gregor! No one's identified him yet. Where?'

'I interviewed him in gaol. At a place called Stein, near Vienna. Before that I went to Altenkirchen. Paul thinks Beckerman killed and robbed the Meissners. He's going to phone you.'

Anna leaned against her desk trying to absorb the blows and felt the first signs of panic fluttering in her throat. 'Stop quoting Esslin at me! He's got an axe to grind. He's out for revenge. Anyway I can't talk now, Monty's here.'

'Anna, unless you identify him within the next couple of days they're going to release him.'

'I can't think about that *now*! Don't you understand?'

'Okay. But before you hang up there's something else . . . Peter's just been to see me.'

'Peter! What for?'

'I'm not absolutely sure. He seemed to think he might want a job on the *News*.'

'Well, well,' Anna said.

She put down the phone and went back into the boardroom.

'Trouble?' Monty asked.

She lit a cigarette. 'You always say you like to know everything. All the facts.'

'Precisely.'

'There is something.'

'Tell me.'

'It's out of the past and out of an earlier life – a different life. It's like an old war-time mine that's been buried for a long time and now the sand has blown away and I can see it and I know I have to defuse it.'

Monty looked at her, frowning. 'I'm listening,' he said.

He had always known that she had worked for the Meissners in Vienna and had escaped with their baby in 1938 while the family disappeared. For obvious reasons she had kept Beckerman's name out of her account. Now she sketched in the facts, but stopped short of his sexual blackmail.

Still frowning, Monty said, 'But I don't see that this needs to be discussed now. We've got so much else – '

'They've found a man called Gregor whom they think is Beckerman.'

'Who is *they*?'

'The French. They say he's responsible for the massacre of more than forty hostages outside Libourne near Bordeaux during the war. He's being held by the Austrian authorities pending possible extradition.'

She told him about Esslin's visit to her and about Nairn's trip to Austria. And the fact that Paul might well seek to interrupt the meeting by calling her.

'That's the background. Of course I won't accept his calls but he might just arrive. He's pathological about it. I wanted you to know in case anything happens.'

Monty leaned back and threw down his pen. 'Let me get this straight. Are you saying that Esslin wanted you to go to Vienna to try and identify Gregor as Beckerman?'

'Yes. Now he's came up with the theory that Beckerman murdered the Meissners for their money. Though how he can be so sure I don't – '

'But Anna, why didn't you go?'

'Don't be silly, Monty. I couldn't just walk out of the building.'

'Why not?'

She looked at him closely. The frown had deepened and she thought she saw traces of anger in his eyes.

'You know why.'

'The meeting?'

'Of course.'

'We could have postponed it by a few days.'

'Why? So I could go off on some wild-goose chase?' Her own irritation was mounting.

'I don't think you could say that the possible identification of a Nazi war criminal was a wild-goose chase. I don't understand you!'

'What are you getting so het up about? No one said the hostages were Jews.'

He looked at her in angry astonishment. Quickly, she said, 'And anyway I don't agree with hounding these people into their senility. There should be a statute of limitations and – '

Monty was not to be deterred. His face had frozen in anger. But he controlled his voice. 'Brutalized human beings don't have to be Jews to earn my compassion,' he said, slowly.

She said, 'I'm sorry, I didn't mean it that way.'

'After all these years I thought I knew you. But I see I don't. Donne said, "Any man's death diminishes me . . ."'

'Don't lecture me!'

'"Because I am involved in Mankind."'

'I *won't* be lectured to, not even by friends as dear as you!'

'You want my advice.'

'Of course.'

'But only if it suits you.'

'Monty, what's got into you?'

He began to draw the papers into a tidy pile.

'It's what has got into you,' he said.

'What are you doing?' She was suddenly alarmed.

'Do you remember once asking me to join you? I said no. You thought I was a chauvinist, that I wouldn't want to work for a woman. You were wrong. Something inside me warned me. I couldn't put a finger on it – '

'Oh, for God's sake, you're not the only one with problems!'

'Half my family, those that stayed behind in Europe before the war, died in Treblinka. I don't believe in statutes of limitation.' He stood up.

'Where are you going?' Her own tension was making her deaf to what he was saying.

'To my office.' He had kept a room on the floor below for many years. 'I need to be by myself for a little while.'

'No one's indispensable, Monty!'

'I realize that only too well.'

In her flat Nairn sat staring at the telephone. She could hardly believe the conversation she had had with Anna. Her attitude to the whole Beckerman affair was so unlike her. What had drawn Nairn, as a rebellious schoolgirl, to Anna was not only her warmth and friendliness but above all her open mind.

During one unhappy period she had run away from school. Anna had found her and taken her back. She had not criticized her but had made her feel that going back was the right thing to do. Then there had been her affair with Neil at university. Both occasions had shown Anna to have a sensitivity with which Nairn did not credit her own parents. Had her father or grandfather refused to go to Vienna she might have understood. But not Anna.

She went on with the rearranging of furniture which had been interrupted by Peter's arrival. The word processor and the camera were still on her hall table. She picked up the camera and looked at it again. Could it be her grandfather's? But how could she take the word of old Novotny, how could she depend on the memory of a sick old man? And did it matter much one way or the other? Cameras were not in themselves important.

A thought, tenuous at first, entered her mind.

She looked at her watch. The staff would be arriving at the *Daily News* and she dialled again, this time asking for Howard Brinckman. He was a Canadian who had once been one of the paper's top photographers but was now so badly crippled by arthritis that Anna had found him a job in the library.

'I've got a question for you,' Nairn said.

'Shoot.'

'In the old days were reporters ever issued with cameras when they went out on stories?'

'They still are. We keep a couple of spares.'

'No, I mean long ago. During the war.'

'I may be a bit old for you, sweetie, but I'm not that old.'

She laughed. 'I didn't mean it that way.'

'Why don't you ask Rogerson? He was picture editor then.'

'Who?'

'Phil Rogerson. He used to come regularly to the Christmas party until a few years ago. Deaf as a post.'

'Do you have an address?'

'Hang on.'

He came back to her a moment later. 'I've got an address for him in Paddington. But it's pretty old.'

'And a number?'

He gave her a telephone number. 'God knows how long we've had these on file. He's probably dead by now.'

But he wasn't dead. When she dialled the number a man's voice said, gruffly, 'Yes?'

'Mr Rogerson?'

'What?'

'Is that Mr Rogerson?'

'Damn and blast!' Then she heard a kind of knocking, then his voice again. 'Hello.'

'Is that Mr Rogerson who once worked on the *Daily News*?'

'Sorry. Can't hear a thing. This bloody machine's gone wonky.' She heard the sound of tapping and thought he might be growing angry either with the telephone or perhaps with a hearing-aid.

'Can you hear me now?'

'Are you Social Services?'

'No, I'm . . . I'll come round!' she shouted. 'Is that all right?'

'Come round?'

'Yes. In a little while. Is that all right?'

'You want to come round?'

'Yes.'

He said, in a normal voice, as though speaking to himself, 'Well, come round if you want to.' Then he put the phone down.

She gathered up her post and took it into the living-room. 'Bill . . . bill . . . bill . . .' she intoned, throwing the window envelopes into a wastebasket. Then she came to an airmail envelope with South African stamps. She looked at it warily. She recognized the handwriting. It was from her father. His envelopes were usually typed – so were the letters, because he always dictated them to his secretary. Even though they were brief notes purporting to give news of himself and her mother, they always seemed to contain an underlying criticism of herself.

He had never got over the fact that she had left university without taking her degree.

She unfolded the pages and found that they too were handwritten. Her father had curiously childlike writing, as though he had been taught copperplate at school but never quite mastered it.

Dearest Nairn, [He usually started his letters 'Dear', she thought]

I have been meaning to telephone you and have a chat, but every time I reach for the phone something seems to come up, so now I've decided to write.

I'm at home and it is after midnight. The south-easter has been blowing and I can hear the waves breaking on the rocks near the seapool.

You have probably been reading in your papers about the changes taking place in southern Africa. Great upheavals. And it is because of these upheavals (God knows where they are going to lead) that we have made an important decision. We have decided to leave.

If I had been on my own I would probably have stayed, for Africa is my country. But your mother has been unhappy about the changes — there is more violence than I can ever remember — and she wants to come back to Britain.

I have gone as far as I can out here. I suppose that one day when your grandfather dies I will take over the African side of things and I will then have to decide what to do about that. But there are young men who want to stay and who are well equipped to run things.

So it looks like once we come over to Britain we will stay. And that is why I am writing. Not only to tell you that but to tell you also that I hope — we both hope — that we can become friends.

I know your mother will be in touch with you about this but I wanted to tell you myself. I also want to say . . . I was going to say how much I'm looking forward to seeing you but it sounds so formal and that's what I'm trying to avoid for once.

I've missed you dreadfully. I often think of when you were little and we used to go down to the seapool. Looking back these seem the happiest times of my life and I wish there had been more or could be more now.

What I'm really saying is, I want to make up for these lost years. I want us to become close again. Is that possible, do you think? Or have I left it too late? I hope to God that is not the case. I love you so much, my dearest Nairn, and regret so much the past and the lost opportunities.

Your loving ~~fath~~ Daddy

She sat back and stared at the letter, reading some of the sentences again. Memories were triggered off and she saw herself as a little girl waiting through the hot afternoons for her father to return so he could take her swimming. She felt again the excitement of having him to herself, the thrill of going down to the seapool and standing on the wall in the breakers, holding his hand.

Four

John Braid looked down at Nico with distaste. He was naked and lying on his back on his bed; his mouth was open and he was making a rattling sound as he breathed.

John had arrived at the flat a few moments before to find the door not quite closed. He had pushed it open, called out, got no reply and gone in. The drawing-room was a mess, cigarette butts everywhere. There were also several empty champagne bottles, an open bottle of vodka and a carton of tomato juice. The kitchen was even worse. Finally, in the bedroom he had found his foster brother.

'Nico,' he said, shaking him by the shoulder. 'Nico!'

'Wha—?'

'Wake up!'

Nico came slowly back to consciousness for the second time that day. 'John?'

'Do you know what time it is? What day it is?'

Nico pushed himself up and rubbed his stubbly jaw. 'Jesus. My head.' He had a vague memory of having had a row then sex with Jacqui but wondered if it had not been a dream.

'Where's Jacqui?' he said.

'There's no one else here.'

'She was here,' he said vaguely.

'Well, she's not now.' John's voice was impatient. 'Let's get moving.'

Nico got to his feet and swayed as the blood left his head. He steadied himself against the wall. 'I don't feel well,' he said.

'Never mind that. It's only a hangover.'

'It may only be a hangover to you, old sport, but it's life and death to me.' Then he laughed. It was a grating, hoarse sound and he held his head tightly as though it might fall off.

'Get moving! We've got to be at the meeting in less than an hour.'

'Oh yes, the meeting . . .'

Nico padded off to the bathroom and had a hot then cold shower. He came out rubbing his head, went into the drawing-room and made himself a bloody Mary. 'Breakfast,' he said.

As the liquor went down he shuddered. He poured a little more vodka into the glass and went off to his bedroom. John followed. Nico sat down on the bed still drying his damp hair. 'I don't like it,' he said.

'What?'

'Anything about this deal. What we're going to do to Mother.'

'All we're going to do is exercise our rights.'

'I still don't like it. It makes me feel . . . squalid.'

'You?'

'Yes, me! Does that surprise you?'

'I didn't mean it that way. Look, we've had this out before. Several times. You needed money. I gave it to you. Remember?'

'I still don't like it.'

'Now's not the time to go into it all again. If I hadn't paid off your gambling debts God knows what might have happened.'

Nico began to dress. 'Don't get dramatic.'

'You were the one who was dramatic. I've still got your letter. You didn't want the family name "brought into disrepute", you said. Well, I don't want the family name brought into disrepute because Mother can't manage the company any longer.'

'Bullshit! *You* want the *Daily News*.'

'That's not the point. The point is if she was running things the way they should be run I wouldn't want to make any changes.'

'I still don't like it. It's sort of putting the boot in when she's down.'

John sat on the bed beside him and reined in his impatience. 'You know as well as I do that people get too old for positions of power. They're like pack animals. They're the leaders but when they can't lead any longer the pack rejects them.'

'And they die!'

'Not necessarily. They hunt by themselves. Human beings retire. Mother is over seventy. It's time to take it easy.'

'Have you told her that?'

'No, but I'm going to this morning.'

'She's not going to be too pleased.'

'I can't help that. Business is business.'

'I knew someone was going to say that. I hoped it wasn't going to be you.'

John watched him dress: designer jeans, a soft blue shirt, gold chain around his neck, expensive Spanish boots. He looked as though he was going to direct a movie rather than attend a board meeting.

'But it's true. It *is* business. We've discussed this. The paper needs new blood, change, a revamping. And you're going to help with that change. The design I mean. You'll be on the staff. On the team.'

'Tally-ho!'

'I thought you wanted that.'

'What I really want is enough money in the bank so I can drink champagne, screw Jacqui and go off to Las Vegas every once in a while.'

John looked at him with renewed distaste. 'Come on, Nico,' he said.

'Coffee. I must have a cup of coffee.'

'Okay, but hurry.'

John stood at the kitchen door unwilling to enter in case something soiled his clothing.

Nico made himself a *filtre* and drank it in gulps.

'Where is Jacqui, by the way?' John asked.

'God knows. All my wives have been unfaithful, you know.'

'You haven't actually been a pillar of loyalty yourself.'

'No, *actually*, I haven't. And I'm not being now – to Mother.'

'Do you want to see a great newspaper destroyed?'

'Of course not.'

'Well, that's what's happening. But we can turn it around. Why don't you have another drink and then we can get going?'

'You think I need the courage?'

'I just think you could do with another drink.'

'Get thee behind me.'

But he gave himself another and looked at the glass for a moment and said, 'Here's to surfboards and all who sail on them.'

'What?'

'Nothing.'

Anna sat alone in the *Daily News* boardroom. All around her she could hear sounds of the day beginning: of talk and laughter, of doors opening and closing, phones ringing, of heels clacking up and down the corridors. It was the beginning of a working day and the staff were arriving. Usually she would have a mid-morning conference with the foreign editor, the news editor and the picture editor to sort out the day's menu of known events. This morning it would have to go ahead without her. She wished she was attending it and that the day was like any other day – the recording of *other* people's disasters.

She sat quietly, like someone in the eye of the storm waiting for winds which she knew were of hurricane force.

Her mind, which should have been focused on what the American assets might fetch if she were able to sell them without advance publicity and the resultant forcing down of the price, was fixed instead on the conversation with Nairn.

She had known when she came into the office earlier that day that the two strands of her life were becoming inextricably tangled. What she could not have guessed was the speed with which it would happen. Now, looking back to those earlier moments when she had stood in her window drinking a cup of coffee and watching the lights of London, they seemed half a lifetime away. And indeed they were, for she had reviewed a span in her own life of well over fifty years.

How would she ever explain to Nairn or to Monty or to Peter or Nico what had happened in those far-off days and which had now come back to haunt her like some restless spirit escaped from its unquiet grave? How could she explain when she did not even know all the facts herself?

How could Esslin – and now Nairn – be so sure that this *was* Beckerman? How were the French so certain? No one had identified him yet. Now it seemed that only she, and possibly Ben, could do that.

The likelihood, of course, was that he wasn't Beckerman at all. And it was clear that the Austrian authorities were becoming restive about holding him. They were probably looking for an excuse to release him. After the embarrassing publicity of their own president being accused of being a Nazi during the war, Austria was not hunting for more. What they wanted was someone to come along and say, 'No, that definitely isn't Beckerman.'

Her skin suddenly grew cold. Wasn't that it? Wasn't that the way around her problem? Wouldn't it be better to agree to visit Beckerman in prison and say no, that isn't him at all, that isn't the man I knew more than fifty years ago, that isn't Cuno?

The beauty of it was that it was so totally reasonable. Why should she be able to identify a man she had not seen since 1938? Only Paul Esslin was convinced she could and he was in the grip of an obsession which he seemed to have transferred to Nairn.

No one knew and no one was ever going to know the real truth about her relationship with Cuno.

She felt a sudden sense of release. She would go to Austria.

She had just reached this decision and was about to go down the corridor and say to Monty all right, I'll do it, when the door opened and her PA put her head through. 'Peter's here,' she said. 'He's asking if he can see you.'

'But the meeting's not for half an hour.'

'He says it's important.'

She looked at the mass of papers in front of her, papers which Monty should have charge of. But Peter was her ally, her strong right arm in this contest. 'I can only see him for a couple of minutes.'

Peter had waited at his phone in Hampstead for more than an hour before he dialled Baxter's private line again.

Baxter's secretary said, 'Peter, I told him you called but there's no way . . . He's got meetings all morning and he's on the phone now. Shall I put you on hold?'

'He's not bloody God,' he said, and put down the phone,

had another quick brandy and drove to Channel 14 in Maida Vale.

Mags gave him a slight smile as he barged into her office. 'I thought you might come.'

She flipped an intercom switch. 'Peter Braid to see you. I told him you were busy.'

The voice came through quite clearly. 'Tell him to wait.'

Then Peter heard a sound he recognized, a kind of 'thunk'. He pushed past Mags and went into Baxter's office. It was empty except for Baxter himself. He was dressed in a yellow Lacoste sports shirt and plaid trousers, and was crouching over a putter. As Peter entered he stroked a golf ball across the carpet and it went 'thunk' as it entered a water glass that had been placed on its side. Peter too had practised putting on the carpet.

Baxter lined up his next putt. 'Hi, Peter,' he said. 'I was just getting in some practice. I'm going down to Wentworth this afternoon to play in a Pro-Am.' He stroked the ball and there was another 'thunk' as it hit the back of the water glass.

'Is it true?'

'Is what true?'

'That you're dropping *Talking Heads*?'

'What made you ask that? The piece in the *Chronicle*?'

'And talking to Roddick.'

'I see.'

He lined up another putt.

'Why?'

'Bums on seats. What other reason is there?'

'When we started you said to hell with the ratings, let's do something well.'

'And we did. Now's the time to change.'

Peter watched him make another putt. A mixture of rage and fear was boiling up inside him.

He wanted to humiliate this hypocritical sod, to ridicule his Australian manner and way of speech, his tycoon's pose. But he kept his mouth shut. Fear dominated. People like Baxter did not like being humiliated, they never forgave or forgot.

He took a deep breath. 'Maybe you're right,' he said. 'Perhaps we were shooting a bit high.'

'Not at the time,' Baxter said. 'It was right then.'

He was about to say, 'What happens to me?' when he suddenly didn't want to ask that question in case he got an answer he couldn't live with.

He tried to keep calm. Uninvited, he sat down in an armchair and allowed one hand to droop over the side in an attempt to show how relaxed he was.

'How's the leg?' Baxter said, making Peter feel embarrassed about sitting down.

'It's fine.'

'You have to keep your head still,' Baxter said. 'That's the secret of good putting.'

'And use your arms as a pendulum.'

'Exactly.'

'The *Chronicle* said you were thinking of expanding into publishing: newspapers, magazines.'

'You don't want to believe everything you read in the papers.' He gave a small laugh and Peter smiled.

'They were right about *Talking Heads*.'

'There are exceptions.'

'You remember our lunch?'

'Of course, Peter.' Thunk. 'Very enjoyable.'

'I've been thinking about our conversation.'

'Which was that? Oh, yes, I remember.'

'What if the *Daily News* did become available?'

'Will it?'

Thunk.

'It might.'

'Go on.'

'It's the AGM today. Just the family. The feeling is that maybe the time has come for a change.'

'I see.'

'But there are certain conditions.'

'I thought there might be.'

'Well, if *Talking Heads* goes down the drain . . .' He left the sentence unfinished.

'Of course. As I understand it, your family owns the shares which can't be disposed of to outsiders because of the preemption clause.'

'You're well informed!'

'One tries to be.'

The Australian accent was almost invisible and Peter wondered if okkerism was something Baxter only cultivated in public.

Thunk.

'But the Articles of Association could be changed in certain circumstances.'

'That's interesting, Peter. I assume that if that happened there would be structural changes.'

'That's what I thought.'

'Involving the editorship?'

'I was thinking of something combining management and editorial.'

'A kind of managing editor.' Thunk. 'It would be an important position, Peter. It would need someone with charisma and talent.'

Peter hesitated. 'That's right.'

'I don't see why not.' He straightened up. 'You must forgive me. I'll have to move it. We're having a photo session before lunch.' He held out his hand. 'Good to see you. Let's talk again after the meeting.'

On the way to his car Peter bought an *Evening Standard*. A story at the bottom of page one carried the heading: AUSSIE TYCOON IN PRESS TAKEOVER. He felt his blood run cold. Then he read the opening paragraph:

Kevin Baxter, the 44-year-old Australian press baron, revealed late last night that he is the new owner of one of the largest publishing companies in Britain.

His £800-million bid for the family firm of Jenkins and Sons, founded in 1827, has taken the City by surprise. Baxter is now owner of a mixture of book publishing, magazine publishing and one national newspaper, the Mercury . . .

He could read no further. He felt sick. Baxter had let him go on and on. Had lured him into making a fool of himself.

'Charisma . . . important position . . .' Jesus!

He turned the car and headed for Victoria.

*

'Hello, darling,' Anna said, as he came into the boardroom. 'I've only got a minute, the others will be here soon.'

He kissed her on the cheek. 'It's about the meeting anyway.'

She registered that his hand felt icy cold, that he was pale and that there were beads of sweat near his hairline. She had long since stopped worrying about the transference of genes, had instead accepted the view that environment not heredity governed human behaviour. But that wasn't the point now . . .

He said, 'I wanted you to know before anyone else – I've resigned.'

'From *Talking Heads*? Oh, Peter! But you loved doing that programme. What's happened?'

'Bloody Baxter, of course. I knew it would be a matter of time. I can't really work for someone like him. The *Chronicle* has a paragraph about him going down-market. My programme is about the only decent thing he's got. I'm not going to be dragged down by some Aussie pseud. You know he's bought Jenkins & Sons?'

'I knew he was interested. When was the announcement?'

'Late last night apparently.'

'I suppose he'll revamp the *Mercury*.'

'Page three girls. Soft porn. All in the name of egalitarianism.'

'He was interested in the *Daily News* at one time.'

'Really?' Peter said, blandly. 'Did he come to you?'

'There were feelers.'

They looked at each other for a moment and she frowned. Peter was lying about something. She said, 'What was it you wanted to see me about?'

'Well, I'll need something to do.'

So Nairn was right, she thought.

'They'll snap you up at the BBC or ITV.'

'Not after the rows I had with them. The trouble is, if you have fights with your producers and they end up as programme controllers it cuts your options.'

It was true, she thought. He had gone from one channel to the next leaving a trail of enemies. He was too acerbic, too unwilling to suffer fools. She had put it down to the pain factor and the need for adrenaline.

'There's always radio,' she said.

'God, what an idea! No, I want something I can get my teeth into. Something important, something that carries weight, something that'll stretch me.'

'That sounds like politics.'

'You must be joking. No, in journalism.'

'You said you hated it.'

'That was years ago.'

'I suppose you might go to one of the new broadsheets. Or what about a Sunday paper? The *Dispatch* is looking for a leader-page "name" so I'm told.'

'No, I thought somewhere closer to home. Something I've an interest in.'

'You mean on the *News*?'

'You sound surprised. Look, it's in trouble. It's my feeling it's got that way because you can't devote all your time to each part of the empire. There's the American Division as well. You should have an overall view. But there needs to be someone who looks only at the *News*.'

'You?'

They stared at each other for a moment, then he said, 'There's going to be a vote today.'

'I am aware of that, Peter. And I'm counting on you.'

His eyes slid away. 'You know that I've always supported you in the past. And I want you to know I'm with you all the way now.'

'But?'

'No, no, there are no buts. It's just that you might try to see things from my point of view.'

'What are you trying to tell me?'

'Basically that I own a large slice of Webster Communications and I would like to work in my family business. That's all.'

'I run the family business, Peter. I've run it successfully since you were a young man. All right, there are difficulties at present but nothing that can't be put right. You see, I've always gone for the *best*, the highest quality in staff, machines, everything – '

'And you don't think I'm the best. Is that it?'

She saw he was angry now but she could not help herself.

'You're superb at what you do. This is different, that's all.'

She paused. 'Excuse me, Peter, we'll have to discuss this later.'

He half rose to his feet and she said, 'No, you stay here. I want to go and see Monty.'

His door was closed. She knocked and went in. It was not a large office and the furniture was simple, just a place to keep his papers and hang his hat, quite unlike his ornate chambers overlooking Trafalgar Square.

'Monty, what are you doing?'

He was going through his drawers and making a pile of papers on his desk. He did not answer and when he looked up at her she saw that his face was flushed and his eyes angry.

She suddenly realized just what she must have done to him. 'Monty . . . Monty . . . God, I'm so sorry . . .' Then she did something she had not done since she had lain next to his naked body. She put her arms around him and pulled his head tightly against her.

But, like the previous time, it did not work. He gently removed her arms and rose to his feet.

'Let's just say we see things differently,' he said.

'No, Monty, I'm not going to say that and I'm not going to let you leave this room without hearing me out first. You are my oldest friend. I love you very deeply. I respect you. I need you. I can't say more than that.'

'I'm afraid that doesn't meet the case.'

Susan, her PA, knocked and said, 'Nico and John have arrived.'

'Show them into the boardroom. Tell them we'll only be a minute.'

Once the door was closed Anna said, 'I want you with me, Monty.'

He did not react.

'I want all of you, all your brains and all your sentiment on my side, otherwise we're going to lose. Peter doesn't know it yet but I think he's preparing himself to vote against me.'

She sketched briefly what Peter had said and Monty said, 'Why don't you promise him something then? You should be able to create a position for him.'

'That's not how we work, and you know it. Everyone earns their place.'

'You can't be just a little bit moral,' he said.

'What do you mean?'

'I mean you are making a moral issue out of a small act of nepotism, a normal business compromise, yet you have no moral guilt about this man Beckerman.'

'Sit down, Monty.' Her voice was cold and he sat. She picked up his phone and said to her PA, 'Take some coffee into the boardroom, will you, Susan? And tell them I'm going to be a little longer than I thought.' Then she turned to Monty and said, 'I'm going to tell you something now that no one else knows. It's something I've kept secret for half a century.'

With carefully chosen sentences she told him what had really happened between herself and Beckerman. Monty's face seemed to sharpen as he listened and his fingers locked in the old familiar way when he was concentrating hard.

It did not take long to tell. When it was over she felt a kind of catharsis. It was as though, after all the years of silence, she had at last found peace by talking to someone else.

Monty looked down at his hands for a moment then said, 'But what has this to do with Peter?'

'He's Cuno's son.'

'Oh God . . . I see. You're quite sure?'

'Yes, quite sure. And if this man is Beckerman he'll try to discredit me. If I'm asked to testify in court and give dates both Peter and Wilson will put two and two together.'

'You can't assume that.'

'Wouldn't it be just *too* coincidental for me in those circumstances to have had a premature child? And I feel sure that Wilson guessed I rushed him into marriage. So you see, I'm not being just a little bit moral. I'm trying to be realistic. All my life I've worried about what this would do to Peter.'

'He's a grown man. He's lived a life and still has a life to live. Think what Beckerman is alleged to have done to those French hostages!'

'But that's all over and finished with! Can't you see how I feel about Peter? Can't you understand that the accident has left scars not only on him but on me as well?'

293

'Yes, I can. And I'm sorry for you. Desperately sorry that you have to make choices, especially at this time, but – '

The phone on Monty's desk buzzed and he handed it to her. 'It's Susan.'

'They're getting restless,' Susan said.

'Right.' Anna put down the phone and said, 'I must go in.'

He turned away from her but she caught his arm and stopped him. 'I want you to know that even before I came into this room, in fact from the moment I knew I'd hurt you . . . Well, I made my decision . . . I'm going to Vienna. I'm going to see Beckerman. I wanted to tell you why I had fought it for so long.'

He frowned. The change had been sudden. 'I don't want you to go because you think you've hurt me. That's no reason.'

'What does the reason matter, Monty, so long as I go?'

He nodded, then picked up several pieces of paper from his desk. 'Let's get the meeting under way,' he said. She led him down the corridor, thinking how easy it was to lie.

Five

Her three sons stood in a group on the far side of the board-room table. They hadn't heard her reach the door and she paused for a moment looking at them and readjusting her thoughts.

They were her sons, yes, but they were also grown men. She must not allow herself to be trapped by memory. They wanted someone new, or thought they wanted someone new. She, on the other hand, wanted to remain at the head of the organization she had created. It was a simple equation and had to be viewed like that. There was no room for sentiment. Business, as so many people had said to her over the years, was business.

She was glad to see that in one way she was right: in her estimate of the clothes they would wear. Nico was in his designer denims, Peter in his blazer and paisley handkerchief, and John in his grey formal suit.

As she moved through the doorway and into the room she was in uncharted waters. There had never been a meeting like this one. Had she had it all her own way for too long? Was Monty right? Was she trying to cling on to power for its own sake?

Thoughts like that could only weaken her and she must not allow them.

'Good morning,' she said briskly. 'Sorry I'm late.'

The little knot broke up and she saw the expressions on their faces. They were uneasy. Nico looked embarrassed. Only John's expression hardened when he saw her.

She went to him first. He held out his hand. 'Hello, Mother.'

She took his hand but moved forward and pressed her cheek against his. 'Did you have a good flight?'

'Not bad.'

'Nico.' She kissed him. 'Have you all had coffee? Good. Let's get started then.'

They took their seats and it was plain how they were divided. Anna and Monty sat in the middle of one of the long sides of the table, while her three sons ranged themselves directly in front of them. The company secretary sat at the far end of the room.

Anna was lighting one cigarette from another. After all the thinking and preparation, the discussions of ways and means with Monty, this was finally the moment. She felt as though a large hand was slowly squeezing her stomach. Neither Nico nor Peter would meet her eyes. Nor would John. He seemed to be watching the door.

Monty opened the meeting by saying, 'Well, this is something of a surprise – I mean, seeing the three of you at an AGM. But you're very welcome. And it's not difficult to understand why this meeting is so important to each of you. You know why and we know why – and we know what we have to do about it. I want to suggest right at the beginning, to save time, that we come to the main business of whether or not Anna retains your confidence.'

'Hang on a minute,' John said, aggressively. 'We've got a lot of talking to do before we get to that.'

Anna had always thought him the least thrusting of the three, overshadowed by Wilson. Now he was the leader . . . and for the first time a feeling that was more than just unease crept into her mind.

'I agree,' she said. 'Let's talk. That's the least we can do for John since he's come this long way. Let's talk about the letter.'

She pulled out a photocopy from the spread of papers in front of her.

'"Dear Mother,"' she read, '"in view of the substantial losses made by Webster Communications and the need to make contingency plans, I write to tell you that I will be attending the annual general meeting to put forward my own ideas. Sincerely, John."'

'Well . . .' Anna said. 'Not the warmest of notes, but brief and to the point.'

John had kept his face expressionless as she read. He might have been made of stone.

'You never told me you'd written to Mother,' Nico said. 'Not like that anyway.'

'I don't owe you explanations for everything I do,' John said.

Peter looked at both his brothers with distaste.

Monty said, 'Let's hear your ideas then, John.'

'Well . . .' John began. 'I thought . . .' He picked up his executive case and pulled out a handful of papers. They waited while he shuffled through them. 'Losses for the last trading year were eight point two million on the UK end of Websters alone – '

'We know all that,' Peter said. 'We get the accounts too. And Mother and Monty know because they see them first.'

'I'm just setting things straight,' John said with a flash of anger. He looked back at his papers. 'The projected loss for the first half of this trading year is already eleven point four million and the way things are going that looks like doubling.'

His voice was monotonous and, as he read on from what sounded, Anna thought, like a prepared statement, she saw that Peter and Nico were becoming restive. Nico was playing with a paper-clip, and Peter was beginning to rub his leg.

Anna said, 'Excuse me, John, but Peter's right. We know all this.'

Nico looked down at his hands. He's out of his depth, she thought. He doesn't want any of this, doesn't want to be here. He must need money. And clearly John had got to him.

He looked down at the statement. 'No dividends have been paid for the period . . .'

Anna thought: he's stalling. But why? Was there another dimension to this? The grip on her stomach tightened.

Just then Monty said, 'There's no point in recapping. I thought you'd come to hear what we proposed to do to put things right.'

'I'd like to hear that,' Peter said.

'So would I,' a voice said behind Anna, a voice she knew

only too well. She turned and saw Wilson Braid and Victor Hardiman standing in the doorway.

'Sorry we're late,' Wilson said and made his way to the far side of the table. John helped his father off with his coat and hat.

Wilson sat down at one end of the table, as if to signal that he was the senior member of the meeting, and Hardiman sat next to him. He took some papers from a briefcase, spread them before him and said, 'Now I want – '

'It's nice to see you, Wilson,' Monty said. 'We're honoured. But I'm running this meeting. We'll get to what you want in a minute.'

Wilson opened his mouth but Hardiman leant across and said something and he subsided.

'Very well, Monty. Or should I say, *Sir* Monty? We ordinary mortals never know whether you people like to be called by your titles or not.'

'"Chairman" will do nicely,' Monty said, smoothly.

Anna knew now they had real trouble. It would be easy to be rude to Wilson, to snub him, but she decided on a different ploy. She smiled at this gnarled and nut-brown man with his bald skull and wintry eyes, whose child she had once borne. 'It's good of you to come. We didn't know. You're looking well.'

He looked nonplussed for a moment and then said, 'Never better. Has John been filling you in?'

'Not really,' Monty said. 'He wanted a chat so we've been chatting.'

John looked angrily at Monty and then flushed as his father said, 'John likes to start slowly . . . don't you, son? The trouble is he often doesn't get up much speed later. Right? What we're going to chat about, with the chairman's permission, are the fucking awful results of the last financial year. Let's have the bumf, Victor.'

Hardiman, whom Anna had not seen for more than forty years, had aged like a matinee idol, all silver hair and sun-lamp tan. He handed Wilson a sheaf of papers.

'I know what you want to chat about: projected figures, plans, restructuring. The point is you're deep in it. You didn't get out of Fleet Street when the other papers left. You stayed on and were clobbered by the unions and you've never recovered. America is where you should have expanded. Instead you went in half-heartedly and now that's going wrong too. Things can't go on like that, can they?'

He turned to face Anna. 'It's the classic mistake. You thought interest rates were going to go down and stay down, so you bought this building and bought your plant instead of renting and having the paper printed out of town. Well, interest rates have gone up and you're being squeezed and we're not going to let it go on. Are we, John?'

'No, Dad.'

'You can bet your bloody life it's "No, Dad." So what we're here to talk about is a very different future. Isn't that so, Nico?'

'I suppose so.'

'You suppose so?'

'That's what I said.'

He turned to Peter. 'And what say you? What does the great Talking Head say?'

'I say I don't like you being rude to Mother.'

'Oh, I can take care of myself,' Anna said, keeping a smile on her face. 'Wilson knows that.'

Wilson ignored her, keeping his attention on Peter. 'You think I'm a coarse fellow?'

'You could put it that way.'

'Coarse, maybe, but I run a successful company.' He turned to Hardiman. 'Give me that story I saw this morning.' Hardiman passed over a small piece of paper. 'This was in the *Chronicle* this morning.' He began to read the media story about *Talking Heads* being canned.

There was a hush round the table and Peter said, when he had finished, 'So? I've resigned anyway.'

'What are you going to do for cash? Baxter's as mean as they come. Well known for it. And you and Laura always lived high on the hog.'

Anna was about to say, 'Get to the point, Wilson,' but checked herself. It was possible, if he went on like this, that he might alienate the entire room all by himself.

'A successful business isn't run by sitting around adding up

299

figures,' he said. 'That's bloody accountants' talk. We know what the losses are going to be and that's all we need to know. Companies are made by people. And all the necessary people are here today: Anna with her thirty-nine per cent holding, Nico, John and Peter with twelve per cent each, and my twenty-five.'

He paused, enjoying himself. 'You see, my dear, at one time twenty-five per cent was a calculated bloody insult by a senile old man. Just short of a blocking minority. Enough shares to be involved, not enough to have any power. Or that's what he thought when he left you the provincial papers. But it's a different game now that you're not paying dividends.'

Anna said, 'Wilson, before we go any further perhaps you'd tell us what you would propose in the way of changes – that is, if you're ever in a position to change things. I assume that's what you want otherwise you wouldn't be here.'

'Oh yes, that's what I want all right. You could call the *News* my alma mater. The first real paper I ever worked for.'

'Yes, well, we're all sentimental,' Monty said dryly, 'but that doesn't answer the question.'

Wilson looked at the huge lawyer with sharp, flickering eyes, but kept his temper. 'I propose to run it *my* way.'

'Which is?' Anna said.

'Make it more popular. Trim the staff. Who needs correspondents all over the world? Most people don't give a bugger what happens in the next village, let alone the next country.'

'Tits and bums,' Peter said. 'Pudenda.'

'That's one of your big TV words, is it? Well, all I have to say about that is, if that's what people want, why not? That's your trouble, Peter, you put yourself above ordinary people. I don't. No, when I take over there'll be changes all right, I'll – '

'Hang on a moment, Dad,' John said. 'I think we should make it clear that I'll be the one running the company in this country.'

'I don't think so.'

'But Dad, we – '

'You think I'm going to stay in South Africa and live under a black government? You must be crazy!'

'But you said – '

Wilson held up his hand. 'Do me a favour, son. Not now.'

Anna looked at John and saw he was stunned.

Monty said, shrewdly, 'I suggest we get a feel of the meeting. Just to see how we stand.'

'Now wait one bloody minute!' Wilson said.

'I've told you before, Wilson, I'm the chairman of the company and of this meeting. The vote is one of confidence in the present management. For?'

Peter put up his hand.

'Against?'

Wilson put up his hand. John, bemused, followed him. Nico raised his hand more slowly and kept his eyes on the table in front of him.

'That's as I figured it,' Wilson said. 'Right.' He turned to Peter. 'Now we do some talking.'

Nairn parked her car and walked swiftly towards Philip Rogerson's flat. He lived near Paddington Station in a road filled with kebab take-aways. The smell of grilling mutton fat lingered in the air. She stopped at number fifty-nine. It was above a dry-cleaning shop and the street door was open. She climbed a staircase made lethal by patches of worn linoleum. There was a bell on the first floor landing. Someone had written 'Doesn't work' on the wall beside it.

She knocked. The surface of the door was dented and the paint was chipped where others before her had tried to gain the attention of the occupant. She took out a coin and used it as a knocker.

After a few moments a voice said, 'Hang on, hang on . . .' She heard a bolt being drawn, then the door opened a few inches on a chain. 'Yes? What d'you want?'

She could not make out the speaker and shouted through the crack, 'I phoned you a little while ago.'

'Social Services?'

In despair she said 'Yes!' at the top of her voice.

He closed the door, released the chain and let her into his flat. It seemed to comprise one large bed-sitting room, a kitchen and bathroom. Philip Rogerson was in his dressing-gown, pyjamas and slippers. He was a large man of extreme age. His tonsure of white hair had not been brushed and there was white stubble on his cheeks. As he walked his dressing-gown flapped open in an alarming way. He wore a bulky hearing-aid of the kind issued by the National Health Service in the early 1960s. Behind him she could see a room in which every surface was covered by an empty cup or plate.

'It won't bloody work,' he said, banging the hearing-aid. 'Why don't you people do something about it?'

'Mr Rogerson, I've come to ask you a few questions.'

'It's no good. Can't hear a thing.' The old fingers ineffectually scrabbled at the square metal case.

'How long is it since you changed the batteries?'

'What?'

'Could I? Would you mind?'

She took the hearing-aid from him, opened the case, took out the battery and said, 'I'll be back in a minute.'

She hurried down the stairs and into the street. There was a chemist's shop three doors down which kept batteries and she was back in the flat in a matter of minutes. She fitted the new battery and said, 'How's that?'

The old man flinched. 'Don't shout!'

'Can you hear me now?'

'Of course I can hear you. If you people – '

'Mr Rogerson, I'm not from Social Services. My name is Nairn Braid. I work for the *Daily News*.'

His face brightened. 'You're a journalist? I worked for the *Daily News*.'

'I know.'

'Is it about the Christmas party? I haven't been able to get there the past couple of years. No transport.'

'Don't you worry about that. I'll lay on transport.'

'It kept me in touch, you know. Just once a year but it kept me in touch. Would you like some tea?'

'No thanks.'

He looked vaguely round the room. 'I had some whisky.'

'No, no.'

'What do you want to ask me?' he said, brightly.

'About when you were picture editor.'

'That's right. I was picture editor.'

302

'That was just before the war, wasn't it?'

'And afterwards. I was called up in 1941.'

'In those days did you give cameras to reporters?'

'Only if we couldn't send a photographer as well. Photographers don't like reporters taking photographs. Bad for business. But we used to keep a couple of cameras just in case.'

'Like this one?' From her capacious bag she pulled out the camera old Novotny had given her and handed it to Rogerson.

He held the square, box-like camera in his hands. 'God, a Rollei. I haven't seen one of these for years. Marvellous. They don't make them any more. It's all miniature stuff now. These were two and a quarter square, you know. You didn't have to be a crack photographer to take good pictures with these.'

He played with the focusing knob.

'Is there any way you could tell whether this was a camera owned by the *Daily News*?'

'Well . . . I don't know. There were lots of these around.' He took the camera out of its case and his old fingers stroked the metal. 'I think we used to put a little sticker in. Has it got a film in it?'

'No.'

He opened the back. 'There. Near the pressure plate. That's where we used to put it. Just a little sticker which said it was the property of the *Daily News*.'

She looked closely but there was nothing there now. She took the camera to the window and in the better light made out a slight discoloration on the black metal which might have been left by glue. But she told herself it was wishful thinking.

'Why?' he said. 'What's it all about?'

'You don't remember someone called Wilson Braid, do you? He was a reporter on the *News* just before the war.'

'Braid?' The old mind began to turn over and she could almost hear the gears. 'Rings a bell,' he said. 'My memory's not what it used to be. You've got to have a good memory when you're a picture editor. I used to be able to look at a picture and say to myself, yes, that was an AP picture or that was a Reuterphoto. I remember once – '

'Braid, Mr Rogerson. Do you remember a Wilson Braid?'

'Wilson . . . There was a young man with a name like that. I remember because I always thought his Christian name sounded like it should be his surname. An Australian, I think he was.'

'This one was a South African.'

'South African, Australian, Canadian . . . they were all colonial types. Yes . . . a biggish sort of chap. Wore one of those hats with large brims . . .' He thought for a moment. 'No . . . Can't say I really do. Why do you want to know all this anyway?'

'I think he might have taken some pictures on the Austrian border of people fleeing from the Nazis. Crowd scenes and queues at the border post, that sort of thing. I'm trying to identify someone who was there. He just might have caught him in a crowd shot.'

'There were lots of refugee pictures. Wait a sec . . .' Suddenly the old eyes brightened again. 'There was something . . . There were some pictures.' She waited tensely. 'No . . . I can't remember. But there was something . . .'

'What sort of something?'

He shook his head. 'When you get to my age things blur. You don't know if you're remembering an event or something someone told you.'

She felt a sudden let-down. 'What would have happened to the pictures if he'd taken some and sent them in?'

'God knows. I suppose they would have been filed. Everything was filed. I mean the negs. We had a huge photo library. We filed all the negs of important pictures, you understand.'

'Would they still be on file?'

'Well now, that's a question. They told me at one of the Christmas parties that all the files and all the newspaper cuttings and all the bound copies and everything like that had been moved when the *News* went to its new building. Not the space, you see. Everything's on microfilm now. Not in my day. Everything was in large envelopes in filing cabinets then. Rooms full of filing cabinets. I suppose that's why they had to move them.'

'Where?' she said. 'Where did they move them?'

'God knows. Timbuktu for all I know.'

'May I use your phone?'

304

She phoned the *Daily News* and spoke to Howard Brinckman again. 'That's right,' he said. 'Everything was moved some years ago. All the old pics and files. They're stored in a warehouse.'

'Whereabouts?'

'Shepherd's Bush. Hang on.'

He came back to her in a few moments and gave her the address. Five minutes later she was on the Westway.

Six

Wilson Braid's idea of a discussion was to listen to himself. He had been talking non-stop for nearly an hour and Anna was reminded of a speech she had once heard Castro make in Havana which had been simultaneously translated into English. Both men seemed to want to weary their listeners into submission.

He took paper after paper from Hardiman. His sneer at accountants had been just that. Now he was doing what he purported to despise. He was using the annual reports from the past five years, and a flock of clippings from the *Wall Street Journal*, the *Financial Times* and *The Economist* to try to show how Anna had mismanaged the company.

Basically she knew he was right, at least about her delay in leaving Fleet Street. That had come from sentiment – as so many bad business decisions did. Fleet Street had been her world and she had not wished to change it for Wapping or the Isle of Dogs. Indeed buying a new building in Victoria, where office space was almost as expensive as the City, had not been much of a saving. But who wanted to work in Wapping? One might as well shift everything to Portsmouth or Thurrock or Slough or a dozen other places that were cheaper and nastier. But there was no point in trying to argue that case with Wilson.

She had thought to strengthen her position in England by expanding in America but that had not worked out. Then the battle with the trade unions had been more protracted than she could have guessed, and because she was slow in getting out of hot metal printing and into the new cheaper technology she had been held to ransom by the printers.

But what Wilson had said in a few words to start with, he now set out to prove by quoting reams of figures. His voice became monotonous. He was doing what John had done earlier, except in more detail.

True to her gut feeling, Anna had decided to keep silent for a time and give Wilson his head, allowing him to alienate everyone else with his aggressive – and now boring – manner. She looked at John as he listened to his father. She would never forget that terrible day she had arrived at Monty's cottage on the Dorset coast to find the children gone. It was one of the worst days of her life, worse even than the day the Meissners had vanished at Altenkirchen.

As Peter had been loyal to her, so John had been loyal to his father.

Clearly John and Wilson had created the scenario for the meeting – drawing in both Nico and Peter because of the loss of dividends – and equally clearly the original plan had been for John to take over Webster Communications in the UK. This had been shattered by Wilson and his talk of not wishing to live under a black government. She supposed that if Wilson came to England to live, then John would get the African empire. But was that what he wanted?

Every now and then he flashed a look at his father. Anna could not make out whether his expression was angry or resentful or both. But whatever was said at this table, she considered that John would remain loyal to his father. He always had. Unless . . .

As Wilson drew breath she said, 'I want to ask John a question.'

Wilson looked up with irritation but she ignored him and, turning to John, said, 'Do you want to live in England?'

'Why?'

'I wondered. You've always had such strong roots in Africa, haven't you? You've got the wine farm near Cape Town and I know you love that. I would have thought that there was too much of Africa in your blood for you to want to live anywhere else. Unless it was Mary's idea.'

'Let's get on with it,' Wilson said.

'No, I want to find out about John. I know Mary was never particularly happy in Africa. Does she want to come back? Is that why you've hatched this plot?'

'It isn't a plot!' John said. It's – '

'I know,' Anna said, 'it's business. But that doesn't answer the question.'

'Never mind about Mary!' Wilson said. 'She's happy. John's happy.'

'Dad, I – '

'Let's leave the psychological stuff to the psychologists. We're here for something else entirely.'

Anna had detected a weakness and she probed further.

'If it is for Mary, and you've decided on the move, then there are other ways.'

'What other ways?' John said.

'Have you thought of leaving Braid International?'

'Why would I do that?'

'I should have thought that was obvious,' Anna said.

Wilson gave a harsh, grating laugh.

John said, 'I don't get it.'

'She's offering you a bloody job, you fool. She's asking you to be a turncoat.'

'That's not true! Anyway it depends on how much John, or perhaps Mary, wants to live in England. Speaking of turncoats, from what I could understand, your agreement with John was that *he* should take over here. And from his expression he thought so too.'

Peter broke in and said to his mother, 'What sort of job had you in mind for John?'

'Never mind that,' Wilson said. 'It's not going to happen. John works for Braid!'

Anna tried to repair the damage. 'All I wanted to know was how much John and Mary wanted to leave Africa.'

'No,' Peter said, 'I don't think that's all.' Then he turned to Wilson. 'Tell me, why didn't you come to me earlier? You clearly suborned Nico.'

'"Suborned"?' Wilson said. 'Another one of your long words! But I understand what it means and we didn't have to suborn him!'

'Of course you did.' Peter turned to his brother. 'What did they offer you, thirty pieces of silver?'

'You bloody smug bastard,' Nico said. 'You sit up in your expensive pad in Hampstead and pretend you're – '

'For God's sake!' Monty said. 'You sound like children squabbling!'

'Smug I may be,' Peter said, 'but stupid I'm not. Things seem to be on offer around this table and I want to know why I wasn't offered something.'

Wilson said, 'John and I agreed that you were the one we would have to convince with facts and figures. Are you telling me something different?'

'I told you I'd resigned. I'm looking – as everyone else around this table is – to the future.'

Anna said, 'Your future's as safe as can be. There are your books, and there's no doubt you'll be offered another TV slot.'

'That's very reassuring, Mother.'

Monty said, 'The BBC will snap you up.'

'Why? They're top heavy as it is. Anyway you can't fight off junk TV with programmes like *Talking Heads*. You were warned about what was likely to happen with a free-for-all, with cable and satellite up against the BBC and ITV. Well, it's happened. Everything's going down-market and that's where the battle for viewers will take place.'

'And you think that's bad?' Wilson said.

'What I think is neither here nor there. I'm telling you the facts. You've made a successful business out of selling tits and bums on the grounds that that's what the people want. Okay. If that's the scenario for the future then we'll all have to try to get used to it.'

'That's a very cynical point of view,' Anna said.

'It's a very cynical business,' Peter said.

'You never used to sound like that.'

'And you never tried to double-cross us.'

'I didn't *mean* it that way. I didn't offer John a job. All I did was suggest another way.'

'Come off it! Remember me? I listened to you say there were no jobs, that the company had slimmed down, that you couldn't create one.'

'You can always create a job,' Wilson said. 'Especially within a family concern. For God's sake, Jock did it, and so did I.' He turned to Peter. 'There's the American Division. The TV stations. Just your sort of thing. How does that sound? Hypothetically.'

'That's blatant bribery!' Monty said coldly.

'I'm looking out for the interests of the company,' Wilson said. 'Which is more than can be said of Anna.'

'If I was hypothetically offered a job in America I would regretfully have to say no. My life's in Britain. Laura would never move. She needs to be in London.'

'What then?' Wilson said.

'I've been thinking about this quite a bit,' Peter said. 'What I believe Webster needs is someone who is above the editor of the *News* with a strong managerial brief as well.'

'You mean a managing editor?'

'Precisely.'

'I don't see why not. I think it's a bloody good idea. Should we have another vote?'

Nico said, 'I don't think it's such a good idea.'

'What difference would it make to you?' Wilson said.

'Ask John.'

They all looked at John. He said to his father, 'You told me to promise Nico a job. So I did.'

'So what's the problem?'

'I'm not working for Peter,' Nico said. 'That's the problem.'

Anna sat back in her chair absorbing the speed of change, the shifting loyalties. She could understand Peter but there was a bitter taste in her mouth.

Peter said, 'Why be unreasonable?'

'Let me spell it out, sport. You've had it all your own way since we were kids. Okay, you had an accident. That was no one's fault. But my God, we all had to pay. Peter this and Peter that . . . and three bags full. Poor Peter, everyone said. Well, to hell with it! I gave up feeling sorry for you a long time ago.'

Peter said, 'Aren't you too old for sibling envy?'

'I'm no sibling of yours. No relation at all. And that makes it easier for me.' Nico turned to Wilson. 'And I'm no relation of

yours either. No relation of anyone's in this room. Now then –
you want another vote?'

They looked at each other in silence.

The industrial estate was a dreary place of small factories and
depositories, most of which had been built in the 1950s. The
one which the *Daily News* owned stood behind a print shop
and next to an office equipment dealer. Nairn parked her car
and went in.

A woman sat in a drab office near the front door. She was in
her sixties, small and grey with a thin mouth. A nameplate on
her desk said 'Miss Cynthia Wiggins'. She had been eating a
sandwich and now hastily put it into her desk drawer.

Nairn explained what she wanted.

'You have to have special permission,' Miss Wiggins said. 'I
can't just get files out.'

'I don't want files.'

'I can't show you any photos either unless you get permission.' She had a sharp face and was clearly relishing her
power.

Nairn showed her a press identification card. Miss Wiggins
said, 'That is not permission.'

Nairn never normally used her position as Anna's granddaughter to gain advantage but she realized this type of woman
– whose empire, tiny though it was, was territorial – would
respond only to the highest authority. She reached for the
phone, dialled the *News* and asked for her grandmother's PA.

'Susan, it's Nairn. I'm at the depository where they keep the
old files. I need to check on something. Would you please tell –'
she glanced at the nameplate – 'Miss Wiggins that I have official
permission.'

She passed the phone to Miss Wiggins and watched her face
flush.

'Yes,' Miss Wiggins said, 'I understand. Yes.' She held the
receiver out to Nairn again. 'She wishes to speak to you, Miss
Braid.'

Susan said, 'I've had a call for you from Vienna. A Mr Esslin.
I said I thought you were at home.'

'Did he leave a message?'

311

'No, but he sounded . . . well, impatient.'

'Okay, I'll check my machine. Thanks.'

Miss Wiggins said, unctuously, 'I'm sorry, dear. I didn't know you were the granddaughter.'

'That's all right,' Nairn said briskly. 'I want to see some photographs of refugees. Austria, 1938. I understand you've only got the negatives.'

'I don't know who told you that. Sometimes we have negs, sometimes photographs, sometimes both. Refugees . . . Second World War . . . Will you come with me, dear?'

Nairn followed her down a corridor where humidifiers controlled the atmosphere. They went into a room where filing cabinets stood like rows of soldiers.

'Refugees . . . refugees . . .' Miss Wiggins tapped the cabinets as if they were old friends. 'France, Belgium, Holland, Denmark . . . Russia, Czechoslovakia, Hungary . . . Lots of refugees weren't there, dear? Ah, here we are, Austria. See Germany.'

She brought out a series of envelopes and placed them on a table for Nairn, then left her.

The photographs were in chronological order but they were not the kind she was looking for. They dated from the early thirties and were largely pictures of famous musicians, writers and scientists who had left Germany. One picture showed the young Einstein arriving in America.

Eventually she found one envelope which bore the heading 'Austria' and opened it with a feeling of excitement. But the people's clothing looked too modern, and when she looked at the captions on the back of each ten by eight inch print she saw these were refugees arriving in Austria during the Hungarian revolution of 1956.

She returned the envelopes to Miss Wiggins.

'Are there no others?'

'No, dear. Were there many refugees from Austria? It doesn't ring a bell. I mean, when you think of refugees you think of old newsreels of the French pushing prams along the country roads.'

'What other files do you have here?'

'Everything that was in the Fleet Street building: all the bound copies going back, well, to when the paper was first started. They were all put on microfilm. And all the personnel files. And all the financial and business files. And the accounts . . .'

'Personnel files?'

'Oh yes. Famous writers worked on the *News*. You know, dear, and I'm not saying it was your grandmother, but a year ago I had a letter saying I should burn all the old files. That they wanted to close this place down. Economies. I said you can't do that. I said this is history. Some day someone will write the history of the paper and they'll want to know who all these people were. The famous people and even the not so famous people.'

'Where are the personnel files?'

Once again she followed Miss Wiggins along the corridor. 'Anyone in particular?'

'Yes, my grandfather. He worked on the paper.'

'I didn't know that! You see what I mean, dear?'

'I can manage now, thanks.'

She put the file on the table near a window and looked at the buff cover for a moment. This file, unlike all the others in the building, was one with which she could identify. She was, in a sense, part of it. She opened it with a mixture of eeriness and fascination.

It did not contain much. There were three letters and a short strip of negative film attached to one of the letters. The first letter was dated 1936 and formally appointed Wilson Henry Braid to a position of reporter on the paper at the salary of eight pounds a week. The second was a commendation for a story he had written about Welsh miners. It was the third – the one with the negatives attached – that she read with mounting concern.

It was dated May 1938 and was signed by the editor, Duncan Henderson.

It read:

Dear Braid,
   I have decided, in view of our discussion yesterday, not to sack you as you deserve but to allow you to resign as you requested.

313

*I do this only because of the great respect in which I hold your
father and in the knowledge of how deeply he would be hurt if he
knew the truth.*

*What you did was despicable and I look upon you with disgust
and contempt.*

It is people like you who bring the press into disrepute.

I do not wish to see you in the office as of today.

Nairn read the letter again and felt her stomach contract. She
held up the negatives to the light but they were underexposed
and extremely dark. She thought she could make out a figure
pointing to something a little distance away from it but what
that something was she could not see. It might have been an
outcrop of rock. But it too was blurred. The photographs seemed
to have been taken from some distance away.

She placed the letter and the negative strip in her bag,
replaced the file in the cabinet drawer and went to Miss Wiggins's office.

'Find what you want, dear?'

'Yes, thank you. I put the file back.'

'If we had destroyed it you wouldn't have been able to see
it, would you? That's what I said to the other gentleman.'

'What gentleman?'

'He was also looking for people in Austria about that time.'

'What people?' She felt a sudden shock.

'I can't remember what their names were.'

'Meissner? Beckerman?'

'All German names sound a bit the same to me.'

'What was he like, this man?'

'Thin. Elderly.'

Seven

Nairn drove back to her flat hardly aware of the traffic. She was on automatic pilot. A whole series of thoughts was racing through her mind, starting with the letter she had read. What was the despicable and disgusting act which her grandfather had committed?

And who was the tall, thin, elderly man who had been at the depository? Beckerman? There was no one else it could be. Who else would be interested in pictures of Austrian refugees of that period?

And why had Paul telephoned? Did he have news about Beckerman? Or was it something else? Something personal?

She had to check her ansaphone to see what Paul's message was. Then she would go in to the *Daily News* and have the negatives processed.

She ran up the steps to her flat, opened her door and the first thing she heard was Balbastre's 'Romance' coming softly, on guitar strings, from the living-room.

'Hi,' Neil's voice called out. 'Is that you, darling?'

He was sitting on the floor letting his long fingers stray across the strings. She saw him in profile with his hair caught behind in a pony-tail. Normally she would have felt a spurt of pleasure that he was so beautiful and that he was hers. But this was not a normal occasion.

The room reeked of marijuana. 'Welcome home,' he said. 'I'm sorry I wasn't here when you arrived.'

She pushed past him and opened the windows. She did not know what to say to him, was not sure of her reactions. It was as though he had never left. Things had happened too quickly. She hadn't had time to register his absence and now here he was again.

'Where were you?' she asked.

'I've been away for a few days.'

'I gathered that. I phoned several times from Austria.'

'Ah.' He strummed part of a paso doble. 'I didn't know, you see.'

'Where did you go?'

He gave her a seraphic smile and said, 'Over the hills and far away.'

'Excuse me a moment.'

She went out and checked her answering machine for Paul's message. All she heard was the hissing of a clear tape; there were no voices, no messages. She opened the machine and saw that the tape had been rewound. She went back to Neil.

'What's happened to the answering machine? There's nothing on the tape.'

'I wiped it.'

'You *what*?'

'It was almost full and I thought you might phone.'

He stopped playing, relit the joint and put his head back against a chair.

It was the feebleness of the excuse that enraged her. The fact that he hadn't even troubled to make it believable.

'You're lying,' she said. 'I can always tell. You've had someone here!'

'Now look, sweetie . . .' He put his guitar down and rose to his feet. 'You're not my keeper. What I do is my business.'

'Not in my home it isn't,' she said.

They stood staring angrily at each other and suddenly he seemed to switch to another stream of consciousness. 'Listen, old love, don't be like this.' He made to put his arms round her but she avoided him. 'Don't say anything we'll both regret. What difference does it make to you what I do when you're not here? It's being together that counts. Anyway how do I know what you were up to in Austria. See what I mean? An open association – '

'To hell with open associations!'

316

And suddenly she saw him for what he was: someone who lived in the theatre of life, both as actor and audience, and one part of him was always clapping and cheering the other. He hadn't really grown up, she thought. And she had.

She said quietly, 'I'm going to the *Daily News*. I don't know when I'll return but when I get back I don't want you here. I don't want anything of yours here. If you take any of my books or anything else that isn't yours I'll get in touch with the police.'

'Now wait just – '

'I want you out!'

She turned from the room and ran down to the car. The reaction didn't hit her until she reached Victoria. She drove calmly and precisely but as she was going up in the lift towards the photographic department she began to shake.

One of the technicians looked at the negatives and said, 'They're pretty thick.'

'Is there anything you can do?'

'I'll try. When do you want them?'

'Yesterday.'

He looked at his watch. 'I'm on lunch in ten minutes.' She waited, he shrugged. 'Okay, I'll do them first.'

'I love you!'

'They all say that.'

She went down to her desk and put a call through to Paul in Vienna. His secretary told her he was at the Ministry of Justice but was expected any minute.

'Would you tell him I'm at the *Daily News* now and to ring me urgently.'

For the first time since the meeting had begun more than two hours before, Anna was afraid. She was afraid she was losing the *Daily News*. Why? That was the question that beat on her brain. How had she reached this point? As the discussion around her grew more heated, she tried to find the answer, to see herself for a moment as others must see her: ruthless, arrogant, privileged.

But wasn't she also the young girl who had fled from her grandmother's farm in Wales? Who had sat up in the train as it raced through Europe towards Vienna, not knowing what her future was going to be, but thankful to be getting away from the immediate past?

She had had good as well as bad luck. She had taken her opportunities when they came. She might be accused of ruthlessness in forcing Wilson into a marriage he did not want. Arrogance? She supposed so. But surely there had been love and compassion and loyalty.

She was still that young woman, but grown old. She herself felt much as she had ever since she could remember. She still did the same things: she slept with Ben and enjoyed it; she walked with a spring in her muscles; she lived her life at the centre of fast-moving events and this kept her young. Or so she thought.

But to Peter and John and Nico and Nairn and all the rest of the staff she must appear to be what she was, a grey-haired woman in her seventies. And she was blocking their particular paths. She looked at the men ranged against her. Three of them she had known since they were tiny and pink and slept in cradles. Now they were middle-aged and each had his own life to live and if he had to use her, then she knew that this was how it would be done.

Blood was thicker than water but there were times, she knew, when that became almost irrelevant. People did what circumstances forced upon them and circumstances were now conspiring to take away from her what she had created.

But her introspection quickly gave way to a stiffening of resolve. She had been leaning back in her chair as though disassociating herself from what was going on; now she leaned forward and placed her elbows on the table-top.

What had caused her fear was the fact that it was Nico who was supporting her, not Peter. Nico was the most malleable of the men and if he could be manipulated by one side, why not by the other?

He was flushed and truculent and was being harassed by John and Wilson while Peter had withdrawn into a tight-lipped silence.

She had lost Peter. That had been clumsy. He had always been the one who had most of her love and who had given her a good share of his. He had been loyal. So something must

have happened to force his resignation from *Talking Heads*. Had
he been humiliated? That was all she could think of. Peter could
not stand humiliation. He needed his position, his dignity, his
power.

Well, she was being given another chance. Nico might be a
weak reed but he needed money. She put her principles on one
side and cut across the conversation.

'We're going round and round in circles,' she said loudly.
'Nico, darling. I've got something to propose.'

Nico swung round to look at her. 'What?'

'America.'

'What about it?'

'You join the American Division.'

Nico played with the gold chain around his neck. The truc-
ulence left his face. Anna could read his mind: he'd be able to
get Jacqui away from the London flesh-pots – the rumours
about her were squalid to say the least – and he would be paid
handsomely.

'A new start,' she said. 'You'd have to learn the business
but that shouldn't be too difficult. You'd have good advisers.
Headquarters in Boston.'

She saw Wilson's eyebrows shoot up in surprise. He said to
Nico, 'You believe that and you'll believe anything. Ask her
what she's going to pay you with.'

Anna said, 'Nico knows very well I've never in my life
reneged on a promise.'

She was aware that Monty was as surprised as the others.
She turned to him now and said, 'Monty believes that too. He
believes in the strength of family loyalty.' She stressed the
word, looking hard at Peter. 'We were talking about this a little
while ago. There's no reason why Nico shouldn't join the
American Division and eventually become a vice-president, as
long as he has the right advisers.'

'They're bullshitting you,' Wilson said. Nico's head was turning back and forth. 'But if you like the idea we can do a deal.'

In all his life Nico had never been wooed like this and he
leaned back in his chair and said, 'What sort of deal?'

'We can get to the fine print later. But sure, if you want to
go to the States, why not? You can *head* the American Division.'

Anna felt the tension in the room. This was like an auction with Nico's greed as the guide price.

'Nico, you know you couldn't run it by yourself,' she said, trying to make Nico recognize the snow job.

'Why couldn't he?' Wilson said. 'You underestimate him. You always have. Nico, we'll give you a brilliant team but you'll be leader.'

His words were chosen well. 'Team' and 'leader' were so much better than 'advisers' and 'vice-president'. And then he put the icing on the cake: 'And you can make your headquarters in New York. That's where the action is.'

But Nico was enjoying himself too much to agree instantly. 'You haven't answered my question,' he said. 'What sort of deal?'

'Okay, if you go for Anna, ask her how she's going to pay you. Or continue paying anyone else, for that matter.'

'I can answer that,' Monty said. 'We've got a line of credit from Erlich.'

'My God,' Wilson said. 'You're up to your eyebrows. You can hardly service your present debts. Now you go to Erlich. They have some of the highest rates in Europe and – hey, wait a minute!' He turned to Nico and said, 'You know what they're going to do? They're going to sell the American Division. They'll give you a few months there while they look for a buyer and then – bang, they'll pull it out from under you.'

Nico flashed a hostile glance at his mother. 'Is that true? Have you been talking about selling the American Division?'

'In a company of this size we talk about a great many options.'

'Have you?'

'We've mentioned it in passing but – and you can ask Monty – we decided it wasn't an option.'

Monty looked uncomfortable and Wilson spotted it. 'They're lying,' he said. 'Anyway it doesn't change the facts. If you went to the States for them you'd be gambling. In your terms you'd be drawing to a straight and you know what sort of odds those are. But Braid International has the money. And we're willing to use it.'

Anna knew then that she'd lost Nico. Monty sensed it too.

320

He said, 'I think we can resolve this. I'd like to have a word with Anna in private.'

They went out into the corridor. 'If they vote now you've lost,' Monty said.

'I know.'

'You've only got one card. Peter.'

'I don't think so.'

'You're his mother. He's your closest. You've got to appeal to him on those grounds. Make it sound like something else but let him know the reality.'

'I couldn't! Not now. He's been humiliated. I'd only make it worse.'

'Nothing's stronger than the love of a mother for a child,' he said. 'It works in reverse too.'

'Not always.'

'Give him what he wants. If he wants to be editor, or managing editor, or God himself, then give it to him!'

'I'm not – '

'I've been watching him. I know he's angry and sore, but there's one thing in your favour. At the moment he dislikes you, but he *hates* Wilson.'

As he spoke she thought, why not? And when she'd won him she'd have her day with the others. She'd flay them! John, pathetic John, dependent entirely on his father and his wife; Nico, shallow and unstable. And Wilson! She would save him for last . . .

They went back into the room and took their seats. 'I have something to say,' Anna began.

They waited.

She took a deep breath. But then, instead of beginning, she let the air in her lungs slowly escape. Instead of three grown men sitting directly opposite her, she saw her three sons. With Nairn they formed her family, all she had after seventy-odd years. If she said the things she wanted to say, first to Peter then to the others, she might save the paper but she would lose their respect and their love, such as it was. She would lose the bulk of her life. For she had no doubt that Peter, when the dust settled, would finally despise her.

'What?' Wilson said. 'We're waiting.'

321

Slowly she shook her head. 'Nothing. There's nothing I want to say.'

'Let's take a final vote then.' Wilson's voice was thick and exultant.

She glanced at Monty. He was looking at her in bewilderment. But there was nothing he could do either; finally this was her company, her family.

'Come on!' Wilson said again. 'Let's vote.'

The door swung open with a crash. Nairn stood on the threshold. She was looking at her father.

'Father! I want to see you!' Her voice was angry, imperative and anguished all at the same time.

Her father said, 'We were just going to – '

'I want to see you. Now!'

Eight

Nairn had waited at her desk for fifteen minutes for Paul's call, and when it didn't come she went into Susan's office.

'How's it going?' she said, indicating the boardroom along the corridor.

Her grandmother's PA was a slender woman in her forties, severely tailored in a grey suit with short hair to match. She looked and was efficient.

'Don't ask,' she said. 'I've been trying to eavesdrop. From what I could hear it's horrendous. I'm waiting for the blood to start oozing under the door.'

'But why?' Nairn was genuinely puzzled.

'The knives are out, that's why.'

She thought of Peter. 'You can't be serious.'

Susan looked up sharply at her. 'I'll tell you this. If Anna loses the paper I'm off. I'm not working for your grandfather.'

'My grandfather! He's here?'

'You didn't know?'

'Of course not. Did you?'

'None of us did. He just walked in with his lawyer.'

The phone on Susan's desk rang and she said, 'Yes, she's here.' She put her hand over the mouthpiece. 'It's Vienna.'

'I'll take it in Anna's office.'

Paul's voice sounded agitated. 'I tried to get you earlier.'

'Yes, I'm sorry. I was out.'

'They're going to release Beckerman!'

'Oh no! When?'

'They're keeping quiet about that. They don't want TV and

journalists waiting outside the prison. I only know because I have a contact in the Justice Ministry.'

'Is there nothing you can do?'

'Nothing. Not as far as extradition is concerned. If we could prove the man is Beckerman and that he had committed a crime on Austrian soil that would be different.'

'I thought the authorities would be only too glad to get rid of him.'

'There's been a change of attitude. Now they think that if they put a war criminal on trial they would show the world that even if our record is bad at least we are trying to make up for it.' He was silent for a moment and then said in a different tone, 'Are you all right?'

'Yes, I'm fine.' There was a pause. 'Paul?'

'I'm here.'

She frowned. His voice had changed again. This time he sounded upset.

'I've been doing some research of my own.' She told him about her visit to the depository and the 'thin, elderly man' who had visited it before her.

'Beckerman, of course!'

'But why?'

'For the same reason you went. To see if there were any pictures on file that could incriminate him. Don't you understand, he has been just ahead of us all this time. Ahead of us in Altenkirchen and now in London. He *knew* he had to work quickly, he *knew* the net was closing. Listen to me, you must get your grandmother here in the next forty-eight hours or it will be too late!'

'I wish I could. I mean I wish I could guarantee that. But all hell's broken loose here. My father's arrived *and* my grandfather. They own shares in the company and I think they're trying to take the paper away from Anna. I *can't* just walk in and say you've got to drop everything and go to Vienna!'

Silence.

'Paul? Are you there? Listen, I have to go.'

'Yes. I'm here. Is that all you have to say? "I have to go"?'

'What's wrong?'

'Everything!'

'I know how you feel but – '

Through the doorway she saw the technician from the photo lab standing at Susan's desk. He had a batch of wet prints in his hand.

'Goodbye!' Paul said abruptly and put the phone down.

She felt perplexed and defensive.

'I'm going off to lunch,' the technician said. 'You wanted them urgently so I thought I'd show them to you wet.' He put them down in a row on a table near the window. There were five large prints. They were grainy and dark. 'It's the best I could do. There's some camera shake as well as underexposure.'

As she looked at them she felt the hair on the back of her neck rise. They were all taken in a forest. Mist was cloaking the dark pine trees.

The first picture showed four people. A group of three and one standing a few yards to the left. The three were what she had mistaken on the negatives for an outcrop of rocks.

In the group she could make out a man, a woman wearing a heavy coat, and a smaller figure.

The figure on the left was another man. She could see his profile clearly. He was wearing a thick white jersey. The man in the group was holding out his arms as though talking, or begging, or imploring.

The second picture showed him falling forward.

The man in the white sweater was pointing at him. Then she saw the pistol in his hand.

The woman had one arm over her face as though to shield herself and she had gathered the small figure into her body with her other arm.

The third photograph showed her falling backwards.

The fourth showed the smaller figure running.

The fifth showed the man in the white sweater bending over something dark on the ground. There were no other figures in the shot, and she knew exactly what she was looking at. It was what Paul had suggested. But here it was in stark black and white. She felt a clammy sweat break out on her face. She had seen nothing like this in all her life; had never experienced such horror.

She was looking at the last moments in the lives of the

Meissners, Michael, Ruth and Stefan. This was how they had disappeared all those years ago, executed in a lonely Austrian forest for the money and the jewels they were carrying. The man in the white sweater could be no one but Beckerman.

'Are you all right?' the darkroom assistant said.

'Yes.'

'What the hell are these? From the war?'

'Yes.'

'A lot of bloody awful things happened then.'

'Yes.'

She wished he would go.

'You want me to put them on the dryer?'

'No. Leave them where they are.'

He looked at her oddly.

She did not even remember to thank him as he left but stood alone in Anna's office as another thought came into her mind; this as shattering in its way as the scenes she had just been looking at. It was only a matter of moments after that that she marched past Susan and along the corridor and flung open the boardroom door.

Now she was back in Anna's office with her father. His face was lined with concern and confusion.

She had been facing the windows and suddenly turned on him. 'You lied to me!'

'What?'

'You lied to me!'

Her voice had risen and he closed the door quickly behind him.

'What's the matter?'

'Your letter.'

'It wasn't a lie. I meant every word of it. I've been wanting to say those things for so many years.'

'Stop it!'

'I won't stop it. It's true. I couldn't seem to tell you myself but –'

'You wrote all those things as a cover. You didn't tell me Grandfather was coming to London! What are you trying to do to Anna?'

326

'We're trying to do what's best for the paper.'

She gave a harsh laugh. 'What would Grandfather know about what's best for a newspaper like this? Nudes on page three? Is that what you've got in mind?'

'Nairn, I – '

'No, listen. Anna spent most of her adult life creating this paper. It's one of the best there is. I'm not going to let Braid International ruin it.'

There was a flash of annoyance on his face. 'You'd better rephrase that.'

'You're going to vote against her?'

'That's why I came.'

'And so is Peter and so is Nico.'

'It looks that way.'

'You knew it all along!'

'We knew about Nico, not about Peter.'

'All I knew was that she had the controlling interest and it only needed one son to vote with her and she could never be beaten. Is that true?'

'It's always been like that. We've known that Peter and probably Nico would vote with her if it ever came to it.'

'I want you to vote on her side.'

'It's too late. That's not possible.'

'Why? Are you frightened of Grandfather?'

'That's an unkind thing to say.'

'Are you?'

'Nairn, don't let's you and me get into a fight now.'

'I want you to vote with Anna.'

'I can't do it. There are other reasons.' He hesitated. 'Look, your mother . . . she wants to live over here. I said I'd come too. That we'd make our home here. Otherwise, well, I have the feeling that she'll come anyway. Do you understand what I'm saying? It could be the end of our marriage.'

'I don't believe that!'

She grabbed her bag and took out the letter written to Wilson Braid by the editor of the *Daily News* in 1938. 'Read that.'

He read it slowly, his face falling into a frown. 'Where did you get this?'

'From the files of this newspaper! Do you understand what it says?'

'It's clear enough. Your grandfather was almost fired from the *Daily News*, that's what it means.'

'He *was* fired. Only they gave him the opportunity of resigning first. That's all it means. Has he ever told you that?'

'Never.'

She stepped aside and revealed the pictures on the table. 'Have a look at these.'

He approached warily, uneasily. He glanced at them for a few moments and said, 'What are they supposed to mean?'

She pointed to the first picture. 'You see that group of three people? Their names are Meissner. They're Austrian.'

'You mean the people – ?'

'That Anna lived with in Vienna. And that is a man called Cuno Beckerman who is in prison now in Austria because the French want to extradite him for war crimes. Look at the second picture. Do you see what's happening?' He peered more closely. 'Beckerman is shooting Michael Meissner. And there – the third picture. He's just shot Ruth and she's falling. And that one – that's Stefan, their son. Only a child. He's running away. He was shot in the back of the head. I know that because the Austrian police have found his skull.'

'If that's true, then it's terrible, but I'm confused. I'm not sure what it's got to do with –'

'Who do you think took the pictures, Father? Who do you think was hiding in the forest? Who do you think could have stopped this execution, by shouting or making a noise or *something* which might have given the boy time to run and hide but instead kept himself hidden and deliberately took picture after picture? Who do you think smuggled them out and so disgusted his editor that he wrote him a letter like this?'

John clutched the edge of the desk and then he slumped into Anna's chair. 'Is all this true?' he said in a voice that already knew the answer.

'Are you all right?'

'Yes, I'm all right. Now what? What are you going to do?'

'It depends.'

'You're not going to make them public, are you? He's an old man. The publicity would kill him.'

'It depends on you.'

'You mean the vote?'

'Exactly.'

He sat staring into space for a long moment and then rose wearily. 'You don't have to threaten. I'm not as far gone as that.' /

Anna watched as John returned to the boardroom. He seemed to have aged five years.

'Well?' Wilson said.

'You wanted a vote, a final vote,' John said.

'Yes.'

'All right, let's vote.'

The hands went up. Three for Wilson, two for Anna – but two was enough.

There was a shocked silence at the table. Anna and Monty were bewildered. Then Wilson Braid leaned towards John and said, 'Are you mad? Do you think you can go against me? You miserable little shit – !'

'Don't go on, Father.'

'But *why*?' Nico said. 'I don't understand.'

'It's Nairn's doing,' Peter said. 'What line did she sell you?'

'That's my business,' John said, 'and it will stay my business.' There was a sudden firmness in his tone that Anna had not heard before.

Wilson, his face corrugated by rage and engorged with blood, said, 'You're finished! You've had it! You'll never work for me again!'

'I know that,' John said. 'Never . . . ever . . . again.'

Don't worry. We'll work things out.

Anna had said this as a kind of litany to Peter and Nico.

After Wilson had stormed out of the boardroom mouthing threats and imprecations, they had sat on looking down at their hands. At last Peter had looked up and said, 'I'm sorry. It was – '

'Please don't say it was only business,' Anna said, smiling. 'Or I'll scream.'

He raised a tired hand and said, 'No, I was going to say it was only selfishness.'

Don't worry. We'll work things out.

Peter rose to his feet and rubbed his leg and said, 'I didn't feel a thing. Not the entire meeting.'

Nico said, 'I remember when we were little. The pain used to go when you were angry or excited.'

'Or scared,' Peter said.

The two of them no longer looked as though they would take knives to each other, Anna thought. That's what catharsis did. It drained you of everything, leaving a vacuum.

But what was the vacuum to be filled with?

Don't worry. We'll work things out.

'Laura and I are getting married,' Peter said, as she walked with them to the lift.

'That's wonderful. I'm so pleased.'

'I'm not sure what we'll do. Probably sell the Hampstead house.'

'Don't do anything yet. Let me think about things. We'll work something out. And Nico – you too. Even if we have to sell the American Division eventually, you could still go out there for a while. Learn what you can. Then we can think again. The point is we'll work something out.'

She kissed them both goodbye at the lift doors and said, 'I'll call you in a few days. How about a family lunch one Sunday?'

They looked at her with some surprise. Family lunches had been traditional in the early years of their marriages, but had then been allowed to lapse when second wives and girl-friends made life complicated.

'We haven't had one for a long time and now John and Mary are in town and I thought it was a good idea.'

Nairn and her father and Monty were in her office. She asked Susan to bring in a bottle of malt whisky. It wasn't a celebratory drink, for the photographs were still on the table.

Anna looked at them and her thoughts went back to that day as she carried Nico in his blanket, Ruth tottering away on her high heels and Cuno in his skiing sweater and long shiny hair,

leading the way. The uncertainty. The fear. It had all been justified.

Just seeing their shadowy figures in extremis gave her an
overwhelming sadness for the Meissners and she felt tears at
the back of her eyes. This was unusual for her. Normally she
felt weepy only when she was very tired.

'Wilson held Nico for me when I went in to see the lieutenant
of police,' she said. 'That's when he must have put the roll of
film into the baby's blanket. I didn't realize it but *I* smuggled
the film across.'

They talked a little longer and then Monty drained his glass
and made to leave. She walked along the corridor and took his
hand and said, 'Thank you, my dear.'

'We're not safe yet,' he said. 'This is only the beginning.'

'I know that.'

Don't worry. We'll work things out.

John and Nairn were still in her office when she went back.
'What now, John?' she said.

'I don't know.'

'Do you think your father meant it?'

'About not working for him again? If he didn't I did.'

'What will you do?'

'I've got savings and shares. Enough.'

'Will you leave Africa?'

'I'll talk to Mary.'

Don't worry. We'll work things out.

'How long are you in London?'

'Another week.'

'Let's have lunch and talk.'

'About what?'

'Before the meeting Monty was playing devil's advocate. He
said, if I resigned and the company had to go to one of my
sons, which would it be? I had no intention of resigning but I
played Monty's game. I said John.'

'Why me? You hardly know me.'

'Because you're a professional.'

A few minutes later he left and only Nairn remained. They
talked about the meeting and then Anna said, 'I'm whacked.
I'm going home.'

331

'I know this isn't the time to mention it but I spoke to Paul on the phone. They're on the point of releasing Beckerman.'

Anna touched the photographs. 'I spoke to Susan before I saw these. She's getting us seats on one of tomorrow's flights.'

Anna walked slowly along the corridor, picked up her jacket and bag and then took the stairs down. The newsroom was in a state of organized chaos. News was coming in from all over the globe, telephones were ringing, keyboards clattering. A great newspaper was racing through its daily cycle.

She drove back carefully through London, stopping in Hyde Park. She walked along the Serpentine. One of her problems was resolved. The other hung over her like a sword.

Nine

Anna and Nairn took a flight to Vienna the following day. Nairn had tried to contact Paul before they left but he was not at his office or his flat. She had left a message with his secretary but he had clearly not received it for he was not at the airport to meet them.

They hired a car and went into the city. Nairn drove and Anna stared at her surroundings. She had not been in Vienna for more than fifty years. A war had intervened, so had a Russian occupation. She hardly recognized anything. Everywhere she saw housing estates built in the sixties. Part of the centre of the city had been shelled by Russian tanks and there were new buildings near the Stefanskirche.

As they drove along the Ring she looked for the hotel where she had waited for Ben, but it too had vanished. What, she wondered, would her life have been like had Hitler not chosen that day to cross the Austrian border? She might have been an American housewife now with a husband who was never at home.

Nairn parked the car and they walked to Paul's office. They had left London in warm spring weather, but here the air was cold, and mist hung over the Donaukanal.

They found Paul's secretary in a state of barely suppressed rage. When they enquired after him she burst out: 'Beckerman! Beckerman! Beckerman! He thinks of nothing else!' Then she unleashed a torrent of German which neither could understand.

'Do you know where Herr Esslin has gone?' Nairn asked when she drew breath.

'To Stein prison. And I have to cancel three appointments. And is coming an American and I do not know his address to stop him.'

She said this as though it was partly Nairn's fault.

They drove north-west out of the city. Again Anna looked for landmarks. This was the way she had come with the Meissners when they had fled the city. They went over the northern hills towards Tulln and picked up the road along the Danube.

Nairn was driving fast and Anna found her foot braking on the floor of the passenger side. 'Austria has one of the highest road casualty rates in the world.'

'Don't worry. I won't have us in the river.'

They crossed the bridge at Krems and soon the walls of the prison loomed up, grim against the leaden sky.

Nairn turned into the parking lot and as she switched off the engine she saw a tall figure come striding from the main prison door, coat flapping and hair blowing in the chilly breeze.

'There's Paul!'

She pressed the hooter and called to him. He turned and came to them as they got out of the car.

'He's gone!' he said, glowering at Anna. 'Two hours ago. The prison department in Vienna would not give me any information so I came here.'

'I phoned you,' Nairn said. 'I left messages.'

'And I left messages for you. On your machine and at the airport.' His tone was sharp.

'I got neither,' she said, remembering what had happened to the tape in London. 'Anyway let's not worry about that. What will you do now?'

'What *can* I do?' He turned to Anna. 'If you had come when I asked maybe this would not have happened!'

She started to say something, thought better of it, then said, 'We're both on the same side, Herr Esslin. Why don't we declare a truce while you look at these?' She spread the photographs on top of the car.

He stared at them, lifting each, looking closely, putting it back in order. Anna looked past him at the bleak prison walls, almost sensing the misery that seeped from them. This was where they had held Beckerman or Gregor or whoever he was.

She shivered. In a way she was glad they'd let him go, but she knew that it was only a reprieve for her. Paul's face was tense with excitement. She knew he would never rest until he had exhausted every possibility of having his quarry gaoled for good.

Slowly, he began to nod his head. He held up the first one, the sharpest. The man in the skiing sweater was clearly defined. 'Where did you find these?' Nairn told him briefly. 'Your grandfather took them?'

'We're not proud of that,' Nairn said.

'But out of his – how can I say? – greed for a story, we may get our man.' He turned to Anna. 'Is that Beckerman with the pistol?'

'Yes.'

'Are you sure?'

'Quite sure.'

'Well, then . . . maybe . . . !'

'What?' Nairn said.

'This is a crime committed on Austrian territory. It is not political. It has nothing to do with the war or extradition. It is a criminal act, the murder of three people for financial gain. We have the photographs, the police have the Meissners' bones. Maybe he won't get away with it after all.'

'But only if this man *is* Beckerman,' Nairn said.

'Just so. There is still the question of identification.'

'Where do you think he'll have gone?'

'Home. Where else? He is a free man.' He turned to Anna. 'I want you to see him, look at him. If you think he is Beckerman there are other wheels we can set in motion.'

Paul drove his Lancia, Nairn and Anna followed in their hired car. They took the road back the way they had come and entered the rolling hills to the north of Vienna. The man who was said to be Beckerman lived, so Paul had told them, near Weidlingsbach in the Wienerwald where he bred trout for the table.

It was a grey afternoon and the trees, though coming into leaf, were black against the sky. The deeper they went into the woods the gloomier the afternoon became. Eventually the Lancia pulled up and Paul came back to them.

'I don't know the roads here,' he said. 'I'm going to ask someone the way.'

He stopped at a *Gasthaus*. They were directed back on their tracks and, after a couple of kilometres, took a small road leading off to the right. Finally they came to an iron gate on which was a notice saying, '*Forellen verkauf*' and in smaller lettering underneath, 'Trout for Sale'. They entered the property and drove up an unmade gravel road until Paul stopped and walked back to them.

'The house is beyond that stand of trees,' he said to Anna. 'Please stay here. Nairn can wait in the trees. If he is there I will say I want to buy some trout. He must come back here.' He pointed to the stewponds a little way off the road. 'We will come past the car. You don't even have to get out. Just look from the car.'

Anna watched them walk up the road and disappear behind the trees.

She had been regretting her decision to come ever since leaving London. But in the face of what she had said to Monty and what Nairn would think of her if she did not, she had had no choice.

But she still did have a choice about what to say after she had glimpsed the man who lived in this remote place. She could hear herself saying, 'That is not the man I knew. That is not Cuno Beckerman.'

And it would all be over. She would have done her best, would have played the moral card. And really, except for Paul and Nairn, no one would care about her lie. The French were involved only for political reasons, the Austrians did not want to be involved at all. Everyone would be happier if the whole situation faded away.

She felt a stab of guilt as she remembered the photographs. There they were beside her in their envelope, the stark black-and-white murders of her friends, the people who had looked after her in her own misery after her parents' death. But how would the arrest of Beckerman help them now?

Was it worth the real possibility of ruining Peter's life? She could not even guess what he would go through if it was shown that his father was a mass murderer. No, life was for the living and it was better that the whole mess be buried. Like the Meissners.

She shivered. That was not a particularly good analogy since the Meissners were no longer buried. Their bones lay in some storage cabinet awaiting an opportunity to tell their story.

Of course it would be satisfying to make Cuno pay for what he had done to the Meissners and to her. But the cost made it unthinkable.

Even though she had told herself that he was an old man now, she was still afraid of Cuno. That's what happened when a man brutalized you. The fear remained, would always remain. And that fear had increased once she saw the photographs. They had seemed to bring him so much nearer.

She thought of Wilson, hiding behind a tree, taking picture after picture of people being killed. It was hard to credit but she was not surprised; he was a mixture of coward and bully and she remembered how he would do almost anything for a story.

Stiff with cold, she got out of the car. A narrow track left the gravel road at right angles. On either side of it were the stewponds where trout were rising to insects, some jumping clear out of the water and landing back with a splash. She had not seen trout rising to flies since she and Ben had lain in the room at the Troutbeck Inn and looked out at the river. It seemed another lifetime. Was she so frightened of giving up the paper because she didn't have Ben? Was it a surrogate for a husband?

To ease her muscles she walked along the track for about fifty metres and stopped between the stewponds. The water was dark under the slaty sky and the fringing reeds bent in the chilly wind. She picked up a handful of dirt and threw it on to the surface of the water. The fish, assuming it was food, fought to get it, causing the surface of the pond to boil.

'Grüss Gott,' a voice said.

She whirled.

An elderly man had come out of the trees and was standing a few metres away from her. She did not know how long he had been watching her. He was thin and dressed in thick dark-green loden, heavy boots that laced to his knees and a peaked cap pulled well down over his forehead.

337

'If you wish to feed them, here is food.' He offered her a plastic bucket.

'You startled me.'

'Forgive me. Try a handful.'

She wanted to go back to the car but he was blocking the path and there was no way around him.

'Have you come to buy?' he said.

'I . . . yes . . . I thought I would. We were passing. My friends have gone to the house to see if there was anyone there.'

'Ah. Ja. Please try . . .'

He held out the bucket again. She took a handful of dried fish pellets and threw them on to the water. Again the fish jumped and fought, thrashing the water into white foam.

'If I didn't feed them well they would turn into cannibals,' the man said, and for the first time Anna realized he had spoken to her only in English. 'Have you ever seen a cannibal trout?'

She shook her head.

'The jaws grow big and long like scissors. And of course the fish grow big too. From eating their friends. You do not think such things happen with trout. So pretty.' He picked up a scoop-net. 'What size would you like? How many?'

'Well . . . I . . . perhaps three. There are three of us.'

She looked past him but the road was empty.

'Half a kilo. That is the best size for eating.'

'Yes. Yes. Fine.'

He scooped up a trout in his net, leaned forward to pick it up, and his cap fell on to the grass. As he straightened, a mane of white hair dropped back into place.

She knew the hair so well, had so often smelled the pomade as his face had closed on hers. She remembered his lips, his tongue, his strong skier's body on top of her, the groaning and the pumping. She felt the same horror she had felt then.

'I'll go to the car,' she said.

'Why is that?'

'To get the money. You pick out another couple.'

'Ah. Ja. The money.'

But he made no move to let her pass. He scooped up two more trout and killed them by putting his fingers in their gills and bending back their heads until their spines snapped. He

338

laid them out on the grass and wiped the blood from his fingers.

He said, 'You know, these ponds are very deep. Deeper than most. They have ledges. Ideal for trout to hide under so that the herons can't find them.'

He took out a clasp-knife and said, 'Would you like me to clean the fish for you?'

'No, don't worry.'

'It is nothing.' He slit open their bellies, pulled out the entrails and threw them into the pond. There was another flurry of feeding.

She looked away. She felt her heart hammering in her ears and she was having difficulty in breathing. Was he playing with her? Toying with her? Or was it possible he had not recognized her after all? It was a hope born of desperation.

'People call it a feeding frenzy,' he said. 'Have you not seen pictures of sharks pulling fish to pieces? No? Trout are like that too. You know, a person could fall into one of these ponds and become trapped under a ledge and after a time when the body rotted, the trout would eat it.'

He held one up. 'Pretty things. Schubert wrote some music about them, I think. But they are not so pretty in their habits. They will eat flies, moths, beetles, worms, maggots. Anything. Even a body. Especially the cannibal trout, the *ferox*. Do you think I have not recognized you? People who have been lovers always know each other.'

'Don't use that word. There was no love in it.'

He smiled. 'Why have you come, Anna?'

'Please let me past.'

'Oh, ja, to get the money. You know I often thought of you. An English girl who pretended to be so innocent. I wondered what had happened to you. I made enquiries. It is easy when you are a policeman. Then later I learned what you did. I must congratulate you. Such a famous newspaper. And then the girl from that same paper. Coincidence? Policemen do not believe in coincidences. I thought, I wonder if Anna will come. I wonder if she could endure everything that would be said in court. How she fell in love with a young skier . . . I may say a brilliant young skier . . . and they had an affair full of passion . . . and then he broke off the affair and she never forgave him . . . But

339

it's too late now. There is no evidence. They cannot touch me. You cannot touch me.' He picked up the fish and threaded a piece of string through their gills. 'Here are your fish. Take them. A present. A payment for favours received.'

It was the last phrase and the contempt in his eyes which touched the fuse, and she felt anger blow through her like a hot wind. 'You may think it's too late but I know it isn't! We have proof. Photographs of you shooting Michael and Ruth and Stefan. They're with my friends.'

She realized then how anger had betrayed her. But there was no going back. The road was still empty. Talk, she told herself. Talk. 'And when we leave here they are going straight to your Ministry of Justice. You may have avoided extradition, but you committed murder on Austrian soil.' She made to pass him. 'Let me through!'

'You're lying.'

'We even know how you did it! First you shot Michael in the head, then Ruth, then Stefan began to run and you shot him in the back of the head. We have the photographs and the police have the bones and skulls.'

'But you still need identification. Can you prove that Herr Gregor was in Altenkirchen in 1938?'

He began to laugh at her.

'Does Herr Gregor have a scar on his right thigh made by a ski-stick?'

He gripped her upper arms. 'Ah, yes, the scar. Do you really think I forgot that? After the war there was an organization for us. Many people had plastic surgery.'

'You can't remove me with plastic surgery, Cuno. You can't blot out memory.'

He was old but strong. His fingers dug into her flesh. 'But I can remove you now! A slip. A fall. The pool is deep. Ledges. An Englishwoman drowns on holiday. My God, how terrible!'

She tried to wrestle free and they stood between the stew-ponds swaying as in some form of primitive dance. He shuffled and pushed, she fought back. But slowly she felt her feet slipping on the grass as she was pushed nearer and nearer to the water.

Her strength was fading. She felt herself grow dizzy. He

was trying to throw her off-balance. Her shoes came off. One stockinged foot landed on the cold, slimy side of a dead trout. She slipped, half fell, grasped him around the waist. He snatched at her hair and began to drag her. She tried desperately to bite his arm through the heavy loden cloth.

She felt herself swaying out over the water. She dug her nails into his neck and cheeks, clinging to his flesh. Her strength left her. A dark film seemed to drop over her eyes.

A voice shouted, 'Anna!' Then, 'I've got him!'

She felt Cuno's fingers suddenly loosen. She landed, half in and half out of the water. Two bodies struggled above her head. They fell. She heard a great splash. The two figures thrashed near the surface. They separated. Hands came up on to the grass beside her. They were going to drag her into the water. She tried to crawl away.

A head appeared. Weed covered the face.

He crawled up the bank. On her knees she fought her way with agonizing slowness through the grass. She heard him come as slowly after her.

Then she could go no further. The strength drained from her like water in a sieve. She could fight no more.

'Anna!'

It was a different voice. She pushed herself up and turned. He was just behind her. 'Ben!' she said.

She heard the noise a sealion makes and Beckerman broke the surface of the pond. He clawed at the water as though to grip it, but his waterlogged loden clothing weighed him down. He made one last effort, then sank. All she could see of him was the palms of his hands, like the white underbellies of dying trout, as they disappeared into the dark depths.

She turned to Ben Ramsey. She was too exhausted to speak but she put out her hand and he took it. Paul and Nairn ran down the track towards them.

Ten

Nairn said to Ben, 'So *you* were the thin, el—' She buried the word 'elderly' in a slight cough. 'The thin man who went to Altenkirchen and to the *Daily News* files.'

'Sure.'

'We thought it was Beckerman.'

'No, it was me. And I was in Paul's office that afternoon after you'd left, and his secretary was spitting tacks because he'd gone off. I'd been at the Justice Ministry too so I knew Beckerman was being released that day and I figured that if the media knew they'd be outside the prison waiting for him and I've been in too many scenes like that, so I went straight to the trout farm. The rest, as they say, is history.'

Nairn, Paul, Anna and Ben were at a *Heuriger* in Sievering. It was late in the afternoon and the air was warm. They were sitting at a rustic table drinking white wine, and the big garden, with apple trees in blossom, was beginning to fill with Viennese making the most of the first warm spring day.

Ben said, 'I always wanted to write something about the Meissners. Anna, you'll remember we talked about that once. But I guess I never had enough time. I started doing some research a few months ago, then the Berlin Wall came down and the whole face of Europe changed and I had too much on my plate.'

Anna sipped her wine and nibbled a piece of smoked cheese. She leaned back, savouring the warmth of the sun on her face. For the first time in weeks she felt wholly relaxed. She glanced across at Paul. He and Nairn were sitting on a bench and his arm was along the back behind her. He had turned his face to the sun and closed his eyes.

Nairn was animated, talking rapidly, recalling with Ben all that had happened. Anna let the talk wash over her.

The last few days had been filled with tension. First police frogmen had recovered Beckerman's body, then there had been the police investigation, the endless questioning – thank God Ben had been with her – then the identification; the grisly scenes in the police morgue, the skin graft on his leg which was almost more damning than the scar itself.

'Yes,' she heard her voice say, 'this is the body of Cuno Beckerman.'

How could she explain to them that whether he had a scar or not, she knew his naked body well enough even after all these years?

And then the press conference. For the first time she knew what it was like to be on the receiving end, the platform end; answering questions instead of asking them. The hot TV lights had been on her and the questions had come thick and fast. She had answered with as much detail as she could, for she realized what a good story this was.

But then the questioning had grown more intrusive: how close had been her relationship with Beckerman? how well had she known him? had they been more than friends?

They might have been innocent questions but not to Anna. All her antennae were alert. She bristled with defences.

It was Ben who came to her aid. 'I can answer that,' he said when a question seemed to probe too deeply about her relationship with Beckerman. 'I was the guy she was in love with. And I was in love with her. Beckerman never had a chance.' He smiled and the room relaxed in soft laughter.

Then it was all over. The papers published their stories, TV carried some extracts from the press conference. And, like so many other stories, it faded into limbo. Homage, as *Le Monde* said in an editorial, had finally been paid to the hostages of Libourne.

'We're running out of wine,' Ben said. 'We can't have that.'

'And cheese,' Paul said. 'I'll help.'

She watched the two men thread their way between the

tables to the open-air counter that served simple food. Ben carried himself well and there was still a spring in his step. If it wasn't for his loss of hair he might have been taken for a much younger man.

She and Ben had been together for the past few days. They had stayed at a hotel in Neustift am Walde, not far from the Althofengasse. She would never have done this by herself for she did not believe in going back. But with Ben it had been different. She had kept the rented car and they had driven all over the northern suburbs, visiting the Meissners' old house, dining at the Urbanikeller, and had even spent a day in Bad Voslau.

It was during this time that she felt the knots in her head begin to unravel and she started returning to normal. The years seemed to drop away. She felt like a young girl again and Ben was that young foreign correspondent who had first kissed her in the shadows of the Amhof. Nairn had been left with Paul.

Now Anna said, 'Paul's a different person. It's as though Beckerman's death has exorcized something in him.'

'He's still full of nervous energy. He's that sort of person.' Nairn swirled the remains of the wine in her glass. 'I'm going to marry him.'

'Darling, that's wonderful! Congratulations.'

'Oh, he doesn't know yet. He was married before. His wife was a biochemist researching into leukaemia and died of the disease. Ironic and sad.'

'I can see you're in love with him, but is he in love with you? He seemed edgy and sharp with you when we arrived.'

'There was a reason for that. He'd left a message on my phone in London. Part of it was personal. He said . . . well, I won't go into what he said, but it was about me and his feelings and . . . I'd stayed in his flat, you see. He said he hadn't had another woman there since his wife died. Oh, nothing went on. He hadn't realized that the gap in his life could be filled. Not only could but needed to be filled. But I never got the message. The tape was wiped. That's why Paul was sharp. He thought I wasn't interested. I'm going to stay on for a few days, if that's okay.'

'Stay as long as you like,' Anna said. 'Come back relaxed. We've got a lot of talking to do.'

Nairn frowned. 'More trouble?'

Anna shrugged. 'Not really. Don't worry. We'll work things out.'

She and Ben flew back to London the following day. Paul and Nairn came to see them off. They stood in the concourse of Schwechat Airport letting the crowds swirl around them.

Ben said, 'Look at them.' He indicated the people. 'Just going about their business. And yet – '

'And yet what?' Anna said.

'I guess I've got a dark mind. I tell myself this is what the Viennese were like before Hitler arrived. Just ordinary people. What if *another* Hitler arrives? Another Beckerman? I mean any one of these could be one of his kids. Do you believe in heredity?'

A cold hand seemed to close on Anna's heart.

'Well, that's one thing we don't have to worry about,' Nairn said. 'He told me he'd never had children.'

'He couldn't,' Paul said. 'It was in his medical papers. He was sterile.'

'Just as well,' Ben said.

Their flight was called.

Anna had no memory of boarding or strapping herself into her seat; no memory of takeoff; or of being given a glass of champagne; no memory of Ben talking to her.

She was numb.

Sterile . . . sterile . . . The word was like a heartbeat in her brain.

No children . . .

Then –

Her thoughts shot back to Vienna before the war. The time she missed her period. It *hadn't* been because she was pregnant by Cuno. Couldn't have been. It was impossible.

She knew now that missed periods could be caused by tension. And just before they had fled from Vienna she was filled with tension.

But then . . .

345

But then . . . to an innocent eighteen-year-old missed periods meant only one thing: pregnancy.

God, the irony of it!

'More champagne?' the air hostess said and Anna numbly held out her glass.

She didn't know whether to laugh or cry. Her whole life, in one moment, had been turned upside down. She needn't have married Wilson, needn't have worried about the effect identifying Cuno would have had on Peter. For that matter she needn't have worried about Peter at all. He didn't have Cuno's genes; no one did.

'. . . and dinner tonight at Lincoln's,' Ben was saying. 'I want a steak, a real Aberdeen Angus steak . . .'

Had her life gone for nothing then?

If she had not married Wilson, how would her life have changed? It might have been better. But it might have been worse.

She started to relax. Relief and gratitude flooded over her. She was closer to her three sons than she had been for years. Wilson was out of her life. And she had Nairn.

Nairn was the future. Anna would fight to save the paper but sooner or later – and maybe sooner rather than later – she would hand it over to Nairn.

And she had Ben. He was the present. The precious, wonderful present.

'. . . a good bottle of wine,' he was saying. 'A really good one. A first growth claret . . .'

'And then?' she said, turning to him.

He raised his glass to her.